NORTH BOY

A big Bollywood dream. A small-town chance.

IQBAL HUSSAIN

unbound

First published in 2024

Unbound
c/o TC Group, 6th Floor King's House,
9–10 Haymarket, London SW1Y 4BP
www.unbound.com
All rights reserved

© Iqbal Hussain, 2024

The right of Iqbal Hussain to be identified as the author
of this work has been asserted in accordance with Section 77 of the Copyright,
Designs and Patents Act, 1988. No part of this publication may be copied,
reproduced, stored in a retrieval system, or transmitted, in any form
or by any means without the prior permission of the publisher, nor be
otherwise circulated in any form of binding or cover other than that in
which it is published and without a similar condition being imposed
on the subsequent purchaser.

Text design by Jouve (UK), Milton Keynes

A CIP record for this book is available from the British Library

ISBN 978-1-80018-314-8 (paperback)
ISBN 978-1-80018-315-5 (ebook)

Printed in Great Britain by Clays Ltd, Elcograf S.p.A.

1 3 5 7 9 8 6 4 2

Our Unbound Firsts titles are inspired by Unbound's mission to discover fresh voices, new talent and amazing stories. As part of our commitment to amplifying diverse voices, Unbound Firsts is an annual opportunity for writers of colour to have their debut book published by an award-winning, crowd-leading publishing house.

Iqbal Hussain is a writer from Blackburn, Lancashire and he lives in London. His work appears in various anthologies and on websites including *The Willowherb Review, The Hopper* and *Caught by the River*. He is a recipient of the inaugural London Writers' Awards 2018 and he won Gold in the Creative Future Writers' Awards 2019. In 2022, he won first prize in *Writing Magazine*'s Grand Flash competition and was joint runner-up in the *Evening Standard* Short Story Competition. In 2023, his story 'I'll Never Be Young Again' won first prize in the Fowey Festival of Arts and Literature short story competition. He was also Highly Commended in the Emerging Writer Award from The Bridge Awards. *Northern Boy* is his first novel.

To Gary, my very own David.

PART ONE
I HAVE A DREAM

One

Despite the years, her handwriting remains unchanged: big loops, rounded forms and circles for dots. I smile, then tut. She's put Sydney on the envelope rather than Melbourne. Judging by the date on the postmark, it's been round the whole of Australia to get here.

I ease out the card, and a stream of glitter and sequins spills out. I laugh. It's like a rainbow's exploded over the table. The glossy black card is decorated with a swirl of tendrils and heart-shaped leaves. Across the middle, embossed in silver, two names:

"Shazia & Majid"

I shake my head. Where has the time gone? One minute, Shazia and I are in makeshift saris pretending to be Bollywood starlets; the next, she's all grown-up and getting married.

Opening the card, I read the invitation inside:

In the name of Allah,
the Most Beneficent, the Most Merciful

Mr Muzaffar Chaudhry & Mrs Heera Chaudhry
Request the pleasure of your company:

Rafi Aziz + 1

To grace the auspicious occasion of the wedding of
their beloved daughter

Shazia Asiya Chaudhry

with

Majid Sikandar Hashim

Beloved son of Mr & Mrs Ramzan Hashim

Saturday, 8 December 2001 (Insha'Allah)
Reception: 12:00 p.m. Nikah: 12:30 p.m.
Lunch: 1:30 p.m. Entertainment: 4:30 p.m.

at Abdul's Buffet and Banqueting Hall in
Pringle Street, Blackburn

RSVP

"Are you *sure* you won't come?"

We're in the kitchen, seated at the island. I play with my salad while he tucks into his carbonara. I stare at him until he is forced to put his fork down.

"You need to do this on your own," he says. "It's been five years. You'll have lots to catch up on."

"Go on, it'll be fun," I insist, forcing an olive down and trying not to choke. "We can do all the sights!" He scoffs and takes a slurp of wine. I blather on: "Come on, you can easily get time off. You're my plus one."

He finishes chewing his mouthful of spaghetti. "Rafi, would you just—"

"I can't believe you don't want to be there for me!" I stab my fork into a tomato, then jump off the stool and pace the room. "Everyone else'll have someone. Just Billy No-Mates here. I can get your ticket if that's it?" I'm shouting, turning sharply with each sentence, flinging my words into the air with a dramatic wafting of arms.

He leans back, his stool creaking. His green eyes track me as I storm up and down the kitchen. The TV is on in the background, and a chat show audience cheers as the next guest arrives on set. I grab the remote control and zap the TV, but accidentally hit the volume up button. The audience roars, as though they're also telling me to shut up.

He takes the remote from me and turns the TV off. "You done, Shah Rukh?" he says, calling me by the name of my favourite Bollywood actor. "Here's the thing." Standing before me, he begins counting on his fingers. "You barely keep in touch with anyone from back there. You've never introduced me to any of them. I don't even know if they know about me. You tell me to shush when you're on the phone to your mum in case she hears me. So, forgive me if I don't fancy flying halfway around the world, with next to no notice, to be judged by a bunch of strangers."

I feel my ears redden. He's right. The years have flown past and as the months rolled by, promises to return to Blackburn became fewer and fewer. Life took over: the house, the career, the relationship. I realise, with a pang of guilt, that I've never put him on the phone to any of my friends or family. Not because I'm ashamed of him, but because . . . because what?

I stutter and try to apologise, but he waves it away. He moves back to the counter and picks up his fork. "No time, mister. You've got to pack. And book that flight!"

Because of the incorrectly labelled envelope and Shazia's belief that mail to the other side of the world arrives in the same time as it does to the UK, there are only three days to the wedding. There's no time to mull over my decision. I can't not go to my oldest friend's wedding.

"I'm sorry for being a selfish prick," I say, going over and taking hold of his hands. The current heatwave means we're almost the same colour. He nods, and I pummel his chest. "You're not supposed to agree! I really want you to meet Shazia. She'd love you. And you her. I know it!"

Spinning me onto his knee while he perches on the bar stool at the island, he kisses me from behind. His strong arms wrap around my chest. I stare at the little hairs leading down to his wrists, bleached white from the sun. "No. This is your moment. You need to reconnect. And, anyway, one of us has to stay and keep Milo company." Our two-year-old labradoodle looks up at his name and wags his tail. "Is your work okay with this?"

I raise my shoulders. That's my next task. I break free from his embrace and head to the master bedroom, my Birkenstocks slapping on the tiled floor.

"Have you got everything you'll need?" he calls after me.

"Everything but the kitchen sink."

Luckily, I'd been organised enough to buy a traditional Asian wedding outfit from Sydney Road a few months ago. Growing up, I'd railed against the baggy salwaar kameez trouser-tunic combination, wearing it only when I attended the mosque. But the wedding apparel is tailored, fitted and flattering. I pack the blue tunic and tight-fitting trousers away. Then I pull on the sherwani that'll go over the top. It's a pale gold, the colour of straw, with red piping and a neckline embroidered with an elaborate snowflake pattern. The buttonholes are in the shape of mango stones, jewelled and sequined. Appraising myself in the full-length mirror, I can't help adopting a range of catalogue poses, modelling for an imaginary photographer. The cotton silk frockcoat rustles satisfyingly.

"Quit admiring yourself!" he shouts from the kitchen. "You've a plane to catch."

I take one last look. There was a time when I'd have been mocked for wearing something so flamboyant. But now I'm grown up and considered a "someone" it will be admired and commented on by all the aunties and uncles. The irony doesn't escape me.

I unbutton the sherwani and carefully lay it on top of the case.

*

The only flight I can get at such short notice leaves after midnight. With little traffic on the road, we reach the airport in record time. The air con in the Jeep hasn't worked for months; I pour out of the passenger seat, my hair plastered to my forehead and my shirt slicked to my back.

Despite the late hour, I slip on a pair of Gucci sunglasses and a Burberry cap.

"Steady on there, Madonna," he says, handing me my suitcase from the back seat. "I think you're safe from the screaming hordes."

He can laugh, but the airport is busy even at this hour. A cool breeze wafts out of the electronic doors of the Departures lounge each time they slide open.

"Have an amazing time." Hugging me, he rests his chin on my shoulder. "Say hi to Shaheeda." He never gets her name right. "I hope your mum and brother and sister are well."

My body tenses, as it always does whenever he talks about them. Although I try to ring every month, this has become less frequent over the years. Work is flat out. There aren't enough hours in the day. And my sister Nabila and brother Taleeb live just streets away from Mother and can pop in and see her any time. But, even as I think this, the angel on my shoulder remonstrates with me – they, too, have busy lives and their own families to look after. As the familiar sensation of guilt works its way through my body, I change the subject.

"I love you," I tell him. He smells of fabric softener, cumin and Dior Fahrenheit.

"Back atcha."

I give him one final hug before he jumps back in the Jeep. "Time to head home to my other man," he says through the open window, "before he starts barking the place down."

As he pulls away, I feel a wave of apprehension. Sighing, I head into Departures.

*

I board and instinctively turn left before stopping at the curtain. Not for the first time in the last few days, I curse Shazia and her bad planning, which means I'm relegated to cattle class. Gritting my teeth, I swing right, pulling my sunglasses and cap back down. Almost immediately, one of the flight attendants recognises me and asks if I'll sign a napkin for her little boy. She thrusts a pen into my hand. As I begin scribbling, I nod over my shoulder. "Would it be possible" – I peer at her name badge – "Kylie, to get an upgrade?"

She shakes her head. "I wish I could, Mr Aziz, but we're a full flight."

I keep the message on the napkin short.

When I get to my seat, I'm dismayed to find it's in the middle of a block of three. My heart sinks further at the man and woman on either side – they are both the size of Sumo wrestlers. Shazia would tell me off for being so judgemental. But shouldn't she have known that I only fly first class? One of the perks of fame is being ferried around with lots of leg and elbow room. I bestow a watery smile to my neighbours and take my seat. As I belt up, I give Shazia another piece of my mind under my breath.

We take off half an hour later. Not feeling sociable, I plug my headphones in and go through the films on board: *Harry Potter*, *Moulin Rouge*, *Lord of the Rings*, all of which I've seen. Then, in the World Cinema section, *Naseeb*, a 1981 Bollywood superhit starring Amitabh Bachchan, Shatrugan Sinha, Hema Malini and Reena Roy. A welcome blast of nostalgia, and it'll shave three hours off the flight.

As the titles roll, I hear Mother's little-girl singing voice. A big fan of Hema Malini, she'd rewind the songs so many times that the tape wore thin, making the images flicker and the sound warble. She'd break into song at the slightest excuse, much to Father's consternation.

I unclip my seatbelt and lean back as far I can go – which isn't far. I force myself to relax. The faded colours and fuzzy edges of the old film help the years rewind. As the villains appear onscreen, a delicious shiver runs through me. I'm ten again – when everything changed. My own Bollywood film plays out in my head.

Two

Mother was in no mood to be toyed with. The bramble roses around her head had slipped and dangled from her ears like mini pom-poms. She was rarely seen without a bloom in her hair.

"Beta, you will grow horns if you continue to play with girls."

I blinked at the absurdity of her comment. And how did she know I'd been with Shazia, dancing to "Super Trouper"?

Mother pinned me with a severe expression, her kameez rimmed with white where she had leaned into the chapatti-floured edge of the kitchen counter. "I am telling you for your own good, young man. You know what happened to the Rizwan's middle boy?"

"Mother, I have precisely zero interest in the life and times of Arshad Rizwan."

Mother snorted. "He was like you. He used to play with girls. Now they say he cannot leave the house. Because of horns! His poor mother."

I scoffed, but I sounded more like a Bollywood heroine than a villain. While I had a grown-up vocabulary thanks to my love of reading, my voice was like a girl's. Any aura of macho-ness was further diminished by my clothes, which consisted of a green T-shirt with Tweety Pie on it, yellow cardigan, red shorts and blue Jesus sandals. I had added a candy bracelet and a chunky, fuchsia-coloured ring borrowed from Shazia.

"It is no joking. Who is going to marry you if you look like an ox?" Mother slapped a freshly rolled chapatti onto the tava, sending up a plume of flour as it hit the hot griddle. "Or a ..." She let the sentence drop while her eyes lingered on my jewellery. I crunched several of the sweets from the bracelet, daring her to challenge me on it.

In her mango-coloured salwaar kameez and jewelled sandals, Mother was a peacock among the Formica. She no longer noticed the lopsided units and peeling linoleum floor or the overflowing Elephant chapatti flour bag serving as a makeshift bin. A well-trodden path was worn between the work surface on which she rolled her chapattis, and the cooker, its gas burners lined with crinkly tin foil that had long lost its sheen.

Nibbling away at another piece of bracelet, I said, "I'm sure I saw him with his dad a few days ago."

"Saw who?"

"Arshad!"

"Oh yes, Arshad. Did you see what he had on his head?" She deftly turned over a chapatti, using her fingers rather than tongs, a skill that always amazed me.

"A cap," I said, swivelling the ring around my finger. "That's nothing unusual."

"And why do you think he was wearing a cap?"

"Because it's the fashion," I said slowly, as though Mother was being particularly stupid. I crunched another two pieces off the bracelet.

She tossed the chapatti into a rattan changher. "It is a funny fashion, wearing it backwards so his hair sticks out the hole. 'New York Wankees' – what does it even mean?"

Chuckling, I skipped to the bedroom I shared with Nabila and Taleeb. With Nabila out, I wanted to style her mop-haired Cabbage Patch doll so that she looked like Agnetha from ABBA in the *Smash Hits* poster on the wall next to my bed. I imagined Agnetha watched over me while I slept, my very own guardian angel with blonde hair and blue eye shadow.

*

Half an hour later, Nabila threw me out. She was back early from a shopping trip with Shagufta-up-the-road, laden with glass bangles from the many Indian shops in Whalley Range, a Boots counter of make-up and a half-eaten Greggs cheese and onion pasty.

Returning to the kitchen, I tap-danced across the lino, relishing the clippety-cloppety sound of my sandals.

"There is a very nice park for you to play in," said Mother, steadying me by the shoulders. "Just like in Lahore! Shazia's brothers will be there. You must not get under your sister's foots." Flipping open the Saxa tub, she poured salt into the pan.

I sighed. "Hussain and Hassan will be playing football, which you know I hate."

She brushed this aside with a flick of her hand. "All boys play football. Just like all girls love to sing." She promptly demonstrated the truth of this by breaking into an Indian film song. While she sang in Hindi, I translated the words into English in my head. Something mushy about how the weather was romantic and how she had to find her sweetheart.

The song was from the film *Pakeezah*, about a dancer. Mother adored her Bollywood films and had even named me after her favourite playback singer, Mohammed Rafi.

I joined in with her, harmonising with the melody. I'd always done this, rarely singing the tune itself, which was too obvious.

"Get them to show you," she said, stopping. "Playing with balls is good for you."

Ignoring her, I thumped out a rhythm on the countertop, adding beatbox noises with my mouth to give vent to the disco number that had just come into my head.

Like an unwelcome party guest, Taleeb strolled into the kitchen. "What's that about playing with balls? You don't mean *her*, do you?"

I looked around to see who he was talking about, before realising he meant me. I shot him a death glare. "What would you know about it?" I said.

"Try being a man, for once."

"I'm ten years old!"

"Just wait till you get to Everton."

A tremor ran through me at hearing the three dreaded syllables of the hated school. "You don't scare me," I said, despite the quiver in my voice. I stood with my hands on my hips, legs akimbo, just as a Bollywood actor would face off a bully.

"The skinheads are going to love you."

My stomach flip-flopped. Why did he always have to mention the skinheads? Apparently they hung around the school gates at the end of the day. As much as I didn't want to believe Taleeb, I knew the skinheads were real – I'd seen reports on *Granada Tonight* of the National Front going on marches. Last week, Mr Khan's shop window was daubed with the NF symbol, leaving me terrified, knowing that either they had sympathisers in our midst or they'd breached our neighbourhood.

I looked over at Mother. Oblivious to our spat, she

stirred the curry and continued to sing about wandering alone and wanting someone to take her in their arms.

Taleeb opened the fridge and swigged milk straight from the bottle, before belching.

"Puthar, please! Not in my kitchen," exclaimed Mother.

"He's disgusting," I said, my fear of skinheads temporarily forgotten at the sight of Taleeb behaving like a junglee. "He's got the manners of a P-I-G."

"Rafi, must you say the name of that unclean animal in my kitchen?"

"You mean him?" I said, pointing at Taleeb.

I hid behind Mother. Startled, she spun round. A dollop of turmeric-tinted curry flew from the spoon, landing with a satisfying splat on Taleeb's white school shirt.

"Watch it!" said Taleeb, jumping back. "Bloody hell. You've ruined it now!"

Tutting, Mother rummaged under the sink, fighting through a stockpile of Vim and Dettol to get to her trusty Daz. With this Holy Trinity, she took on the world and all its ills.

Without undoing the buttons, Taleeb tugged his shirt off over his head. I looked enviously at his taut frame, comparing it to my own pudgy tummy. Catching me staring, he balled his shirt at me, hitting me in the face. "Does he have to be my brother? Can't we send him back to Pakistan?"

He said this in such a calm voice it caught me unawares. For some reason, it hurt me more than if he had smacked me. As much as I hated him, I still wanted him to like me.

I ran out, tears not far behind.

Three

It was my last year at St Matthew's before "big school" next year. I quickly squashed that thought. It was enough dealing with losing sunny Miss Newton for super-strict Mrs Entwistle, without pondering on the horrors that awaited me at Everton.

"St Matthew's is a good-good school," Father would say. His opinion chimed with those of the other Asian parents. Despite it being a Church of England school, most of its pupils were Muslim. "We all believe same-same. But, remember, puthar, Jesus was a prophet, like Muhammad, peace be upon him. *Not* the son of God." He intoned "thoba, thoba", asking for forgiveness for the misguided Christians.

I was getting ready to leave for the first day of term. It had taken much persuasion to convince Mother to let me walk to school by myself.

"My precious burfi!" she exclaimed. "How will you cope with the roads? What if you get lost? You might fall and hurt yourself! Oh, my gulab jamun! My heart is being torn in two!" In between each dramatic exclamation, she showered the top of my head with kisses.

Her comparison of me to various Indian sweets did not go unnoticed by Taleeb, who was shuffling his way out the door, dragging his school bag by its broken strap.

"Gulab jamun? Ha, that suits this round, syrupy, sickly-sweet ball," he said.

He always had to make a comment about my weight. I made to trap him in a web from my Spidey wrists, but Mother clutched me to her bosom.

"My sweet jalebi. My little boy is growing up so quickly. Oh, rasmallai of my heart. I could just eat you up! How will I last the day without you? Ya Allah, why do you test me so?"

*

St Matthew's was a handsome Victorian structure hewn from fudge-coloured stone. The thick walls were studded with high-set mullioned windows, which Mr Mobsby, the caretaker, opened with a hooked pole. The steeply pitched slate roof was adorned with gables, gargoyles and a weathervane in the shape of a shuttle. On the rare occasions Father wasn't at the mill and could drop us off, he'd religiously salute this nod to Blackburn's weaving heritage.

From the sombre expressions in the queue, we may as well have been awaiting a firing squad. Mrs Entwistle's reputation was legendary. Only Zaiman Malik and Shirley Gibbons carried on as normal. She gave him a rundown of what she was having for her tea, both oblivious to Ashiqah Ibrahim glaring at them with her grey-green eyes.

Ashiqah and I barely tolerated each other. We went through each school year determined to best the other: there was a constant comparison of grades; seeing who could gain the most gold stars; showing off new expressions we'd learned; and baiting each other at every opportunity.

She was looking superior – as well she might, for she had a fetching blue-and-white Pan Am sports bag over her shoulder. I moved my battered satchel to the front and exaggeratedly tightened the buckled straps. Ashiqah glanced over. Her hair was tied into pigtails and piled on top of her head in the shape of a large pretzel.

"Oh, hi, Rafi, I didn't see you there," she said. "You look well. A rounder face suits you."

I squared my shoulders. "Nice bag. My dad's got the same. He keeps his tools in it."

Before Ashiqah could retort, Mohammed Seedat thumped me between the shoulder blades. "Give it a rest, you big girl."

As I rubbed my back, the classroom door shot open. Mrs Entwistle loomed in the doorway. She was dressed in a lime-green jumpsuit, like the one Judith Hann wore on *Tomorrow's World* last week. She had the same big hair too. The chatter ceased immediately.

"Zaiman Malik, get away from that wall. Asghar Hamedi, wipe that finger at once! Not in your hair, you horrible little boy!"

As we filed in, Mrs Entwistle stood behind a large desk at the front, glowering at us. Behind her was a blackboard recessed into the wall, with metal strips to move it up and down. Cupboards lined the perimeter of the room, filled with books, art supplies and assorted stationery. The smell of newly painted walls hung heavy in the air.

"Shirley, the exercise books. Ashiqah, the pencils and rulers. Quickly!"

I was piqued at not being asked. Ashiqah looked like the cat that had got the cream. She slapped a sharpened pencil and wooden ruler on my desk, making me jump. I glared at her.

Mrs Entwistle picked up the chalk and wrote on the board, making us write our names and then copy her words onto the cover of our exercise books.

I reluctantly rubbed out the "h" I'd added in advance. Unconvinced at her spelling, I drew a heart over the "i" to make up for it. There, that looked better!

> Rafi Aziz
> Autumn 1981
> Mrs Entwhistle

Four

We were a month into the school term. Seating arrangements had settled, friendships and enmities established or rekindled, and everyone had mastered their fountain pen – except for Zaiman, who insisted on using it like a biro, splitting the nib like a fish's tail.

Monday rolled round with a gale that rattled the windows in their frames. I tried to drag out the morning. This was the first day of the end of my life: I was visiting Everton High, the school I'd be attending next year. For weeks, I'd protested in Bollywood tears, wails and overwrought tantrums that had left even Mother speechless. But she wasn't budging.

"No more nakhras, young man. If it is good enough for Nabila and Taleeb . . ."

The real reason was the school was a twenty-minute walk from our house, which meant we didn't have the expense or inconvenience of taking a bus.

My biggest concern was running into Amjad Bashir. Though just two years older than me, he was double my size. For some reason, my mere presence was a red rag to this bully – he'd spot me playing hopscotch with Shazia or skipping to Khan's Korner Kabin for a Jubbly and charge over. There'd be no escaping him if I was at the same school.

As I dawdled in the lounge, Mother bustled in with tea and a changher on her head piled high with toast. Even though I wasn't hungry, I claimed the two topmost slices, as I only ate toast when it was fresh off the tava. I looked at it as it lay on my plate. Normally I'd have chomped my way through both slices in a matter of seconds.

"I don't think he's well, *Maam*," said Nabila, studying me. We were the only family who used this regal-sounding title rather than the usual Ammi or Amma. No one knew where it came from, but it sounded odd if we called Mother anything else.

Mother inspected me closely, but, not finding anything obviously wrong, kissed the top of my head before returning to the kitchen.

I tore my toast into little squares, forming a pile on the table. "We're coming to Everton today," I said to Nabila. "Will you be there?"

"I'll make sure *I'm* not," said Taleeb, walking in and flicking the back of my neck with his finger. "I don't want anyone thinking you're my brother."

"I wasn't talking to you," I retorted, shoving him away.

Taleeb mimicked my reply, but in a higher register.

"What time are you there?" said Nabila.

"Lunchtime. Just four of us. And Mrs Entwistle." It wasn't an illustrious party – me, Asghar, Zaiman and Shirley. Banished to the same school as a trio who rated Dollar over ABBA.

Mother returned with a platter of sliced fruit: melon, papaya, guava. Before she left, she kissed me on each cheek, wafting behind the scent of Tibet Snow face cream.

"So," said Taleeb, shaking cornflakes into a bowl and wolfing them down without any milk, "are you ready for the skinheads?"

My hand jerked, causing the tower of toast squares to collapse.

"Ignore him, little bro," said Nabila. "He's winding you up."

"Fatty Boom Boom knows I'm doing it for his own good," said Taleeb.

"Why would I believe you?" I said, debating lobbing the rest of my toast at his head.

"Believe what you like." Munch. "I've seen them picking on new kids." Crunch. "They really hate sissies. Why do you think you haven't seen your mate Arshad lately?"

My blood ran cold. Could it be that the skinheads had beaten up Arshad? He went to St Paul's and had visited Everton a few weeks earlier. I hadn't seen him since.

"Stop scaring him," said Nabila, punching Taleeb on the arm. "You'll be fine, Raf." She ruffled my hair and headed upstairs to pack her bag.

Taleeb continued reading the *Daily Mirror* with which Mother had lined the changher. He picked up a slice of toast and bolted it down in just four bites. He rubbed his greasy fingers on the arm of the sofa. I turned on my heel with a flounce, hoping he'd noted my dramatic exit.

*

We were greeted by a tall, serious-looking woman in tortoiseshell Reactolite glasses. In the murky light, the lenses were the colour of strong tea. Mrs Entwistle made us line up in a neat row before the woman. She was draped in a black smock covered in white blots, cinched at the waist with a rope-like belt with a massive tassel. It was like being greeted by a Friesian cow.

"I am Mrs Hebblethwaite," she said, sounding like

Margot from *The Good Life*, "Head of Music at Everton High and your guide for this afternoon's open visit."

I glared at the school: a featureless concrete building, flat and long with hundreds of windows. There had been an attempt at colour – random squares of blue and red – but this was lost against the slate-coloured Northern skies. My heart sank. This was going to be my home for the next five years? A prison, more like.

"Coo, it's amazing, isn't it?" said Shirley, mouth agape. I scowled at her.

Having arrived during lunch, the grounds teemed with students. They were giants. It was also a jolt to see so many white faces. I scanned the grounds for Amjad and skinheads. Both were thankfully missing.

Then I spotted a familiar figure, hands in pockets, strolling towards an outbuilding: Taleeb. He kept looking over his shoulder, then hurrying on. Taking comfort from even his presence in this alien environment, I called after him, but a group of students jostled past at that moment, spinning me around. Mrs Entwistle told me off. When I righted myself, Taleeb had vanished. Wisps of smoke puffed out from around the outbuilding. Wait till I told Mum later!

*

"And this is the Canteen," stated Mrs Hebblethwaite unnecessarily. A queue of kids snaked into the room, trays in hand, jostling each other. A blast of chatter assaulted my ears while malt vinegar and battered fish did the same to my nose.

A rumpus broke out as I surveyed the rows and rows of tables and chairs in the room, with my fingers spidered over my nose and mouth. A blonde girl, with legs like

Grecian columns, bumped into a short, curly-haired boy getting up as she went past. Crockery, food and boy scattered everywhere. A cheer went up. The girl whacked the boy around the head with her tray and had to be dragged away by a teacher. I stared, transfixed, appalled.

"High spirits," said Mrs Hebblethwaite to Mrs Entwistle.

To think this was the school I was coming to. My heart thumped out of control.

A trio of boys walked past. "Just what we need – more pakis," one of them muttered. It was like he'd punched me. I stepped back. He made a gun-shape with his fingers and took each of us out with a "pa-choo" sound. His mates laughed. My stomach shrivelled and I tried to become invisible. Mrs Entwistle and Mrs Hebblethwaite remained oblivious.

*

After taking in the science labs, PE hall and reception, we wound up at the music room. Mrs Hebblethwaite pointed out various instruments, naming them one by one, even obvious things like guitars and drums. How would this woman teach me anything?

"Explore, children. Play to your heart's content," she said, before turning to Mrs Entwistle, who looked less than enthusiastic about the instruction.

"What's this?" said Zaiman, picking up a triangle, before bashing it on a pair of bongos. Asghar shook a maraca in his ear. Shirley strummed a guitar tunelessly.

Ignoring them, I sat down at the piano and bashed out a tune I'd composed on my toy piano last week. It sounded so much better on a real piano, which also had proper black keys rather than painted ones. I closed my eyes and pictured the tune as a song in a film. Jeetendra and Hema Malini leaping about on a Swiss mountainside, madly in love. Not that I knew what love was, but it involved lots of running and synchronised dancing. I finished with a Richard Clayderman-style flourish, as the camera zoomed in on the two lovers and branches of oleanders hid them from sight just as their lips touched.

I opened my eyes. The others were staring at me, their mouths open. I stood up, taking a bow, and finished the performance off properly. I turned to Mrs Hebblethwaite, keen to hear what she'd thought of my impromptu performance.

She cleared her throat and looked at her watch. "Is it that time already?"

*

As I tore the shiny toilet paper, the main door banged open. Laughter, snorting and bad language ricocheted off the tiled walls. Amjad and his mates. Shine a light! Why couldn't I have waited?

They began kicking open the cubicle doors.

A voice from the stall next to me pleaded for them not to hurt him.

"Hurt you? Why would we do that?" Amjad said. "Let's be having you."

As they dragged out the unfortunate fellow, I heard the sound of taps being turned on, followed by the more sinister sounds of spluttering, crying and choking.

Though terrified, I took advantage of the commotion to sort myself out. Then the taps turned off. The parchment-like Izal in my hand crackled like flames. Their victim legged it. They didn't stop him – not now they had a new target.

"Knock, knock!" said Amjad, walloping the door of my cubicle. "Who's there? Jester. Jester who? Jester friend." He laughed a hollow laugh.

Drawing up my trousers, I pulled my feet onto the seat and hugged my knees.

The door clanged open, the bolt flying loose. Bodies rushed in, hands grabbed my arms and I flew off my toilet perch.

Just two years older than me, Amjad was built like a double-height fridge freezer. Bad skin, bad breath, bad attitude – and now bad luck as he walked towards me. His tie was askew and his shirt covered in ink – and what I hoped was ketchup. He slammed me into the wall. With the air knocked out of me, there was no chance of screaming for help.

"I'm counting down the days, you fucker," he said. "You and me's gonna be best pals, innit?" He cupped my chin in his huge, sweaty hand and moved my head up and down. He laughed and his mates joined in. His other arm pressed across my chest, pinning me to the wall. If I hadn't just been to the toilet, I would have soiled myself.

His face lurched close. "You're mine, yeah?" He again made my head nod. "You'll come when I snap my fingers, yeah?" And again. "You'll do as I say, yeah, pretty boy?"

He laughed and breathed vinegary fumes over me. I tried not to retch. I took a deep breath, ready to cry for help, but he clamped his hand over my mouth.

"Right, time we had a bit of fun."

Manoeuvring me into a headlock, he dragged me backwards towards the cubicles. I tried to release his arm from around my throat, but it was like fending off a bear.

"The other sod got a proper soaking," he said. "I'll go easier on you, 'cos I like you. Just one dunk, yeah?" He mimed the flushing of a chain and broke into more laughter.

I kicked out, trying to stop him. He just laughed, then picked me up and slung me over his shoulder. I screamed for him to stop, but he kept walking towards the cubicles.

Then, miracle of miracles, a thumping on the door!

"Rafi! Are you in there? We need to go. The others are on the coach."

"Mrs Entwistle!" I shouted in relief.

Amjad dropped me to the floor as quickly as he'd lifted me.

Mrs Entwistle walked in. "There you are! What are you doing on the floor? Get up!" Then, seeing Amjad and his cronies: "What's going on here?"

Amjad stood aside, holding a hand towards the door. "Nothing, miss. Just showing our guest the bogs."

I scarpered out, my heart as loud as the bongos Zaiman had bashed earlier. The sound of mocking laughter followed me. My cheeks flamed red.

I tumbled into the seat next to Shirley, unable to speak. I had been that close to being dunked headfirst in the toilets! The others jigged up and down, babbling, but the breath caught in my throat. My insides bucked and heaved. I hated Mother with all my heart. She was the one fixated on this hellhole. She'd vetoed the much more suitable choice of Pleckgate because it involved two bus journeys. I'd have taken ten buses.

"I bet they have fish and chips every day," said Shirley to Zaiman and Asghar, poking her head through the gap in the seats in front.

"Did you see how big the footie pitch was?" Zaiman leaped up and drew a large rectangle in the air, before being told to sit down by Mrs Entwistle.

"I can't wait to wear a tie, so I can take it off!" Asghar said. His face beamed, as though this was the best thing. Fools! How could they not see what an awful school it was?

There was no way I could go to Everton – not if I wanted to carry on staying alive.

As the coach pulled away, the Bee Gees' song of the same name played in my head; its disco beat mirroring the pounding in my chest.

Five

Sitting cross-legged on Shazia's bedroom floor, I tried not to lose myself in the busy pattern of red, orange and brown chrysanthemums woven into the carpet. We'd listened to both sides of the *Bucks Fizz* album and had moved on to *Can't Stop the Music* by the Village People.

"Do you think Bobby's better-looking than Mike?" asked Shazia, her mind still on the wholesome foursome.

"They look the same to me," I said absentmindedly. I flicked through last week's *Look-in*. "But I like their hair. Oh, look at this one! She looks gorgeous," I said, jabbing at a picture of Agnetha in a cornflower-blue jumpsuit.

Shazia gave it a cursory glance. "Bobby's got a nicer face," she said, opening the cassette insert and scrutinising the tiny pictures on it, "but Mike's got better hair."

"Are we still on Bucks Fizz?" I said.

Shazia glared at me. "Even if I could find a jumpsuit like that, I'm not sure I could carry it off," she said, taking the magazine from me. "Agatha's got really long legs."

"Agnetha," I corrected, snatching the magazine back. "And yes, she has."

Shazia leaped up. She ran to the stacked hi-fi and turned up the volume. Then she paraded up and down the room, her salwaar billowing as she scissored her legs like we'd seen models do. Unable to resist, I joined her, casting haughty glances to the audience as we strutted our stuff to "I Love You to Death".

"Shazia! Rafi! Samosas!"

In an instant, we abandoned the world of pop music and high fashion and hot-footed it downstairs. Mrs Chaudhry's samosas were legendary.

I jumped on the sofa, sliding along the protective plastic film. Unlike Mother, Mrs Chaudhry had sacrificed comfort to preserve her settee's pristine state.

I tipped my head to Shazia's brothers, Hussain and Hassan, who had turned around from the TV. "All right?" I said, the greeting awkward in my mouth. I was never able to say "All right" without pronouncing each word separately.

The nine-year-old identical twins stared at me, not blinking. I was reminded of the cover of *The Midwich Cuckoos*, which Nabila was reading for English.

Mrs Chaudhry brought in freshly fried samosas. I bit into my triangular treasure of spiced potato and peas and watched the screen through a haze of steam. Local news. Hussain got up to change the channel.

"... to sing with the group ABBA, with Lancashire having been selected in the initial draw. Schools across the region were entered into a random ballot. And, we can announce that the winning school is St Matthew's, Church of—"

I let out an almighty shout. Hussain jumped back from the TV. Had I heard right? Our school was going to be singing with ABBA? How had I not known about this? ABBA were my favourite band in the whole world, and they were coming to Lancashire! But I didn't remember reading about it in *Look-in* or seeing it mentioned on *Multi-Coloured Swap Shop*.

"Too much chilli?" said Mrs Chaudhry, rushing back with a tumbler of water.

I shook my head, before getting up and skidding on my knees to a stop before the TV. Mrs Chaudhry warned me I'd ruin my eyes, but I waved her concerns away.

"The band are in the North filming a music video," said the announcer. "The ballot was held in secret to avoid hordes of adoring fans descending to the scene." That explained it. "St Matthew's school choir will join the Swedish supergroup on a special episode of the BBC's *Pebble Mill at One*."

I had stopped chewing. Hussain tutted about the "rubbish music" and once more made to switch channels. I roared "NO!", surprising us both. I cranked the volume all the way up.

A clip of ABBA in concert exploded onto the screen, with the song "Gimme! Gimme! Gimme! (A Man After Midnight)". The shrieking fans mirrored the excitement racing through my body. We'd be singing with ABBA! I couldn't believe it. I'd dreamed about this. I joined in the chorus, waving my samosa in the air.

The bespectacled newsreader concluded: "And if appearing with Benny, Björn, Frida and Agnetha wasn't prize enough, one lucky young singer will get to perform a solo with Benny on the piano. To quote the Swedish Fab Four, the winner really will take it all. And now over to John, for the weather."

I said goodbye to Shazia and dashed home. Mother was in the kitchen. With the speed of a sputtering telex machine, I filled her in with the news. We'd be on TV. I'd be famous! I might even become the fifth member of the group. I needed to bag that solo. Who knew which talent scout might be watching *Pebble Mill*. If that awful St Winifred's choir could be on *Top of the Pops,* so could I. I'd compose hits on my toy piano, get rich and go to a school of my choice. This was my Get Out of Jail Free card. I broke into a medley of ABBA songs.

"Rafi, please!" said Mother, waving a spatula at me. "Why this hungama? What do you mean you are not going to school? And why are you singing these baqwaas songs?"

I forgave her ignorance. I needed her on my side. Without her, I couldn't compete.

I switched to an old Bollywood number. Mother couldn't resist. Dropping her spoon with a clatter, she waltzed me around the kitchen, the sizzle of the pan and the sticky slap of our feet on the lino marking out the beat. Her dupatta flew behind her as we danced.

Six

"Good morning, ladies and gentlemen, this is your captain speaking. We're currently cruising at an altitude of 35,000 feet at an air speed of 400 miles per hour..."

I'm jolted out of my thoughts by the announcement. We are only twenty minutes into the film. I yawn. The lady next to me is also watching something on her little screen, but the man is already asleep, his head resting on the window. I can hear his bear-like snores despite my headphones and over the rumble of the engines.

I need the toilet, even though I went just before we'd set off. Some things never change – I've never been able to go a few hours without needing a wee.

I pull off the headphones and stir in my seat, letting the woman next to me know I'm ready to get up. She remains engrossed in her film and doesn't move. I tap her on the arm. She jumps, then inspects herself as if expecting a spider to have landed on her.

"Excuse me," I say loudly, rising from my seat. "I just need the bathroom."

She blinks, beams as though noticing me for the first time, blushes, giggles, then draws her knees back. It's not much help, as I still need to clamber over her various bags and blankets on the floor. I can't be sure, but I'm pretty sure I feel a pat on my bottom as I lurch past. When I look back, she's staring at her screen.

I make my way to the front of the plane, trying not to elbow people in the head as I shuffle up the narrow aisle. The toilet is occupied, so I wait my turn. As I lean against a seat, a dark-haired steward walks past. I take in his fine features, snake hips and long legs. He catches me staring and flashes me a smile. Embarrassed, I look away.

The toilet door opens and I slip inside.

I return to my seat and put on my earphones just as the food trolley pulls up. The dark-haired steward mouths something to me. His badge says Pedro. He smiles and dimples appear on his cheeks. My stomach flutters. I'm further distracted by the lady beside me already tucking into her dish with gusto, her elbow digging into me. The man on the other side continues to sleep his noisy sleep. On the screen, a song breaks out and the music seeps out tinnily as I remove my earphones.

"Chicken or beef?" repeats Pedro.

He must think I'm an idiot. I gather my wits. "Sorry, I think I ordered the vegetarian?" I know I did – I didn't fancy a heavy meat dish just before sleeping – but years spent living in Australia makes the statement come out like a question.

He consults a piece of paper in his hand. "Ah, I can see yours was a last-minute booking, sir. It looks like the system didn't catch up in time. What are we going to do?" He looks at me with eyebrows raised.

Again, my tongue sticks to the roof of my mouth. He looks like a Spanish version of the actor Aamir Khan. I'm a sucker for a handsome face and an accent. He ducks and rummages around the bottom of the trolley. A minute later, he straightens and hands over a dented box with a flourish. "Protein-free, lactose-free, fat-free, salt-free."

I stop myself adding "and taste-free". As our fingers touch, a tingle passes through me. I need to get a grip. What am I, a Bollywood heroine?

He asks if he can get me anything else. Not trusting myself to reply, I shake my head and shovel in a plastic forkful of under-cooked, under-seasoned vegetables.

Seven

Walking into the music room for the first Project ABBA choir lesson, I stopped in my tracks. What was Jeetendra doing in the building?! The man handing out the sheet music was surely the Bollywood actor himself. The same thick head of hair, the fair skin, the little moustache on that handsome face. Clothes-wise, he was dressed as Jeetendra would have been, too: the slightly tight trousers, the cowboy boots and a combination of T-shirt, shirt and hooded top in various shades of blue.

"Come in, class, welcome. Gather round. Take a copy of the music and pass it on."

These simple instructions proved impossible for anyone to follow. The boys dropped the stapled pages and proceeded to walk all over them.

"It's him, innit?" said Zaiman. "The bloke from the market. Sells radios."

It was obvious to anyone with even half a brain who this vision was.

The girls gathered in bustling flocks, putting their hands before their mouths so they could whisper to each other. But they were so excited, you could hear every word.

"It really is him!" said Moti, glancing around at the

teacher before swivelling her head back with such speed she risked giving herself whiplash.

"Tell me it's not who I think it is," said Shirley, fanning her face, which had gone a shade of strawberry.

"But who *is* it?" said Ashiqah, looking between Moti and Shirley. As she turned, the huge swathes of fabric in each leg of her pink-and-purple gharara swished and settled.

I couldn't help myself. "Really?" I said. "You're pretending you don't know who that is?"

She squinted at me. "Oh, hi, Rafi. I didn't see you there."

"That's funny," I said, looking her up and down, "because with that get-up I saw you from a mile away."

Her best friend Izmat cut in before she could retort. "Ohmygod, ohmygod, sir is well fit, innit? Ohmygod, I'm proper dreaming. Pinch me, quick, before I faint. I swear to God I'm gonna faint; I just can't believe it. What's he doing here, Ash?!" She spewed this out while chewing gum at a hundred miles an hour.

Jeetendra beckoned us over to the music stands, rewarding us with a big smile. I'm sure I wasn't the only one who went wobbly at the knees. Shirley puffed in and out like a pair of bellows, and even the boys had stopped their chatter and grinned at him with large teeth, like the birds in *Roobarb and Custard*.

"Welcome to the choir," he said, speaking English in an American accent. "You've done incredibly well to make the cut. I've known Mrs Entwistle for many years" – he did? How was she friends with a Bollywood star? – "and she has very high standards."

I admired his English, which had no trace of a hard Indian t or d. He spotted me gawping and grinned, making me instantly shy. I looked at my feet.

"I need to get you guys shipshape for the ABBA

recording. You're gonna have the eyes of the nation on you – well, the lunchtime brigade – so we've got our work cut out."

Why wasn't he in Bombay finishing off another film? He must have been in at least ten films last year, so maybe he needed a break.

"We've got forty-five minutes of show to fill. That's a whole lotta songs, folks."

I glanced at the music in my hand, noting what was on page one: "Mamma Mia". My fingers began playing the marimba intro on my leg.

"Plus, we need to think about the choreography, to keep things interesting visually," said Mr H. "Does anyone know what choreography is?"

Several hands shot up.

"It's when you bust your moves and stuff, innit?" said Zaiman.

Jeetendra wasn't fazed by this ugly response. "Spot on, young man!" He put a hand up, palm-side out. Zaiman smacked it with his own. "High five, sir – cool!"

"Oh, before I forget, I'm Mr Haqq. That's H-A-Q-Q. But feel free to call me Mr H. I answer to both."

Two q's – how exotic! And who knew Jeetendra even *had* a surname, let alone a Muslim one? Like other A-list stars, such as Rekha, Dharmendra and Vyjayanthimala, the actor was only ever known by his first name.

After cries of "Ohmygod, Allah ni kasam, wait till I tell my mum!" (Izmat), "Thank you, sir" (Ashiqah) and "You were well good in *The Burning Train*" (Javed), Mr H handed out the song sheets.

As the others went through the lyrics of "Chiquitita", which I knew off by heart already, I scrutinised Mr H some more. I admired his hair, which was thick and quiffed, with not a strand out of place. He wore thin leather straps around his wrists and a Celtic band on the little finger of his right hand. As he passed, he trailed a scent of Denim. I couldn't believe Bollywood royalty was taking our class. Wait till I told Mother later!

*

It didn't take us long to realise Mr Haqq and Jeetendra were not one and the same. While disappointed, we were heartened at having the next best thing.

"Where's your accent from, sir?" said Mohammed. "Is it Bolton?"

Mr H chuckled. "A bit further. I lived in San Francisco for ten years."

Music lessons were much more fun. Mr H brought in cassettes of music from around the world. "A good musician casts his or her nets wide," he said. One choice was the soundtrack for *Sholay*. Anyone who liked the Bollywood composer R. D. Burman clearly had good taste.

While we rehearsed "Thank You for the Music" again, Mr H tapped me on the arm.

"Hey, Raf, what're you doing there?"

I didn't know what he meant. "Singing, sir?"

Mr H laughed. "Yes, kiddo, but I noticed you weren't doing it like everyone else."

I blushed. I didn't always sing the tune, but I harmonised and came up with a secondary melody that blended with the first. Was I wrong?

Ashiqah smirked. "Was he out of tune, sir? Rafi does that when he gets carried away."

I glared at her. "There's more than one way to sing a tune, don't you know?"

"Yes, a right way and a wrong way," she said, doubling over with Izmat.

"And the truly gifted way," said Mr H. Ashiqah stopped mid-titter. "When you hear the same tune over and over, you're crying out for something different – right, Rafi?"

I scrunched my nose up at Ashiqah, before we all launched into another verse.

Mr H stopped me again. "Man, where are you getting those harmony lines from?"

This time, I looked at him blankly. Didn't everyone hear harmonies?

"Ah, of course, you've practised the song with Mrs Bainbridge?" he said.

Mrs Bainbridge, the old music teacher, had nothing to do with it. Tunes whirled around my head all the time. Once I had the melody pegged, I experimented to see what counter-melody fitted on top. It kept my interest. I'd always done this when singing and couldn't see how others weren't able to do the same.

Mr H asked me more questions. Most of the time, when I talked about music with anyone their eyes glazed over or they walked away, but Mr H was genuinely interested.

"Kid," he said, taking me by the shoulders, "you and me are gonna get along A-one."

*

"Why are you so late, my pumpkin?" said Mother, scooping me up and showering me with kisses. "Your paratha has gone cold. Let me heat it up on the tava."

"No need," I said, tearing pieces off the cooling buttery bread. "I'm starving. Mr H kept me back. He said I should go for the solo part."

"Mr Itch?" said Mother.

"He's our new music teacher. He's—"

"What kind of name is that?"

"It's short."

"He is short? That is not his fault, puthar. I have raised you better than this."

It wasn't worth correcting her. As I gobbled down the paratha, in between sips of sugary, milky cardamom tea, I told her about the conversation between Mr H and me. "He says I have one of the best voices in the choir and that I'm the only one who can harmonise. He thinks I can go for the solo spot. He said I'm the best person for the role, and that I'm going to be famous and I can be anything I want, even a Bollywood actor or pop star or disco dancer!" I gulped my tea and dramatically wiped my mouth with the back of my hand.

Mother dabbed my lips with kitchen roll before wiping my fingers one by one. "Puthar, a popping star, an actor, a dancer – these are not respectable jobs. You will become an accountant, or a doctor, or an engineer like your Uncle Shaukhat in Pakistan. Your uncle has so many letters after his name, ma'shallah," she said, thanking God for her brother's success.

"Mr H says that—"

"No, you listen to your mother, who has raised you, fed you, loved you."

I rolled my eyes. She was being very Bollywood. She even looked like Nirupa Roy, an actress who had cornered the market in sentimental maternal roles.

"You will learn proper subjects at Everton. No time for music, no singing-shinging. You are too old for those." She hummed a tune and got up, smoothing her kameez.

I looked at her askance. Mother was always singing and dancing and went out of her way to encourage me to do the same. When had she become the Sharia'a police?

I pushed away the paratha, my appetite gone.

Eight

It took an hour for Mrs Entwistle and Mr H to whittle down the choir to decide who'd get the ABBA solo spot. In the end, it fell between Ashiqah and me. We had to sing a verse and chorus of "Money, Money, Money", accompanied by Mr H on the piano.

As much as it hurt to admit it, Ashiqah could hold a tune and had an excellent sense of rhythm. But – thank the gods on high – there was an issue.

"Ashiqah, you're hooting," said Mrs Entwistle. Ashiqah fought to control her big mouth and tried again.

Then it was my turn. Heeding Mr H's advice, I thrust my chest out, shoulders back, diaphragm engaged and opened my mouth.

All went well, until I got to the end of the verse. I should have waited two bars before the chorus, except Ashiqah nudged me in the ribs. Off-guard, I came in early. Mr H looked around, but I kept going, extending the words across what seemed like a thousand bars until the music caught up. I was then out of breath for the next line.

It was no surprise when Mrs Entwistle announced the winner. Devastated, I fought back the tears.

"You gave it your best, bud," said Mr H, coming over and consoling me.

"Bad luck, Rafi," said Ashiqah in a fake sad voice.

I shoved her out of the way and ran out.

*

I pedalled home, my legs pumping up and down like *The Beano*'s Billy Whizz. I *dring-dringed* at every perceived obstacle: cats, children playing and old ladies gossiping on street corners. The whoosh of the wheels created a kind of percussion and, despite my anger and frustration, I found myself singing, first under my breath and then more loudly. Unable to face an ABBA number, I laid into "Save Your Kisses for Me" by Brotherhood of Man.

As I passed Mrs Kapoor, I belted out the chorus at the top of my lungs, the words popping out before I could stop them.

Mrs Kapoor stumbled off the kerb. I screeched to a stop. Dad would want me to make sure she was okay. Luckily, she was steadied and wrenched back by her friend, Mrs Mamood.

"Besharam," cried Mrs Kapoor, waving her bony fist. "Singing dirty songs at me, shameless monkey! I will be telling your father."

As she came after me to box my ears, I put up my imaginary Wonder Woman metal cuffs, kicked up the pedals and set off again. Mrs Kapoor's hand dived into a blue tartan trolley and a bread roll bounced off the back of my head.

*

"What's up with you, Droopy?" said Shazia, pointing at my face. I ignored her. She went to a different school, Our Lady of the Rosary, a car ride away. Mrs Chaudhry said it was worth it because, with few other Asian pupils, unlike St Matthew's, Shazia would stand out.

Shazia was home alone, with everyone else out, visiting. As we went to her bedroom, I told her how Ashiqah had robbed me of the starring role, and how I hated her and how I wished she'd get swallowed up by a black hole or be run over by a truck and preferably both.

Shazia made all the right noises, then announced she was going to give me a make-over to cheer me up. "I'm going to turn you into Agnetha from the *Waterloo* album cover," she promised. Although I didn't believe her skills matched her ambition, I managed a weak smile.

She sat me down in front of the full-length mirror, then shoved a blonde wig on me, pinned a crocheted beret on top, wrapped a sequinned dupatta around a shiny tracksuit top and Velcroed me into velveteen bell-bottoms atop six-inch-high stacked white boots. For good measure, she coloured my eyelids blue, inspired by the "Winner Takes it All" video.

As each item of clothing went on, I tried looking on the bright side. I was still going to get to sing with ABBA, even if I didn't have the solo spot. I reflected on last week's assembly about counting our blessings. But it was one step forward, two steps back. How would anyone hear me singing with the choir? Benny, Björn and the ladies wouldn't get a chance to hear my voice. Ashiqah had denied me my chance to be the fifth member of ABBA. She'd also consigned me to the prison that was Everton. I forced myself to keep my rage in check by focusing on the vision of loveliness in the mirror. Shazia had done a surprisingly good job. I looked amazing!

Now it was my turn.

"Sidal Vassoon at your disposal. What can we do for

yourself today, Madam?" I asked, clicking Shazia's mum's fabric scissors.

Shazia pulled back. "I'm not sure about that, Raf – I mean, Mr Vassoon."

"Sidal, please."

After some persuasion, Shazia relented. I began with the back. The good news was I snipped in tiny, careful strokes. The bad news was there were rather a lot of strokes. It wasn't easy keeping the hair in line, so I had to keep going back to try and even the drop.

Similarly, once I started on the fringe, I couldn't stop. The scissors were tricky to hold at an angle, and I wasn't helped by Shazia bobbing her head around like a nervous pigeon.

Finally, I was done. "Remarkable! Even your own mother wouldn't recognise you."

I'd shaped her fringe into a big, droopy "W". Although it went in rather high at the edges, it hung nice and heavy over the forehead.

I passed Shazia a hand mirror. She gasped, but I couldn't tell if in a good way or bad. I reassured her she'd be the talk of the town. She took a deep breath, admiring herself from various angles, flicking the fringe from one side to the other. At last, she allowed herself a smile.

Giving one last toss, she got up and said, "I'm sure I'll get used to it. Right, since you want to be an actor, let's see how well we can pull off our disguises."

Before I could protest, she'd pulled me out, arm in arm, in the direction of Khan's Korner Kabin. It was hard work keeping my balance in such high heels. I minced through the streets like a runaway geisha.

Dark, pigeon-coloured clouds rolled across the sky. This wasn't quite the lighting I'd wanted for my starring role. The wind had picked up and I was grateful for the Kirby grips holding my beret in place.

Shazia turned around halfway, remembering she'd not locked the door. "My mum'll kill me if we get robbed. The TV and stand are her pride and joy. See you at the shop."

As I waited at the kerb, a Volvo driver tooted, wound down the window and wolf-whistled at me, asking if I "need a lift, darling". I thought this odd, until I remembered I was now an Agnetha lookalike. I waved back with the tips of my fingers and said something non-committal in a high-pitched voice, before crossing the road, gratified at having fooled at least one person.

*

I pushed open the door of the shop. The familiar scents of spices, flowery agarbathi and bleach assaulted my nose – and something metallic. I wrinkled my nose in distaste, but I couldn't back out now.

With the bank of clouds outside, the shop was even darker than normal and it took a while for my eyes to adjust. Large jars of sweets and snacks lined the shelves behind the counter. A hotchpotch of goods, from foodstuff to footballs, ironing boards to aspirin, hung from the ceiling, leaned against the walls or crammed onto the maze-like shelving units. A fluorescent tube on the ceiling flickered apologetically, casting little light into the interior. A chest freezer skulked under the window, emitting a high-pitched whine.

"I will be with you in a minute, Modom," said Mr Khan, glancing up from the far end of the shop, before manoeuvring a huge side of lamb through a vertical blade. That explained the iron-rich smell. I tried not to gag. I rarely ventured into that end of the shop, piled high with meat and a pan scale hanging off the ceiling on a vicious hook, and Mr Khan butchering away in a bloodied white doctor's coat.

I looked to see who Mr Khan was talking to, before realising he meant me!

The customer at the meat counter glanced over. Mrs Kapoor. I groaned. Was I destined to keep bumping into her today? She peered at me through the gloom of the shop, pondering if I was worth greeting. A piercing shriek from the blade as it sliced through a bone decided it. She floated towards me, spectral in her white sari and chadar shawl.

"Hello, dear. Sun gone?" She gestured towards the window, looking at the strip of sky visible over the family-pack of toilet rolls. "This awful country. Always so dark."

She sounded so like Mother, I struggled not to smile.

"A pretty face," she said, reaching for my chin with her gnarled hand. I stepped back. I couldn't afford to let her see me close up, as she was bound to see through my disguise, even if she was half blind. "If you could just lose some kilos now," she added.

Bloody cheek! I wanted to answer her back, but I couldn't risk it. Lowering my face, I looked up at her with raised eyes, like Princess Diana. Mrs Kapoor's mouth worked itself with a camel-like motion, chewing something. I focused on the clump of moles over her right cheekbone, which made a W-shape, like the constellation Cassiopeia.

I started as lightning lit up the shop, followed by rain clattering against the window.

"Now, now, dear. I am only being kind for your own good," said Mrs Kapoor, stroking my hand. It was like being rubbed with sandpaper. "Are you married? No? I did not think so."

The doorbell chimed and a wet Shazia ran inside. The fringe looked less attractive in the dim light of the shop. The rain had also rendered it lifeless and it stuck to her forehead like Uncle Shaukhat's wig in the pictures we'd seen of him.

Mrs Kapoor did a double-take, her knobbly hand going to her own hair. "What in Bhagwan's name?"

I wanted to defend my haircutting skills, but I was worried my voice might give me away. Mrs Kapoor had the eyesight of a mole rat, but there was nothing wrong with her ears. Mother claimed she could hear gossip from several streets away.

"Keep clear of that one," said Mrs Kapoor to me. Shazia moved away from her gimlet gaze, diving into the biscuits and boxed cake aisle. "The whole khandaan is altu-faltu. Only the father is a good man."

I realised she thought Shazia was Nabila.

"As for that young boy of hers . . ."

Maddeningly, she broke off to tell Mr Khan not to fob her off with fatty cuts.

I cleared my throat to get her back on track.

She continued: "As for that boy of hers. Well . . ." Mrs Kapoor flicked her teeth with her thumb, before hastily jiggling her mouth to reset the denture she had unsettled. "He is trouble from tip-top to tip-top. He nearly drove his bicyclette over me!"

This was a blatant lie. She'd stepped off the kerb into my path and only my superior cycling and bionic reflexes had helped avert an accident.

"There is something wrong with him. That's what happens when you marry cousins."

I had no idea what she meant. All I knew was I needed to get away from the wet slap of her lips, which, together with the heat in the shop and the iron-rich smell from the meat counter, was making me queasy.

"Another time," she continued, talking to the shop in general, "and strike me dead if I tell a lie – he was wearing a skirt over his trousers. Have you heard the like?" She spat out red juice from the paan she was chewing, just missing my feet.

Mr Khan, returning to the counter laden with bags of meat, made to remonstrate with Mrs Kapoor; a look from her and he backed down.

"I blame the mother," said Mrs Kapoor. "Not a sensible bone in her body. More interested in flowers and clothes and make-up."

I didn't see how these were bad things, but I kept schtum.

"That'll be £9.87," said Mr Khan.

Mrs Kapoor let out a moan. "Including the mangoes, Mr Khan?"

"With the mangoes, it comes to" – he totted up on a paper bag – "£11.34."

Mrs Kapoor collapsed against the counter. Fanning herself, she remained at a forty-five-degree angle, complaining bitterly about "thieves and robbers".

Unmoved by Mrs Kapoor's overwrought display, Mr Khan addressed the next customer. "Yes, Modom?"

It took a moment to realise he meant me. "Ten pence of fried please, peas," I said.

Mr Khan's head jerked, as though I'd asked him for the keys to the shop.

Of course, I'd got my words wrong! "Sorry, Mr Khan, fried peas, please."

He still looked confused. Of course – in all the excitement, I'd forgotten I was in disguise and had used my normal voice. "And five pence of fried chickpeas, my good man," I added, in a higher pitch and with added nineteenth-century formality.

Mr Khan shook the chickpeas slowly onto the scales. Mrs Kapoor squinted at me.

"Anything else, Modom?" said Mr Khan. "Or should I say, young Rafi?"

Mrs Kapoor righted herself in an instant, revived by invisible smelling salts. "That ruffian. Where is he? Let me give him a piece of my mind!"

At that moment, the door shot open. I barely registered the blur of golden marigold flowers, the floral scent of Anaïs Anaïs and the chinking of bangles, before I was being dragged out of the shop.

"Mother – my peas!"

"Be quiet!" She hauled me with such force she nearly wrenched me out of my boots.

Shazia followed us out. "Mrs Aziz! Please, stop, you'll have an accident!" she called, as Mother stepped off the kerb without looking, causing an Austin Metro to swerve.

Mother stopped in the middle of the road. "Shazia? What ... what have you done with your ...?" Realisation dawned on her face and she shook me, before turning back to Shazia. "I'll be having words with your mother, missie. And I suppose these are your clothes?" She wrinkled her nose and slapped me on the head. Rain droplets flew off my nose.

"Ow!" I cried, putting my hand up. "What was that for?"

"The tamasha this boy has given everyone," she said, talking about me in the third person, loud enough for the street to hear. Luckily, the only people out were a couple of kids floating lolly sticks in the gutter. They looked up as we passed. "Besharam," she continued, shaking me, "wait till your father hears about this." She scrubbed my lips clean with her dupatta, shaking her fist at any drivers foolish enough to slow down to gawp.

Nine

"Why, why, why, why, why?" Mother demanded upon her return, each word getting higher and higher, matching her rising arms. She threw a bundle of dry clothes at me. They missed me and landed at my feet in a bunched-up mess. Nabila snorted. I shot her a death stare.

"Why what?" I wouldn't give Mother the satisfaction of a straightforward reply – not after I'd been dragged home like that. I snatched my shirt off the floor and flung it on, twisting each button viciously, my fingers trembling.

She tutted. "Ai-hai-hai, how he talks to me. Why were you dressed like that? Why was there make-up on your face? Why did you bring disgrace to the whole family? Why, why, why?" She paced the room, raising a draught.

I sat down heavily on a pouffe. I couldn't trust myself to pull on my trousers while standing up, in case I fell over. Every part of me was jittery.

Nabila was on the pouffe next to me, taking in my appearance, which was now less Swedish bombshell and more Worzel Gummidge. Help, I mouthed, nodding to Mother.

Nabila sighed. "*Maam*, calm down. Don't be so hard on him."

"And you be quiet, little madam! Letting him play with your make-up and dolls."

"It's not like he went out in a bikini," said Nabila.

Mother recoiled, collapsing against the fireguard.

"Please – you're such a drama queen," continued Nabila.

Gasping, Mother clutched her throat. "Is that any way to talk to your mother?"

"No one died," I muttered. "It was just a bit of make-up."

"A bit?" Mother straightened and turned her ire on me once again, the marigolds in her hair shaking loose. "I did not recognise you. Your own mother! And my dupatta – ruined!" She slapped the wet cotton onto the fireguard, narrowly avoiding Nabila. Steam rose instantly from it. "Your father is also to blame. If he was around more often . . ."

I didn't see what that had to do with anything, but now was not the time to argue.

"I have been too spoiling with you. Same with you, besharam," she said to Nabila, who looked justly put out at being described as shameless. "You are twelve years old. No more make-up. No fancy-schmancy clothes. You need to start dressing more like a young woman."

"But you make her clothes yourself," I pointed out. She glared at me. "And you don't normally mind me playing and using my imagination."

Mother flared her nostrils. "There is playing, like Taleeb's cricket and Shazia's brothers' football, and there is bringing shame on our heads, like what you've done with Shazia."

I thought the choices stark, but she waved my protestations away. "Did you not see Mrs Kapoor's face? She will be telling everyone in the village back home."

"That old bag hasn't a good word to say about anyone," said Nabila, taking out a lipstick, only to have it snatched away by Mother. She slashed it around her own mouth.

"Show respect for your olders," she said, finishing off her make-up before the mirror and sticking the marigolds back in her hair. "The sour old churail will be telling everyone how I am raising boy-girls."

I shot up. "Who cares what she thinks? And you've just called her an old witch!"

Mother waggled her head at me. "That is no way to speak about Mrs Kapoor."

She was impossible. I tried to keep my cool. "You've always encouraged me to dress up and dance and sing and stuff. You say I remind you of Rajesh Khanna, and how—"

Nabila scoffed at this comparison to Mother's favourite actor.

"Enough!" said Mother, slamming the lipstick down on the mantelpiece. "There is playing. And there is playing. I keep telling you to spend time with Shazia's brothers. Play footy-ball. Cricket. Tennis. Balls are good. Guns are good. Dresses are not good."

I dropped back onto the pouffe. "You've never minded before when I've tried on your shoes or used your chadar as a skirt. You've even shown me how to wrap a sari."

Mother sighed and spoke slowly, like the white shopkeepers in town often did with her. "Son, there is *inside* the house and there is *outside* the house."

The cogs in my brain whirred, triggering off a series of lights. It was all about what the neighbours would say!

Not what Mother thought. My behaviour was acceptable as long as it remained behind closed doors, in purdah.

Mother continued: "Often, I let you be. I think, 'He is my little boy, he is only playing. It is no harm. He will grow out of it.' But you are getting older. People are talking."

My stomach cramped. I was sick of this message. Shazia's brothers giggled each time I opened my mouth. Mohammed said I "ran like a girl". Everyone else saw and heard something I didn't. I wasn't trying to be anything other than me.

"No more playing with Shazia until you drop this music and make-up and dressing-up baqwaas," said Mother.

"But," I began, but she cut me off with a raised palm.

"No but. I forbid you to see Shazia. Not until you can learn to be a good boy."

How could I contemplate not playing with Shazia? What did being "bad" even mean? Mother wanted me to give up being me. The things she'd once loved about me were now the things causing her issues. It was like me asking her to stop putting flowers in her hair.

I shot up and roared – a scream of pure frustration. Nabila jumped, alarmed. Mother told me to stop right now. I screamed louder and kicked the pouffe. Mother grabbed at me, but I swerved and kicked again. It felt good. Straw bled out of the faux leather sides.

Nabila tried to calm me down, but I couldn't. The world had turned red.

Mother sank on the sofa, shaking her head. She hid behind her chadar, the end of which she raised to her face, just her eyes visible, staring at me as if she didn't recognise me.

The front door slammed. It was Father, home from the

mill. Mother ran out, not even giving him time to drop his tiffin tins in the kitchen. Their whispers swiftly turned to raised voices. The next minute, he'd wrenched open the living room door. I got up from the pouffe, trying to plead my case, but he cut short my objections with a whack on the head.

I fell on the sofa. I had no idea what I was being hit for. Going to the shops dressed as Agnetha? Cutting Shazia's hair? My rage at the pouffe? Before I could register what had happened, I was hauled upstairs, thrown into my bedroom and the door slammed behind me.

I landed by the table, my palms on fire from skidding on the carpet.

The room was in darkness. My legs trembled so much I couldn't stand up to switch on the light. My head swirled with fractured thoughts. Was it me? Or was it everyone else? I was powerless to change either. I moaned. Spasms emanated from within my body. I heaved, taking in dry air in between deep, racking sobs.

From downstairs, Mother called up the stairs before I heard creaks on the steps. Father shouted something and she stopped. She yelled back at him: "You work, work, work. I get no help. It is no wonder he has turned out like this." Her footsteps retreated.

I shook my head in disbelief. Who *was* this woman? For all my ten years, she'd encouraged my play-acting and love of dressing-up and make-up and singing and dancing – and now she was complaining I had *turned out like this*?

In the lulls between my parents' argument, snatches of gameshow laughter escaped from the TV in the living room, as though mocking my plight.

Gradually, my sobbing grew quieter. The room didn't seem as black; the silhouettes were less sinister and the edges had softened. Getting up on shaky legs, I tottered to the bed and collapsed in the middle in a foetal position. My face stung from the salt in my tears.

I drifted off into a troubled sleep.

That night, I dreamed of dragons.

Ten

Although school was going well, thanks largely to Mr H, nights were a different matter. I endured a succession of nightmares: falling down the stairs; my teeth falling out; hiding from a masked man; evading churails and their backwards-pointing feet.

The evening in the bedroom had terrified me. Not Father hitting me – although that had been shocking enough – but my reaction afterwards. Something was gnawing away inside me, but in my waking hours it disappeared with the dreams and the dragons. Whatever was tormenting me, one thing was certain: unhappiness lay therein.

No one understood me, least of all myself. I wasn't like the other boys, but I wasn't like anyone else I knew, either. I could have talked things over with Shazia, but I wouldn't have known where to begin unpicking the layers to get to the root of my sadness.

Lately, I'd received a lot of unwanted attention, the message the same: that I had to change. As though it was as easy as swapping a shirt: a blue for a red. But, like Joseph in the musical, my shirt had many colours and I wasn't prepared to give up any of them.

*

Mr H rushed in, out of breath and apologising for being late. He looked like the Milk Tray man: black polo neck, black jeans, black belt, black cowboy boots.

"Whose funeral is it, sir?" said Zaiman.

Everyone laughed, including Mr H. "Okay, settle down. Lots to get through today."

As Mr H put his paperwork on top of the piano, he cleared his throat, which set off a cough. The papers slipped off the edge and scattered. Ashiqah and I ran over to help.

I gathered up a photo: it showed Mr H, on a beach, with a dark-haired man, about the same age and height. They looked into the camera, each with an arm over the other's shoulder, dressed in almost identical vests and shorts. The photo had fallen out of a letter, which I instinctively began to unfold. Ashiqah slapped the back of my hand.

Mr H approached, flushed. "Thank you, both. I can take those." He reached down.

Ashiqah made to hand them over, but something caught her gaze and she held on for a few extra seconds. I followed her gaze. There was a blotchy rash on Mr H's wrist, like the birthmark above my belly button. Seeing us staring, he pulled down his sleeve and got up.

"Listen up," he said, back at the piano. "Today, we'll be working on your diction. No, Javed, that doesn't mean reading the dictionary. Think soft, think American."

As Mr H explained, the problem was our Punjabi consonants, especially the hard t's and d's. They were a boon for comedians like Jim Davidson and Bernard Manning, but embarrassing for the rest of us. Ashiqah and I didn't pronounce them hard, but everyone else did. Mr H had his work cut out. It took half an hour before we'd vaguely softened anything.

Exhausted, I scanned the lyrics to see what was coming up. Two paragraphs down: *"Pitter patter patter, pitter patter patter, here comes the rain."* The Punjabi t had the aural finesse of a dried chickpea dropped into an aluminium pan from a height.

Mr H caught my eye, winked and nodded. "To paraphrase Shakespeare: to t or not to t – that is the question."

*

After school, Father asked me if I wanted to join him on a trip to the auction house. I was still angry at him for having slapped me, but the lure of the auction proved too hard to resist. I couldn't bring myself to speak to him, so I just nodded yes. He smiled.

He clipped my seat belt in for me, then reached into the glovebox and drew out a bar of sesame seed brittle. Breaking it in two, he offered me the bigger piece.

Father turned the engine. It wheezed like a dying man. "Come on, bloody bastard."

It took several attempts before the car rattled into life. He let the engine run for a few minutes, before pulling away. At speed. He screeched right into Windham Street, narrowly missing the lamppost. I sent up a prayer and focused on the red, fur-lined interior of the car, drawing patterns in it with my finger.

"Son," said Father, popping the last of the brittle in his mouth, "I hope you understand why ... why I did what I did?"

I didn't answer. I traced an elephant in the side panel.

"We cannot behave like junglees," said Father, picking at his teeth with a thumbnail. "People will be saying this and that. How we have not brought you up properly."

I wiped away the elephant in three angry strokes.

"I know you were just doing what you enjoyed," continued Father. "You have a friend you trust. You were going with your heart, not your head. But you know what people are—"

Father broke off to bang the horn and let out a string of expletives in English and Punjabi. A Mini Metro had pulled into our lane without indicating. The driver flashed his rear lights in apology.

"Puthar, we must be respectful of others," said Father, pressing the horn one more time for good measure. "We know many people here. Everyone's families know each other in Pakistan. What if they wrote to Mirpur and said you had gone out dressed up as a girl? Our good name would be laughed at."

I pressed my lips tighter. The incident in the shop seemed like an age away.

"Your mother complains all the time. She says – move, you bloody donkey!"

I thought that unreasonable of Mother, before realising Father was shouting at a cyclist.

"She says she never asked for any of this," said Father, indicating the street outside. I looked at the empty mill we were passing. It sat like a large brick dinosaur, with chimneys for horns and smashed windows for scales. I couldn't blame Mother. "I give her silk, money, gold. I let her come and go as she pleases. I try to be a good husband. She says there are some things you can't buy."

I knew they often argued, but I'd just assumed everyone's parents did. I must check with Shazia to see if her parents ever had cross words with each other.

"She is a wonderful mummy to you all, a good cooker, a seamstress, a maker of . . ." He listed Mother's attributes on his fingers, leaving the steering wheel unmanned. I sunk into the beaded seat, closing my eyes, not wishing to witness the manner of our imminent deaths.

"Sometimes I wonder what I did by bringing her to this country. She has everything she needs, yet she is not happy. Kya baath hai? If only to know."

I also couldn't see what Mother had to be unhappy about. She was always singing and dancing and wearing new clothes. I had never seen her wear the same outfit twice.

"She talks and laughs and the sun comes out," Father said in a quieter voice. "Then, the next day – for no reason – the clouds come back." He sighed, a mournful sound that made the hairs on my neck stand up.

I opened my eyes. It had started raining. Father flicked the wipers on before returning his hands to the ten and two position, the knuckles white. He looked straight ahead, his back stiff and arms locked tight. Muscles and veins throbbed in his throat.

"The land of plenty, puthar – that's what they called it," he said. "So much jobs, they said, you will be making bunglas everywhere. Two, three, four houses. You will send money back to Pakistan. You will want for nothing." He stopped at a junction, waiting longer than necessary, given there was no traffic from either direction. Just as I thought the car might have stalled, he pulled away. "Why would I want nothing? The bloody fools."

A brown Toyota Estate overtook us, with two children sitting cross-legged in the boot. "I know I am lucky. I have a job. For now." He shook his head. "I have health-wealth. I have a home. I should feel like a rich man. And I do. In so-so many ways." He chucked me under my chin, his finger rough against my skin. "But at what cost?" He sighed.

I stuck my tongue out at the kids in the boot of the Toyota. They did the same.

"Don't be like me, son. Make something of your life. There is no future in the mills," he said. "That bloody woman has seen to that."

Mother could be tricky, and ruled the roost, but I had no idea she had this much power outside of the house.

"Bloody Thatcher!" said Father, banging the horn, making the Toyota speed up.

Now it made sense! So many kids at school said their fathers had lost their jobs because of her, as the mills had shut down one by one, with no new jobs to go to. I didn't want that to be us. Before I could ask him more, he made a sharp left. The flashing mosque ornament on the dashboard slid towards me. I pushed it back to the centre.

"Study hard. Respect your teachers. Get a good job. Like a doctor. Or a lawyer."

"I want to be a pop star," I blurted out. "Or an actor. Maybe a dancer."

Father didn't say anything. The indicator clicked in the background.

"I want to make music," I continued, my voice fighting against the noise of the rain. "I want to sing. Dance. Entertain people."

"Son, have you not listened to a word I have said? I told you already, you need to—"

"I won't give up my dreams! I need to perform. I'll die if I can't!" I claimed dramatically and thumped the side panel.

The car juddered as Father stepped on the wrong pedal. "Everton is a good-good school. In Mirpur, we did not even have school. Come, now, I expect better of you."

I flumped back into my seat, crossing my arms and staring out of the passenger window. Thoughts ran around my head in time with the hypnotic thwack of the wipers:

No to Everton. I won't go. No to Everton. I won't go. No to Everton. I won't go.

Father turned into Freckleton Road and pulled into a free space, killing the ignition and yanking the handbrake. The ticking of the cooling engine matched the patter of rain on the roof and my racing heartbeat. Father remained seated, looking at his hands, which were clasped on his lap. His fingertips were blackened with oil or grease from the mill. We sat in silence as the rain quickly overwhelmed the windscreen.

Finally, Father sighed and squeezed a thumb and finger over his eyes before turning to me. "Okay-dokay, shall we see what they have this week, puthar?" He unclipped my seatbelt. "Maybe we will find one of those tap-tap machines you have been wanting?" It was like the previous conversation had simply not taken place.

Normally I'd have bounced out, excited at the thought of getting a typewriter. But I felt unsettled. I opened the door with a heavy hand and an even heavier heart. Rain wetted my head and I pulled up the hood of my duffel coat.

The auction house dominated the street, a Victorian hulk built of sand-coloured stone, Gothic sash windows and fancy finials. I followed Father. As he pulled open the heavy door, the heat of many bodies and the smell of dust, polish and mildew wafted over us.

Before I went in, I turned and looked back. The Capri sat at a rakish angle on the cobbles, an outsider in its two-tone raspberry and cream livery, the only splash of colour in the otherwise grey and brown street. A small part of the heaviness inside me lifted.

Eleven

I yawn. I smile thinking of the Capri. I get up and stretch my legs, determined not to get a DVT from my enforced stay in cattle class. On my third lap, I spot an elderly man towards the back of the plane, in a window seat. For a moment, time scrolls back and Father is here with me. The same flat, pale topi on his head, the chest-length white beard and prayer beads in his knotty hands.

My legs buckle and I must call out, for he looks up, his fingers pausing on the beads. The spell is broken. It is not Father. Father had a straight nose, but this man's is aquiline. He smiles at me, revealing a set of snaggle teeth.

"Assalam alaikum, uncle," I say, greeting him in Arabic.

"Walaikum assalam," he replies. "Aap teek ho?" he adds in Punjabi, asking if I'm well. I nod. The woman at the end of the row looks between us and mutters something.

He indicates for me to join him in the empty middle seat. I excuse myself past the lady, who doesn't budge. I stumble over her bags and she glares at me. I shrug.

He places a hand on my upper arm and talks. I struggle to keep up. I'd never got beyond the basics of my mother tongue before English took over. I nod and smile.

He shifts in his seat and I catch the floral scent of attar. I'm reminded of Father. The smell would linger in the house long after Father had left for the mill. I remember the moment when I kissed his cold forehead and breathed in his favourite attar for the last time.

A hand touches me on the shoulder, and I jump. I'm back in the present. The man is looking at me. He asks if I'm okay. I nod. I get up to take my leave. He passes a hand over my head. "Khush raho, beta." Stay happy, son. Tears prick my eyes.

As I edge out of the row, the woman says something. This time I hear her: "Terrorists".

I make no effort to avoid her feet on my way out.

When I get back to my seat, my female neighbour grins at me. "Say, don't I know you?" She has a strong American accent. I shiver as I'm reminded of someone I once knew. The woman doesn't notice. She offers her hand. "Eulalia. Eulalia Johnson."

Her grip is firm. "Rafi. Rafi Aziz," I say in return.

She squints. "The name don't ring a bell, honey, but the face sure as hell does." She crosses herself at her blasphemy.

I reach for my headphones. Uncharacteristically, I don't feel like talking about myself. Eulalia clicks her fingers. "Oprah!" Even with my imagination, I struggle to see how she can confuse me with a middle-aged Black woman. Seeing my bewilderment, she guffaws. "Coupla month back. Talkin' 'bout Islam." She nods.

My shoulders rise at the mention of Islam. Since September, it's become a heated word. I try to correct her. "You might have seen me on stage?" I proffer. "*Mamma Mia?*"

She scrutinises my face. "You Eye-talian? Why dincha ever say?"

I give up. I say I need to get back to my film and pop my earphones back in.

Twelve

Despite being in Mother's bad books, nothing could sour my weekend. It was the season of mists and something else, according to a poem Mrs Entwistle read to us. In my hand was a letter from school confirming I was taking part in the TV recording at the end of the month along with the rest of the choir. It was the golden ticket to Willy Wonka's chocolate factory.

Clutching it to my chest, I spun around on the spot: if the magic missive in my hand wouldn't let me become Wonder Woman, nothing would.

*

For all my determination not to tell Mother about the ABBA show, I needed her signature on the slip allowing me to go to the recording. Normally I'd have gone into the kitchen leaping and dancing, but today I approached her as one might a skittish horse.

"*Maam*, could you sign this please?" The letter quivered in my hand.

Mother hacked away at a whole chicken on the counter. She preferred to butcher it herself as, like Mrs Kapoor, she didn't trust Mr Khan to give her all the pieces. "Sign? Sign what?"

"My letter." I waved it like a white flag.

"Letter?" she asked, steadily chopping.

"The one about appearing on TV."

"TV?"

She was being particularly obtuse. I doubled numbers in my head. "You know, because St Matthew's won the competition?" This failed to elicit any recognition, so I reached for a further explanation. "To sing on TV?" Still nothing. "With ABBA?"

"Abba? You are singing with your father on TV?" I gritted my teeth. I was clearly not saying the Punjabi word for "father", which was pronounced quite differently.

"ABBA! The band. You love their song, 'Knowing Me, Knowing You'."

On cue, she began humming the chorus. She stopped abruptly a few seconds later, no doubt remembering I was still out of favour with her.

"Anyway, could you sign? They need everyone's letters back on Monday."

Yanking open the door of the fridge with such force that it wobbled, she grabbed a second chicken from inside and thudded it on the counter. "I know you, my boy. Now, it is time for you to know me. I will not be signing-shining anything."

The letter, which had taken up the full screen of my imagination, shrunk to a dot, like when the TV was turned off.

"All this singing and dancing and behaving like a besharam . . . it has turned you bad." She gave such a tug on the skin of the drumstick that the bird shot across the counter like an enormous pinball. "Now look what you made me do," she huffed.

She washed the runaway bird under the tap. "I will send you to Pakistan with your father. You have forgotten your roots. More and more you have become like the goray – but we are not English. We are Muslims."

"We can be both!"

Harrumphing, she thumped the second chicken on the counter. She ripped the skin off both legs – with a gut-wrenching tearing sound. She lobbed the skin over her shoulder into the Elephant flour bag-cum-bin.

"Wow, you could be a basketball player," I said, hoping to butter her up. She didn't crack a smile. Her cleaver flashed in a blur of silver.

Nabila wandered in and opened the fridge.

"This one is growing up fast, and not in a good way," Mother told her, pointing her spoon at me. "Make-up. Hair-cutting. Saris. Playing with girls. Going to the shop dressed as . . ." Unable to finish the sentence, she turned to the pan and stirred the contents around with unnecessary force. "Such tamasha. Such dhoom-dhadka. Where will it end?"

Dumping the pieces of chicken into the pan, she stirred them around vigorously.

"But you've never minded before," said Nabila, pulling out a strawberry-flavoured Ski yoghurt. "You're always singing and dancing together. And you laugh when he dresses up and give him more bits and pieces to try on."

"Well, it is different now," said Mother, riddling the pan over the hob.

"Why?" we both asked in unison.

Mother didn't immediately answer. Giving the contents of the pan one final noisy stir, she reached for the brass mortar from one of the cupboards and let it thud onto the counter, making us jump. She emptied fistfuls of spices into it and pounded away as though breaking rocks. "I have told him: what happens at home is okay, what happens outside is not." She tipped the spice mixture into the pan; the sizzling spices made me cough. "Like your father says about Big Muzaffar: tall people have their sense in their ankles. By the time the sense reaches their head, it is too late. Just like this one."

Nabila took the letter off me and scanned it, before offering it to Mother. "Go on, *Maam*. He really wants to do this. I'm sure he didn't mean anything by whatever happened. You're sorry, aren't you?" she said to me.

"Yes, I am," I said, willing to agree to anything for that signature.

Mother studied my face. Then, as if she couldn't help herself, she squeezed my cheek. She took the letter and started reading it, tracing a turmeric-stained finger under each line. After a minute, she lay it face up on the counter, staring at it some more, before turning back to the pan. She dismissed us with a wave over her shoulder.

I glanced at the letter. It was upside-down. She hadn't even read it. "Actually, I'm not sorry," I said, trying to control my breathing. "I enjoyed dressing up and going out and fooling Mrs Kapoor. And I'd do it again." My voice rose with each sentence.

Mother turned around, sighing, her eyebrows knitted in disappointment. She picked up the letter and tore it in half, then half again, before dropping it in the Elephant bin bag.

Like in a Bollywood film, I heard the shriek of high-pitched violins when the heroine has been told she's got cancer and only three days to live. I gripped the counter.

"No TV recording. Do your schoolwork. No more make-up-shake-up."

I heard Mother as though she was in a different room, her voice muffled. The Bollywood camera panned in and out on my face and then pulled back to show my increasingly bent frame, my knuckles in my mouth.

Mother shook the pan and turned up the heat, filling the room with a frenzied sizzling and spluttering, the chilli burning the back of my throat.

Nabila put a hand on my arm, but I brushed it away. "I hate you!" I shouted at Mother, making her jump. She continued stirring the pan.

In the end, for all her eccentricities, Mother was no different from anyone else. She wanted me to change, to become someone else. But her betrayal was the worst because her approval meant the most.

I grabbed the torn letter from the bin and ran out of the kitchen.

*

I picked up my walkie-talkie and buzzed Shazia to come over on the pretence of doing homework together. Father had bought me an introductory set from the Empire Stores catalogue after he'd done a month of nights. They didn't have a great range, unlike the ones in *The Three Investigators* books, but luckily Shazia only lived a few doors down.

I imagined her eyes wide in horror as she listened to my account. "She tore it up?" she said, incredulous.

I sniffed. "Into four."

I heard her new fringe swish as she shook her head. "I don't get it. What's so bad about taking part?"

I paused. "Well, it's not the concert she's got a problem with. Remember when she dragged me out of KKK's that time?" I said, meaning Khan's Korner Kabin.

She sighed. "Why do parents never get the joke? Right, we can fix this. Didn't you say you'd got a typewriter?"

When Shazia arrived shortly after, Nabila was at Shagufta's, who was going to show her how to do a French plait, so there was no one to chuck us out. Reaching in the gap under my bed, I pulled out the orange Olympia Father had got me from the auction. While Shazia dictated the contents of the torn letter, I typed the words on a blank sheet of paper. I typed much slower than usual, as I didn't want to make any mistakes. I followed the layout of the original letter, even ending each line at the same point.

Shazia whipped the finished letter out. She compared it against the four torn pieces. "Perfect," she said. Then she grabbed my four-colour pen and pushed down the blue button. "Just your mum's signature to add. What does it look like?"

I tried to remember how Mother signed our sick notes. "Well, she doesn't write her name as such. She goes more like this." I traced a series of elliptical scribbles in the air.

"Fab. Makes it easier."

"But, we can't just forge her . . ."

Without waiting for me to finish, Shazia signed the letter with a flourish and handed it back to me. "My work here is done," she said, fanning herself with the letter.

Thirteen

It was happening! I'd counted down the days with increasing anticipation, careful not to let slip in Mother's presence. In a few hours' time, I'd be in the same room as ABBA!

As we waited for the coach driver to let us on, I careered down the queue like a spinning top. Mohammed and his cronies booed, but today nothing would get me down.

Five minutes later, Mrs Entwistle blew the whistle, indicating it was time. Quickly handing my letter over to her, I made to get on the coach.

"And what do you call this?" she said, stopping me, holding my wrinkled-up letter by the corner. She didn't even look at the signature. I'd purposely scrunched up the page, hoping the creases would deflect attention from the different typeface.

"Sorry, Miss. My brother," I lied with surprising ease.

She tutted, then looked at her watch before signalling me up the steps.

Mr H couldn't make it. He wasn't feeling well, said Mrs Entwistle. I'd miss him, but I was too excited to think about anyone or anything else except what was to come.

In twenty minutes, we hit the M6, following directions to the mythical SOUTH.

*

Three hours later, we were at the studios in Birmingham, on our way to the make-up room, guided by Beverley, a poodle-permed woman in a fern green jumpsuit and liver-red leg warmers. She trailed Avon Charisma, a flowery scent I recognised from Mother's collection. Unlike Mother, Beverley was about eight feet tall in her stacked boots.

"Kids, look sharpish – only forty-five minutes till broadcast," she said, referring to her clipboard with a noisy flick of the pages. "That's not a long time in the world of TV." Except it came out "Tie-vie" with her strong accent. "One episode of *The Adventure Game*. Not that I watch it – goes right over my head. But me other half, he loves it, like!"

I called out a greeting from the programme: "Gronda, gronda!"

"And the same to you, bab!" she said. "Is that Pakistani?"

Before I could answer, she'd turned the corner. "Keep it moving, kids: move and groove, that's what my old granddad never said!"

I chattered to myself. I couldn't take it in: the impending meeting with my idols; my senses assaulted by the photos on the walls and the smell of new carpet; and all the while processing Beverley's stories and vowels.

"Stick to the left – busy corridor, this. Some days it's like the bleedin' M40!" She ignored the sharp look from Mrs Entwistle. "The great and the good – not to forget the ugly ..." she gave a braying laugh "... they've all walked down these hollowed walls. Just yesterday: Terry Wogan – a good head of hair, I said to me mam. This morning: Hot Gossip – nice wenches. All legs and leotards, like, but bugger me if they don't get under your feet faster than you can say 'Where's the one with the dodgy teeth?'"

Mrs Entwistle cleared her throat, but the Pied Piper of Edgbaston was oblivious.

"Take it in, kids. The high octave world of television. Smoke and mirrors. 'Never mind the talent on screen,' I says to our George, 'it's the talent behind the scenes that counts.' Without us, we'd be in No Business, not Showbusiness. Oh, that's bostin', that is: No Business!" She clutched her stomach. "I'm a bugger for making meself laugh."

"Pardon me," said Mrs Entwistle, her nostrils flaring. "Brenda, is it?"

"Who, me, love?" said Beverley, looking over her shoulder. "I'll answer to most things. You can call me Brenda if you like, doll."

I tried not to laugh. There was no one less like a doll than Mrs Entwistle.

"Yes," she said. "Would you kindly temper your language in front of the children?"

"Don't mind me, sweetie. You should hear me on a Friday night with the girls. A few Babychams and Lambros ... Lamborghini chasers, and I'm effing and blinding like a—"

"Brenda!" Mrs Entwistle's hair bristled. "Is that really any way to—"

"Hold that thought, Teach," said Beverley, putting a finger to her lips while tottering to a halt before a door with a large star on it. "Righty-tightie, I'll see if they're ready for yous. Knock, knock! Coming in, ready or not!" Banging on the door with the subtlety of a giant coming to tea, she barged inside. "Ta-ra a bit!" she hollered back at us.

I trembled. Behind the star on the door were four even bigger stars: Agnetha, Benny, Björn and Frida. Mumbled voices and laughter seeped through.

Then the door opened. It wasn't ABBA. And it wasn't Beverley. Instead, a short man in cowboy boots stepped out, blocking our view into the room. "You can't come in!" he snapped. "*They* are still in there."

He stressed the word as though talking about otherworldly creatures. Which, I suppose they were. His tone implied that if our paths met, ABBA would explode in a shower of starburst. I was disappointed. I'd desperately hoped we could chat to ABBA before we all went on. Now it looked like it wasn't going to be so.

Mrs Entwistle took charge. "We have no intention of upsetting anyone. But we have been brought here by that . . . by Brenda. Where is she?"

On cue, Beverley snuck out of the door. "Boo!" she said from behind the short man, who leaped into the air. We giggled. Beverley beamed at Mrs Entwistle. "A slight glitch, Teach." Then, to the man, "Nothing to get your knickers in a twist about." Mrs Entwistle and the man remonstrated, but Beverley brushed it off. "Now, would you be loves and stand back so that there's room for their Highnesses when they come out? Then we can get you in for a bit of powdering and what not. That do you, titch?" she asked the man. "Oh, get me! Teach and titch! That's bostin'!" She patted him on the head, which made him jump again as though he'd been electrocuted.

The man, who must have been ABBA's manager or agent, glared at Beverley. He'd gone a shade of raspberry and his eyes threatened to pop out. "I have NEVER . . ."

he began, but couldn't find the right words. He spun on his Cuban heels, shouting, "Woe betide if anyone tries to come in before *they* are ready to leave!" He slammed the door shut.

From inside the room, came raised voices. Beverley tittered nervously, then filled us in about some of the celebrities she'd worked with. I hadn't heard of any of them. The louder the protests from behind the door, the louder she spoke. I tried not to yawn as she began a boring story about Dickie Davis. I wanted to kick the door down. I drilled through the wood with my X-ray vision, crossing my eyes along with my fingers, hoping to glimpse my idols. I just ended up making myself feel a bit dizzy.

Finally, after what seemed like hours, the door inched open and the man stepped out again, even more red in the face than before. "*They've* been very gracious and asked that you come inside," he said in a clipped tone. "Highly irregular, and it goes against all my advice. But *they* have spoken. Consider yourselves honoured. Come in – quietly!"

We twittered and flapped like a bunch of sparrows. I couldn't believe it. We were going to meet ABBA before the performance. An unexpected bonus! Mrs Entwistle marshalled us into a neat crocodile, ably hindered by Beverley who preferred a more natural line-up. Then we went through the fabled door.

It was like the moment in *The Wizard of Oz* when Dorothy steps out of the fallen cottage to a world of Technicolour after the black-and-white of Kansas. As we filed in, we let out hushed variations of "Oh my god!" and "Wow!" and "I can't believe it!" There were A, B, B and A, in that order, on barbers' chairs, hair and make-up ladies buzzing around them, the light throwing haloes around their heads. They waved at us. Agnetha's fuchsia-coloured mouth – those dazzling teeth – smiled at us. I went fluttery.

Ashiqah couldn't stop at a gasp or exclamation of surprise. She swooned. Putting a hand to her forehead, and taking a quick look around first, she dropped like a felled oak.

"Is she okay, the little girl? What happened?"

Agnetha! Those perfect purple-red lips had moved and formed words! I considered swooning myself, so Agnetha could save me, but no one liked a copycat.

Like a newly born giraffe, Ashiqah clambered up, supported by Mrs Entwistle and Beverley. Agnetha flashed her a smile and blinked her a little wave. I couldn't believe it. That should have been for me!

Beverley corralled us before my very own Fab Four. "Now then, kids, say hello to our special guests. It's not every day you get superstars of this calliper."

I was too excited to supply her with the right word. We applauded, hooted, whistled and cheered.

"Hey, hey, hey," said Björn. "Who have we here, then?" He rocked a figure-hugging silver trouser suit and boots with soles the size of the phonebook. He flapped away a make-up lady going for his eyebrows with a pair of tweezers.

We introduced ourselves.

"Izmat Begum, ten-and-a-quarter, and I've always loved your music, ever since I was a little girl, because my Mum remembers me dancing to 'Waterloo', even though I wasn't speaking, but that's because I was a late developer and my Mum says I'd—"

"Thank you, Izmat," cut in Mrs Entwistle.

"Ashiqah Ibrahim, ten. I have all your records." The liar! She curtsied. I felt hot rage.

"Mohammed Seedat, eleven. I don't dig your music, but Miss made me come." Javed had fallen ill, so Mohammed was a last-minute addition. Björn broke into a cough.

Then they turned to me: Benny while being fitted into a cape; Björn adjusting his neckline and fending off Eyebrow Woman; Frida having her lips blotted; and Agnetha having rollers taken out of her hair. My stomach puffed up like a puri in hot oil.

Frida told me not to be shy. Benny winked at me. I gurned to help me relax.

"I see we have saved the best for last," said Björn.

"What is your name, Mr Red?" asked Agnetha. The blonde goddess had spoken to me! And she had noticed my favourite shirt! My cheeks flushed the same colour.

"Rafi, your majesties." I cringed. I'd been thrown by Ashiqah's sickly curtsey.

Björn laughed and clapped Benny on the back, knocking his cape loose, making them laugh even more. "Well, we have been called many things before," said Björn, a twinkle in his eyes, "but never 'your majesties'. I think I like it! Don't you, Frida?"

"It suits me very much." She mimed putting on a crown.

"Sorry, I got a bit nervous," I said. "I just . . . I just really love your music. I'm always playing it on my piano. I can do all the parts from 'Dancing Queen'."

Benny looked impressed. "It is not so easy to play, no? Now, tell me, which song is your favourite?"

It was like being asked to choose my favourite sweet. "I couldn't possibly," I said.

"Puh-lease," muttered Ashiqah without moving her lips. I clenched my fists.

"But if I had to ... probably 'Fernando'," I said. The boys snorted. "I'm normally Agnetha." The boys found this even more hilarious. I reddened. "And ... and my friend Shazia – she's usually Frida. But she doesn't sing as well, and she can't do harmony."

"I hope you are meaning your friend, and not me?" pouted Frida, crossing her arms.

I stuttered an apology.

"I am just joking on you," said Frida, allowing the wardrobe lady to fasten a choker around her neck. "You are too ... hm, I don't know the English. Agnetha, how do you say ..." And she gargled a Swedish word that sounded like "goo-lig".

"Ah, yes, 'cute'!" said Agnetha, blowing me a kiss.

Without thinking, I caught it and brought my fist up to my heart. Mohammed muttered "idiot". Frida told Agnetha she had a young admirer. The boys jeered. Mrs Entwistle slapped a few heads. Björn raised an eyebrow – allowing Eyebrow Woman finally to land her tweezers.

Frida and Agnetha got up – shimmering visions in maxi dresses and cross-your-heart straps. I thought I was going to faint. The most famous person I'd seen until then had been the flautist Atarah Ben-Tovim, who I'd thought was the blond one from Status Quo.

"So, Mr Red. You like to sing 'Chiquitita' with me?" said Agnetha.

This wasn't happening. There *was* a God! If I couldn't have a solo with them on the show, this was the next best thing. "S-s-s-sing a song? With you? Like, now?"

She laughed. "Ja, but I hear Frida is also available."

Mrs Entwistle swung into view and blocked out the light, turning Agnetha and Frida back to mortals. "Are you sure, Miss Fältskog? You don't need to rest your voice?"

Agnetha shook her head. "It is quite all right," she said. "Nothing is trouble. We have a talented young musician here."

I glowed.

Ashiqah put her hand up. "Miss," she said, meaning Agnetha, "could I please do the backing vocals? I know all your songs." Bare-faced liar.

"Sure," said Agnetha. "You had bump? Ouch!" She circled her hand above her head.

Ashiqah beamed.

Beverley rustled up. "Twenty minutes, everyone, twenty minutes. Are yous all right for time, Agnes, bab?" She asked this as if Agnetha was suggesting going skydiving.

Agnetha nodded and sang the first verse. Frida clicked her fingers and the snipping of scissors and hiss of hairspray provided further percussion. Agnetha indicated for me to come in with the chorus. Ashiqah hooted in her backing vocals. I moved to the harmony lines, glancing at Frida, who normally did them in the song. She gave a thumbs up.

I added more intricate harmonies. Agnetha looked at me with her eyes wide open, hands held palm up. Frida clapped and Benny and Björn shouted "Bravo!" Björn mimed playing a guitar and Benny a piano in the air. The whole choir joined in the next verse. The hair dryers fell silent as the make-up ladies swayed from side to side.

When we finished, everyone applauded. Beverley, to Mrs Entwistle's horror, put a finger and thumb in her mouth and produced an ear-splitting whistle.

Benny and Björn came over and shook our hands.

"Wow!" said Benny. "Bravo to your music teacher."

"Just amazing," said Björn, patting me on the shoulder. "You blew us away, truly."

I almost cried. I reached out to hug Ashiqah, magnanimous in my moment of fame, but she shoved me away. I didn't care. I'd sung with Agnetha! We'd all made such a wonderful sound together, too. The best group in the world had loved our performance.

"I do believe," said Agnetha, "we have found the number five member of ABBA!"

She pecked me on the cheek. I stopped breathing. Time stood still. How many times had I stared at that poster on the wall? I would marry Agnetha. Mother would thread roses through her golden locks, copy her blue eye-shadowed look and communicate in Punjabi-inflected Swedish.

As I came out of my reverie, I clocked Mrs Entwistle deep in conversation with Agnetha, while they both looked between me and Ashiqah. What was going on?

*

With the foursome now in the TV studio having their sound check, Beverley took charge again. "Ten minutes, ladies and gents," she bellowed. "Stop yer riling, come out smiling! Ooooooh, I like what I did there. I'm a poet, and I don't even know it. Oh, again! Bostin'."

We were marshalled into the recently vacated chairs, to be powdered and our hair combed and brushed. Janice – "but everyone calls me Jackie" – set to taming my hair with just a comb and liberal sprays with something she called "good old Corporation Hair Oil". It had none of the slickness of Mother's Himalaya Hair Oil, nor its cranberry red colour.

"Can you get it in Boots?" I asked, as Jackie squirted on more of the wonderstuff.

Jackie chortled. "You're a bab, and no mistaking."

Ashiqah yelped as she was bundled in my place. Jackie

eyed the backcombed bouffant with suspicion. It was leaning perilously after her earlier fall. "Well, did you ever – not in a rain of pig's pudding!" Ashiqah looked shocked. It was bad enough being insulted, without the "p-i-g" word being thrown in as well. Jackie quickly dismantled the lopsided beehive, replacing it with a scalloped fringe, like my beloved Parveen Babi.

"You look well bostin'," I said to Ashiqah, meaning it.

"Language!" barked Mrs Entwistle.

*

Just before we went into the studio, Mrs Entwistle called me over. "It seems like you have a fan," she said, breaking into a rare smile. "Agnetha was most taken with your rendition and has made a special case for you to share the solo."

Ashiqah's ears flapped from the back of the room. She charged over. "Miss, that's not fair! He didn't win. I did!" She looked tearful and murderous at the same time.

My mouth dropped open. I couldn't speak. Mrs Entwistle's news was like being gifted a chocolate factory, a trip to the moon and a starring role in a Bollywood film all in one.

The noise around us continued. It coalesced into words "... and he didn't even get his lines RIGHT!" – uttered with such venom that the make-up ladies looked up.

"Ashiqah, remember where you are," said Mrs Entwistle.

"It's not fair," said Ashiqah. "He's being rewarded for losing. I hate him!"

"That's quite enough," snapped Mrs Entwistle. "You are to sing the first half of the song and Rafi the second. And that's the end of it."

*

Marian Foster, the presenter, introduced us and we arranged ourselves in a semi-circle behind the seated four. The sea of grey heads in the audience smiled and clapped politely. Cameras blinked and sailed into position. As the lights dimmed, Benny played the introduction on a white grand piano.

The next forty minutes passed in a blur. We went through all the songs we'd rehearsed over the weeks at school, but this time accompanied by the Fab Four. Mr H had trained us well and we sang our hearts out, conducted by Mrs Entwistle. We performed our choreography without any hitches, the boys getting into it as much as the girls – except for Mohammed, who just shuffled about and looked uncomfortable.

The final song was "I Have a Dream". This was the solo number. Normally my least favourite track, today it was the best song ever. I couldn't stop grinning.

Accompanied by Benny on the piano, Ashiqah sang first. Never one to hold back, she opened her mouth to full "O" and delivered her lines with the vigour of an anthem.

Then it was my turn.

"Go for it, bud, you've got this," I heard Mr H's voice in my head.

A camera came in close. I caught myself on the little monitor next to it. My red shirt looked splendid, my Brylcreemed hair slicked tidy and my mouth open just so.

I enunciated each word. I remembered Mr H telling us: "There's poignancy in the song and it's often missed."

The last part was to be sung completely a cappella. I paused, as I'd been told to do back in the dressing room. Looking into the camera, I gave my best Colgate twinkle. Ashiqah elbowed me, but this time I was expecting it and held my ground.

I breathed in, mindful not to shrug my shoulders. The

audience was completely silent. I sang the final lines, hearing my voice echoing around the studio. Inside my head, a metronome ticked off the beats, keeping me steady.

As the final "dream" hung in the air, Benny wrapped things up with a flourish of keys. The audience clapped, Marian thanked everyone and the titles started rolling.

Agnetha came up and kissed me on the cheek. A surge of electricity shot through me. I'd never wash again!

After that, the memories turned into the pages of a flick book: ABBA coming around one final time and shaking our hands and ruffling our hair and Marian saying something to us and everyone wishing us a safe journey back and Beverley rounding us up and taking us in reverse through the corridors to the coach waiting to drive us back and being warm and tired and saying something to Ashiqah and being rocked in the seat with my head resting on Shirley and driving up the motorway and struggling to keep my eyes open.

Fourteen

I checked in daily with the school receptionist, in case talent scouts from the world of pop, TV or dance had been in touch. Incredibly, the answer was the same: no. It was with a bitter heart that I accepted fame wasn't going to follow me as it had the shouty singers of St Winifred's. The threat of Everton loomed just as strong. Thankfully, I had another ten months until then, so I tried to put it out of my mind for now.

Passing the piano in the Hall, I breathed in the comforting smell of beeswax. Mr Mobsby must have polished the wood recently. Checking to make sure I was alone, I lifted the lid up and ran my fingers over the ivory keys, marvelling at their smoothness.

Five minutes later, I was on the stool, thumping out passable covers of Bucks Fizz's "Making Your Mind Up", the chorus of ABBA's "Honey, Honey" and "Memory" from *Cats* – until the sound of clapping made me jump. Mr H leaned in the doorway, a big smile on his face.

Slamming the lid shut, I shot up, the stool scraping on the parquet. "Sorry, sir."

Mr H walked over, the heels of his cowboy boots rapping on the parquet. He wore a brown Stetson. "I come in peace," he said. "I won't tell, if you don't. The only crime was a few bum notes and a sketchy left hand, sure, but otherwise it was bang on the money."

I blushed from the compliment, even if I didn't understand every word of it.

Mr H looked around the piano, the stool and finally me. "Where's the sheet music?"

"Sheet music? Oh – no, sir, there isn't any."

Mr H raised his eyebrows. "Okay, hit me with something else."

"Like what, sir?"

"Surprise me." He jumped over the stool and sat next to me. I detected the spicy lavender scent of Brut. He placed his hat on my head. I grinned from ear to ear.

My hands weren't used to bridging such spans and the keys were heavier than I was used to. But I muddled through, occasionally doing a Les Dawson with the wrong notes.

As I signed off with a baroque flourish of keys, Mr H started coughing.

I looked over at him anxiously. "Was it that bad, sir?"

Mr H laughed, setting him off again. "Sorry," he said, when it finally went away. "Just a cough I can't seem to get rid of. But, bravo, my man! That was a masterclass in melody. A neat tune, with plenty of light and shade. I wasn't able to place the song?"

I came over uncharacteristically bashful. "It was ... it was one of my own."

Mr H tilted his head. "You wrote that?"

I nodded.

"I've been teaching for almost ten years," he said, "but these moments are few and far between, believe me."

What moments? I was just playing something I'd written. Didn't everyone do this?

As if reading my thoughts, he said, "No, it's not common.

I was at music school before I could even do half of what you've just shown me. Way to go!"

He stuck up a high five, which I clapped straight back. Inside, I was on fire. No one had ever complimented me on my music before.

Mr H asked me for another tune. And another. I was more than happy to oblige.

*

Mr H persuaded Mrs Entwistle to let me use the piano. He said I had a gift. He'd teach me twice a week after school. In between, I was to practise by myself.

"Rafi, could I have a word?" said Mr H at our next lesson. He was in his signature denim, like the man in the Denim aftershave ad. A chunky gold chain disappeared into the open buttons of his shirt. Tan-coloured cowboy boots completed the outfit. I made a note to ask Mother if she would buy me a pair from Mehbooba's School Outfitters And All The Latest Fashions For Men, Women's And Children, a local clothes store run by the short but formidable Mrs Mehbooba.

"Yes, sir?" I said.

He passed me a brochure with a red-brick building on the cover, with hundreds of windows, and an ornate glasshouse on the side. "The Conservatoire. Do you know of it?"

The pages were full of students dressed in navy blazers, grey trousers or skirts, and maroon-and-yellow striped ties. I shook my head.

"It's a French word," said Mr H. "It means a school that specialises in music and the arts. The Manchester Conservatoire is one of the best in the country."

I flicked through the pages: laughing students carrying their instruments around campus; scenes from a play that looked worthy of the BBC; a double-page spread of a concert hall with an orchestra of pupils on stage watched by proud parents.

"I can't believe it's real," I said. "It's like Disneyland."

"Well, you don't have to fly to Florida," said Mr H. "Just an hour on the train from here, although most of the students are boarders."

Visions of *Malory Towers*, *Billy Bunter* and *Jennings* popped into my head: midnight feasts, crazy French teachers, receiving cake in the post. My eyes bulged.

"You like the sound of it, Rafi?" Mr H leaned back, tipping his chair onto its rear legs so he could stretch his cowboy-booted feet before him.

"It would be a dream come true!" I tried to tip myself back, too, but quickly righted myself. Returning to the brochure, I let out gasps and moans as each new page boasted further glories available to the students. Here a girl was playing a harp! There a boy conducted an orchestra!

"Why should it be a dream, Rafi?"

"Because it is, sir. It's not for people like me," I said wistfully.

"People like you?" Mr H brought his chair back down and scrutinised me. "I'm looking, Rafi. What am I meant to be seeing?"

Mr H couldn't be this blind or stupid.

"Sir, how could I get into a school like this?" I rustled the book. "No one looks like me." Mr H shook his head, not understanding. "They're all white."

Mr H wasn't fazed. "And?"

Why was he pushing me? My eyes filled up. I didn't know why I even cared about the stupid school – it's not like I stood any chance of getting in. In any case, we all knew which school I'd be going to.

"Rafi, let me tell you something." Mr H leaned in. "You and those students all have one thing in common: talent. They – and you – have a reason for being at that school."

As much as I wanted to believe him, I did what the adults around me usually did: knocked myself down and stifled any dreams. I kept my mouth shut, not trusting what might come out.

He pointed at a couple of pages. In one was a student from an Asian background, and, in the other, two Black teenagers. "Keep an open mind. Don't see what you only want to see, Rafi. At the risk of sounding like the Dalai Lama, you can follow paths well-trodden or you can forge your own. It's easier to go along a familiar route – when there are no tigers to fight or rockfalls to negotiate. But where's the challenge in that?"

I didn't know what he was talking about. It was suddenly hot in the room. I needed to go.

Mr H went on: "Some of these students will have parents who work in the mills. But they'll have received financial help because of their talent. Hard work. Determination." He tapped the brochure at each point. "Not money. Not family. Not the colour of their skin."

The clock in the back of the Hall chimed the half hour. Through the open windows, I heard the slamming of a car door and an engine firing up.

Mr H had stopped talking. "You okay, bud?"

I stared at the brochure. "I seem to get into trouble for my so-called talent, sir. Or told to stop doing it." I blinked quickly, to bat away the tears that were threatening.

Mr H grasped my shoulders. "You have music and performance and dance running through your veins. Don't let *anyone* tell you that's not a good thing, or for you to stop being who you are."

The fluorescent strip behind Mr H's head glowed like a light sabre. "I'm not like the other boys," I said. "There's something wrong with me." It was out, the thought that had haunted me for years. "I don't fit in. The girls won't let me play with them, either. Sometimes, I'm so lonely I . . . I . . ."

Mr H passed me a lilac handkerchief the shade of a sugared almond. I wiped roughly at the tears that spilled over. What was wrong with me? Why was I always crying lately? What must Mr H think of me?

Embarrassed, I stood up, turning my face away. "You don't understand, sir. I'm . . . my family . . ." I pushed around my chair, looking for my jacket. "You're normal. Everyone's normal. The whole world's normal. Not a freak like me!"

I leaped up, sending the chair toppling, the crash echoing around the Hall.

Mr H put his hands up. "Hey, easy now. You know you can talk to me any time, right? Not just about school stuff. About anything. Okay, bud?"

I continued searching for my jacket, barely able to see through the tears.

Mr H got up. "Believe me, Rafi, we are more similar than you think."

I felt like I'd run a marathon. Mr H was letting me down, just like the other grown-ups – only he was giving me hope, when he knew there was none. I began walking away.

"Stay, Rafi. Talk it through. Maybe I can help?"

I scoffed. He didn't know Mother. There was no getting around her prejudices or her stubbornness.

"Keep the brochure. Show it to your parents. I can come and speak to them?"

I turned around and wiped my nose on the handkerchief, which I still carried. "Posh boarding school ... music and dance ... Manchester. They'll never agree. They won't ever understand. I'm going to Everton, and that's that."

Mr H visibly blanched. "The rough school on the hill? Jeez, no!" He came over to me. "Let me have a word with them. I'm pretty sure I can make them understand."

His continued kindnesses were like stabs to my heart. I shook my head and roared. Mr H put up both hands, as if holding back a wild animal. As I tossed my head from side to side, a scattergun of fresh tears fell on the parquet. Mr H said something and slowly walked towards me, but I couldn't make out the words. I edged away from him, then broke into a run.

As I pulled open the door, Mr H called after me. "Rafi. Who wants to be normal?"

*

I flung stones into the canal, firing them off as fast as I could pick them up from the towpath. The conversation with Mr H played out in my head. I couldn't bear the fact he had seen me so vulnerable: crying, wailing, snot running from my nose.

I was surprised at my worn-down attitude. Normally, the idea of boarding school would have had me skipping around with excitement. But it was as if I was determined to punish myself. Perhaps I didn't think I was good enough for the Conservatoire? Or maybe I knew I'd never be able to persuade Mother? She was unlikely to agree to a school that focused on the very singing and dancing to which she now objected so strongly.

The thought of ending up at Everton made me clench

my jaw and hands. As my breathing grew shallow, black dots appeared before my eyes, a precursor to getting a headache or fainting. I sank down onto the verge. Everything I'd heard about the school made me despair. It had the worst grades in the county. Only a tiny percentage of pupils got A to C in their O levels. Even fewer went on to university. I'd be lucky to get a CSE, especially with Amjad tormenting me each day.

I covered my face with my hands. I was tired of the fighting, both mental and physical. I couldn't risk another argument – with Mr H, Mother, Father, whoever – in case it proved to be the one to topple me.

Fifteen

As the days passed, the dragons visited my dreams less frequently, and I was to meet a mythical creature of another sort: David Harrington.

When he started school mid-way through November, it was like our own episode of *The Boy from Space*. Like the alien boy, David spoke a new language: Australian English. Unlike the boy, David was tall, outgoing and with a luxuriant head of conker-coloured hair. I'd also just read and enjoyed *I am David* by Anne Holm, so I was intrigued to see what this real-life namesake would be like.

With his fair skin, green eyes and perfectly straight nose, he was a unicorn in our midst. He caught me staring and flashed a dazzling smile. I pretended I was looking at the noticeboard behind him. He came up and introduced himself, replacing my handshake with a warm hug. I stood stiff as a tree, arms by my side.

We were soon joined by the others.

"Can you keep kangaroos as pets?" asked Ashiqah.

"Do people walk upside down there?" That was Asghar.

"In a fight, who would win – Australia or America?" said Mohammed, throwing punches with whoosh-whoosh sound effects.

Everyone wanted to be his friend – whether it was the

girls linking arms with him and gossiping in his ear or the boys involving him in football games or teaching him the boring intricacies of itti-danda, a game played with two bits of stick.

*

In our first music lesson together, Mr H paired us up, despite my best attempts to look invisible. I was so used to others thinking me odd, I didn't want to see the disappointment in David's eyes when he realised I wasn't one of the cool kids.

We had to recreate a popular song in any method of our choosing.

"So, what kind of music are you into, Raf?" said David. "Is it cool for me to call you that?"

I nodded. Certain he wouldn't like anything I did, I asked him to go first.

"Do you know 'Eagle'?" he said.

I had vaguely heard of the American band. "I'm not very good with rock, though," I apologised. I looked at the clock over the door: it was going to be a long hour.

David clapped me on the back. "No, you dill. I meant the ABBA song."

My head did jerky pigeon movements. He had chosen one of their lesser-known numbers. Had someone put him up to this? Told him how to wind me up?

"But, no worries," he continued, "we can do something else if you—"

"You know 'Eagle'? Really?" I said, my voice squeaky with excitement.

"ABBA are massive back home, mate."

The rest of the lesson flew by. We performed the song without instruments. David had a good singing voice, deeper than mine, and he took the melody while I sang harmony. Mr H raised an eyebrow at our choice of song, his mouth raised at the corners.

As we finished, I looked over in Mohammed's direction. Normally, he would have said something but today he kept quiet.

*

David and I started to hang out during break times. He'd play football or British Bulldogs or cricket with the other boys, then seek me out. We'd walk around the playground, chatting, his arm often around my shoulders. It was a wholly novel experience for me, as normally I spent my break practising the piano, reading or trying to latch onto the girls' groups.

Mohammed and Co. would look over, wondering what David saw in me. I wasn't sure myself. I think he found me funny. I had a way with words. I could tell a story with silly voices and actions, pretending it was a scene from a movie. And, since I had an opinion on everything, we could talk about most things, not just cars or football.

He went through the rules of football with me after I asked him if a free kick was the same as a penalty. He showed me how to angle a cricket bat to avoid giving away an easy catch. How to remember the names of the bones in a skeleton in biology lessons, which he loved. How to cleave the water to make my front crawl more efficient. He told me about his camping holidays in the Outback, showed me how to read a compass, how to make a whistle out of a twig, and a hundred other things. He also taught me self-defence moves, using tricks he'd learned from Bruce Lee films.

I showed him how to use milk to write secret messages

that only became visible once the paper was held next to a light bulb. I taught him different types of knots. I introduced him to Punjabi swear words, which I realised were largely animal-based: bhandar (bear), ullu ka patta (son of an owl) and bhara khotha (big donkey). I even revealed to him Mother's unique paper plane design, which was far better than any other.

As a result of our association, I found myself being teased less. I even became halfway decent at PE. David made a point of choosing me for his team, rather than the usual state of affairs where I ended in the bottom two with Asghar (who had the excuse of having a glass eye). His faith in me paid off, as did his private lessons, and I learned to kick a ball so that at least it went in the direction I wanted it to.

My logic was a good match to his skill and strength. We were the fastest at the wheelbarrow: I would grip his plim-solled feet and tilt him up at the most efficient angle, while he would spring along on his hands with powerful strides. I tried not to get distracted by the faint blonde hairs on his tanned legs.

In the piggyback race, his face would be close to mine, shouting out encouragement. Then it would be my turn to jump on him. He'd set off at a sprint, his arms pinning the backs of my legs. As I minimised the drag and jostle by pressing into him, my face came into contact with the back of his head, his hair brushing my cheeks. I marvelled at its softness and willed for the race to go on a little longer. I held on tighter.

It was an autumn where, for the first time, I belonged. It was an autumn I didn't want to end.

Sixteen

Intermission. I press Pause and stretch my arms overhead. Time for a walkabout again.

The lights were dimmed shortly after dinner. The man on my right hasn't stirred. Eulalia is still awake, playing poker. Each time she wins a hand, she crosses herself.

I pace the aisle, restless. The flight's going to be another five or six hours. Cooped up in here like a rat in a cage. Most of the passengers are asleep. A handful of screens glow in the dim light. I'm the only one on my feet. The captain has wished everyone a good night and even the crew have retired to their quarters. I pace stealthily and carefully, mindful of dangling limbs and slumped heads.

As I approach the first-class curtain, it pulls back. I stifle a yelp. The spicy waft of Kouros. Pedro. His face in shadow. His eyes glitter from the faint light of the Exit sign.

"Can I help you, sir?" he whispers. I hear his accent even in those five simple words.

A shiver runs through me. What's the matter with me? I'm as good as married, yet here I am, behaving like a teenage girl out on a secret tryst.

"I . . . I . . . I'm just having a stretch," I say. As if to demonstrate, I rise up and down on the balls of my feet. The tendons in my ankles click like castanets in the night. I stop.

Pedro doesn't say anything. Is he smiling? It's hard to tell in this gloom.

"Actually, could I – would you have some water?" I ask.

"Water?" he says, teasing out the syllables as if saying the word for the first time.

I cock my head. "Agua, sí," I say. I bite the inside of my cheek. Why have I suddenly switched to Spanish? It's not like he doesn't speak perfect English.

"Estás seguro de que es todo?" he answers, a suggestive quality to his voice.

I blink. He flicks his head and motions for me to follow him through the curtain. I hesitate for a second, then head after him into first class, the blood thumping in my ears. *What are you doing?* says the angel on my shoulder. *You do this, he'll never forgive you.*

What happens in Vegas, stays in Vegas, I tell myself. We might not have an open relationship, but he knows I have dalliances when I'm travelling around the world. Doesn't he? All gay couples do. Don't they? What's a boy to do when a sexy opportunity comes up? Stay at home like a nun? No, he'll understand. It's just a bit of fun.

Pedro pushes open the door of the toilet. The light flickers on. He looks back at me before entering. This isn't quite what I'd hoped for, I think, but I follow him in.

The first-class facilities are no more spacious than those in cattle. The toilet is cramped enough for one, let alone two. He pulls the door shut and snaps the bolt home.

I breathe through my mouth – no amount of Kouros will blot out the smell of disinfectant. The strip light casts a urine-coloured hue. I glimpse myself in the mirror and immediately turn away – I don't need to see my conscience staring back at me.

Pedro locks his lips on mine, his hands like a blind

man's all over me. He pushes me back against the sink. My head bangs into the light unit. Pedro grunts in satisfaction and presses into me with even more frenzy, making my head thud with each thrust. With nowhere else to go, I'm concertinaed onto the ledge of the sink, water seeping in through the bottom of my jeans.

I try to relax and meet Pedro's kisses with the same passion. He tastes of nicotine and spearmint. I wrap my fingers in his hair, to hold his head steady, noting how the strands feel so different from the ones I know so well, more coarse and straight. I experience another stab of guilt. What the hell am I doing? I make to get down from my precarious perch, to get back to my seat. But Pedro isn't letting me go that easily. His leg locks between my crotch, pinning me back. He thrusts himself at me with even more fervour.

As his fingers rip my shirt open, a button flies off and lands with a rattle in the toilet bowl. I peer over Pedro's shoulder. I could rescue it, but I've just had my nails buffed. Twenty dollars literally down the drain. I grit my teeth. *Focus.*

His fingers play with my nipples. I can't help but gasp in pleasure. At the same time, another wave of guilt floods through me. I bat it away. It's too late for that.

Pedro's hands move south. I moan and nuzzle his neck. The light fizzes angrily behind my head but all I can think about are the incredible spasms running through me.

"Y qué tenemos aquí?" he says. He finishes unbuttoning my jeans and sinks to his knees. I vaguely worry about the wet floor, before all sense leaves me. I close my eyes. I forget about everything else. Australia may as well be a million miles away.

*

When I return to my seat, Eulalia is asleep. Her screen lies unloved and untouched in her lap, showing an unplayed poker hand. She snores as loudly as the man by the window. He's changed position and his head now lolls into my seat, as does Eulalia's. I sigh. It's going to be a long flight.

I briefly contemplate removing my wet trousers but decide against it. I shudder as I picture the headlines. "Star of musicals caught with his pants down!" "Going down under!"

I stumble past Eulalia, then inch gingerly down into my seat.

Naseeb is still on pause. I should sleep, but my mind is racing. I slip my earphones on and press Play. The comforting sounds of Indian melodrama fill my ears.

What was all that about? I ask myself. When did I become someone who has sex in a toilet? I shake my head, trying to dislodge the image. We've been together for five years – mostly monogamous. Yes, like a magpie, my attention is easily caught by anything shiny and new, but I don't always act upon it. What made me do so this time? Was it the anonymity of the situation? Even that's not true, as I recall his name badge looming in my face each time he thrust me back into the mirror. The fleeting nature of the encounter? Knowing that I'll probably never bump into him again? Being so far away from home?

The excuses spin round and round in my head in a knot as complex as the plotline unfolding on the screen. I need a shower. I'll pop into the first-class lounge at Dubai.

Eventually, my eyelids feel heavy and I drift off. Back to more innocent times.

Seventeen

It was Saturday morning and Mother and I were visiting Aunty Tariqa, a distant relative. Working with complementary colours, I'd teamed a royal blue shirt with a burnt-orange tank top. I looked the biz, as Mr H often said about some TV actor or another.

Mother concluded a tale about the men in her village with a surprisingly positive reaction towards the Brylcreemed quiff I had spent all morning perfecting. "They have a whiff, just like yours," she said. "A man is judged by how much cattle he has, if he has his own teeth and how big his . . ." She tailed off, having reached our destination.

The house was right at the end of Pitt Street, on the corner of Meadow Street. It must have been a shop in a former life, as it had a huge downstairs window that ran the entire length of the wall. Heavy net curtains, the colour of teabags, covered the glass. Eyeing them distastefully, Mother knocked on the door.

"They may be at the butcher's, Reshma," said a voice from behind us. "Tasleem was at the shop earlier and mentioned she was making keema mattar."

It was Ashiqah's mum. She wore a black raincoat belted over a baby-blue salwaar kameez, with a fluffy yellow scarf knotted around her neck, her feet in marshmallow pink trainers. She looked like she was made out of Liquorice Allsorts. "Just on my daily walk," she said. "Exercise is so important for women of our age."

Mother didn't say anything but stared at her as though she was a mirage. I couldn't take my eyes off her, either.

"We sell trainering shoes," said Mrs Ibrahim, unperturbed, wiggling a pink foot. "Do pop in. There is something for most feet." She said this as though Mother had hooves.

"You are very kind, Ghazala," growled Mother.

"You must be so proud of him," said Mrs Ibrahim, patting me on the head, before registering the quiff and withdrawing her hand.

Mother stepped back. "Proud?"

"Come, my dear. It is not every day our children come to such attention."

"It certainly is not!" Mother huffed.

They were talking at cross purposes – and I had a horrible feeling I knew what Mrs Ibrahim was referring to. I tugged at Mother, to get her to turn away, but she resisted.

"You must have wanted to shouting it from the rooftops, my dear?" said Mrs Ibrahim.

Mother knotted her dupatta under her chin. "The less people who know, the better."

"*Maam*, can we go home? They're not in," I said.

Mrs Ibrahim frowned. "I did not see you as the modest type, Reshma."

"Modern? I am very modern, Ghazala jaan, but I am not *that* modern!"

I tried again. "I should get back and do my book review. Miss said—"

"It was on TV. Everyone in the khandaan has seen it. It is the talking of the town."

Mother gasped, then fired off questions like machine gun

bullets. I tried to divert the conversation by asking after Ashiqah, but Mrs Ibrahim was now equally determined.

Her forehead creased with lines, reminding me of the staves in my sheet music. "It was on the B . . . B . . . C." She strung out the letters like they were precious jewels. "All singing-shinging. With that popping group – you know, AMMA?"

Despite Mrs Ibrahim getting the name wrong, Mother twigged. Her embarrassment immediately morphed into anger. Her fingers dug into my arm, kneading it as though it was chapatti dough.

Mrs Ibrahim went on: "Baby and your Rafaz in wah-wah close-up. Big, big faces, ma'shallah!" She adjusted the belt around her coat. "You will insist on keeping me talking, Reshma," she trilled. "Come soon. We do not normally do credit, but as it is you, my jaan . . ." She left her generosity hanging.

Mrs Ibrahim called over. "I will send you the VHS. Baby's father recorded it on the JVC. Her and Rafiq's big day – we cannot be forgetting. Khuda Hafiz!"

With that formal goodbye, she speed-walked away in her pink pumps.

Mother spun me round. "Bathameez child. Is this true?"

I was spared by the door opening. Mother vented her fury on Aunty Tariqa's young daughter, who, in panic, tried to shut us out, further igniting Mother's rage.

*

When we got home, Mother continued from where she'd left off. "You went against my wishes, behind my back, over my head! I told you I would not sign your letter. I tore it up! But you still went. How? Why? When?"

Without waiting for an answer, she dropped to her knees and rummaged under the sofa. She pulled out my piano. "No more this for now, young man."

"Not my piano!" I made to take it from her, but she raised her arm like the Statue of Liberty, holding the piano out of my reach.

"You need your father to chandna you again." she said, referring no doubt to the incident when he'd slapped me. "He has been too easy with you. And I have spoilt you. This is how you thank us?" She rattled the piano, shaking out a series of broken chords.

"Be careful!" I implored. If she damaged the piano, I knew she'd not get me another one.

"Making a tamasha in front of everyone. On national TV! What will people say?"

"Probably how good I sounded," I said, making another grab for the piano. She held her arm aloft even higher. "I'd forge your signature again if I had to."

She slapped me on the back of the head. "You shame me in front of Mrs Kapoor. You run around the street wearing make-up and a dress. Your father—"

"It wasn't a dress."

"—has to apologise to Mr Khan," she bulldozed on, slapping me again. "You cut Shazia's hair. I have to apologise to Mrs Chaudhry. Then I forbid you to go to TV. And what do you do? You go to TV, making even more show of yourself and me!"

She emphasised each accusation with another shake of the piano. It rang out dolefully. As I took in all the charges, she stormed out, taking my precious, blue baby grand with her.

*

A couple of hours later, the bedroom door opened. From downstairs, I heard the roar of a football match. *Grandstand*. Every bloody Saturday, as predictable as the Back to School posters which appeared as soon as the summer holidays started.

"*Maam* asked me to have a word." It was Taleeb. It must be important if he was prepared to leave a game unwatched. Normally, he was glued to the box from midday till five, shouting at anyone foolish enough to walk in front of the screen.

I sighed. "What about?" I was on the bed, playing imaginary keys on the duvet. He'd interrupted me just as I was getting to the chorus of an Arabian-inspired melody.

Taleeb perched on the edge of the bed. "Is everything okay, Raf?" he said in a soft voice. I looked behind him to see what they'd done with the old Taleeb.

I drew my knees up and hugged them. "Why shouldn't it be?"

Taleeb paused. His face was even longer and more serious than normal, making him look even more like Champion the Wonder Horse. "*Maam*'s worried about you. Says you're not yourself at the moment."

Not myself? Surely, the problem was I was being *too* much of myself for her.

"You have to start growing up. In a few weeks, Dad'll probably be out of work. What's he going to do then? Thatcher's shut everything down."

Up until recently, Margaret Thatcher had just been a name I'd heard on the news. Now she was in our house. I shivered, picturing her like the Evil Queen from *Snow White*.

Taleeb placed a consoling hand on my knee. "I'd love to play for England, but it's not going to happen. We've all got to step up. You can't be nine forever. Just think before you do something. Ask yourself, how will it look on the rest of us?"

"I'm ten, actually, and I'm fine the way I am," I said, removing his hand from my knee. "I don't know what your problem is."

Sighing, he scratched his Jimmy Hill chin. "My mates tease me about my 'little sister'. You sound like a girl. You even *walk* like a girl. I'm fed up of defending you."

So, that was what this was about. Never mind what I might want or think.

He wasn't done. "Look, all I'm saying is don't have people talking about you. You'll become an embarrassment."

The dark piano chords of the Madness song "Embarrassment" sounded in my head. "Leave me alone," I said, blinking away the tears. I tried to leave, but he pushed me back.

"You can't keep running away," he said.

With trembling hands, I dug out a folded-up tissue from inside my shirt sleeve.

"Come on, I'm telling you for your own good, looking out for you," continued Taleeb, his grip easing and his voice softening. "No more dressing up. No more silly games. No more playing with Shazia. Just be yourself. Okay?"

Again, the mixed messages of what being myself meant. I shot out of his hold and bounced off the bed, nostrils flared, arms akimbo, teeth bared. "I've had it up to here!" My hand sliced above my head. "If being a boy means being like you, then forget it!" I windscreen-wipered my index finger in front of his face.

Taleeb laughed. "You're consistent, I'll give you that."

I growled and Taleeb jumped. Mother called up to see if everything was all right.

"Just be myself? Well, guess what, I *am* being myself. This is me." I swirled my hands down from my head to my hips. "And if you – or anyone else – don't like it, well you can just . . . they can just . . . fuck the fuck off."

I swept out of the room, noting with satisfaction his shocked expression. My first swear word. And I'd said it twice!

Eighteen

It was going to be a perfect Sunday. No doubt feeling guilty about her bad mood yesterday, Mother was being extra nice to me. Apart from promising to make my favourite aloo gobi for lunch, she'd given me a crisp £1 note, to get onions and garlic and to spend the change as I pleased. Later, Father said he'd take me for a spin in the Capri over Darwen Moors. Just a half-hour drive away, the moors were a world apart from the cobbled streets and smoking chimneys of the town. Father hared through the green and purple heather-strewn hills like he was Gilles Villeneuve. He'd stop at the top so we could take in the lights of Blackburn glittering in the dusk. With the car doors open, the hypnotic sounds of traditional Pakistani qawwalis sung by Nusrat Fateh Ali Khan would echo around the very English countryside.

After a breakfast of crispy, buttery parathas, I wheeled my Grifter from the backyard, through the house, scraping the handlebars on the walls of the vestibule.

Baines Street was quiet – it was still early. I spotted Shazia sitting on her doorstep. I hadn't seen her for a while, as I'd been so busy with my music lessons.

"Where are you going?" she asked. She was playing panj-geete, throwing four stones into the air and trying to catch them on the back of her hand while tossing up a fifth stone.

"KKK's – want to come? My mum's given me extra money to spend on stuff."

Shazia flung the stones into the road. She popped into her house and, a minute later, joined me on her scooter. We wheeled bike and scooter along the pavement, so we could talk, the big and small wheels trundling over old hopscotch games on the flagstones. With my CHiPs-style sunglasses and Shazia's dark green visor, I imagined we were Frankie and Joanne from *The Red Hand Gang*. I wore a blue cardigan over a candy-striped T-shirt, biscuit-coloured shorts (with a curry stain on the pocket) and imitation Converse from Tommy Ball's. They were a roomy size seven, Father saying I had more years to grow into them.

"Mum's shown me how to make spicy scrambled eggs," said Shazia, filling me in on what she'd been up to. "I'll make you some when you come round next. School had to close for two days because everyone got nits." She scratched her head and I nudged my bike away. "What else? Oh yes, Hussain and Hassan are going with Mum to Pakistan next month. It'll be nice having the bedroom to myself! And my dad's lost his job."

She said it matter-of-factly. Mr Chaudhry had worked at a different mill to Father. Waterfall Mill was still open, but who knew for how much longer? Soon, all the looms would fall silent. The beating heart of the town would be stilled.

"What will he do?" I ask. "My dad says he'll fix people's geysers and gas fires when his time comes."

Shazia looked surprised. "I didn't know your dad knew how to do that?"

"He doesn't."

Shazia raised an impressed eyebrow. "Dad says he'll drive a taxi." Mr Chaudhry was a dreadful driver. I worried for his future passengers. "I almost forgot! Mrs Ibrahim's shop got Rubik's Cubes in, so I got you one as well."

I gave Shazia a one-armed hug. I'd been wanting a go on the colourful cubes since seeing them on *Swap Shop*.

When we reached the top of Baines Street, we turned around. The road ran far into the distance, snaking the length of the neighbourhood from the corner of Culvert Street, where we were, crossing Windham Street at the midpoint and feeding into the equally long Pitt Street on the other side. With no cobbles, it was perfect for cycling down, especially on this quiet morning.

"Let's see if we can do it in one go without brakes," I said to Shazia. "We can go to the shop later."

Before she could say no, I launched myself off, pedalling just enough to get going. After a few seconds, I heard Shazia do the same, propelling herself with one salwaar-clad leg before stepping with both feet onto the scooter body. We freewheeled down the gently sloping street. I waved at an imaginary audience in the doorways of the identical red-bricked, white-windowed, black-stepped houses.

I'd attached tinsel to the handlebars, repurposing it from the boxes of mangoes Mother bought from Khan's Korner Kabin. As I hurtled down the road with my feet off the pedals, belting out Captain Caveman's battle cry, Shazia close behind, the golden threads fluttered gratifyingly in the slipstream.

*

An hour later, when we were on our seventh or eighth freewheel down, Shazia's mum popped her head out. She screamed like a washerwoman and told Shazia off for behaving like a junglee. She dragged her inside, glaring at me. She hadn't forgiven me after the hair incident.

So I went to Khan's Korner Kabin on my own. I came out fifteen minutes later with Mother's groceries and packets of Potato Puffs, a Marathon and a Curly Wurly bent in half, together with assorted small sweets stuffed into my pockets. Mounting my bike with a rustling of packets, I cruised into Culvert Street, a tree-lined alley that was the quickest way to the canal. I wasn't ready to go back home. Mother wouldn't need her onions yet.

I hummed "Yeh Dosti" from *Sholay*, a jaunty number in which buddies Dharmendra and Amitabh Bachchan rode around on a motorbike and sidecar. I stood up on the pedals and sang lustily, throwing my head around in the exaggerated way they did in the film, but drew the line at lifting my hands in case I crashed. Shazia should have been my wing woman.

As I turned the corner, I juddered to a halt. A few feet away: Amjad Bashir.

"Oi! Sissy boy!" he greeted me.

I frantically began a clumsy three-point turn, muttering kotha under my breath.

"Who are you calling a donkey?" said Amjad, his eyes bulging.

Shoot! He'd heard me. I stuttered that I'd been talking to a cat.

"Are you taking the—"

I didn't wait. Having wheeled round, I powered down hard on one pedal. My foot slipped, my ankle catching on the chain. I bit my cheek to stop myself from screaming.

The golem thudding towards me was the only thing stopping me from throwing myself on the floor and writhing around in agony. With gritted teeth, I stood up on the pedals. Bad move. I lost control of the handlebars, swerving head-first into the wall. The jolt threw me onto the crossbar. I'd barely enough time to register the new pain, before a third type joined it – a fist in my stomach. I rolled to the ground, tears blurring my vision, unable to breathe.

"Get up!" A pair of scuffed blue and yellow Pumas the size of skateboards swam into view. "Here, let me give you a hand."

"I'm fine. Just a bit—"

Amjad yanked the bike off me. Tossing it to one side as though it was made of cardboard, he hoisted me up by the front of my T-shirt, the fabric ripping. My feet dangled several inches from the ground.

"Weren't you going to stop and say hello?" taunted Amjad, breathing pickled onion Monster Munch in my face.

Half-choked, I croaked a greeting.

Amjad continued: "Why were you running away, softie?" A whack on the head. "I was talking to you." A prod in the chest with a finger the width of a broom handle.

"I wasn't running away," I wheezed. "Honest!" Squirming, I tried to get a foothold on the ground. "I . . . I just remembered I had to get something . . . at the shop."

"The shop? How much cash you got, sissy boy?"

How had such a promising day taken such a turn? I'd gone from hero to zero in mere minutes, just like in a Bollywood film – and true to form there was no one around to rescue me. The police always came along well after the villains had scarpered.

My heart beat so hard I was sure he'd hear it. I tried a different tactic. "My brother – Taleeb – you might know him?" He looked blank. "Calls himself Tee? Says you're a top lad," I lied.

A smile spread across Amjad's acne-strewn cheeks. "Tee? He's mates with me uncle. Thinks you're weird. Says it every time. Ain't that funny?"

A fresh wave of tears threatened to burst out.

"What's he doing with a weirdo like you for a brother?"

Not waiting for an answer, he shook me some more before stepping back. He grinned, his eyes flitting between my face and my shorts. Had I wet myself?

Before I could check, he dropped me. The relief was short-lived. Amjad grabbed the waistband of my shorts and thrust a hand into my pocket. More tearing of fabric.

"No!" I shouted. "I'll tell Tee! He'll sort you out."

Laughing, as though I'd said something funny, he withdrew his bear-like paw and, with it, my stash of sweets, crisps and chocolates. "Ace! What else you got for me, poofter?"

He slammed me against the wall. While I caught my breath, he tugged at the strap of my calculator watch. In a few seconds, it was secured around his own wrist. I cried out in frustration and anger. Amjad clamped a sweaty hand over my mouth.

"Anything else?" he said. Once more, his eyes went back down to my shorts. He'd already cleared out my sweet stash. What more could he want down there?

He pressed me into the wall, trapping my hands behind my back. My face was clammy, like I was about to black out. He reached down, this time between my legs. I almost threw up. I kicked out and the blow connected with his shin.

He roared and let me go. "So, the soft lad wants a fight? C'mon then."

As he released me, I charged. He moved aside, snorting with laughter. I came back at him. He held me at bay with a huge hand cupped over my head. I flailed around uselessly with my fists. This made him hoot even more.

"You fight like a girl. You sound like a girl. You even *walk* like a girl."

Where had I heard that before? I didn't have time to mull it over. Tiring of his game, Amjad pushed me into the verge and strode purposefully towards my Grifter. "And what have we got here?"

"I'll get into trouble! I can get you money, as much as you want," I bargained wildly, tears streaming down my face, my hands clutching the air for invisible notes. Father had paid two pounds for the bike at auction. How would I explain to him that I'd lost it?

Amjad swung a leg over the crossbar and revved the handlebars as though it was a motorbike. "Nah, I like this. Suits me, innit."

He stepped on the pedals and bore down on me. I dived out of the way, landing heavily on the gritted path. Amjad laughed and flipped me the finger. "Lo-ser!"

He ripped the tinsel streamers off and threw them back at me. They landed with a sad rustle next to my feet. Amjad sped past, his monstrous frame hunched over the bike, ringing the bell amid a final volley of Tarzan-style whoops and jeers.

I watched the bike disappear into the distance. I swiped my face with the back of my grubby hand, palms hurting from where I'd scraped them on the ground. Wincing, I slowly got up. There was a damp patch in the crotch of my trousers.

I hobbled home.

Nineteen

It took Mother barely a second to take in my dishevelled state before letting out an ear-splitting shriek and clasping me to her bosom.

Taleeb got up to increase the volume on the TV. "What's the fuss about? I've had worse playing football."

Mother rocked me in her arms. "My chandh ka tukra," she said, "what happened?"

Taleeb snickered at this description of me as her "piece of the moon".

Anger bubbled up inside me. "If I could get hold of him, I'd . . . I'd . . ."

"Sing a song to him?" said Taleeb. "Play your piano at him?"

Mother sat me down on her knee and inspected my leg. She picked out the stones, wincing in sympathy whenever I yelled. Then she dabbed at the skin with a spit-moistened end of her dupatta before sending Taleeb into the kitchen for the Dettol.

"He also took my money," I said. "And my watch. And my bike. Everything." I sobbed at each loss. I'd been doing so much crying lately. I hated myself for it, but I couldn't stop.

"Who, puthar?"

"Was it Amjad?" asked Taleeb, returning with a mug full of diluted Dettol.

I look at him. "How would you—"

"The boy who looks like a buffalo?" interrupted Mother, squinting at Taleeb.

"Yes, him. Ouch!" I said as Mother cleaned the cuts with the milky solution.

Something shifted in my memory. "Amjad – he said the same thing."

"What thing?" said Taleeb.

"What you said yesterday, about how I walked and talked."

"You walk and talk like a prince, my pumpkin," said Mother, dabbing away.

Taleeb snorted. I glared at him. He shrugged his shoulders. "I asked him to have a few words, that's all. The stupid get went too far."

A stupid get? I could think of worse names to call him. I thumped Taleeb in the chest, so that he stumbled. Mother told me off, saying this was no way for her nabob to behave. She cradled me, crooning softly.

Taleeb laughed, twisting a spiral finger next to his temple, indicating either me or Mother were mental. "Right, I'm off. I can't take more of his nonsense," he said. "He just has to blink and those cow eyes fill with tears. You fall for it, every time."

Mother kissed me. "Yes, my little one has fallen for it today."

"My eyes are one of my best features, actually!" I shouted after Taleeb.

He called back: "It's no wonder you get beaten up. Wait till you're at Everton."

At its very mention, my tears dried in an instant.

*

Hell hath no fury like Mother scorned. She charged through the streets, Godzilla on the warpath.

At Amjad's house, the door wasn't even half open before Mother launched into a verbal assault on his mother. She fired off words in a rapid stream of anger, barely pausing for breath. Amjad himself was absent, presumably kept inside for his own safety.

Net curtains twitched and doors popped open in quick succession down the street, like a giant Mexican wave. Mother gave the neighbours their money's worth: she jangled her bangles, stamped her kitten-heeled feet and raised her voice to a pitch that sounded like the recorder in the upper register.

Mrs Kapoor and Mrs Mamood approached, arm in arm, walking with a stiff, jerky gait as though powered by clockwork. They hurried to the scene as fast as their aged legs could handle.

"Really, Mrs Aziz, this is no way to conduct yourself," said Mrs Kapoor, breathless, putting a hand on Mother's shoulder both for support and attention. "You are not in India now."

"Pakistan, Mrs Kapoor, Pakistan," corrected Mrs Mamood, hiding her mouth behind her chadar.

Mother shot them a basilisk glare. "My dear Mrs Kapoor, how nice to see you," said Mother, the sharp edge to her voice suggesting otherwise.

Mrs Kapoor wasn't fazed. "I do not care how you choose to behave in your own home, Reshma," she said, pausing and shuddering as if seeing something awful in her head, "but in the street, you are not to behave like a goondi."

The entire terrace held its breath at Mrs Kapoor having

likened Mother to a common thug. Children were urgently recalled and doors slammed shut.

Mrs Bashir made to follow. Lightning quick, Mother shot a pink-muled foot in the opening and had her say for another ten minutes. Doors popped back open.

*

When Mr Bashir saw Father at the mosque that evening, he promised to give his son "much, much thuppar". While this satisfied my need for justice, something didn't feel right. Had this been a Bollywood film, the hero himself would have given Amjad a hiding. Even Babra Sharif, in *Miss Hong Kong*, karate-kicked her own way out of trouble. Yet here was Mother fighting my battles for me.

The experience had left me bruised – and not just physically.

Things that Amjad had said kept popping into my head. He had gone on about my "girly-ness". Called me a sissy. Mimicked my walk. This wasn't new, as Taleeb did the same on a daily basis. What had been different was the violence, and from someone I barely knew.

Twenty

Mr H did a double-take when he saw me. He actually choked and spluttered, which I thought was a bit much. It took him a while to catch his breath. "Jeez, what happened, bud? You take on Muhammad Ali?" He pointed at my split lip and black eye.

The bruises from Amjad's battering looked even worse today. "Just a stumble, sir," I lied. I didn't want him hating me for being a sissy, like everyone else did.

He joined me on the piano stool. The woody notes of Old Spice aftershave wafted my way. "Rafi, I meant it when I said you could talk to me about anything. Is everything okay?"

I nodded. What was the point of telling him anything? He couldn't change a bean, even if he'd wanted to. He couldn't banish Amjad. He couldn't magic away Everton High. He couldn't make Taleeb nicer.

I practised my scales, but my fingers kept slipping and I had to start over again.

To fit in the extra lessons from Mr H, I told Mother I was helping Mrs Entwistle with tidying up the classroom at the end of the day. Or playing football with David. Or having extra Arabic lessons at mosque. The lies popped out with surprising ease. I felt bad. Father was a stickler for honesty, and even made us go back to KKK's if Mr Khan totted up wrong and gave us too much change. But my relationship with Mother was changing and the lies protected me from this new version of her. Lying also gave me control when I increasingly felt I had none in the rest of my life.

While I'd agreed to the Conservatoire audition, I still had concerns. "Mr H, my mum said not to tell anyone, but my dad's going to lose his job. How will we pay for it?"

"I'm sorry to hear that, bud," said Mr H. "If it helps to know, the Conservatoire offers full scholarships, including boarding. They're looking for talent – which, without making your head any bigger, you have in spades. You're a butterfly among the bricks."

Mr H's words reminded me of the moths we'd learned about in history, which evolved to blend in with the sooty mill chimneys to avoid predators. The white moths were picked off more easily. I had no idea how to blend in – and nor did I want to – but I was determined not to suffer the same fate as the white moths.

*

There were two months before the audition, which I thought was loads of time. But Mr H wasn't having it. He put me through my paces, with no break in our after-school lessons.

As I came for another day's practice, he motioned for me to take a seat at the piano while he wrestled with a large envelope. "Perfect! Nothing beats a bit of Mozart."

I could think of a million things – anything by R. D. Burman, for a start. I bashed out a medley from the Bollywood composer's soundtracks. Mr H put the Mozart aside and propped a different piece on the piano stand. "Right, time to lay off R. D. Let's try this."

Sight-reading: I'd have to sing or play music I'd not seen before and perform it without practice. This was tricky, especially when it was in a key I didn't like. The music was nearly always classical, so I couldn't even rely on having heard it on *Top of the Pops*.

As I played a few bars, I stopped. "I know this one – it's from *The Omen*!"

Mr H looked aghast. "You've seen it? I need to have a word with your parents." I pulled a face. "Seriously, the lousy dialogue alone would give you nightmares!" I chuckled. "This is *O Fortuna*, by Carl Orff – not in the movie, but certainly similar."

The audition panel also wanted to hear a song of my choice, sung unaccompanied.

"Any song at all, sir?"

"Within reason. For instance, it can't be—"

"Oooh, can I do 'Making Your Mind Up'?!" I'd recorded their appearance on the Eurovision Song Contest and knew all the moves. "I could put a skirt over my trousers, tape it with Velcro, then rip it off. Please, sir!"

"I think you know the answer to that one."

I was dejected – for about a second. "How about 'Japanese Boy'? I know all the moves. And I could wear a kimono!"

Mr H shook his head. "Definitely not. It needs to be something that shows your range. They'll also look at how you interpret the song. You can't just sing it as you would in the choir – you'll need to show emotion and acting through the music."

My eyes lit up. "I can just go for it, without anyone telling me to tone it down?"

Mr H smiled. "Again, within reason."

He suggested a song called "Buenos Aires". I looked blank. "You know, from *Evita*?" I shook my head. He launched into the chorus of another song from the show. Something about Argentina, but I was none the wiser.

Mr H had his work cut out, exorcising my bad habits. I threw in beatbox sounds during musical interludes. The first time I did this, he spluttered on his water, which set off a coughing fit that took a good minute or two to stop. He also tackled the trills I liked to add, a familiar feature in Bollywood songs. "Let the music speak for itself," Mr H said.

With my acting, I was prone to throwing my arms up in the air and putting my face through a vigorous work-out. Once more, the blame lay at the door of my beloved Bollywood, where everything was performed at the high end of melodrama.

"Dial it down, Rafi."

"Is it too much, sir?"

"Just a tad."

"Even that last line?"

"Especially that last line."

One unexpected result of the lessons was my voice began to change in real life, too. Mr H taught me how to hold myself, using advice from some man called Alexander. As he adjusted my chest, shoulders, tummy and head, I felt taller and more confident. He showed me how to breathe deeply and how to use my diaphragm to support my voice.

*

Later that day, when I spotted Taleeb on the street, I couldn't resist trying out the new techniques.

"You, boy – yes, you. Move yourself, jaldi jaldi!" I bellowed, diaphragm taut, bouncing my words out in the manner of the Sergeant Major from *It Ain't Half Hot, Mum*.

The joy of seeing Taleeb jumping in the air, startled by my booming voice, was worth the subsequent smack when he caught up with me.

Twenty-one

December rolled in with bitter winds. Even I had to concede and ditch my T-shirts and shorts for shirts, jumpers and long trousers. The streets smelt of coal and applewood, the smoke barely out of the chimney pots before it was torn apart by the gusts.

When I got home on Tuesday, having first popped into Shazia's to exchange our customary "pinch and punch" for the first of the month, Mother was in the lounge. She had her Pfaff out on the round Formica table. She was never more content than when flooring the pedal of her sewing machine. She'd also been kinder to me since the incident with Amjad. So now was a good time to canvass her thoughts on the Conservatoire. I grabbed the brochure from where I'd hidden it under the mattress and raced downstairs.

"*Maam?*"

I could barely see her behind an eruption of sparkly pink fabric.

"*Maam!*" I called, louder, hovering in the doorway.

She fed a never-ending supply of flamingo-coloured cloth through the machine. What was she making – a hot air balloon?

"*Maam!*"

Mother screeched. She drew out the cloth, stitches staggering drunkenly across the fabric.

"Can I show you this?" I said. I wafted the brochure gently over my head, trying not to make too much of it and yet needing to catch her attention.

"What is it? Can it not wait?" She rustled around in her basket for her seam ripper.

"Sorry. But I just wanted to show you before you got stuck in," I said, nodding at the mountain of fabric around her.

She unpicked stitches at a furious rate.

"You don't even need to read anything," I said. I pointed at the glossy visuals. "It's a new school," I said. "Well, it's not new – it's old – but it'll be a new school for me."

"New-old-new. Puthar, you are making my head hurt." Pushing me away, she worried away at the stitches.

I let a few minutes pass, before I lay the brochure on her lap.

Mother blinked at it. "What is this?"

I counted to ten. "The new school."

"Everton?" she said.

"NO! NOT EVERTON!"

"Puthar!" Mother put her fingers in her ears. "What is this baqwaas? You are going to Everton. No ut-but."

I grabbed the brochure and rifled through more pages.

Mother tutted. "All these white children! Everton is much much better: half-half Pakistani, half-half English."

"This school is much much better," I said, mirroring her language. "Look at how happy they look. How good the facilities are. How modern the chemistry lab is."

She looked blank so I showed her the gardens. This shameless appeal to her love of flowers worked. She took the brochure off me. I pressed the advantage. "They only take thirty students a year. Mr H says there's no reason why I can't be one of them."

"Mr H? Who is Mr H?"

"Mr Haqq. I've told you about him hundreds of times!"

"Oh, him," harrumphed Mother, with the same lack of enthusiasm she reserved for our neighbour, Mrs Moto's husband, who was Indian.

"Look at the orchestra!" I said. "I could learn a new instrument. Like the cello."

Mother handed the brochure back. "Challo," she said, mishearing me and encouraging me to leave. "Two weddings next week and I don't have a stitch to wear."

"You're not listening! I'm not going to Everton. I want to go to this school. I'll be able to really work at my music – and acting and dancing."

Her face clouded. She fixed me with a gimlet stare. "Beta, when you are young, yes. But you are older now. It is time to put away your childish fancies."

"But you're always singing and dancing!"

"Boys are boys, girls are girls."

This made zero sense. I glared at her.

She sighed. "Okay, sing, dance even, but in private." She looked at me, expecting me to be grateful. I ground my teeth. "People talk. There is a name for boys who sing and dance in Pakistan." She shuddered. Then: "Your Mr ABC has put ideas into your head."

"Mr H!" I snapped. "Get his name right!"

Mother stared at me, the chrysanthemums in her hair quivering. "Is that any way to talk to your mother?" She pressed her foot down, stitching in a perfectly straight line.

I waited until she got to the end of a run. "Anyway, I'd be out from under your feet, as I'd be boarding." One of her eyebrows moved northwards. "I'd stay there during the week and be back at the weekends."

Mother sprang up, sending the scissors flying. She ran to the mirror, dabbing at her eyes with her dupatta. Her chest heaved. "Leave me, son? Your own mother? I who have raised you, brought you up, looked after you, fed you from the moment you were born. You could leave me?" She broke into a sad song, then trailed off. "You belong *here*," she said in a broken voice, her hand pressed to her heart.

Mother was being absurd. I had to manage her carefully, else she'd spiral off into another Bollywood-style overreaction. "I'll still be with you, just not every day," I said. "I promise." She looked unconvinced. "But I really need to go to this school." Her eyes narrowed. Diplomacy wasn't winning. I needed to fight histrionic fire with histrionic fire. "I'll die if you send me to Everton. I won't go, even if you paid me a million pounds. It would be the end of me!" I shouted out the last line, the veins throbbing in my forehead.

"What is this drama-shama?" she said. "I do not know where you get this from."

I stared at her in disbelief.

She continued: "You turn your nose up at a school that is good enough for everyone else, including your brother and sister."

"I am not them!" I screamed. She flinched. I needed to calm down. "I'm happy for them if they're happy at Everton. But I want to go to the Conservatoire. Please, I want to be around people like me."

Mother sighed. "For the last time, puthar, put these altu-faltu ideas out of your—"

"I hate you!"

She recoiled, as though I'd slapped her. She flung the brochure to the floor. "You will not bring shame to this family," she warned. "No singing, dancing, acting. You are going to Everton. And it is not as if we can even afford this fancy school." I opened my mouth to tell her about the scholarships, but she was in full flow. "You children think money grows on trees. Your father works hard, but look where that has got him. In three days, he has no job."

She sat down, her dupatta at her mouth. But it was too late. The secret was out.

I gasped. We'd all known it was coming, and yet it was still a shock. Dad was going to be jobless? He'd worked at the mill for all my life.

"I should not have said anything," she said, picking up her sewing.

I grabbed the brochure off the floor. "But what happened?"

"What happened?" she said, her eyes boring into me and her voice rising again. "What happened? That bloody ironing lady, THAT'S WHAT HAPPENED!"

It took me a moment to work out she meant the Iron Lady. I'd never heard Mother swear before. I'd also never seen her this angry. She gripped the Pfaff, her knuckles white, the dupatta around her neck sliding up and down as her chest filled with quick bursts of air.

As sorry as I felt for Father, I felt sorrier for myself. It was now even more important that I escaped this hellhole. I had to grasp whatever opportunities came my way. As much as I didn't want to incite Mother's anger again, I had no choice. Taking a deep breath, I waved the brochure at her. "Just take one more look, please."

Mother turned to me, cranking her head round slowly, disappointment written all over her face. She stared at me with blank eyes, as though not quite registering me. Then she turned her attention back to the sewing machine. Dialling round the stitch selector, she flicked down the presser foot and floored the pedal.

I'd been dismissed.

Twenty-two

The lights flicker back on. I wince. I must have nudged my eye mask off. I pull it back down, but it's no good. There are signs of life all around, including from the flight deck.

"Good morning," says the captain. "I hope you managed to catch some sleep. We're expecting to land in Dubai in just under two hours. The cabin crew will shortly begin the breakfast service."

I yawn and stretch, removing my mask. The man on my right is still asleep. For a moment, I wonder if he's died in the night as he's not moving or breathing, but then he emits a thunderous snort that kickstarts him back to life. His eyes remain shut. Eulalia beams at me, before stretching her arms overhead, then rising and heading to the bathroom.

I groan as memories from my sordid night-time tryst come back to me. I spot Pedro, trolley before him. I shrink into my seat.

As he makes his way down the aisle, it strikes me – as well as being a dead-ringer for Aamir Khan, he reminds me of Paul. I haven't thought about him in years. But the same nose. Cheekbones. Even the way he holds himself in that slightly pissed-off way.

It took several aborted visits to the university's gaysoc before I bit the bullet and went inside. I didn't know what to expect – from the horror stories I'd heard growing up, I wouldn't have been surprised by fire-breathers with two heads and six arms. I'd been on the verge of scarpering, when a voice had shouted across the room.

"Fresh blood!" It was Paul. Everyone had laughed, including me. I was immediately drawn to his hazel-coloured eyes and brown hair. He reminded me of another and I momentarily saw that youthful face again, before it morphed back into Paul.

Before the day was over, we'd shared our first kiss.

I smile at the memory. I'm taken out of it by the smell of Kouros and bacon. The trolley has stopped at our row. I can't meet Pedro's eyes as he hands over the foiled container.

"Whaddya say you did, Rafique?" says Eulalia, back in her seat and forking a hash brown into her mouth.

"It's Rafi," I say, prodding a slab of egg, "and I work in—"

"Say, Rafique, could you be a doll and give Sleeping Beauty a nudge?" She waves her plastic knife at the man next to me. "My dearly beloved," she explains. "Chuck, Rafique. Rafique, Chuck. He's cute, huh?"

I don't know which of us she's referring to. Chuck nods at me, yawns, then rips open his foil lid. He tucks in. I wish I could, but I can taste the smoked salmon I should be having in first class. Instead, congealed scrambled egg lies in my mouth like a dead sprat. I spit it into my napkin.

"Chuck and I always buy window and aisle seats," says Eulalia. "We figure no one'll sit in the middle." I blink. "No offence, honey."

"None t—"

Eulalia screams and jolts me, sending the juice flying. I grab it. Made from concentrate.

"ABBA!" she yells. "We saw you Friday." Eyes shut. "Sky! Sky Masterson!"

She's almost right. "Did you enjoy the show?" I ask.

She looks across me at Chuck. "Baby, looka who it is. We got us some royalty!"

Sighing, Chuck turns to me. "It was you or *Annie*. Sorry." He goes back to his breakfast.

Eulalia gives me a plot rundown of my own show. I tune out, back to my memories.

Twenty-three

The living room was bathed in a soft light, thanks to the Chinese lantern-style shade I'd persuaded Mother to put over the bare bulb.

The gas fire sputtered, flames licking all four of the ceramic tiles. Strewn on the fireguard was an assortment of washing, steaming gently and releasing the comforting aroma of Daz into the room. The hiss of the fire and the pebbling of the rain on the window created a hypnotic sound; we lounged in the room like a slink of contented cats.

I leaned against the table, flicking through an old *Whizzer and Chips*. Nabila was threading her fingers for a game of cat's cradle. Taleeb lay by the fire, pasting football stickers into an album. Surely he was too old for that?

The TV was on in the background: *The Generation Game*. We looked up now and again, the show an insight into a strange world where white families willingly made fools of themselves on national TV for a cuddly toy.

Mother clattered into the living room, making us all jump. She held a tape recorder before her and a serious expression on her face.

"Children, where is the speaking thing?"

She meant the microphone. Every month, we recorded a tape for relatives in Pakistan, telling them our news. We did this in place of an airmail letter. Mother said it was quicker as, instead of being posted, it would be sent off with anyone in the neighbourhood flying to Mirpur, and also a way for us all to get involved.

Taleeb finally found the microphone tucked down the side of the sofa.

"Nabila, beti, TV off. You can watch that baqwaas later." Nabila, her cat's cradle still on her hands, turned off the TV with her elbow. Larry Grayson and Isla St Clair shrunk to a small white rectangle in the middle of the screen.

"Where's the tape?" I asked.

"Is it in the machine?" said Nabila.

Taleeb looked through the aperture. "Boney M. Must be his, the big brown girl in the ring," he said, misquoting one of their finest hits. "It's okay – we can tape over it." He looked at me while corkscrewing his finger down to the red Record button.

I shrieked, grabbing the recorder and hitting Eject.

Five minutes later, a blank C-60 cassette having been found, we were ready.

Mother sat on the sofa, microphone in hand, tape recorder on the table. Taleeb sat next to her, while Nabila and I arranged ourselves on the floor, like courtiers before a queen.

We hushed, as Nabila pressed Play and Record. Mother let the tape wind on for thirty seconds, never trusting the beginning of a cassette. She cleared her throat several times, flicking her hair and readjusting the sprig of rose-hips behind her left ear.

"Tasting, tasting," she began, speaking in a loud voice and holding the microphone at arm's length as though it was a cobra about to strike her. She scrutinised the tape through the aperture for confirmation that it was spooling.

The others relished the opportunity to put their voices

onto tape. They recorded in Punjabi. I relied on a mixture of Punjabi and English, stepping out of one language whenever I needed a word or phrase from the other.

Nabila spent her five minutes talking about clothes: what she was wearing, what she was having made and what she would like the relatives to send to her.

Mother took the microphone back. "Ammi, forgive my greedy girl. She still thinks she is ten," she said, as though it was a whole generation away. "If you know of any good families, please find a good rishta for her."

Nabila made a strangled noise and snatched the microphone. "Gran, please, please, please ignore that bit. I'm twelve years old!"

"Don't be fooled," said Mother, taking the microphone, "she has a budda roo – she is twelve going on thirty-two. Old enough to think about settling down in a few years."

Nabila tried to grab the microphone, but Mother twisted away. "Anyway, twelve is not so young, Ammi. You were that age when you married Abba. And girls here grow up so fast. I was fourteen when I married, and ... well ..." She trailed off, not finishing the sentence. "It will give me comfort to know Nabila has a good match for when she is a little older. Is Penghi Janat's son still available?"

Nabila let out another squawk. I shared her horror – any son of a woman named after her squint was not a promising prospect. She stormed out, telling Mother she hated her. Mother shrugged and passed the microphone to Taleeb.

It amazed me how someone as surly as Taleeb could find so much to say, and to relatives he had never met. Tonight, as on previous occasions, he enthused about football and cricket, going into long details about recent games he'd played or watched. No doubt the Pakistani relatives fast-forwarded his bit.

Once Mother had related all her news, she and I each supplied a song with which to wrap up proceedings. I was going to do "Matchstalk Men and Matchstalk Cats and Dogs".

"Look at my little mothi, in his shishay ki koti," said Mother, stroking my black velvet waistcoat, with golden braided swirls inset with penny-shaped mirrors. As I screwed in the legs on my piano, the waistcoat cast a glitterball of lights across the walls.

"Mothi?" said Taleeb. "Surely you mean moti?"

Mother tutted at him turning me from a "pearl" to a "fat girl" with the removal of just one letter. "Do not make fun of your little brother," she said. "You will give him a stutter. Now, my pumpkin, are you ready? Nabila, beti, please!"

Nabila thumped back down the stairs. Mother handed her the microphone and recorder. Nabila was the only one who knew how to adjust the settings so they recorded songs and my piano without the sound distorting.

I counted to four, then launched into Brian and Michael's hit song.

Taleeb literally rolled around the floor, laughing.

I soldiered on, thumping out dramatic chords to accompany my impassioned singing, complete with pumped-up Northern vowels to mimic the original singers. Taleeb laughed even harder.

When I finished, I unscrewed the legs off the piano and threw one at Taleeb. It sailed into the darkness beyond.

Mother went to the mirror and experimented with her dupatta, finally settling on it half-draped over her head – a demure look she rarely visited. Her dome-shaped gold earrings glinted in the firelight. Grabbing a mascara pencil from the mantelpiece, she daubed a beauty spot on her cheek – just like her beloved Noor Jehan. She lit the agarbathi that poked out from the links of the mirror, releasing the scent of rose into the room. Satisfied, she sat down.

She swayed gently from side to side, singing an R. D. Burman track from the film *The Great Gambler*. As she lost herself in the song, her delivery became more confident. I didn't understand every word, but it was about the story of the heart, which it claimed could be summed up in two words: love and youth.

Her girl-woman voice gave me goosebumps. More so tonight, with the cold and dark outside and the flickering glow inside, which threw shadows deep into the room.

She stood up, her eyes closed, head thrown back, lost in the minor-key melody of the song. Her dupatta had slipped off her head. As she sang about the joys of life, her hand spiralled heavenward; as she balanced it with the many sorrows, the hand sunk floorward.

As she entered the last third of the song, I accompanied her on the piano.

Her singing got quieter and quieter. By the final line, she was barely whispering. She staggered unsteadily, her head lowered and the microphone dangling from her hand. The tape continued to spool, clicking its lonely beat. The fire burbled and hissed. Mother brought up the microphone slowly, as though it was now much heavier.

"That was for you, Ammi," she whispered in her thin, breathy voice, addressing our grandmother. "Your little bulbul may have flown far away, but she still likes to sing. One day, I will sing before you once more. Like no time has passed."

Her eyes remained shut and her lips fluttered, little

mewing noises escaping from them. In the hypnotic heat of the room, she seemed to sway on her feet.

Nabila coughed nervously. "*Maam?*"

With each deep breath, Mother's necklace rose and shimmered in the firelight. She sighed and opened her eyes, cradling the microphone. Otherworldly, somehow smaller than usual, rosehips threaded through her beehived hair, bejewelled fingers wrapped around the microphone and a sad Mona Lisa smile across her face. Her eyes, ringed with surma, unblinking, sparkling, as though they had a candle behind them.

I approached cautiously, as one might a woodland creature. I hugged her, laying my head on her shoulder. Despite the heat in the room, she was cold. She was so still I could barely sense her breathing. A wave of guilt washed over me. How could I lie to this woman? Right now, she needed me. These tape recording sessions often affected her. It's like a part of her went back with the cassettes. I had to protect her. Could I put my own desires behind hers? The gnawing in the pit of my stomach gave me my answer.

She gently unclasped me. Still looking at some far-off sight, she made her way out of the room, towards the kitchen, the tape still spooling. In the dim light, she seemed to float around the furniture. The way she held the recorder before her, dangling by the handle, reminded me of a small suitcase. I got a flash of Mother disembarking from a plane, wearing just a salwaar kameez, buffeted by the wind skimming off the runway, her worldly belongings in the battered brown suitcase, which now lay on top of the wardrobe.

As Mother closed the door behind her, a wordless refrain drifted back into the room.

"*La la la laaaaaaaa, la la la la-la laaaaaaa.*"

After a few minutes, we followed her into the kitchen, to make sure she was okay. She was in near darkness, having stopped by the sink, staring out of the window. Behind her, the front hob was on, like it always was – an Eternal Flame. It cast the only light in the room. Something glinted on the window ledge: Mother's wedding ring, a golden nugget among the cobwebs, Fairy Liquid and turmeric-stained Marigolds.

"A thousand pities I came to this grey, cold country," she moaned, shivering. "Why your father could not choose somewhere warm? These Mirpuri men and their love of England. They think the streets are covered in gold."

She collapsed against the worktops as though the string holding her upright had snapped: shrinking in size, hugging herself in her Aztec-patterned cardigan and looking mournfully at her sandalled, glittery-socked feet.

"Ya Allah. This country has made me old. I do not want to end my days here."

Nabila attempted to tell Mother a funny story. I joined in and laughed uproariously, encouraging Mother to smile. Taleeb came in; we shook our heads: Mother was elsewhere.

"Dear Anjam, Zubeida, Ruksana... Shabnam, Fareeda and sweet little Najma..." She reeled off the names, like a list of exotic flowers. "I can see them so clearly – sitting in the courtyard, under the orange tree, picking through the rice, laughing, talking, teasing Najma, singing... oh my darling Najma. Where did those years go?"

Like pieces on a chessboard, we tracked around the tiny kitchen, trying to engage with her. While she was bodily with us, her spirit had soared over the oceans. She was home, the years having fallen away. Father was yet to cast a shadow in the adobe rooms of her childhood.

Nabila embraced her in a hug. I joined in. Taleeb awkwardly patted her on the back.

Mother started singing again. This time, a song from the film *Bobby*, about a pair of lovers locked inside a room, the key lost.

We propped her up as though she was a storm-damaged tree, letting her know we were there, even if she was someplace else. Her chest rose and fell as she sang her sad song, the hiss of the hob, the howl of the wind and the scatter of rain on the window providing percussion. I played imaginary piano keys on the small of her back.

Mother uncoupled from us and left the kitchen, making for the door that led to the staircase. She floated away, head to one side, still singing, a mermaid heading for the horizon.

She slowly ascended the steps. Like the train of a wedding dress, the song drifted down, fainter and fainter, until the bedroom door shut and we heard no more.

We didn't see her for the rest of the evening.

*

Next morning, Mother was back in the kitchen, putting together our sandwich boxes, packing satchels, sewing buttons on shirts, dispensing money for the book club, smoothing down hair, kissing foreheads and telling us to work hard – as though nothing had happened the night before. Only the dark circles underneath her eyes told a different story.

Twenty-four

Bedlam greeted us when we came back from school that afternoon.

"We do not want him to think we keep a dirty house," said Mother, flapping a dupatta around the room. She was dusting, something I'd never seen her do before. David was coming to tea. She normally discouraged visitors to the house, but she'd been so relieved I had a friend who was a boy, she'd insisted I bring him home.

While I arranged dahlias I'd "borrowed" from a neighbour's garden into milk bottles, Nabila fitted a new cover on the settee. Mother had made it on the Pfaff, adding extra wide frills to the red and yellow floral fabric, creating a jaunty, calypso look.

"What to cook?" said Mother. "Will he eat chicken?" She threaded a garland of plastic flowers around the mirror, adorned already with prayer beads, peacock feathers, a sandalwood agarbathi stick, a timetable of prayer times and several wedding invitations.

"Chicken's the least of his worries," said Nabila, booting the pouffes around the room until Mother's Paddington Bear stare stopped her. She had a point – even we had fish and chips every Friday to counteract the heat and spiciness of the rest of the week.

"English food – why is it so brown?" said Mother, shuddering. Having once seen Delia Smith ladling out a beef bourguignon, this had literally coloured her view of English cuisine. She broke into an old Bollywood number, as if to dislodge the unsavoury image.

*

Two hours later, David's mum dropped him off. She refused to stay, saying, "foreign food gave her a dickie tummy and we weren't to mind". Normally, Mother *would* have minded, but she was so thrown by seeing a white face at the door, that the insult went over her head.

We sat around the gold-and-black Taj Mahal table. As guest of honour, David had pride of place in the middle of the sofa. I was next to him, pointing out various things in the room, especially the origami garlands I'd made and draped around the mirror. Nabila sat on a pouffe, gawping at him. We'd never had a white person in the house before. Father and Taleeb were out, which was just as well, as neither took to strangers well.

Mother bustled in and out with various plates and bowls of food. The front of her kameez was spattered with oil from where she'd been frying. "You like?" she asked David, as she watched him bite into a pakora.

"It's delicious, Mrs Aziz. If they had these in Melbourne, there'd be a riot."

Mother beamed. "Let me know you need anything. Salt okay? Not too much hot-hot?" For some reason, her English had taken a turn for the worse.

"I wish my mum cooked like this, Mrs Aziz."

Mother giggled, hiding her face with her dupatta. "You good boy. You come again." She returned to the kitchen, taking the empty changher and her missing words with her.

I high-fived David. Mother liked him! She'd been so weird recently, I'd no idea how tonight would go. But, so far, so good.

I showed him how to tear off a piece of chapatti and use it as a scoop for the curry. He made a mess. Nabila leaped up with the kitchen roll.

"Thanks," he said, wiping his fingers. "You must think I'm a real idiot."

"Not at all," she simpered. "It's tricky if you're not used to it."

I stared at her, marvelling at her Cadbury Caramel Bunny voice.

Nabila looked bashfully at him, like Princess Diana, her eyelids smooshed with orange eye shadow and her hair coiled around her ears, like Princess Leia.

Mother brought in a tray of samosas. "Davy, you want fork? Knife?" Without waiting for an answer, she handed him a wooden chip shop fork and a butter knife before returning to the kitchen to rustle up more food.

The front door slammed shut. I recognised Taleeb's loping gait on the plastic runner in the hall. He flung the lounge door open.

"So, Fatty Boom Boom, you stuffing your—" He stopped, registering the new person at the table. "Who's this?"

"G'day, mate. I'm David. You must be Taleeb."

David got up to shake hands. Taleeb ignored him and lobbed the football he was carrying into the void created where the two sofas in the room met at right angles.

Mother came in, a water jug in one hand, a platter of kebabs in the other and a changher of chapattis on her head. "Puthar, eat, eat," she said to Taleeb.

"I'm fine. I'm not hungry," he said. "What's *he* doing here?"

Mother slapped him on the back of the head. She turned to David. "So sorry, Davy."

"No worries, Mrs A."

I beamed. Nothing could faze him.

"Davy, you have brothers? Sisters? Where your mummy?" She filled his glass.

As David answered, Taleeb remained standing, rubbing his head and glaring at David.

"Your daddy not here?" said Mother.

"Oh, they don't live together, Mrs Aziz," said David. "They separated last year."

Mother looked puzzled. "Sep-ray-ted?" She tested the word, syllable by syllable, her expression indicating she didn't care for the taste of it.

Taleeb saw his chance. "He means they're divorced."

Mother gasped, spilling water from the jug. I shot Taleeb daggers, but he just grinned back, pleased at the effect he'd had. Mother was old-fashioned, and the idea of divorce was anathema to her. She pinched her ears and intoned "thoba, thoba" to ward off the evil energies we'd unleashed by mentioning it. "You good boy," she said to David, edging towards the door. "I pray for you." She left in a hurry.

David looked confused. I told him divorce wasn't a thing in the Asian community – not that it didn't happen, but it was seen as shameful and so was dressed up as something else. Someone had to go back to Pakistan for a dying relative or move for a new job.

"So, what do you see in this sissy brother of mine?" said Taleeb, butting in.

Nabila turned and punched him in the shin. "If you can't be nice, shove off!"

I glared at Taleeb. "Yeah, rack off," I said, both

emboldened by David's presence and glad of an opportunity to use one of the Australian phrases he'd taught me.

"Just asking, that's all," said Taleeb. "Little Fatty normally plays with girls."

David put his chapatti down. "If you mean Rafi," he said, "then he's a top bloke. I'd be proud to have him as my brother."

A glow spread through me. "I wish you *were* my brother. Not that oaf!"

Taleeb reached over to knuckle my head. David leaned forward, his hands balled into fists. Taleeb hesitated, then nabbed a samosa, as though this was his intention all along. "Anyway, what brings you here, you and your mum and dad?" he said, demolishing the samosa in three bites with his big horse teeth. "Oops, I mean, your mum."

David's body tensed. I put a hand on his knee. From the kitchen, Mother sang a sad song about break-ups and lost loves. Nabila offered David another pakora. He politely declined. "My aunt's not well. Cancer. She probably won't make it into the new year."

Nabila dabbed her nose with a tissue rescued from her sleeve. "I'm sorry, David."

I squeezed his knee. He squeezed my hand back. It felt good.

Taleeb didn't say anything. He rubbed his greasy fingers on the arm of the sofa.

Mother walked in with glasses of Quosh. "Thank you for look after my baby."

David spluttered. "Your baby, Mrs A? I didn't know that you—"

"You show him pow-pow-pow!" She punched the air three times. I'd told her David had been teaching me self-defence. After the Amjad incident, I wasn't taking any chances.

David laughed and pretended to spar with her. "It's the least I can do for a mate."

Taleeb knelt on a pouffe. "So, what happens after your aunt . . . you know?" He whistled while making a cutting motion across his throat.

Mother slapped Taleeb, before hauling him up by the ear. "Enough!"

Taleeb protested, but Mother wasn't having it. She pushed him out before her.

David's foot nudged mine. I thought he'd knocked it by mistake, but he kept it there, same as he did with his hand on my knee. I swallowed my pakora without chewing it.

*

Before she let him leave, Mother presented David with a Stork margarine tub, its lid secured with a strip of pink fabric tied in a fancy bow. "Samosas. For your mummy."

I wasn't sure Mrs Harrington would be keen on the spicy snacks, but David was delighted. "Mrs Aziz, you are the best," he told her. "Thank you."

Mother giggled, her dupatta at her mouth.

As she went inside, David gave me a goodbye hug and whispered in my ear: "Meet me Friday eve."

Before I could ask him anything further, he'd sprinted down the street, crossed Windham Street and disappeared into the shadows of Pitt Street.

Twenty-five

When Friday finally came, I realised David and I hadn't agreed where or when we'd meet. I couldn't go and knock for him, as I didn't know where they were staying.

I couldn't face spending my evening watching *Blankety Blank*. So I spent a happy hour creating butterflies with the Spirograph Dad had picked up at the auction – a bargain 20p, even if it lacked some of the toothed wheels. As I tacked the finished drawings up on the wall, I glanced out of the window and noticed a flashing light. It was my name in Morse code, except there were two f's. David! I ran downstairs, nearly knocking over Nabila, who was coming up no doubt to turf me out. I grabbed my coat and raced outside.

"Last one to the bridge is kangaroo poo!" said David.

We ran up the cobbled alleyway, crunching deep footprints into the snow that had fallen and accumulated into drifts over the past week. We made and lobbed snowballs during the length of the alleyway, before leapfrogging each other on Pilkington Street and puffing up the incline of Windham Street while trying not to slide back. We reached the bridge at the same time, but we kept on running – through the patch of vegetation on Coronation Street separating the houses from the canal. I weaved in and out, the wings of Mercury on my heels. Victory was short-lived. Hollering like Tarzan, David felled me with a rugby tackle. I thudded into the snow.

I flipped myself round and tried to get up. David straddled me, pinning my arms.

"Say 'I give'," he said, looking down at me.

"I give what?"

"I give up."

"Never!" Mustering all my strength, I lifted him up and over, karate-chopping him before applying a figure-four leg lock like I'd seen the wrestlers do on *World of Sport*.

David cried out and tapped to be released. Horrified, I unhooked my leg and David fell back, cradling his ankle. As I got up to fetch help, he rolled towards me and pinned me down, his hands meshed in mine, a grin on his face. "Got you!"

It took a few seconds to realise what was going on. "You're not hurt?"

He shook his head.

With renewed energy, I tried throwing him off, but it was no good. "Okay, you win."

David let go and rolled next to me. Our chests puffed and sank, our breath rising like a pair of smoking chimneys, hanging in the damp evening air before slowly breaking apart. The moon was just rising, not full for a couple more days. As we made snow angels, with fresh snow falling and settling on us, I picked out Cassiopeia directly above. The W-shaped constellation always reminded me of Mrs Kapoor's moles. I chuckled.

David squeezed my hand. He'd left his woollen-gloved hand entwined in mine. I dared not breathe in case he pulled it away. The wind soughed through the trees, the branches scissoring the sky into hundreds of shards. Bats wheeled drunkenly overhead.

I was lightheaded. My heart was going to burst from my chest. My body tingled all over. I'd never felt like this before – happy but nervous, content but scared. I shivered with delight and immediately kicked myself, expecting David to move his hand. He didn't.

After a while, I trusted myself to speak. "Do you get the same stars Down Under?"

"Hm? I'm not sure," said David, stirring. "What's that one?" He pointed at it, taking my hand up with his.

I traced the contours of the constellation. "The Plough."

"And that one?"

I followed his finger. "Orion. You can see his belt. Look."

As I recounted the names of the constellations, David made me trace the shapes in the sky, still with my hand on his. I wanted to hold his hand forever and ever. I wanted the night to claim us, to keep us hidden, safe. While he was by my side, everything was okay. I sighed.

An owl hooted. A curry-scented breeze wafted in from the direction of the houses on the other side of the vegetation. The spell was only broken by the sound of a woman's voice in the distance, calling. The evening was getting colder, but neither of us moved.

"Raf, there's something I need to tell you," he said.

My gut contracted. Hot bile climbed up my throat. Something in his voice warned me this wouldn't be good news. Inside my head, I began to chant. "La la la la la la la la."

David got up and sat cross-legged before me. He looked as serious as he sounded. My heart sank. "You know my mum and I are only here until my aunt passes away?"

I tried to change the subject. "Did I tell you what happened to—" I began.

"Well, she's not in a good way."

I put my fingers in my ears to stop myself from hearing what I knew was coming. Tears sprang to my eyes, but they weren't for David's aunt. Instantly, I hated myself. But each time I tried to give David my condolences, I just felt sorry for myself at what was to come.

"La la la la la la la la la." If I couldn't hear him, it couldn't happen.

The woman's voice called again, this time louder and nearer.

"Listen, Raf, I know it's hard, but this is important," said David, gently uncovering my ears. "Mum says we need to get back. She wants to book the flights soon."

My heart thudded in my chest. "How long until she does?"

David shrugged. "I don't know, mate. But it could be anything from a few weeks to a couple of months. It depends on—"

"No!" A clamour of rooks took off from a nearby tree, releasing a squall of snow from the branches. "You can't go! Not now!"

"Raf, please, you know I'd stay if I—"

"You can live with us! We'll find the room." Even as I said it, I realised how hopeless it was. "It's not fair!" I sobbed, clasping his hand. "Best friends don't leave!"

"Rafi, get back home this instant or you will feel my chappal on your backside!" It was Mother – the woman calling. She had made it all the way up to Coronation Street. Normally, such a threat would have made me titter. But, tonight, the laughter had gone.

David and I held our breaths. My whole body shook.

David held me. He smelt of fireworks and shepherd's pie. I felt myself calm. We were well hidden in the overgrown strip of land. After a few minutes, we heard Mother call again, indistinct, further away.

I breathed out. My limbs felt heavy, as though I'd done a circuit around the dreaded Apparatus in PE. As I looked out to the ever-darkening sky, the stars bled and became glowing blots. I bent over and couldn't speak.

David laid a hand on my back. "Come on, mate. I've no choice."

I heard him as though he was speaking from another room.

"My dad's not seen me for all this time," he said quietly. "He needs me."

"*I* need you!" I thumped his chest with my fists. David let me hit him, let me vent my fury and disappointment and grief. "I need you! I need you! I need you!" I sobbed into his shoulder. He stroked my hair and told me it would be all right.

Eventually, the tears spent themselves. I stopped shivering. Being held by David felt good. I didn't want to pull apart. My crying ceased.

Mother's voice sounded faintly one final time. But the threat had gone. For now.

David said something, but I didn't catch it. He tilted my head up. The silvery light of the moon had turned his blond hair grey. I stopped breathing. He looked like a Roman statue. He stared down at me. I didn't dare to blink in case I broke the spell. Then his head moved towards mine, in exquisite slow motion. His hands reached out. I thought he was going to wipe away my tears, but he cupped my face. Drawing me closer, his mouth was centimetres away from mine. Millimetres. Then our lips met.

The most incredible surge flooded through my body, I imagined a Ready Brek glow emanating from me. The tension I'd been carrying over these weeks and months finally released itself. The worries about school, Amjad, the audition, skinheads and Mother – all melted away. The gnawing feeling I'd had inside me since the night Father had slapped me – everything fell into place. There was nothing wrong with me. It had merely taken until this moment to find myself and for David to help me get there.

I trembled uncontrollably. I laughed. I cried. It was like the night before Eid when the excitement of what was to come made sleep impossible. Bollywood songs rang in my head along with images of roses and doves and Swiss mountaintops. Glitter coursed through my veins. The moonlight dusted us in silver, wrapping us in a protective cloak.

My eyes shut, in anticipation of a second kiss. The wind whisked the falling snow around us. It was even sweeter than the first.

*

The next day, Shazia and I were in my bedroom, making collages while Nabila was out with Mother. We had a stack of comics and catalogues before us, scissors in hand and Pritt sticks at the ready. To keep ourselves refreshed, we nibbled on Smith's crisps and drank raspberryade through twisty straws.

"David said I should be nicer to Ashiqah," I said, snipping around a male model in brown Y-fronts. He was the centrepiece of my collage, rising out of the water like Neptune.

"Really?" asked Shazia, cutting out the paper doll costumes on the back page of *Bunty*.

"He says it's better to be friends than waste energy

being negative." That was hard to do, especially after Ashiqah spilt ink on my raffia mat, pretending she'd tripped. I flicked through an Empire Stores catalogue for a trident. "David's teaching me more karate moves," I said, stopping at the angling section. "They get the Jackie Chan films first in Australia."

"Australia?"

I took a big slurp of my drink. "I've told you like a million times. It's where he's from." I rapidly clicked my scissors, like "Mr Snip-Snip", the barber who cut our hair in his living room in Helen Street. From downstairs, the smell of biryani wafted up. It was the only time Mother used the oven; normally, she used it for storing her pans. I'd been instructed to turn it off after an hour. "Would you go down and check?" I asked Shazia. I couldn't let my collage concentration lapse.

She didn't hear me, so I repeated my request.

"Did you want me to feed you crisps as well?" she snapped. "Now look what you've made me do." She held up the paper doll, one of its legs chopped at the knee.

I changed the subject. "You know what David said to me?"

Shazia sighed, scrunching up the doll. She wrenched open a catalogue and began butchering a page, seemingly at random.

"Well, I'll tell you," I continued, snipping carefully around the tines of a garden fork. "He said that when he went to Hong Kong last year, the first thing—"

Shazia slammed a Thomas Cook brochure down, sending crisps flying out of the open packet. What *was* the matter with her?

I counted to ten. "Anyway, David – he said when they got off the plane, they—"

"And that spade looks ridiculous there." She glared at my collage.

"Spade? It's a fork. Anyone with even half a—"

I stopped, forcing myself to follow David's advice about befriending those who annoyed you. "I like what you've done there," I said, pointing at Shazia's gaudy effort. "It's really effective. Even with the yellow."

She didn't comment but continued to snip and glue images at a furious rate.

I returned to my collage. For Neptune's mermaids, I raided the bra section of the catalogue – shot from the waist up, the models would look like they were standing in water. As I snipped, I whistled the theme tune from *It's a Knockout*.

"Did I tell you what David said when I—"

"Yes, only a million times!" she said, slamming her Pritt stick down so hard that it rolled off the table. "It's all you ever talk about. David this, David that, David three bags full. David, David, DAVID!"

I backed away. I looked at her, aghast. What had come over her? She was screeching like a churail. "Why are you being so—"

"You sound like you're in love with him!"

My scissors slipped, severing the arm of the second mermaid. Shazia's accusation hung heavy in the air. I flushed and my heart thudded as though I'd run a race.

I got up, mumbling something about the biryani. I ran down to the kitchen and shut the door behind me. Leaning against it, I bent down, my hands on my knees, trying to process what Shazia had said.

The cumin-scented, close heat of the kitchen enveloped me. I couldn't breathe. I yanked open the window, tearing a hole in the net curtain in my haste, adding to the holes already there. It took a few minutes for my breathing to return to normal. I looked around, trying to focus my eyes. The kitchen was as cluttered as always, with pots and pans, mugs and dishes, rolling pins, cans of vegetable oil, plastic racks of vegetables, drying plates and sacks of rice laying claim to every surface. But, without Mother, the room felt empty.

I turned off the oven, taking care not to switch off the Eternal Flame by mistake. I was convinced something bad would happen if it ever went out.

A few moments later, steps thundered down the stairs, followed by the front door slamming.

Twenty-six

Christmas came and went. It was just a normal day in our house, as in all the other Asian houses in the neighbourhood. Nothing marked it out as special, apart from the inconvenience of everything being shut. KKK did a roaring business, and Mrs Kapoor went around telling everyone that Mr Khan hiked up the prices on certain goods just for the day.

As the year ended, so did David's stay in the UK. His aunt had passed away just after Christmas. His mum sold the aunt's house to a cash buyer, so they had no further reason for being here. Their time in Blackburn was done. They were heading back to Australia.

David had been in my life for just two months, but I felt I had known him for much longer. For the first time in my ten years, I'd found a male friend who liked me for who I was. Who didn't call me out for being different. Who encouraged me to be me. Who had brought out feelings I didn't know I had. And now he was going.

As Mrs Entwistle blew the whistle on the end of the second week of January, David and I headed to a quiet spot at the bottom of the playground, his arm around my shoulders. This was his final day. I dragged my heels, wanting to eke out the last minutes.

"I'm gonna miss you, mate," he said, looking me squarely in the eyes. "You're a one-off. Don't ever bloody change." His voice quavered.

I studied his face, knowing this was the last time I'd see him. "Don't go," I said, even though I knew it was hopeless. I knew I sounded pathetic, but I couldn't stop myself. The tears started, and I hated myself for crying, yet again, in front of him.

He just held me. "It'll all be fine," he whispered.

I didn't know what he meant. I tried hard not to cry. There had been so many tears. I heard the thud of my heartbeat, the blood pumping round my body. If I held on to him, maybe he'd miss his plane and have to stay. I pressed my arm tight around him.

His breath tickled my ear. My cheek pressed against the wool of his duffle coat. He smelt of Imperial Leather, sweat from playing football and the roast chicken he'd had for lunch. I stored the scents away, along with the feel of his strong arms around me, the softness of his hair against my temple, the pulsing warmth of his neck against my lips.

When I eventually allowed him to pull away, his mouth brushed against my face. I reached up to touch my cheek. As he began to say something, a train of kids jostled past.

I shook my head, clenched my hands into fists and bit my lower lip: rites for a spell to try and stop the inevitable. The beginnings of a deep ache rumbled inside me. I wanted to speak, but my mouth refused to form consonants. A mishmash of vowels vomited out.

David's mother was at the gates. I scowled at her, resenting her for taking him away from me. "Oh, love," she mouthed, seeing my tear-streaked face. She hugged me and kissed the top of my head. She smelt of Charlie by

Revlon. More tears, this time into her chest, her coat scratchy against my skin, a harp-shaped brooch pressing into my breastbone.

"Can't you stay?" I sobbed. "Just for a bit longer. Please?"

She stroked my hair and let me empty out my anger and sadness. As the playground thinned out, the excited shouts and cries of the other children grew fainter. The gates behind us creaked and slammed into each other, animated by the wind. A pair of wood pigeons thrashed around in the trees. From inside the school, Mr Mobsby moved desks around.

Eventually, my tears cried themselves out. My breathing had calmed down but remained juddery from all the sobbing. I pulled away, knowing I must look a mess.

"Be good to yourself, love," said Mrs Harrington. She kissed my head one last time.

And then they were gone. One minute, David was there; the next, he had vanished – from school, from my heart and out of my life.

My head whirled with the chorus of ABBA's "SOS". Mr Mobsby whistled tunelessly.

The world continued to roll on; night followed day, but the magic was spent.

Twenty-seven

Thanks to the executive lounge card I treat myself to every Christmas, I'm showered and halfway human again. It also feels good to wash away the incident with Pedro.

Despite being just after 9 a.m. here in Dubai, I help myself to a glass of champagne and, as an afterthought, a small plate of sliced fruit. After the sleepy first leg of my journey, the busy lounge is an assault on the senses. I huff as a man in a shellsuit and box-fresh white trainers elbows past me, his plate laden with bread rolls.

Finding a seat in the corner, I go over the songs I'll sing at the wedding. Shazia had added a note inside the card, begging me to perform some of her favourite Bollywood numbers. I'll need to rehearse as it's been a while since I've sung them.

The clink and scrape of crockery and cutlery is like percussion in the background. Before long, I'm humming to myself – a song by the late R. D. Burman, a favourite of mine since childhood. I start off quietly, then get louder and louder. As the music in my head swells, I lean forward, perch and finally stand, sending the plate on my knee tumbling. I'm no longer in the lounge, waiting for my flight to be called, but on stage, looking out at the audience. The

Hindi words feel good in my mouth. The orchestra inside my head keeps a galloping pace befitting the jaunty cabaret number.

When I finish, applause rings out. It takes a moment to realise it's not in my imagination. I grin and make a flamboyant bow to all corners of the room.

"Bravo!" says a snowy-haired woman in a polka dot frock. "I didn't understand a word, but you were great." Then, after a few seconds: "Say, aren't you that guy?"

"That's him," says her friend, pushing up her sunglasses. "I never forget a face. If I was twenty years younger..." The sea of grey and white heads around them nod and giggle.

They surround me, chattering, thrusting pens and napkins to sign. My heart swells.

*

I take a deep breath as I leave the Lounge. It's shuffling-room only in duty free. I haven't had time to get wedding gifts. Actually, that's not strictly true. It's not like I hadn't known the big day was coming, even if I didn't have the exact date until a few days ago. But rehearsals and the show itself have taken up so much of this year. Shazia will understand.

There's a large crowd in the electronics section. Never one to miss out, I brave the scrum. The credit card-flashing mob is ooh-ing and aah-ing over MP3 players. There's an impressive range, but, as always, I'm drawn to the bitten apple logo.

"The iPod can store up to a thousand songs," promises the fast-talking assistant.

A likely story. But I pop one into my basket – then another. If it's good enough for Shazia... The iPods join the silk scarfs and pashminas I've already got in there.

Next stop, perfumes. Even when we were kids, Shazia would be enveloped by a cloud of scent. I chuckle, remembering how she'd squirt herself with her mum's Elizabeth Arden, dousing it liberally over her jumper. I drop in several bottles. Then I look for perfumes for myself. I try out various colognes, spritzing the air and walking through the mist.

"Definitely that one," says a voice behind me. It's Pedro. He's close enough for me to smell him. The spiciness of bergamot. He sniffs the air around me. "Good choice."

I grin and hold out two bottles. "This one has the citrus I like," I say, "but this one's got more musk."

"We all like a bit of musk," he says, his eyes twinkling. "Isn't that right, *guapo*?"

I blush and look away. Before I can say anything else, he winks and leaves the store. I stare after him. He makes his way to the toilets, turning back to me before he goes in. I quickly focus my attention back to the colognes. Unable to decide, I put both in the trolley.

There's a huge queue at the till. I look at the exit. I could leave the basket. Follow Pedro. *Behave*, says the angel. I sigh. I prepare for a long wait. My mind wanders instead.

Twenty-eight

The display of royal wedding memorabilia was covered in dust and star-shaped sale cards, all blaring out "New Year sale!" and "Basement Bargains!"

"All half-half price," called out Mr Khan. "Everything must go!"

I dithered between a Princess Di mug and a cereal bowl. It wasn't for myself but for Shazia. She loved Princess Di and was keeping a scrapbook about her, so I figured a gift would go down well after our strange evening making collages. As I deliberated, the door opened behind me, and a few moments later, I heard a familiar voice. "So, what is the difference between those two? They look kinda similar."

It was Mr H! He was at the counter, pointing to the jars of Bombay mix on the shelves behind Mr Khan. Mother used the same jars for her homemade pickles. Mr Khan squinted at him as though debating whether or not to call the police: Mr H was clad head to toe in denim, with dark brown cowboy boots and thin leather straps wrapped around his wrist. A chocolate-coloured Stetson perched at an angle on his head. "Mr H!" I called out.

Mr H looked around. "Hey, whaddya know?" He approached me and proffered a fist. I clutched it, not knowing what else to do. He laughed.

"Sir, what are you doing here?"

"Right now, I'm trying to work out what's what with those two jars."

"That one's spicy, and that one's not. Otherwise they're the same, but the spicy one costs more," I said, incurring a scowl from Mr Khan.

Mr H laid down a one-pound note. "I'll take a bag of each, my good sir."

Mr Khan beamed at being addressed thus, then held the note up to the dim light.

"Isn't this neat?" said Mr H, spinning around and taking in the shop. "All these amazing things in one place? Just look at it!" He flung his arms out. "*'Oh, wonder! How many goodly creatures are there here! How beauteous mankind is!'*"

I must have looked blank, as Mr H added, "*The Tempest.*"

I was none the wiser. The smell of spices in the shop had clearly sent him doolally.

Mr Khan must have thought the same. He glanced over. "Your friend need doctor?"

The door blew open. Mrs Kapoor creaked in, pushing an empty pram before her. "One minute rain, next minute sun," she said, out of breath. "How to live with this?"

Mr H helped lift the pram over the threshold. Mrs Kapoor tilted up at him. "Such good manners. Not like some." She shot me a look.

"The pleasure's all mine, Ma'am." Mr H proffered a hand, which Mrs Kapoor shook by the tips of his fingers. "Maaz," he said.

"Namaaz? Already?" she said, blinking at the sunburst clock behind Mr Khan.

"He means his name is Maaz," I said, realising I'd not known this until now.

"Maaz... Maaz..." She rolled the name around her gums. Satisfied, she moved closer to him. "What fair skin. A sign of good breeding." Then, at me: "Usually."

Mr Khan passed over the chickpeas. Mr H handed me the spicy ones and offered Mrs Kapoor the others. She demurred. "Very kind, beta, but I must not ruin my appetite."

More like her dentures. I had to get him away. "Mr H, could I take you to my—"

"Where is your wife?" she said. "You have children? How old?" With each question, she threw different dry goods into the pram: lentils, rice and, bizarrely, a Pot Noodle.

Mr H laughed. "Oh, well, Mrs... er..."

"Kapoor." She held out her hand. Mr H kissed it. "Your wife is a lucky lady."

"Wife? No, Ma'am, just a partner."

This was news to me! I'd have to grill him later.

"And no children – that I know of!" he added.

Mrs Kapoor tittered and tossed a bag of cashews into the pram.

"Being around them all day is plenty fine for me," said Mr H. "And when you have smashing kids like Rafi here, it's a hard act to follow."

Mrs Kapoor looked around, as if expecting another boy of the same name, before reluctantly smiling at me. Reaching to pat me on the head, she couldn't bring herself to do it and pretended to stumble, throwing in an exclamation of "Save me, Allah!"

"No children? Why not? Such a handsome face." She squeezed his cheeks. "Own hair..." She tugged at his sideburns, then pointed at his quiff. "A little long, mind."

Mr H offered her the chickpeas again. She rummaged around, finally picking one out and sucking on it. "You are a good boy. You have respect for your elders. Not like some. Why no wedding ring?" She ran a bony thumb over his fourth finger.

Mr H's eyes crinkled at the corners. "My dear Mrs Kapoor, like I said, no wife. The other half, yes, and we are as good as married."

"No wife?" She collapsed into the biscuit aisle. I shook my head at her histrionics.

Mr H hoisted her back up. "A nice wife you need. A seedhi-saadhi girl. Someone to cook and clean. I find for you." She helped herself to a fistful of chickpeas.

Mrs Moto's children rushed in, tearing around like they were on *Runaround*.

"No running!" shouted Mr Khan. "Any breakings and you will pay for."

"Such sweet children," said Mrs Kapoor in such an insincere tone I was surprised her nose didn't grow. Then: "Even if they are half-and-half."

Mr H unhooked his arm. "Forgive me, Mrs Kapoor, I don't get your drift."

"Jif?" she said. "In the back, beta, but Vim is much-much better."

Mr H indicated Mrs Moto's children, who were head-first inside the big chest freezer. "I was curious what you meant by 'half-and-half'?"

"Oh, nothing, puthar. Just life was simpler. Black was black, and white was white." She consulted a non-existent watch. "Is that the time? I must get back for namaaz."

"She means that their dad is Indian and their mum is Pakistani," I piped up.

Mr H leaned back against the counter, his legs impossibly

long in front of him. "A bringing together of cultures can only be a good thing, no?" He smiled. "Your name ... Hindu? No doubt you know Muslims and Sikhs. Look at our friend here, who serves everyone, regardless of who they are." Mr Khan looked confused at being brought into the conversation. "We should be building bridges, right, not knocking them down?"

Mrs Kapoor drew herself up to her full four-and-a-half feet. "Just because something is possible does not mean we have to act on it!" She began dragging the pram backwards.

"Ma'am, I didn't mean to upset you," said Mr H. "Let me help you."

Mrs Kapoor flapped the end of her chadar at him.

"I know what it is like to be a 'half-and-half'," said Mr H. "My dad was Pakistani, my mum English. And I have known nothing but good because of it."

Mrs Kapoor and I gasped. I'd assumed Mr H was fair-skinned, like my beloved Jeetendra, but he was half-English. How exotic! Mrs Kapoor backed away, raising her chadar to her face as though Mr H had set out to hoodwink her.

From the counter, Mr Khan called out: "Mrs Kapoor, would you liking to credit?"

Mrs Kapoor ignored him, instead looking Mr H up and down. "No ring ... dressed like a loafer ... no wife. Oh-ho, now I see you, you lufanga!"

"She called you a yob, sir," I translated.

"I've been called worse," he said. "And Mrs Kapoor is entitled to her opinion."

Mrs Kapoor wrenched the pram backwards with a strength normally found in someone decades younger. A bag of kidney beans slid to the floor. Ever the gentleman,

Mr H grabbed it. As he straightened up, he winced, as though he'd pulled a muscle. I made to give him a hand, but he began to cough and got out his handkerchief.

Mrs Kapoor hissed. "Shoo! Dhaffa haun ja!" She slammed the door shut behind her.

"Kid, you've got interesting neighbours," said Mr H, shaking his head and coughing again into his handkerchief. He slowly unfurled himself. "Ouch! I'm getting old. Dodgy joints. Or I'm coming down with the flu."

I must have stepped away, as he laughed. "Only kidding. Probably just slept funny. Anyway, she's the real deal, that one – nothing escapes her, that's for sure!"

While he adjusted the bag slung around his shoulder, I grabbed my moment. "Sir, can you come to my house? My mum's making kebabs! My dad might even be home."

"Sounds great, Raf, and I'd love to shoot the breeze, but there's a kid with a guitar and a Grade 6 exam coming up who needs me."

Mr H taught somebody here? I swallowed the jealousy that rose in me.

Seeing my disappointed face, Mr H ruffled my hair. "You can show me the best way there, if you like?"

I grinned. I popped more chickpeas into my mouth. All was well in the world again.

Before we left, I remembered Shazia. I grabbed a Princess Di mug *and* a bowl and asked Mr Khan to put it on our account. I'd explain to Mother later. Shazia was worth it.

*

As we walked, Mr H brought me up to speed with news on the Conservatoire. He'd sent my application off a few weeks ago, which we'd completed together. "It's just been accepted," he said. "You've got an audition, buddy!"

I stared at him, mouth agape. "They'll have been bombed with applications, so you should be rightly proud."

I whooped and hollered, skipping and dancing alongside Mr H, too happy to speak.

We made our way along Pitt Street. It was a longer street than Baines Street and with more cars parked on the road. The houses were also not in as good a condition, with lots of the window sills needing repainting and the roofs showing slipped tiles like missing teeth. The sky was the colour of a dead fish. What sunshine there'd been was now properly gone. Mrs Kapoor was right. How was one to live with such changeable weather?

As we walked, I found it harder to hear Mr H. What I'd thought was the drone of cars now sounded like a football crowd: a rhythmic ebb and flow of massed voices, with bursts of raucous laughter. And it was getting louder.

Then, as if someone had turned on a tap, the empty street ahead suddenly flooded with people, all pouring in from Grimshaw Park Road. White faces, and lots of them. They swung and jabbed banners and Union Jacks in the air, accompanied by rattles, drums and whistles. There must have been a hundred or more, walking towards us, in the road, on the pavements, thumping on car bonnets, banging doors, heckling, shouting, chanting. I couldn't make out what they were saying, but the message was clear: they were trouble.

"Mr H," I said, tugging at his sleeve. "I think we need to go back."

Mr H narrowed his eyes and surveyed the scene, not breaking his stride nor his gum-chewing. We were the only other people out on the street. Front doors, normally open in the summer, were now shut. In panic, I banged on a couple, but they remained closed. With no trees on the street or indeed, any of the streets in the neighbourhood, we were totally exposed. Just iron lampposts every few hundred yards, tall and imposing but not wide enough to hide behind.

"Stay close," said Mr H, taking my hand, the thud of his cowboy boots audible over the chants. "If we go back, it'll be a red rag to a bull. I've met these types before. I've got you." He squeezed my hand in reassurance. "I'll protect you. I promise."

I was finding it hard to breathe. As the mob got closer, I made out their signs:

"*Rights for Whites!*"

"*Britain for the British!*"

"*STOP immigration. START repatriation!*"

How could something as banal as a piece of cardboard create such terror? Father always told us not to go into town on match days, but this was a hundred times worse, as trouble had come looking for *us*. Even though my heart beat so hard I thought I'd pass out, my body was freezing cold, and not just because of the January cold; the blood had pooled to my feet, readying them to flee.

Mr H continued walking, taking me with him. "We'll be fine, trust me."

I looked at him in astonishment. Outside of the classroom, he looked thinner than normal. How was he going to protect me against a big group of NF thugs? Why was he leading me into the lions' den? Couldn't he hear the chants?

"*What do we want?*"

"*Pakis out.*"

"*When do we want it?*"

"*Now!*"

Taleeb's threats of skinheads had come true. And not at

Everton, but in our own neighbourhood. I struggled to keep my feet moving, which had turned into medicine balls.

"Oi! Paki! Talking to you, paki!"

My stomach cramped. It was like I'd been punched. I put my head down and shrunk away from the pavement, willing us to become invisible among the red bricks.

"Who let you out the corner shop, paki?"

I recoiled. The last time I'd heard the dreaded p-word was during our visit to Everton. To hear it spoken again now, repeatedly, and by grown men, made it much more threatening.

I pulled back, but Mr H encouraged me to keep on walking. "Don't show them any sign of weakness. Nearly there. You're doing great. Don't look at them."

A trio of skinheads in tight jeans, bomber jackets and big boots ran towards us, making monkey noises. They walked three abreast on the pavement, forcing us to stop. I thought I'd stop breathing. This was the stuff of nightmares. I was in my own horror movie.

"Oi, paki – I asked you a question."

My hands trembled so much I dropped the thin blue plastic bag containing Shazia's mug and bowl. It landed with a crack. The skinheads cheered, and the nearest one booted it into the road.

"Leave him alone," said Mr H. "He's a kid, for Chrissake."

The leader bared his teeth, yellow and sharp. "A Yank? You can fuck off, an' all."

"Mind your language, else I'll mind it for you," said Mr H.

The skinheads made an "ooooOOOOoooo" sound to show how un-scared they were by the threat. It should have been comical, but the effect was chilling. A shiver ran through me and I shrunk further into the wall. I'd wake up in a minute. This wasn't happening.

"Get out of our way and let us pass," said Mr H, seemingly unconcerned by them.

"What's the magic word, paki-lover?" taunted the second, looming into Mr H's face.

"Fucking nonce," said the third, tipping Mr H's hat off and flipping it repeatedly into the air like a coin. "Should be locked up."

Mr H grabbed his wrist and twisted it, making him cry out in pain and drop the hat. Mr H picked up the hat and placed it back on his head, tilting it at the previous angle.

"Hard man, eh?" said the ringleader.

"Smack the fucker," urged the third, nursing his wrist, his face contorted in pain.

The ringleader moved his head back and I thought he was going to headbutt Mr H. He did something even worse: he spat at him. Luckily, it missed.

I wanted to throw up. It was the kind of thing Amjad would do. How had such a nice day turned into this nightmare? Terrified, I forced myself to keep looking at the three thugs. Just like when in bed, fearing the churails were coming for me, I knew it was better to keep my head out than under the blanket. Know where your enemy is at all times. Each time one of the skinheads scowled at me, I maintained eye contact despite my bowels contracting and my breath catching in my throat.

"Try that again, and so help me God," said Mr H, his hands clenching into fists.

The ringleader squared up to Mr H, his fist up. "Try what again? You want some of this? Do you? Do you?" With each question, he chest-bumped Mr H. Mr H stood his ground. I'd never seen him look like this – his face rigid and no trace of his usual smile.

Before anything more could kick off, police sirens cut through the din. As they got louder, the crowd moved faster down the street.

Mr H pushed me behind him then barged into the skinheads, shouldering them aside. He walked on, now moving me in front of him, his hands on my shoulders.

"If I see you again, I'll kick the fucking shit out of you," yelled the ringleader. "Yankee bastard!" Without breaking stride, Mr H stuck a finger up at him. The skinhead shouted something, but the sirens sounded and his mates bundled him away.

Blood pounded in my ears. I tried not to be sick. I was too scared to even blink, in case it brought them back. In our wake, we heard car windows smashing and the thunk of beer cans lobbed at doorways. Jeers rang out each time a fist, boot or brick met its target.

Whatever else had gone through my mind during the terrifying last five or ten minutes, one thing had become crystal clear: the Conservatoire was my only hope. I had to get in – or die trying.

Twenty-nine

Monday, 1 February. The day of the audition. I could barely open my eyelids. I'd tossed and turned with terrifying dreams of skinheads chasing me down the street, with Mother at their helm. I'd called out to David to help me, but he'd flown up into the sky like Superman, saying he had to go back to his dad, leaving me to my fate. I'd shouted myself hoarse in my dreams. Had I called out for real, too? I tentatively tested my voice. It was fine.

While David haunted my dreams, in the daytime I was too busy to think about him. Which was just as well, as I didn't have enough room in my head to take on his loss. It was all I could do to hone my audition skills. Mr H told me repeatedly not to underestimate what was to come.

I didn't want to get up. I didn't want to face the world. I wasn't ready for what today meant. But I knew that lying in bed wasn't going to rescue me from my predicament.

The thought of breakfast made my stomach heave. Mother was suspicious, so I took a piece of toast, played with it, then chucked it under the sofa when she went out.

As I got to school, a dark blue BMW with tinted windows pulled up. Ashiqah stepped out. Her mother hollered through the open door: "Dear Rakesh – such round, round cheeks, ma'shallah. Tell your mummy we have new purses in. From Taiwan. They are not the same quality as India, but better for *her* purse." She tittered as she drove off.

"Why are you all dressed up like a dog's dinner?" said Ashiqah, pointing at my tweed jacket, which I'd found in the Children's Society shop on Darwen Street where Nabila and I had sheltered in one rainy day, worn over a paisley shirt, the lavender swirls a complementary match to my mustard-coloured trousers.

"That's for me to know, for you to find out," I said. Arms wide, I did a Wonder Woman spin on my imitation Golas so she could get the full effect.

Before she could comment, Mr H's black Mazda screeched to a stop in front of us. Mr H reached over and popped open the passenger door. He was in triple denim: jacket, shirt and jeans finished with a black Stetson. "Hop in, kiddo!"

Easing off my satchel, I narrowly missed poking Ashiqah in the head with an elbow. She thumped me, making me stumble into the car.

"Whoa there, bud," said Mr H. "We don't want you breaking a leg. Not this way!"

Ashiqah's head tracked our departure, a scowl on her face.

*

"Are you all right, skip?" said Mr H. "You've not said a word!"

My stomach hadn't stopped bucking and heaving since I'd got up. I opened my mouth, but just a croak came out.

"What was that?" laughed Mr H. Then he flinched, as though in pain. He forced a smile on his face. "What have they done with the old, loud, full-of-beans Rafi, scourge of Mrs Entwistle and tester of patience of choirmasters?"

I laughed, then I flipped his question round. "Are *you* all right, Mr H? You don't look so good." He didn't. He sat at the edge of his seat, hunched over the wheel, as though the car had got too big for him. His blazer swamped him, as though it was two sizes too big.

Seeing me staring, he eased back. Again, he winced. "Darn headache. Comes and goes. But don't worry about me. Today is all about you. We are on a mission."

Mr H gently punched me on the arm, making me smile. "That's better," he said.

"Sorry, Mr H," I said, "I just can't stop thinking about what's going to come up and worrying if I'm going to do it right and what happens if I don't and I muck up and they think I'm an idiot and then I'm back to square one and I can't—"

"Whoa! Ease up, buddy. Take a breath. Can't have you passing out before we've even got there."

He made me follow his slow breaths for a minute. Gradually, I felt less light-headed and my heart stopped beating quite so fast.

"You can do this, Rafi," said Mr H. "Don't let the nerves get to you. They just mean you're ready to perform."

My stomach flipped. I moaned and launched into another rapid monologue.

Once again, Mr H calmed me down. "Think of your nerves as butterflies. The way you feel at the moment, those butterflies are all over the shop, flying where they want. Just focus. Train them to fly in formation. Like we talked about in lessons."

Slowly, he took me through some of our old exercises.

While the nerves didn't go away, I felt I was a little more in control of them. The butterflies weren't quite so wild.

*

The gardens reminded me of Corporation Park, with beds of crocuses, snowdrops and early daffodils in between immaculately clipped lawns, crisscrossed with shingle paths. Students of all shapes, sizes and colours milled around the campus in their smart blazers, various musical instruments in tow.

"Mr H, it's like another world." Set in several acres of ground, you'd never know you were in a busy city. I couldn't even hear the traffic.

"Ready for your close-up, Mr A?" Mr H zoomed in on my face with a viewfinder made from his fingers.

I looked blank. He laughed, explaining it was a line from one of his favourite films.

A group of students went past, chatting animatedly. They looked so relaxed in each other's company, walking around campus like they were strolling around a park.

The butterflies in my stomach took off all at once, bumping into each other in random, skittish flight. "I can't do it!" I cried. "Let's drive back." I felt exposed, as though the students would turn around and ask what I was doing here and send me off to Everton.

"Wait. I know what you need." Mr H took out a dusky pink silk handkerchief with a monogrammed MH in the corner. "My lucky charm." He popped it into my shirt pocket.

That was the second time Mr H had given me one of his handkerchiefs. I was grateful for its presence. It would be like he'd be with me in the audition.

Mr H performed an exaggerated head-up-chest-out-deep-breath-hair-comb sequence, which I mirrored. He flipped his Stetson in the air so that it landed on his head. I did the same with my cap. Then we strode purposefully, side by side, arms curved out, legs bowed, cowboy boots and plimsolls crunching on the gravel, announcing our arrival.

*

The audition room smelt of beeswax, which reminded me of the piano I practised on. The space was twenty times the size of our lounge, seemingly made entirely of wood. Portraits of old white men peered down from the walls. Chandeliers hung from the ceiling. A large mahogany table dominated the room, behind which sat two women and a man. I told myself to keep breathing. What was I doing here? These people would see right through me. I turned, wondering if I could scarper. My eye caught a square of pink in my blazer. I touched it and felt my breathing slow down.

"And who do we have here?" said the lady in the middle, in a pink-and-blue checked wool twinset, her hair like a swirl of Butterkist popcorn. I stared, transfixed. She motioned me to the wooden chair in the middle of the room. I sat down and nearly slid off – polished to a high sheen, the curved seat provided little friction against my corduroy trousers. Her mouth twitched and she brought a hand up to cover it.

"Rafi Aziz, Miss," I said, righting myself. "I'm pleased to make your acquaintance."

"Likewise. Now, Rafi" – she pronounced it "Rah-Fee" – "could you tell us why you want to come to the Conservatoire? We have many applicants and only a few places, so our task, as you can appreciate, is not an easy one. Why should we choose you?"

Mr H and I had rehearsed this question many times. Acknowledging each of the panel in turn – Pinched Mouth, Popcorn Head, Olive Oyl – I squared my shoulders, engaged my diaphragm and got ready to speak. "I've been a performer all my life," I orated. "There wasn't a time when I wasn't singing or dancing or acting. It's just part of me. Mother says I danced before I walked."

Popcorn Head smiled at the last line. Maybe she also recognised the reference to "Thank You for the Music".

"But," I continued, my confidence growing, allowing me to go off-script, "more and more, people around me have got less and less tolerant. They tell me I should keep quiet. I will grow out of it. What will the neighbours say?"

Pinched Mouth, who had been making notes, looked up. "How does that make you feel?" He peered at me over the top of his glasses. He looked like Clark Kent.

"Sad. And angry." I unclenched my fists. "But it makes me even more determined to be true to myself, sir. I belong here. I want to be in that brochure."

Olive Oyl smiled and nodded, animating the feathers woven in her hair. "We certainly encourage all forms of creativity and expression in our students," she said.

"How do your parents feel about you being here?" said Popcorn Head.

I was going to tell a lie, but she pinned me with such a penetrating gaze I knew it would be pointless. "They don't know, Miss."

All three exchanged glances with each other.

I continued: "They would have stopped me. But I can't let them ruin my life."

"Ruin your life?" said Olive Oyl, blinking her eyes. "In what way, young man?"

"If I don't get accepted, I'll have to go to Everton – the local secondary school."

"Presumably, the school has a music department?" Pinched Mouth took off his glasses and chewed on the stem.

"Yes, sir, but the music teacher wasn't interested in what I had to offer," I said.

"I see." He slid his glasses back on.

"Mr H – my current music teacher – said she wouldn't know talent if it jumped up and bit her on the ar – I mean, nose."

Pinched Mouth looked at me over his glasses but didn't say anything.

"It's like *Grange Hill*," I continued. "One girl hit a boy over the head with a tray." All three blinked. "They flush your head down the toilet." Coughs from the panel. "You also don't know Amjad." Heads to the side. "Or the skinheads." Creased brows and pursed lips. "I won't survive there." Clicking pens. I thought I'd best stop there, as I wasn't sure if their reactions were good or bad.

Finally, Popcorn Head spoke. "We do need parental consent, you understand?"

I nodded. "When I get accepted . . ." She raised an eyebrow. "If I get accepted, Mr H will come and explain to them. Once they realise how prestigious the Conservatoire is, they'll want to tell the neighbours – *and* send a tape to Pakistan!"

"A tape?" said Pinched Mouth.

"Not to worry, Mr Beecham," said Popcorn Head. "Time is against us. We can cross that bridge if . . ." she paused and held my gaze ". . . and when we come to it."

"Touché, miss," I said.

Popcorn Head again struggled to hide a smile. "Very

well, let us hear your audition pieces," she said. "Shall we start with the speeches?"

*

Half an hour later, Popcorn Head sat back and folded her hands atop the pile of paper before her. Her face gave nothing away. "Thank you, Rafi," she said. "That was, certainly, a unique audition. I think we'll all remember that for a long time." She looked at her colleagues, who nodded in agreement. My stomach plunged. They'd hated it. That's why they'd remember it. For the sheer awfulness of it. I wanted the ground to swallow me up. "We will be in touch next month once we have interviewed all the shortlisted candidates. We appreciate you coming to see us today, and we wish you a safe journey home."

*

I ran out of the room in tears, with Mr H calling after me. He'd been waiting outside in the corridor. I didn't stop crying until we were in the car and back on the motorway.

"But, what happened?" said Mr H, his voice quiet and full of concern.

I couldn't speak, but just let out a growl and thumped the dashboard.

"Easy now, tiger," said Mr H. "I'm sure it wasn't as bad as you think."

"It was worse!" I blared out. "I was a frigging mess!"

Mr H nudged into the slow lane. "Frigging? What kind of . . . anyhow, that can't be true, buddy. I'm sure you slayed it."

"I did! I killed it stone-cold DEAD!" I shrieked, letting out all my anger, hurt and embarrassment.

Mr H shook his head as though tipping water out of his ear. "Steady on, Regan."

Who the hell was Regan? Wasn't that the name of the new American president?

"Could you say that a bit louder?" he continued. "I'm not sure I got it."

Was he trying to be funny? How could he be making a joke at a time like this?

"Come on, Rafi. Talk me through it. How did the speeches go? We'd got those down to a tee, hadn't we?"

I shuddered. Who did I think I was kidding, thinking I could bamboozle the judges with a speech Amitabh Bachchan gives in *Deewaar*, pleading with the gods to spare the life of his dying mother? I'd kept slipping into Hindi whenever I forgot the English bits of the translation Mother had done for me. I'd told her it was for a school project, and the sentimentality of the speech had also appealed to her. She'd never have helped if she'd known it was for my audition.

"What about the sight-reading?" said Mr H. "You're an ace at that. That must have been fun, no?"

"If you like beggars and operas," I snapped. I hadn't known the piece, but I'd managed to sing the words to the melody on the page minus any flair as I was so worried about getting the tune wrong. The piano sight exercise wasn't much better, my confidence knocked by seeing four flats in the time signature.

As a fleet of lorries overtook us, Mr H hugged the car further into the hard shoulder. "How about 'Buenos Aires'?" he said. "You loved doing that."

Remembering the audition, I shuddered all over again. This time, I'd gone the other way and put too much of myself into the performance. In what was meant to be a pure vocal, without accompaniment, I couldn't stop myself from shimmying and shaking as the samba rhythms of the song took over. No wonder Popcorn Head had kept leaning into her colleagues and whispering each time I let myself go. I ground my teeth.

"And the dance? You'd totally nailed the piece from *Fame*."

I had, while rehearsing it a million times with Mr H. But, for reasons known only to myself, at the last minute, I'd switched it for something completely unrehearsed. Freestyling, I'd enacted moves from the film *Zamaane Ko Dikhana Hai*. As if the frenetic Bollywood stylings weren't enough, I'd thrown in bhangra, street dance and disco moves as well. The judges had raised eyebrows again, scribbling so much they all needed new sheets of paper. Cringing at the memory, I thumped my forehead on the dashboard.

"Rafi!" cried Mr H. "Stop! You'll hurt yourself!"

Mr H reached over to stop me from banging my head again. I wasn't going to try it again, as it had hurt. But I didn't want his sympathy. I roughly pushed his hand away. He let out a surprised yell, which turned into a coughing fit. It racked his body, making him double over. He coughed into his hand, but the spasms were so strong that his free hand lost its grip momentarily on the steering wheel.

After that, the world lost its crisp edges and became a grey blur. The Mazda swerved from the outside lane into the middle, clipping a lorry. Traffic screeched around us. Beeps and horns sounded, a strident din over the screech of rubber burning on tarmac. The car skidded and slid across all three lanes, zigzagging first one way, then the other. Mr H yelled and tugged at the steering wheel, but the car had taken on a life of its own.

The blood drained from my face. I couldn't breathe. Everything slowed down, like in one of my nightmares. An awful noise filled the car. I realised it was me screaming. Mr H shouted something. As the wheels skidded hard across the cats' eyes down the edge of the road, the tyres burst in quick succession. I called out for David to save us. The car bucked, like an out-of-control bull. There was a screech, followed by a colossal bang as a car slammed into the boot. My teeth rattled in my skull. Mr H was launched forward, his head smashing into the steering wheel. He remained slumped across it, the horn blaring.

The last thing I remembered was hot white pain shooting through me before the curtain came down.

Thirty

"If you were home more, this would not have happened."

"Woman, how you can blame this on me?"

"I blame you for many, many things, believe me."

It took a while to register the voices. "*Maam?* Abba?"

There was a dreadful ringing in my ears. I tried to shield my eyes, but I couldn't move my left hand for some reason. I turned my head away from the light. Random beeps went off all around me, like someone playing on a Spectrum. Where was I?

A heavy weight landed on me. I winced and opened my eyes. It was Mother, sobbing into my chest, in an emotional Bollywood scene worthy of her facesake, actress Nirupa Roy.

"Give the boy room," said Father, coming into view and peeling her off me.

I was late for school! I made to get up, but once again couldn't find my left arm. What was I doing in bed? And what was that awful echoing in my ears? I stared at the white sheets. Whose bed was it? We had floral sheets at home, rustled up by Mother on her Pfaff.

"Come, Mrs Aziz. It looks much worse than it is."

What looks worse? Worse than what? Who was

speaking? My head felt woolly. I sank into the bed, my body as heavy as a tree trunk. I tried to speak, but it was too much effort.

A nurse in a blue uniform came over and led away Mother, before tucking me back in.

"Where's mm-hm?" I mumbled when my tongue finally engaged with my brain. Frustratingly, I couldn't get all the words out. I tried again. "Mm-hm H?"

Mother fussed around me and told me not to worry about anything.

"Mm-hm all right?"

She shushed me. Tears ran down my cheeks, which she wiped away. She sang me a lullaby, as though I was a baby. I asked more questions, but the words stretched out like elastic, never quite forming correctly. Within minutes, I'd drifted back to sleep.

*

The hospital released me three days later. Miraculously, apart from a broken arm, I had no other injuries. I ran my hand over the cast, tracing the names of the nurses and doctors. I sat on the chair by the bed, slightly fuzzy and with a dull ache all over, but otherwise fine. The curtain was drawn back, so I was in full view of the rest of the room. The twenty or so other beds were filled with kids and teenagers of all colours, most sitting up ready to receive their visitors. On cue, the bell rang to announce that visiting hours were open.

Mother ran in as if she hadn't seen me for a year. My bedfellows observed her with awe. With her emerald-green salwaar kameez and scarlet dupatta, gold jewellery, glass bangles and blooms in her hair, Mother was as exotic as the peacocks on the lawns of the Conservatoire.

Thinking about the music school made me groan. My memories had come back, day by day, slowly, then with the speed of an out-of-control lorry. I groaned again.

Thinking I was in pain, Mother clasped me to her bosom, raining kisses on my head.

"Mrs Aziz? Very pleased to meet you. I'm Dorothy, the Ward Sister."

Mother shook her hand, then looked around at the busy ward. "You have a very large family, Mrs Dottery." She pointed at me. "He okay now?"

"He's fine to go home, bless his cockles – our very own Superman. He was lucky, all things considered." She crossed herself. "I wish I could say the same for his teacher."

"We need to see Mr H!" I said, getting up.

Mother shushed me, as she had done each time I'd brought up his name since I'd been here. Finally, knowing I wasn't going to be quiet, she forced herself to address the issue. "How ... is ... he?" she asked Dorothy, cranking out the words with difficulty.

"The ambulance arrived within minutes," said Dorothy. "But the gentleman was in a bad way, the poor duck. He's only just woken up. Do you know if he has any family?"

I said we would go up and see him, but Mother glared at me. She fired off the same questions she'd asked me several times already in the last few days. "Why were you in Manchester? Why were you not at school? Why was that man with you?"

I was struck dumb. I couldn't shake the image of Mr H lying sprawled across the wheel. And now knowing he was lying unconscious somewhere in the hospital, without anyone around him. I looked at Mother, unable to comprehend her cold manner.

"Rafi's had quite a shock, Mrs Aziz. Maybe you'd like to—"

"I will give him shock!" snapped Mother. "This rascal boy should be in school."

No, I should be with Mr H. He was all alone. He needed me.

"Hopefully next year, yes, Mrs Aziz," said Dorothy. Seeing Mother's puzzled expression, the nurse clarified: "Rafi was telling me all about it this morning." She ruffled my hair. "Fingers crossed for the audition, young man."

"Audition? What audition?" Then the penny clicked. Mother seemed to grow an extra two inches. Without waiting for an answer, she grabbed my right hand and hoisted me up. Without saying anything else, she began dragging me from the ward, her various necklaces and bangles clinking and clanking our getaway. A couple of nurses stopped what they were doing and stared at us. I stumbled in Mother's wake, my legs stiff and in pain.

"Mrs Aziz," called Dorothy after us. She caught us up and held the door open. "Mrs Aziz, would you like a cup of tea before you set off?"

There wasn't time for tea. "We need to see Mr H!" I insisted. "It's the least we can do."

Mother ignored me. "Thank you, Mrs Dottery. His father is waiting for us."

"We can't leave him. He's got no one." I began to cry. "Let me go! Let me GO!"

I slipped my hand free and lurched down the corridor, holding onto the walls for support. Ignoring the shooting pains in my legs, I peered into the wards and rooms, hoping to see him. Mother clack-clacked after me in her glittery sandals, followed by Dorothy in her sensible white lace-up shoes.

"Mr H!" I called, as though he could hear me and call back. "Mr H!"

As I got to the end of the corridor, I came to a door with a glass panel. I peered through it. The room contained just one bed and some machines. Lying in the bed was the Invisible Man, his head swathed in bandages and a cast around one of his arms. I didn't recognise him at first, but a gap in the bandages revealed a familiar moustache. Yanking open the door, I fell in.

"Mr H! Thank God – you're okay!"

He opened his eyes and cracked a smile. "Hey, buddy! Good to see you. I was worried sick. Hey, I *am* sick!" He laughed, which set off a bout of coughing.

I laid my hand on his arm, waiting for the cough to subside. "I'm so sorry, sir! I didn't mean for any of this to happen." I indicated his prone body and the wires coming out of it. "I've kept asking to see you, but they wouldn't let me—"

"Come here, bathameez child!" Mother rushed in, yanking me away from the bed. "Wait till your father hears of this." Despite being out of breath, she was still able to issue threats.

Dorothy ran in. "Rafi, Mrs Aziz, I must ask you to leave. The gentleman needs complete rest." I noticed Mr H had already shut his eyes. Then, more gently, turning to me, the nurse said, "You can come and see him tomorrow, duck."

"It's all my fault," I said. "If I hadn't come for the audition, this would never have happened! If I hadn't had a tantrum in the car, he'd be all right! If I'd done a better audition, this would never have happened!" I yelled each declaration louder and louder.

"Stop this hungama right now," said Mother, shaking

me by my good arm. "What will people say? You are embarrassing Mrs Dottery! This man, this Mr Itch, is not our problem. Let his own family look after him. We need to get home. Enough tamasha."

I gasped at her choice of words. How could she be so heartless? "It's Mr Haqq! He's on his own here. His family's in America. We can't leave him." I ran back to his bedside. Mr H's eyes fluttered open sleepily and he waved at me.

Mother breathed out loudly through her nose. She marched me out, ignoring Dorothy's exhortations to go easy on me and how they didn't want the fracture to worsen. As I turned round, I spotted Mr H's cowboy hat on the chair next to the bed, his boots underneath. They looked strangely forlorn and lifeless.

*

Mother yanked open the back door of the Capri and bundled me in before slamming the door so hard the whole car shook. I caught my breath, winced, then sat up and turned my head, taking one final look at the hospital.

"Do not think for one second you will be coming here again to see him," she said, getting in the front with another slam, ignoring Father's protestations. "Or the fancy school. All these nakhras; I have spoiled you and you have become a little maharajah." She jammed her seatbelt into the socket with a click so loud it ricocheted like a gunshot.

"I hate you!" I shouted. "I don't know what's happened to you. You used to be fun. You used to laugh. Now you're like the Ayatollah."

"Thoba, thoba," said Mother, horrified at me comparing her to a Shi'ite.

"I'm *glad* I went for my audition without you knowing!"

Mother let out a screech. "How many times must you disobey me? What have I done to deserve this? Hai Allah, what devil child have I raised?" She looked at Father.

"We should be back in an hour," he said, keeping his eyes firmly on the road.

Mother flicked her dupatta at him before turning to look at me through the gap between the seats. I flinched. "You have lied to me. Again. And now your teacher is in hospital. I told you many times not to see him at school as he is filling your head with drama-shama nonsense, but you will not listen to your own mother! This is Allah punishing you for misbehaving."

"My dear, please," said Father, "can this wait until we are home?"

Mother ignored him. "No bicycle for you, my boy. This is what happens when you do not do as your mother tells you. Singing and dancing, making a showboat of yourself. Allah punishes you. And your teacher, too, for teaching you haram things."

Her callous words rang in my head.

*

I couldn't stop thinking about Mr H. Each time I closed my eyes, I saw him in the hospital bed, linked up to all those tubes, his eyes sunken and dark, his face skeletal, drawn and tired under the bandages, looking so frail. Was it because of the crash, or had I been so absorbed in my own problems that I hadn't spotted Mr H was having problems of his own?

Now he was lying in a hospital. And it was all my fault. No one could tell me otherwise. Not Mother. Not Shazia. Not Nabila. It was my fault we'd crashed.

While Mother did indeed lock away my bike in the

shed, she plied me with my favourite foods to make up for it. But not even potato-stuffed parathas or freshly fried samosas could assuage my guilt. I kept replaying the conversation in the car and then the way I'd shoved Mr H's hand away, setting off the chain of events which led to him now being in a hospital all on his own, groggy and unloved.

Clutching the taweez around my neck, I began to pray. First in English, then in Arabic. After I'd exhausted the kalimahs I knew off by heart, I picked up my Qu'ran from the high ledge where it was kept in our bedroom and began to read. I didn't know what the words meant, but the guttural words were a direct line to God. He would hear my prayers.

Thirty-one

A week later, I returned to school, my arm still in its cast. Nothing had changed – and yet everything had. There was no David. Mr H was still in hospital. The pain I felt was inside me rather than in the twisted scaffolding of my broken arm.

Mr Brindle took the final assembly of the week. The darkness outside threatened to encroach inside, so all of the Hall's lights were on. The heat from the cast iron radiators sent dust motes whirling. The parquet blocks threw up their comforting scent of oak and polish.

A cough from Mr Brindle brought me back into the room. He gazed down at us from the lectern. His hair was combed with a sharp crease in his parting. His nicotine-stained fingers thrummed against the wood.

"I am sorry to have to announce..." he began. My heart thumped in time to the rhythm of his tapping fingers. No good came from those seven words. Mr Brindle cleared his throat. "I am sorry to announce that Mr Haqq will not be returning to the school." I gasped, along with everyone else. Surely he'd be better by now? "Mr Haqq had been ill for some time."

What was going on? He'd been ill? Since when? Surely, Mr Brindle meant Mr H had been in a car crash and that's why he wasn't here. He'd be back soon, like I was. I know he coughed a lot, but it was just a cough. No big deal. But then a niggling doubt came into my mind. I remembered how unwell he'd looked at the hospital. How he'd seemed so thin the last few times I'd seen him, like he wasn't eating. Was Mr Brindle right? I'd been so wrapped up in getting to the Conservatoire that I'd not taken much notice of what was happening right in front of me. I'd brushed it away each time an alarm bell had rung.

"There were complications from the illness." Mr Brindle looked around. "Doctors weren't able to treat it." He paused. From behind him, on the chair she was sitting on, Mrs Entwistle pressed a handkerchief into her face. Miss Newton patted her on the arm. The bile rose up my throat. I was going to be sick. "I'm afraid to say, Mr Haqq . . ."

Cries and shrieks, including my own, drowned out the rest of the message. Black dots descended before my eyes. How could this be possible? Mr H would never be coming back? He was the only teacher who understood me, the only adult in my life who believed in me. He'd encouraged me to do my best, to want more, to think big. One of the last things he'd said to me in the car journey to Manchester was: "Shoot for the moon, Rafi. Even if you miss, you'll land among the stars." I cried at the memory, wishing I could rewind the clock and speak to him one last time.

My body felt like it had been plunged into a cold bath. This wasn't happening. A vacuum sucked the sound out of the room, like when I went swimming and my ears got blocked. From somewhere far away, Ashiqah asked if I was okay. Or I might have imagined it. All I could think of was how I'd never hear his cowboy boots echoing on the floor. How I'd never hear that laugh as he tipped his head back. How no one would call me "kid" again.

I felt a sudden rage rising inside me, making me grind my teeth. Why hadn't Mr H told me he was ill? Why couldn't the doctors fix him? What illness could be so bad that there wasn't a cure? How had he caught it? Had he given it to me? I'd spent a lot of time in the classroom with him. Should I tell Mother? Did I need to see Dr Yusuf?

Just as quickly, I flipped to red-hot shame. How could I be thinking about myself at a time like this? I'd rarely asked Mr H questions. I didn't know what he'd been doing in America. If he had a girlfriend. And when I'd seen him coughing or looking ill, I didn't think to check if there was anything wrong before turning back to my favourite topic: me.

Teachers weren't meant to leave. You were meant to leave them. Mr H hadn't stuck to the rules. He was gone. I bit my lip. I tasted iron. The pain jolted me back to my senses.

"Now, let us pray," said Mr Brindle, putting his hands together. "The Lord's Prayer. *Our Father, who art in Heaven, Hallowed be thy Name . . .*"

Thirty-two

The news of Mr H's death did what nothing else had managed so far. It toppled me. In the weeks following, it was as though I was Pac-Man, a wedge missing from what was once a perfect circle.

Mother plied me with gripe water for the pain in my stomach. When that didn't work, she fed me ajwain seeds. My mouth was dry and it took several minutes to get them down. Their bitter crunch masked the sugary-sweet water, but the ache remained.

Confined to bed, and despite many blankets, I struggled to keep warm. Mother bustled in and out, cooing and clucking her concerns, plumping up the pillows and encouraging me to eat. I kept my mouth shut, afraid to give voice to whatever was inside me. With my arm still in a sling, eyes open, body rigid, I was Tutankhamun, seeing everything, registering nothing.

Shazia came every day, usually straight after school. She brought me something with each visit – a copy of *Look-in* magazine with Boney M on the cover, a multipack of Seabrook crisps and even membership to the Puffin Club. She lent me her Walkman and said I could borrow it until I was better. I couldn't believe it. She was the first one on our street who had one. I put the orange foam headphones over my head and, with a trembling finger, pressed play. An eerie synth intro, followed by Frida's voice. ABBA. Their new album, *The Visitors*. Tears sprang to my eyes. I couldn't speak. I hugged her. She said the tape was mine to keep.

Nabila lent me her favourite doll and filled me in on what had happened in *Dynasty* and *Charlie's Angels*. Even Taleeb dropped by. He was sleeping on the sofa while I recovered. Leaving me the week's *Dandy*, he promised to take me to The Happy Haddock when I was better.

My mind raced with images of David and Mr H, screening in the cinema of my head as flickering black-and-white movies. In just two months, I had lost them both. It had taken ten years to find a friend like David. Even though he'd left for reasons beyond his control, I insisted on tormenting myself. Had he gone because of what happened on the canal? Had Mother said something to his mother? Australia may as well have been on the other side of the moon. When would I ever go there?

I felt Mr H's absence even more keenly. His loss was fourfold: he'd been my confidant, mentor and inspiration. He was also the older brother I should have had. No one had stood up for me the way Mr H had. Yet I'd been vile to him in the car. I was so wrapped up in my own selfish plans I hadn't even noticed how ill he'd been. Our last conversation was me moaning and being ungrateful; then I'd slapped his hand away. Mr H might have been around for years yet, even with his illness. I'd behaved abominably. All for a scholarship I wasn't going to get anyway. *You don't deserve it,* whispered the voice in my ear. It was right. I'd give it all up just to feel Mr H's reassuring hand on my shoulder once more.

Mother's harsh words kept coming back to me. I *was*

being punished. I'd be going to Everton, where Amjad would beat me up every day. It was what I deserved.

*

The moon went from full to a sliver and back to full before I felt strong enough for school. My arm was still in a sling, but there was nothing wrong with the rest of me. Mother would have had me home for the rest of the term, but the dragons wouldn't be vanquished on their own.

The first dragon was Ashiqah Ibrahim, my old nemesis, who was playing with Izmat and Shirley in the yard. Ashiqah was throwing two balls against the wall, chanting a rhyme.

"*'Have a cigarette, sir.'*"

"*'No, sir.'*" (She flung the ball at the wall in an overarm.)

"*'Why, sir?'*" (She threw the ball under one of her legs.)

"*'Because I've got a cold, sir.'*" (Then the other leg.)

Normally, I would have tried to join in, but I skulked past, trying to be invisible. She dropped the balls and glanced at Izmat before running over. "Hi, Rafi. I hope you're well? I've – we've missed you."

I rolled my eyes, wondering what sarcastic comment would follow. To my surprise, none came. Instead, she gathered up the balls and dropped one into the hand of my uninjured arm. I looked at them as though they were phoenix eggs. "Your turn," she said. "Go on, I'll show you how."

Izmat flipped out a stick of chewing gum from a packet, unwrapped it and broke it in half. "Say aaaaah." She lobbed one half into my open mouth and the other into her own.

Zaiman rocked up with Asghar. "It's good to see you back, mate," he said.

"You been on holiday, bruv?" asked Asghar. Zaiman elbowed him.

Moti, Javed and some of the others joined us, creating a circle in the centre of the yard. My cheeks glowed red. I rolled my shoulders up into the side of my face. After weeks alone, I wasn't used to people. Ashiqah gently pressed my arm.

Zaiman handed me a small parcel from behind his back. "From all of us." It was wrapped in *Willo the Wisp* paper – Evil Edna glared at me. I allowed myself a little smile.

I eased off the paper. In my hands was a framed pencil drawing Zaiman had done of Mr H, leaning against the bonnet of his Mazda. The likeness was startling. Mr H's head was thrown back, his eyes crinkled shut, mouth open as he laughed at something, sunlight catching his teeth. His thumbs were tucked into his belt; his denim-clad legs stretched in front of him, his cowboy boots crossed over at the ankle. Any minute now, he'd lower his head, wiping away tears of laughter, and say, "You gotta be kidding me, you guys. For real?"

*

I woke; I washed; I dressed.

I ate enough breakfast to appease Mother.

I went to school; I came back home; I did my homework.

I ate enough dinner to appease Mother.

I brushed my teeth; I said my prayers; I went to bed.

*

I put Mr H's picture in pride of place on top of the TV.

Mother, walking in with a changher balanced on her head, clocked the frame and pursed her lips. "Puthar, what is this? Be a good boy. He is gone."

She lifted it off. I snatched it back, thumping it down on the TV, sweeping aside the plastic flowers, golden tissue box and dancing dolphins.

"Come and eat," said Mother, patting the sofa. "You are too old for this ghusa."

It wasn't just anger. I was frustrated, sad and confused – a hundred and one negative feelings all rolled up into one. Dinner was the last thing I wanted. I remained standing.

"We need you nice and strong for big school," she said, setting the changher on the table before sitting on the edge of the sofa.

My stomach flipped. "That's six months away," I said, glaring at her.

"It will soon come round, my little bulbul. Now, come and—"

"I won't be going," I said, crossing my good arm over my broken one.

She shook her head. "Do not be a silly willy, puthar."

"I'd rather be dead."

Mother clutched her throat. "Thoba, thoba. You must not say such things, pumpkin."

My heart beat hard. "I'm not going. I'll lock myself in my bedroom. I'll run away. I'll leave the country."

Mother shook her head but didn't say anything.

I wiped a tissue over the glass frame. "Why couldn't he fight it?" I said. "With all their medicines and machines – they can make anyone better."

Mother reached over to stroke my cheek, but I shrugged away. She sighed. "Puthar, your teacher was not well.

I know you liked him, but he was not what . . . he was not who you thought he was."

She was talking in riddles, trying to fill my head with bad things about Mr H. I wouldn't let her. How dare she. Trembling, I made myself try to forget her hateful words.

Mother broke off a piece of chapatti and offered it to me. I turned away. She pouted, before popping it into her own mouth. "He did bad things. And Allah has punished him."

I put my hands up to my ears and banged my head against the back of the sofa.

"Thank heavens you did not catch it," she said. "Now, come on, have your gobi. I've added peas – your favourite, no?"

*

As life slowly got back on its usual tracks, so did everyone else. Ashiqah sniped at me once more. I realised how much I'd missed it. Izmat's bubble gum deliveries shut up shop. Mohammed found his shoulder again and resumed barging into me whenever we passed in the corridors. Mrs Entwistle's voice recovered its nasal tone, and she threw the chalk at me when I got an answer wrong.

The bell went for the final choir lesson of the week. Mrs Bainbridge had been coaxed out of retirement. I gathered my satchel. Standing up tall and taking a deep breath, I followed the other members of the choir into the Hall. I wasn't struck down by lightning. I didn't collapse. The room was just a room and it had kept on ticking even when I'd been absent. It would carry on ticking.

While everyone milled around and chattered, I leaned against the piano and closed my eyes. I blocked out the sounds and thought of him. In a few moments, I could hear only his voice. "Climb every mountain, Rafi."

That was a bit ambitious in Blackburn, but I racked my brain. "Like Pendle Hill, sir?"

He answered with another bit of advice: "Ford every stream."

With no streams, I wasn't wading through the canal. "Is it from the Bible, Mr H?"

He laughed and then broke into song, waltzing around, his arms skyward. Giggling, I joined in. We whirled like a pair of dervishes, my faux-Converse squeaking and his boots scraping across the polished parquet.

A nasal voice cut through my thoughts. "Rafi, are you with us?"

I opened my eyes. Mrs Bainbridge was at the piano and Mrs Entwistle had her hand aloft, ready to conduct.

The twirling ghost in the checked shirt had taken his leave for the last time. Just his laugh lingered.

Thirty-three

The flight to Manchester is shorter and less crowded. I have a row to myself. The gods have been kind. Actually, one god – a blond, six-foot-tall Mancunian head steward called Jason – to whom I appealed for a different seat when I found myself once more the sandwich filling in a block of three.

"Let me know if there's anything else you'd like, sir," he says, reaching up and shutting the overhead locker. His crotch is dangerously close to my face.

"Oh, I will," I mutter, forcing myself to look up.

He meets my gaze with startling blue eyes and I feel myself blushing. Thrown, I rummage in my Louis Vuitton messenger bag and hand him a signed CD of the show.

Looking from the cover to me and back, he raises a pierced eyebrow and the corners of his mouth lift. He's about to say something but is called away by a colleague.

I track his arse down the aisle, then tell myself off. Being on a plane, and in no man's land, makes the rules go out of the window. I'm not normally like this.

I beg to differ, says the angel on my shoulder. *You're your mother's son. Your head's easily turned by shiny, bright things.*

I'm not sure she'd appreciate the comparison, I say.

Be that as it may, need I remind you that you're spoken for?

And happily so. Five years and going strong, with a lovely man who accepts me for who I am but who isn't afraid to put me in my place when I get grandiose notions. And yet, there is always this side of me that needs the thrill of the chase. Who enjoys catching someone's attention. Who wallows in that attention. Why would I jeopardise what I have for a few moments of carnal pleasure? First Pedro, now Jason. And who knows how many others, had the flights had even more changes. I'm a walking-talking cliché, a man in every port – or every stopover. It's no coincidence, surely, that I've ended up in a career built on insecurity, a carousel of rejections, seeking validation in the admiration and support of others.

"Rafique! Over here! Coo-ee! Talking to yourself, doll? First sign of madness."

Eulalia and Chuck – two rows in front – an empty seat between them. She ripples her fingers at me. I wave back at her, then plug my earphones in.

Just as I get comfortable, Eulalia sinks into the aisle seat with a thud. She spends the next half hour regaling me about Chuck's bad habits.

"And don't get me started on his toenails. Like claws, I tell you." She shudders. "But I love that big ol' lunk. The good, the bad and the ugly. That's what it's all about, ain't it?"

I nod. That's exactly what it was about – even though I was pretty sure it was me who brought the "bad and the ugly" to our relationship. I cringe, remembering some of the tantrums I've put him through. The last one was about me making it clear I didn't like the shirt he'd got me for my birthday. The man is a saint and doesn't deserve me going behind his back for a quick how's-your-father with every Tom, Pedro or Jason.

"I blame his mom," continued Eulalia, offering me pretzels. "Treats him like he poops gold. Pardon me! Anyway, no wonder the man don't know a goddamn thing."

I shift in my seat as a twinge of recognition shoots through me. Mother's smothering love is almost certainly responsible for my spoilt streak. She'd call me her prince. Her rajah. Her nabob. And all manner of endearments based on Indian desserts. I chuckle.

"Ain't no laughing matter, Rafique," says Eulalia, tapping me on the arm. "You tried talking sense to a man who don't know his left from right? Well, honey, let me tell you . . ."

I'm missing my own "big ol' lunk". Picturing his easy smile, I find myself smiling back. Jason pushes a trolley of duty-free down the aisle at that moment. He picks up a couple of aftershaves and asks if I'm interested. He raises an eyebrow. To my surprise, and his, I say no. As he continues down the aisle, I mentally pat myself on the back. The angel on my left shoulder tells me off for being smug. I know, I know, I should really confess all when I'm home. But what's to confess? One tawdry encounter in a poky toilet and lustful thoughts for a blond Adonis? No, he doesn't need to know. He's easygoing, but even he has his limits. He might not see it as a "bit of fun". We don't have an arrangement for extracurricular fun, as many of our friends do, so why rock the boat?

Not for the first time, I wish he was with me on this trip. It would make things so much easier. Not just as my plus one but as my equal. Mind you, it's probably better that he isn't. I'd have to introduce him as my "friend" or colleague or something. He'd hate that. And rightly so.

But it's easier to tell them a white lie than the truth. The Indian languages don't even have a word for "gay". I shake my head. Eulalia, thinking I'm disagreeing with her, slaps me again. I nod and crank up a smile.

When Eulalia finally leaves, I close my eyes. I can't face watching more films. My head hurts. I keep coming back to whether or not I should 'fess up when I get back home to Melbourne. Whichever way I square it, I'm not happy with the answer.

Thirty-four

Ashiqah's mother at last came good on her promise. Mother finally saw the tape of the *Pebble Mill* show.

Nabila filled me in when I got home from Shazia's to exchange a pinch and a punch for April. She said Mother had watched the performance, perched on the sofa, straight as a telegraph pole, barely blinking. Not surprisingly, she'd got something in her eye and by the time of my solo, she was dabbing away with her dupatta. Nabila had to rewind and play the song three more times, she said, before Mother managed to get the grit out. She then called Father in, to watch it with her.

She sent Nabila "chop chop" to Mohammed's dad, who rented out bootleg Bollywood films for 50p and had two video recorders, to get copies made of the tape.

When I walked into the lounge, Mother wrapped me in a big hug. Father joined in, saying how proud he was of me. He smelt of cigarette smoke, engine oil and Brylcreem. I hugged them back, confused at the fuss but happy to let it ride. It'd been so long since I'd had praise, or something to be happy about, I'd take it even if I didn't know what it was for.

I finally extricated myself. "What's going on?" I said.

"Your mummy is very happy today, puthar," said Dad, ruffling my hair. "As am I, as am I."

"You should have told us, my jaan," said Mother, cupping my face in her hands and beaming at me. I flinched, not used to this glowing version of her.

"Told you what?" I asked, once more trying to break through her inane grin.

She squinted at me as though I was being obtuse on purpose. "Your TV show, puthar! You have made us very proud! The camera loved you and kept coming back for more – and why wouldn't it? How smart you looked in your red shirt, my gulab jamun! To think my little one is such a star, and I never knew!"

I was taken aback by her praise. She was lauding me for something she'd been adamantly against and for which I'd gone behind her back and even forged her signature. I shook my head. "But, you . . . you didn't want me to do it. You said I wasn't going to make a show of you. You tore up the—"

"She thought she would get one over me," said Mother, wrinkling her nose. "Like I could be angry with you, my own sweet jalebi." Father made to say something, but she silenced him with an imperious back of the hand. "She will hate that. Such a jealous woman. Never a nice quality."

Ashiqah's mum! So, that was what this was about. Like my continuing battle with Ashiqah, Mother had a never-ending one-upmanship with Mrs Ibrahim. Mrs Ibrahim, with her fancy ways and money, usually had the upper hand, but not this time. The fact that I hadn't disgraced Mother on TV was only a small part of her largesse now; the bigger part was I'd got a starring role on TV that had bested the daughter of her nemesis.

I sighed. It wasn't quite the affirmation I'd wanted, but Mother wasn't entertaining my reticence. Having quickly checked her appearance in the mirror and jabbed a gerbera behind her ear, she ejected the cassette from the video recorder and told me to get ready. "I must return this to Ghazala. I don't want her telling people we keep things that are not ours. Quick, quick, get your coat, my bulbul. We must get there before she shuts."

*

Mother and I made the journey to Mrs Ibrahim's shop in record time. She stayed open till seven on Fridays ("to catch the Jum'ah crowd"). An LED sign flashed "Open". As we approached, the door swung inward by itself, emitting an electronic ding-dong as it did so.

"What jaadu is this?" said Mother. Not that it was magic, just that Mrs Ibrahim had invested in hi-tech upgrades to the shop since we'd last been.

Our feet sunk into the grey-and-white zigzag-patterned shagpile carpet, and my nose recognised the lemony scent of Shake 'n' Vac. Mother had tried it once, before declaring she'd use talcum powder for half the price and a better smell.

Mrs Ibrahim was behind the counter, surrounded by glass display cabinets full of telephones, calculators and various glass and brass ornaments. She had an elbow on the counter, her head in her hand, listening to Mrs Kapoor dispensing gossip while shaking her way through a tray of snow globes of the Badshahi Mosque.

"Dear Reshma," said Mrs Ibrahim, turning to us while touching her ears to cleanse her mind of whatever image Mrs Kapoor had planted there. "Are you come for the purses? I set some of the smaller ones aside for you. They will be just right for your purse!" The joke was as unfunny as the first time she'd said it to me.

Mrs Kapoor caught me rolling my eyes and glared at

me, wielding a snow globe like she was about to lob it at my head. Mother pushed her aside and took her position at the counter. She took out the video cassette from her handbag and slid it across. "I just came to returning your cassette, Ghazala jaan. Very thoughtful of you. It was a splendid sight."

Mrs Ibrahim pulled the tape out of its cover and inspected it. I don't know what she was looking for, but she spent several seconds shaking it about. The Casio on her wrist beeped the hour. I looked at it enviously – we never did get my things back from Amjad, who must have sold them. Mother eyed the watch with distaste, her bangles trembling.

Mrs Kapoor, clocking the video cassette, squinted between it and Mother. "You are not a young girl, Mrs Aziz. Singing and dancing is not for—"

"Rafi was quite the sitara," declared Mother, cutting her and addressing Mrs Ibrahim.

"Your *Rafique* was the star?" Mrs Ibrahim stumbled. "You mean *Baby*, surely?"

"Baby's face did fill a lot of the screen, that is true," conceded Mother. "But, ma'shallah, when my little boy sang those final lines, the camera staying on him . . ." She broke off, staring into the distance, her hand on her chest.

Mrs Ibrahim rammed the cassette back into the cover. "Of course, Baby is not one to hawk the landlight. Not like some."

"My little one will be famous," declared Mother. All three swivelled in my direction. I raised my eyebrows and smiled. "He will be a Bollywood film star, market my words. He sings and dances and acts beautifully. We have always encouraged him."

I broke into a cough, astonished at this lie. Mother thumped me on the back.

Mrs Kapoor moved her mouth around as though to spit out some paan, but a frown from Mrs Ibrahim stopped her.

Wrenching open the door so hard the chimes got confused and skipped the first bars, Mother finally acknowledged the old woman. "Mrs Kapoor. I hope you find medicine for your eye. Oh, it is always like that, you say? I will pray for you. Allah helps even the most wretched. Khuda Hafiz!"

*

The next day was the Easter concert, which panned out better than I could have hoped for.

Firstly, Ashiqah got hit on the head by a pair of falling maracas thrown by Izmat. She had to be helped off the stage, limping, even though there was nothing wrong with her legs. None of the chorus girls felt up to taking the lead role, so I stepped in, even persuading Mrs Entwistle to let me model Ashiqah's exotic turban-style head-dress. Mrs Bainbridge had choreographed a trio of calypso numbers with suitably colourful outfits. I was in Bermuda shorts, a Hawaiian shirt and a garland of plastic hibiscus flowers around my neck. I'd left the shirt unbuttoned and knotted it at the bottom, to give it some flair. What would Mother think? I looked out into the audience. She winked at me, nodding in time to the jaunty beat of "Mango Walk", the pink carnations in her hair threatening to slide out. She was still in a buoyant mood after her showdown with Mrs Ibrahim.

Taking advantage of her recent about-turn towards me and my need to perform, I shimmied, jiggled and high-kicked across the stage with wild abandon.

Then Mr Brindle developed a frog in his throat. He

tried to power on through, but he sounded like Norman Collier and his faulty microphone. Mrs Entwistle asked me to stand in, as I wasn't shy of public speaking, and I knew how to mind my t's and d's.

And, towards the end, Mrs Bainbridge fled to the toilet, having lunched on a prawn sandwich. Mrs Entwistle didn't even have to ask me before I'd taken a seat at the piano. I launched into the opening chords of "Christ the Lord is Risen Today". I didn't strictly follow the sheet music, which looked complex, but bashed out a passable alternative, playing half by sight and half by ear. I smiled, thinking how Mr H would have told me off for the flourishes I kept putting in. "Easy on the extras, Liberace," he'd have said.

As we approached the final chorus, I found myself getting hot behind the eyes. It had been a day full of emotion and expectation and it was nearly over. I furiously blinked away the tears. I hadn't cried since Mr H's death. Crying didn't change anything.

I looked up from the piano. In just three months, this group of children would never be together again. Mrs Entwistle, Mr Brindle and the other teachers would leave our lives for good. I would miss Izmat's babbling, Shirley's stories, Zaiman's artwork, Asghar's goofiness and Moti's kindness. My goodwill didn't extend to Mohammed, whom I'd gladly never see again.

"Sing, ye heavens, and earth reply, Alleluia!"

Most of all, I was astonished to realise I would miss Ashiqah. We'd spun round each other like orbiting planets, sometimes coming perilously close to knocking each other off course. And yet we couldn't survive without the other. Being more like me than I cared to acknowledge, she'd added much-needed masala to my life. Now she'd be off to Pleckgate, where she'd become somebody else's sparring partner, while I'd be condemned to Everton, where I'd be Amjad's punching bag. My fingers faltered.

"*Where, O death, is now thy sting? Alleluia!*"

Today, I'd performed on stage in all the ways I'd dreamed of. I should have been grinning from ear to ear. Yet I felt less and less merry.

"*Where's thy victory, boasting grave? Alleluia!*"

Flickering sensations: wafts of incense, hair oil, furniture polish; rowdy singing from the audience of parents, bursts of laughter, the wind outside; the dry taste in my mouth; the increasing slipperiness of the keys; the April cold outside encroaching within.

"*Hail the Lord of earth and heaven, Alleluia!*"

I made more mistakes, my fingers trembling. David and Mr H should have been here. Why couldn't David stay? Why couldn't the doctors fix Mr H? It wasn't fair. I sensed them all around. David's green eyes looking at me. Mr H's checked shirt. I heard both of their laughters.

I froze before I could play the final sequence of chords. The notes I'd just played hung in the air, heavy and mournful. The choir, confused, finished off the hymn unaccompanied.

Then the scent of Tibet face cream and a flash of purple and yellow petals: Mother was next to me on the piano stool. I lay my head on her shoulder. Despite my best attempts to stop them, the tears came out in a torrent. There were murmurs from the parents in the Hall while the choir shuffled uncomfortably around us.

Mother stroked my hair. "It will all be fine, my little one. It will all be fine."

Thirty-five

The Easter holidays flew by. I spent most of them with Shazia or composing music on my baby grand. Before I knew it, the two weeks were up and we were back to Sunday, the most boring day on the planet. If it was a packet of crisps, it would be Smiths Salt 'n' Shake, but with the blue salt packet missing. There were no shops open, except Khan's Korner Kabin. I wasn't allowed to go to the cinema on my own, and I wasn't old enough for the arcade.

TV consisted of back-to-back religious programmes. The exception was *Nai Zindagi Naya Jeevan*, an Urdu-language show on BBC1. One of the few programmes with brown faces on it, we watched it religiously instead. Amidst a clattering of noise from the kitchen as Mother prepared breakfast, Nabila and I settled onto pouffes around the Taj Mahal table while Taleeb and Father reclined like Moghul kings on the settee, their majesty diluted slightly by the blowsy, flower-covered sofa cover Mother had run up on her treasured Pfaff.

"*Maam*, Noor Jehan's on!" shouted Nabila, causing Father to take a big slurp of tea and chastise her for making him burn his mouth.

At the sound of the harmonium firing up, Mother

rushed in like a comet, a tail of smoking burnt butter behind her. Quickly checking herself in the mirror to adjust the pansies in her hair, she sank to the floor amid a clinking of jewellery.

Mother adored Noor Jehan, not least because they looked remarkably similar. Although Mother was slimmer than the solidly built folk singer, they were both fair-skinned and had large expressive eyes and full lips. They arranged their hair in towering sculptures, favoured make-up and plenty of it, and they weren't afraid of a bright fabric.

When the song finished, Mother leaped up with a start. She ran to the kitchen, then returned with a changher of parathas on her head and a letter in her hand. "This came yesterday. I forgot all about it," she said, waving an envelope at Taleeb. Taleeb peered at it, then handed it to me.

Although it wasn't unusual for me to receive post – I sent off for things advertised in Bazooka bubble gum packets – I'd never received such an important-looking envelope before. The cream-coloured paper was stamped with the motto of the Conservatoire. My heart sank. Memories of the awful audition came flooding back. And my last time with Mr H. My stomach threatened to bring up the breakfast I'd just eaten.

I made to slide the slim letter under the pouffe. It was clearly a rejection.

"Who is it from?" said Mother. "Open it, quick-quick! Don't keep us waiting."

I sighed. I knew what the letter would say. What was the point of opening it? But Mother had taken a perch on the sofa, blinking at me like an expectant finch.

I toyed with the edges of the envelope. Mother clucked her frustration. Reluctantly, I picked at the seal, my bitten nails struggling to make a purchase. Taleeb offered to tear it open for me, but I snatched it back.

With trembling hands, I eased the stiff paper out of the envelope.

"Well?" said Mother. "What does it say?" Her voice was rising. "Who is it from? What does it say?"

Father shushed her as a report about the Citizens' Advice Bureau came on.

My heart thudded like a jackhammer.

"Dear Rafi,

Thank you for coming to the auditions last month. Having seen all of the candidates, it was a very difficult decision selecting the final thirty. As you can appreciate, we had to . . ."

I dropped the letter, unable to read on. The wording was clearly setting itself up to deliver a big fat no. There was little point in continuing. Disappointment flooded through me like I'd stepped into a cold bath.

Taleeb scooped up the letter and scanned it. "He's only bloody got in, hasn't he?"

My mouth dropped open. I stood up, but my knees buckled and I rolled off the pouffe. Taleeb helped me to my feet and thumped me on the back. "Well done, bro! I knew you'd get in."

"Get in where?" said Mother, so loudly that Father jumped before turning up the volume. "Why is no one telling me anything, your own mother?"

"The Conservatoire!" said Nabila.

For a few seconds, no one spoke. The TV blared out a news story about an Indian satellite launched by NASA. My heart boomed in my ears. I couldn't allow myself to believe Mother would let me go. She was only happy about the TV recording because it had given her a one-up on Mrs Ibrahim. Her change of heart could never extend this far.

I turned in her direction. She gawped at me, her mouth open and her head tilted to the side. The pansies she'd threaded in her hair this morning had worked loose and now dangled perilously.

Before she could say anything, she was interrupted by Nabila jumping from her pouffe onto mine, grabbing me in a bear hug and yelling her delight. Even Taleeb piled in, encircling his skinny, long arms around us both, as we hollered and jumped around on invisible pogo sticks.

"What is all this hungama about?" said Father, finally accepting that something was up and he couldn't ignore it any longer. He half-heartedly shooed us away from the TV, but we were too giddy with excitement to take heed.

"Dad, he's got in!" said Nabila, jumping wildly, her pigtails flying behind her.

"The Conservative school?" he asked. Nabila nodded. Father turned to me and attempted a smile, but I could see the worry behind his eyes. In a quiet voice, he said, "Times are hard, puthar. How will we afford it? I want to say yes, because I know how much this means to you, but we have to be sensible."

"Dad, it's fine," said Taleeb. "Listen to the rest of the letter:

"*Your unique interpretation of the exercises for the audition charmed and beguiled us, and we all agreed we wanted to see more. We are therefore delighted to announce that you have secured a full scholarship at the Conservatoire, which includes your tuition and board during term time. Well done on making it through – this year's selection was particularly competitive.*

"*We will send out details in the next few weeks of what*

you can expect from your first term with us and information about items you will need to purchase before you arrive."

For once, my prayers had been answered. Thank you, thank you, thank you, Allah!

Father cleared his throat and put out his hand for the letter. Taleeb gave it to him. We all stood still. The programme switched to a boring church broadcast.

As an organ launched into the intro of "All Things Bright and Beautiful", Father looked at me over the page in his hand. "They have said yes? And they will pay?"

We all nodded.

He ran a finger over the words on the page as though not believing what they said. "And this is what you want to do?"

More than anything in the world, I wanted to say. But I couldn't speak. It also meant I wouldn't have to go to dreadful Everton. And I'd be spared any more torment from Amjad. I nodded.

"Fine," he said. "If it is good with your mummy, it is good with me."

I screamed like Penelope Pitstop, before rushing over and hugging him. He seemed surprised, then chuckled and hugged me back.

Then we all swivelled our heads in the direction of Mother, whose mouth was still open. I knew what was coming. She was going to shake her head, letting the pansies in her hair fall to the ground and crumple. I closed my eyes. I didn't need to see it.

But I was wrong. She outstretched her arms and beckoned me into them. "My baby boy! I am the proudest mother today. Forgive me for not having believed in you." Her voice quavered, as she threatened to break into

Bollywood-style tears. "I was protecting you. I know how important it is to have dreams. And how easy it is for those dreams to be broken." She glared at Father and he gave her a sorrowful look. "If you had failed, my delicate flower, it would have broken you."

I found it hard to agree with her dramatic analysis of the situation. That wasn't how it had come across at the time when she'd put her kitten-heeled foot down on one plan of mine after another. She'd been spiteful and overbearing. But I couldn't hold a grudge. She was on my side now, and that was what mattered. I hugged her back.

Ever the drama queen, she sobbed into my shoulder. "My little pumpkin is growing up. He will leave me. How will I live without him? How will I mend my broken heart? Don't forget me, my chandh ka tukra. I pray, don't forget me!" She ran into the kitchen, sniffing loudly, her dupatta at her face.

Father looked after her, shaking his head. "Your mummy is always with the drama. She is not easy to understand. Crying, but happy. And if she is happy, it is as well to agree with her. It might not be the future I had dreamed for you, puthar, but what is there for you here?" He held me before him, looking directly at me. "I am very proud of you. We have so little to give you, and yet you have made so much of it. Continue to follow your dreams, my son. They will take you far."

*

When I was able to get away, I grabbed my coat and ran to the canal. Running up the crooked bridge, my breath puffed out before me like smoke from a steam train. It might have been spring, but no one had told the weather.

I leaned over the curved walls of the bridge, brushing

against recently plastered posters for a Showaddywaddy concert at King George's Hall. I gazed out over the water. A pair of swans glided past, cleaving a path through the morning mist hanging over the water. A jogger huffed and puffed and disappeared under the bridge. To the left was the vegetation in which I'd lain and held hands with David and where we'd said goodbye. Tears pricked my eyes.

A car door slammed shut, followed by the engine sputtering into life. A gust of wind tugged at the letter in my hand, entreating me to take another look. Pulling my jacket closer, I read the typed words from beginning to end. This time out loud, engaging my diaphragm, wanting the whole world to hear my news.

When I finished, my face flushed and something landed on the fluttering page. Snowflakes. At this time of the year? I looked up at the sky. Huge banks of cloud had drifted in, the colour of the water after Mother washed Father's overalls.

As the unseasonal snow flurry fell, I slid down and put my head between my knees. Racking sobs ripped through me, but it felt good. I was saying farewell to the old me, to David, Mr H, Everton, to Blackburn itself.

The tears extinguished the last of the dragon's flames and, from the blackened grey ashes of the year past, colour and new life stirred inside me.

Thirty-six

Three months later and school was out, not just for another year, but forever. I said tearful, overwrought, Bollywood-style goodbyes to everyone, even Ashiqah. She gave me an unexpectedly tight hug back. I gifted Mrs Entwistle my raffia mat, which had taken weeks to make, especially after Ashiqah had spilt ink over the old one. Mrs Entwistle said she'd find a special place for it. Then she blew the final whistle and closed the gates for good.

*

Mother and I were in the lounge, the tape recorder before us. Despite it being the middle of summer, it was a grey, gloomy evening. Little heat penetrated the thick walls and high ceilings, so the fire was on two bars. It sputtered and hissed. Father had taken Nabila and Taleeb in the Capri for a drive through Darwen Moors. Mother had asked me to stay with her.

The sky darkened further, throwing the room into an early twilight. Mother was on the edge of the sofa, dressed in a green salwaar kameez and sequin-rimmed magenta dupatta. She'd threaded a wreath of sweet peas around her head, like a floral crown. The sweet smell wafted over each time she nodded her head.

"Tasting . . . tasting . . ."

The cassette spooled for a good half a minute. I adjusted my position on the pouffe.

Mother counted me in. As I played my piano, we did something new, and at Mother's request: we sang together in English – an ABBA song, "When All is Said and Done", from their latest album, which I'd played non-stop since Shazia had gifted it to me.

Mother imbued the already poignant song with her haunting, girl-woman voice. Although she struggled with some of the words, she kept going, her Pakistani-accented vocals taking on the melody while I added the harmony. Our voices blended as one.

As we finished the first chorus, we paused. In the song, dark clouds covered the sun, marking the end of summer and the couple's relationship. For Mother and me, the clouds had parted – at least for now.

As the tape wound reassuringly on and the fire continued to heat the room, a shaft of light broke through the net curtains.

*

The next six weeks flew by in a blur. Before I knew it, I was in my bedroom, where Mother was helping me with the tie. My fingers trembled too much. She pulled up the knot, then folded the stiff collar down. She stood back to admire her handiwork. Pleased with what she saw, she kissed me on both cheeks. "My little boy is all grown up," she said. "So handsome. I cannot bear to let you go. But I must." She showered me with more kisses.

"*Maam*! I need to get ready." I wrenched free of her embrace.

She mopped her eyes with her dupatta. Then she gave

me her tenth hug of the morning, once more engulfing me in the scent of buttery Sunblest toast. "Now that you are not going to be a doctor" – she gave a sniff for old times' sake – "I want you to become a famous actor like my beloved Rajesh. I want everyone to know! I am so-so proud of you."

Humming one of her Bollywood idol's songs, she went to get ready herself. She'd found work in a bakery, along with Shazia's mother. As well as money and a structure to her day, she'd gained a sense of purpose. Father was also busy, word of mouth keeping his DIY skills in demand. I didn't have to worry about either of them while I was away.

I pulled on the grey flannel trousers, with their crease worthy of any Army officer, and marvelled at the turn-ups. I'd never worn formal trousers before.

I saved the best till last: the navy-blue blazer lined in dark maroon with shiny buttons that glinted in the light. Stroking the gold piping around the breast pocket, I mouthed the words embroidered around the image of a phoenix rising from the flames: "Pro amore musicae."

Admiring myself in the full-length mirror, my chest swelled in pride. I almost didn't recognise myself. My hair was shorter and neatly combed to the right with nothing more than the famous "Corporation Oil". My shirt gleamed white rather than the reds and yellows I normally favoured. Instead of tatty Converse, I wore smart black leather shoes which Father had bought from Curtess rather than Tommy Ball's.

As I grabbed my satchel, the bedroom door opened. It was Taleeb. He hesitated, then stepped inside. "Just a little something." He thrust a newspaper-wrapped package in my hands and was gone.

I stared at the rectangular-shaped parcel, turning it in

my hands, before picking at the taped ends with nails that were no longer bitten. Inside was the ABBA 1981 annual. I gasped. Although nearly a year old, it was new to me, not having been able to afford the £2.50 price tag. I traced a finger over the red cover, scrutinising the sixteen small images of the foursome, remembering how I'd been in the same room as them. With rumours that the band were breaking up, it felt even more important to hold onto that memory.

I slipped the annual into my briefcase where it joined my pencil case – no longer fluffy, but a plain fabric – a can of Tango, a Nutty bar and a Tupperware of aloo dhal sandwiches Mother had made especially for me.

Leaving the room to join Father, who was tooting the car horn outside, I realised I'd forgotten something. I dashed back to the bureau. Where were they? I was sure I'd put them here. I pulled out all the drawers and sifted through the contents.

There, at the bottom, between two jumpers: two handkerchiefs, one pink and the other purple. Embroidered with curlicued initials *MH*. My breathing returned to normal. I'd kept both, squirrelling them away, needing them near me but not able to take them out. Until today. Gently pulling out the folded-up squares, I brought them up to my nose: the faint scent of Brut still clung to them. I bit my lip. I would not cry. Not today. He wouldn't want it.

I folded and slid both handkerchiefs into my blazer pocket, next to each other. The two-tone strip of pink and purple stood out proudly against the dark blue of the blazer.

Returning to the mirror, I took in my reflection one final time.

"I'm ready for my close-up, Mr H."

PART TWO
DOES YOUR MOTHER KNOW?

Thirty-seven

"Ladies and gentlemen, welcome to Manchester, where the local time is three p.m. It's a rather chilly five degrees, so do wrap up warm. Cabin crew, prepare doors for cross check."

I yawn and stretch. I'm groggy, even though I was able to lie across all three seats and get some sleep. As the doors are opened, a raw wind races through the cabin. I shiver.

I'm among the last to shuffle out. I'm in no rush to embrace the grey and cold. Eulalia sails down the aisle before me, Chuck in tow. Hearing my tread, she turns around.

"Well, hello there," she says. "That gonna be enough?" She means my windcheater.

I grimace. "I packed my jumper in the hold. Not thinking straight."

"Been a while since you were home, honey?"

Home? It takes a few seconds to realise where she means. I nod. "My last visit here was Dad's funeral. Five years ago." My mouth is dry and I swallow. Where does time go?

Eulalia reaches past Chuck's shoulder and squeezes my arm. "I'm sorry," she says.

To my surprise, tears prick my eyes – whether from her

kind gesture or from memories of Father, I don't know. She nods and I look away.

"You, young man, are a doll!" Her shriek makes me jump. Jason is by the front door, where Eulalia has him clamped against her bosom. "Will you be on our flight back?"

I try not to laugh as the head steward extricates himself with some difficulty. "I'm sure that can be arranged, madam. The pleasure was all mine." A true professional.

"Call me Eulalia," she says, slapping him on the lapel, before finally disembarking.

Jason turns to me, smooths his locks, grins and puts out a hand. Formal, I think, but I take it anyway. His grip is firm and there's something else – a note left behind in my palm.

I don't open it until I'm inside the terminal. His number and hotel. My heart races.

The angel on my shoulder picks up his pen. I ball the note up and shoot it in the bin.

*

"Hope u gt there ok? M & I miss u. Have gr8 time. Give Shahida my love. House v quiet without u. XXX"

I grin. He's never mastered Shazia's name. Looking up from the small screen on my Nokia, I note the heightened security at the airport. Police with guns and dogs walk past, making me feel instantly guilty. A mere month since 9/11, the after-effects have clearly hit even here.

"Where have you come from, sir?" asks the Border Control man when it's my turn.

"Melbourne," I say. The man stares deeply at me and I feel compelled to fill the silence. "I live there. I'm here visiting family. And my best friend's wedding – you have to, don't you, else they'd never speak to you again. You know what women are like." I'm babbling *and* spouting casual sexism. The man holds my passport up to the light while flicking his eyes back to my face. Unnerved, I hum ABBA's "Hasta Mañana" in my head.

"I see you were in New York for six months last year. Why was that, sir?"

"For work," I say. "I'm an actor. I was on Broadway."

The man isn't impressed. He observes me with the implacable stare of an Easter Island statue. "Where will you be staying while you're in the UK?"

I give him details of the hotel. I can't stay at Mother's as my old room is now a sewing space or something, according to Nabila.

"And where do you live in Melbourne?"

Again, I fill him in.

He types away, then looks back at me. "Is someone meeting you here today?"

"Yes, my friend," I say. "You know ... getting married?"

He sits up straighter. "You're getting married?"

I bite my cheek. Is he being obtuse on purpose? The last time I flew, six months ago, I was waved through with just a cursory glance at my passport. Today, I'm being given the third degree. But, as annoying as it is, I get it: given current events, I'm a prime candidate for scrutiny – a young Pakistani male, travelling on his own, with a name setting off a barrage of klaxons in the system. "Not me. My friend. I'm back for her wedding."

I continue to answer his questions as politely as I can. Each time, he looks up and purses his lips, before tapping the details into his computer.

"Do you have family here, Mr ..." He looks at my

passport. "Aziz? What is that – Muslim or something?" He says it as an aside, but I know exactly what he means.

It takes ten more minutes before he stamps my passport with a thud. "Next!" He waves me through impatiently, as if I've been the one wasting his time. Meanwhile, the queues on either side of me have continued to move at a steady pace.

*

After collecting my suitcase, I head for the exit. I pass through the "Nothing to declare" channel, stepping up my pace to shorten the time it'll take to be outside.

"Would you mind coming this way, sir?"

For the love of Sondheim, what now? Am I to experience every form of bureaucracy?

A whip-thin security guard in an oversized suit and knuckles tattooed with LOVE and HATE appears from behind the Perspex screen, blocking my path. He leads me to a curtained-off area. "Could you pop your case open for me, sir? This won't take long."

"My case? It's taken me ages to get it all in there," I protest, lifting it onto the counter. I'm past caring about repercussions. "Is this really necessary?"

He pulls on a pair of latex gloves. "Just routine, sir. Nothing to worry about. We'll soon have you on your way."

Through the gap in the curtains, I see my fellow plane passengers strolling past, some with huge luggage, unchecked by his colleague. Not a brown face among them.

As I click open the case, he works from one end to the other, dumping the contents onto the counter. It isn't long before it looks like he's running a bring and buy sale.

"*Catcher in the Rye?*" he says, pulling out the book.

"I remember this from school. Didn't read it, mind. Any good?"

I shrug. He riffles the pages and I have to bite my tongue. He stops midway and chortles at something, before handing the book back to me and continuing his search.

"Where have you come from, sir?" he says, sifting through my underwear.

"Melbourne. I live there." I'm in a parallel world where conversations are repeated.

He unfolds my jumpers. "You don't sound Australian," he says accusingly.

I count to ten. "I was born here. I didn't go out there until the '90s."

He nods. "I see." He unpacks a stack of T-shirts. "Mind you, you don't sound like you're" – he circles my face with an extended finger – "either, if you don't mind me saying."

"Like I'm what?" I say, knowing where he's heading but not quite believing it.

"You know . . . no 'but-but-but'." He imitates the hard consonants of an older Asian person speaking English.

I breathe through my nose and don't say anything. His casual racism isn't worth rising to. I've heard worse.

Reaching the end of his inspection, he snaps the case shut and taps it smartly. He shakes my hand. "All done, sir. You have a good day, now, won't you? Mind how you go."

Thirty-eight

As I come out of Arrivals, a screaming banshee in a purple salwaar kameez and a two-foot-high beehive launches at me like a runaway bowling ball, almost knocking me over.

It takes a few seconds before I realise it's Shazia, who has gone all-out retro, including Aunt Sally-style dabs of lilac blusher, surma on her eyes and false eyelashes the size of moth wings. She looks fabulous, and she beams when I tell her so. I disentangle myself from her myriad of necklaces and lockets. My suitcase careens down the corridor.

"What took you so long?" she shrieks, coming back for more hugs. "And where is he?" I can't move. We're causing an obstruction in the exit aisle, but Shazia refuses to let go. People stare at us, no doubt wondering why I'm being attacked by Barney the Dinosaur.

"Back home," I say, catching my breath. "Looking after Milo. And I was grilled like a criminal back there. A whole half hour. I've never had that before."

"I really wanted to meet him! Next time – promise, Allah ni kasam? As for the airport... welcome to the 9/11 effect. They're coming down hard on anyone who looks like us."

"What, gorgeous and glamorous, you mean?" I say, affecting a catalogue pose.

She titters and slaps me. "Everyone I know has a story about the extra hassle they're getting at the moment." Pulling away, she appraises me, squeals, quivering with delight, then grabs me in another hug. "Anyway, the main thing is: you're back!"

"I came as soon as I could," I wheeze, trying to ease her python-like hold around my neck. I attempt to retrieve my case, but Shazia clings on, rooting me to the spot.

"Five bloody years?" she yells into my ear. I can't move. She smells of Timotei, McDonald's fries and Chanel No. 5. "You call that soon?" Her voice breaks.

A pang of guilt shoots through me. Having left for Melbourne a few years after graduating, I've been back just once, for Dad's funeral. I find it difficult to breathe: not just the overbearing scents and sounds, but from connecting with my past in such a physical way. Even the air feels different. I'm back home. Except it hasn't been home for years.

I peer over her shoulder. There are no clamouring fans. I put away my sunglasses. Taleeb and Nabila know I'm back, but they can hardly be expected to drop everything to come and collect me. Part of me is relieved, as the jetlag is already setting in and making my head woolly. But part of me is undeniably disappointed and affronted. Mother will no doubt roll out the red carpet when I see her, but my sister and brother were in no rush to drive over.

*

Kylie's "Can't Get You Out of My Head" plays us out as we peel off the M65 in her Ford Sierra. Shazia tells me she's got her eye on a Porsche. I raise an approving eyebrow.

We've been on the road for an hour. It's just past four o'clock and it's already dark. Having left Melbourne in a blazing summer, the cold and gloom are a bit of a shock. As is our conversation, which is strained. I'd imagined we'd be talking non-stop, but once the car doors slammed shut, I didn't know where to pick up the threads. Emails are no substitute for speaking to someone face to face and hanging out regularly with them.

"I must be mad letting you talk me into picking you up," says Shazia, flipping on her full beams as we turn into a smaller road, free of traffic. "Today of all days!" She's referring to her Mehndi later, when female friends will come around and the mehndi artist will draw elaborate henna designs on their hands and feet. She thumps me on the arm, the paste jewellery on her fingers like a multi-hued knuckleduster.

"Ow! You horror," I say, jumping back. "It's not my fault I only got the invite a hundred years too late. I've not lived in Sydney for ages."

She snorts. "I also emailed you the date. Months ago."

That's true. I'd meant to write it on the calendar but, as always, got distracted.

"Anyway, give me a break – I've only got a big wedding to organise," she says.

I groan. "Please tell me the whole of Blackburn isn't going to be there."

She chuckles. "And Darwen."

As wonderful as it is being back with Shazia, I'm relieved the journey is almost over. She's driving like a maniac, rarely leaving the fast lane of the motorway, her Ugg boot pressed firmly on the Sierra's accelerator pedal.

"Listen," I begin, as another wave of tiredness sweeps through me, "can you drop me off at my hotel? I'd love to meet Majid and see your place, but honestly, I feel like death warmed up."

She shrieks. "No way, mister! He's looking forward to it. And we won't be long. I haven't seen you in years. I'm not letting you go just yet." She gives an evil cackle.

There's no point arguing further. I yawn again, my jaw cracking – I'm genuinely exhausted – but she's not taking the hint. As we join a dual carriageway, she leans across to open the glovebox.

"Hey, guess what?" I say, trying not to notice her full attention isn't on the road. "My name's up in lights. At the theatre. Just like I always wanted."

She squeals in delight and drops the packet of toffees she's retrieved. She hugs me, before bending forward, scrabbling around in the footwell. The car weaves across the lane, and for a moment, a memory flashes in my mind and I'm in another car, with another driver, in another time. I catch the scent of Brut. I hear my panicked screams and Mr H's shouts as the car spins out of control. My fingers grip the seat, my whole body rigid.

"Fuck's sake! Watch what you're doing!" I yell.

Shazia jumps back in her seat as though I've slapped her. "Really?"

"Sorry. I didn't mean to—"

"I see you once in the last bloody five years, and that was at your dad's funeral, and you have a go at ME?"

This wasn't going well ... I close my eyes and silently count to ten. I deserved that. It always comes back to this, even in her emails. Why I left. When I'm coming back. Why I don't return more often. But it's not like I've moved to Spain and can just pop back for a pound on Ryanair.

Shazia sniffs and angrily wipes her eyes.

I'm taken aback. I lean over and put a hand on her arm.

"Come on, I didn't mean to leave. But I had to go. I had no choice. You know that."

She gives another sniff. "But did you have to go all that way? Couldn't you have starred in bloody *Blood Brothers* or something here?"

I laugh. "It's complicated. But I'm back now. For a bit. So, let's not argue. Please?"

I peck her on the cheek. Her skin is hot.

A smile appears back on her face. She pops a Werther's Original into her mouth. She offers the packet to me.

"They've even spelt it right," I say, unwrapping a toffee and popping it in my mouth.

"Spelt what? Werther's?"

"My name . . . in lights."

I should hope so!" she says, her jaw working hard. She beeps at a car in front. "Road hog!" she yells as she overtakes it.

A minute later, she takes a sharp exit onto quieter side roads. I breathe easier.

"I wish you could see it," I say. "The show, I mean. It's had rave reviews."

"I'd love to. But that flight . . . and the cost. We've got the house to do up. Luckily my parents have paid for the wedding so at least we don't have that expense. Imagine!"

I can. Asian weddings are no small thing. Hundreds, if not thousands, of guests is quite normal. The whole community usually turns up.

We're now in the familiar residential streets of Lower Audley, where she has to drive slower. I relax back into my seat. "I'll fly you over – business class," I pledge.

"You might regret that."

"You're part of this. All those years ago, pretending we were Bollywood stars or models on the catwalk."

Shazia chuckles. "Or that bird Agatha," she says, tyres crunching loudly into the kerbside as she parks expertly into a tight space without thinking twice.

"Agnetha! After all these years, you still can't get her name right."

"I say it to wind you up," she says. I scoff. "She always was your favourite."

I get out and wince. The icy, damp air settles around me like a cloak. But it feels good to be on terra firma after twenty-four hours in the air. The street is empty, apart from a handful of children on bikes in the distance.

Shazia joins me and I loop my arm through hers. "No. *You* were always my fave."

"Don't be soft." Despite her words, she can't keep the smile from her face. "Now, come on – I can't wait for you to meet Majid." She rummages in her sequinned handbag for the keys.

I grab her coat sleeve. "Seriously, you were," I insist. She looks up, surprised. "You never judged me. You were my rock."

Under the streetlight, I see her cheeks turn red under the lilac blusher. She turns away and kicks the front wheel.

"You've no idea how much I needed you growing up," I continue. "I may not have told you, but I'm doing it now." I spin her round so she's facing me. "In the words of *The Golden Girls*: thank you for being a friend."

Shazia splutters. "The show with the old biddies? What're you saying?" Her oversized eyelashes blink rapidly, and she looks for something in her bag.

"Just what I mean." I sweep her up in a hug. She giggles. "And I won't leave it so long the next time, Allah ni kasam," I promise.

"You'd better not. Else, I'll take your passport away.

And break your legs. Now, put me down before people talk!"

As we walk to their front door, I spot the sign on the wall: Meadow Street. Just a few minutes' walk away from Baines Street. "Have you seen anything of my mum?" I say.

Shazia nods. "As bonkers as ever. Even more colourful, if you can believe."

I smile. Some things never change.

*

"All right?" says Majid, getting up from the plastic-wrapped scarlet and gold sofa.

"G'day," I answer, without thinking, shaking his hand. "All right?" Even after all these years, I've never mastered how to say the word in one fluent sound.

Majid's my height, with fair Pathan skin, hazel eyes and a proud, straight nose. He boasts a thick mop of hair, which he flicks back with his free hand. I note the Rolex on his wrist – surely a fake, I think, before telling myself off for being so judgemental.

"Good to meet you, bro," he says. "Shaz never stops going on about you. Each time she gets a letter or email, she talks about nothing else for days. I feel like I know you even though I've never met you!"

I grin. " 'Shaz' does that?"

"It's Shazia to you, mister," she says, dumping her bag on the sofa and kissing Majid on the cheek. She leaves a purple mark behind.

"Thanks for coming over, mate," says Majid, wiping his cheek in a well-practised move. "Long way 'n' all. And for doing the songs. Appreciate it."

Shazia begins fluffing up a score of gold braided cushions on the sofa. "Mags, my jaan-e-man, there would *be* no wedding if Rafi couldn't make it. You think I'm joking..."

Majid grabs her from behind and nuzzles her neck, kissing her repeatedly, making her squeal in mock embarrassment. She thumps him with one of the cushions. "Behave!"

Chuckling, he makes his way to the kitchen. "Get you a drink, Raf? Kettle's boiled."

"Amazing, thanks. A proper brew. Just a splash of milk."

As he leaves, I turn to Shazia. "Gor-geous," I mouth.

"I know," she mouths back, taking a seat next to me. Then, louder, she says, "Now, tell me all about your fella. What's he do? Where did you meet? And, most importantly, what does he see in you?"

I slap her and she slaps me back. We end up parrying like kangaroos, before dissolving in giggles. Just like that, we're ten years old again and it's like no time has passed.

Thirty-nine

I'm awoken by the cleaners. I must have slept right through, as I'm still dressed and on top of the covers. They apologise and back out through the door in a series of small bows.

I look at my watch: 12:05 p.m. Shit! I rush into the shower. I've missed the reception, but I've got to be there for the Nikah, the wedding ceremony itself.

My knee-length navy-blue kurta is speckled with gold polka dots, with a heavily embroidered Nehru collar and an equally elaborate dagger neckline. I've teamed it with gold pyjamas, which are a tighter fit than the normal salwaar, and a matching silk dupatta draped over one shoulder. I finish the outfit with the gold sherwani, my fingers struggling to button it up. On my feet are embroidered moccasins with curled toes. The clothes are stiff and make me stand ramrod straight. I could be in the adverts that used to be in Nabila's *Stardust* movie magazines. I concentrate and force my hands to stop shaking. Why am I so nervous? It's not about me. This is Shazia's big day. I'm just playing a small part in it. I breathe out.

Too late for breakfast at the hotel, I grab a coffee and a pastry from a cafe on the corner. The lady behind the counter does a double-take when I walk in, before wiping the tea urn with a J Cloth and saying how it looks set for rain later.

*

I'm in a taxi on the way to the wedding venue. The radio's tuned to a qawwali station. I'm reminded of Father and our trips to the Moors. Islamic calligraphy decorates the windscreen. A tiny Rubik's Cube dangles from the rear-view mirror next to a crescent moon air freshener.

"You groom?" asks the driver, who introduces himself as Mr Mirza. He has a big white beard, an equally wide grin, but only one lone tooth at the front.

"No, just a guest," I say. "Is it far?" I thrum my fingers on my knees.

"No, no, not far." He waggles his head. "You not from here. Where you from?"

It hasn't taken long for my imposter status to be found out. "I was born here. Audley Range. But now I live in Australia."

The man considers this. "Where your wife?"

I sigh inwardly. Here we go again. "No wife."

"I find you wife. No problem." He catches my eye in the mirror, his face full of hope.

I shake my head. "I am too busy with work, my friend, but thank you."

He gives another waggle. We sail past streets named after jewels: Jasper, Pearl, Emerald, Ruby, Topaz. Each is filled with identical red-brick terraces – the pavements still with their pebble-coloured flagstones and the side streets still cobbled. Everything looks familiar – the people, the houses, even the corner shops with their windows full of huge packs of toilet rolls – and yet I'm a stranger looking in. None of it *feels* familiar. Having got used to the wider streets and bigger houses of Australia, not to mention the sun and the sand, it's hard to imagine this was once my normal.

"What job you do?" The taxi driver's voice cuts into my thoughts.

"I'm an actor," I say, resisting the urge to pronounce it actooooooor.

"Indian fillums? I know so!" Mr Mirza thumps the dashboard with the palm of his hand. "I will telling wife. She watches fillums night and day, big-big eyes. This is something. Kya baath hai."

There's no point in correcting him. Most Asian people don't go to the theatre. When I begged to see *Joseph and the Amazing Technicolour Dreamcoat* at King George's Hall, Mother looked at me like I'd asked to go to midnight mass. Yet a stage musical and a Bollywood film have so much in common – songs and dances; larger-than-life storylines; and enough melodrama and colour to magic you away for a few hours.

The taxi slows down as we approach the venue. There are cars parked everywhere, reminding me of the drive-in theatre we go to now and again back home.

"How much money you make?" asks Mr Mirza, turning in his seat as I hand him the fare. He drinks in the grandeur of my costume, his eyes wide and head waggling.

I'm taken aback by the directness of his question and gaze. "Oh, is that the time?" I say, looking at my Bulgari. "I don't want to keep the bride waiting. She's a monster when she's angry, believe you me."

As I step out, shivering in the cold (why didn't I bring my coat?), I'm mobbed by a gang of children, smart in their little suits. I look over their heads but don't recognise anyone among the impeccably dressed throngs shuffling in through the double doors. The whole of Blackburn really is here, in all their finery. My costume is sober by comparison. The air resounds with car doors shutting and people shouting to each other.

Taking a deep breath, I join the crowd. I've not been around this many Asian people for years. It takes me aback. They look at me, no doubt wondering who this interloper is in their midst. I look like them, but they can tell I'm not one of them. I feel the colour reaching up my neck. I force myself to put one foot in front of the other.

Luckily, the children come with me. They think I'm Hrithik Roshan, an up-and-coming Bollywood actor I've vaguely heard of, and fire off a hundred and one questions. I embrace the game and tell myself this is another acting gig. I joke and tell them I'm in between films. This draws more kids and more questions. They sweep me along and, like a glacier moving in time-lapse through a valley, we carve a path through the other guests to the open doors.

*

Stepping inside, a wall of noise assaults my ears. It's as packed inside as outside. I'm greeted by hundreds of bodies pressing into me, with faces in every shade of brown. Trains of small kids with scrubbed faces and oil-slicked hair weave through the throng, exploring the corridors and side rooms, getting thwacks on the head from weary parents.

It's like being thrust into a tandoor oven. Sweat forms under my armpits, and I am baking like a masala chicken in all my layers. Everyone's at least a head shorter than me. My height draws attention. Women whisper to each other and men openly appraise me. I also note I'm one of the few men in traditional dress – most are in suits or shirt and trousers. The West has caught up with the East, even here in Blackburn.

I try to shrink myself down. Then I tell myself off. I have nothing to hide. I become Hrithik Roshan again. I take a bow. They draw back, giving me room, thinking I'm part of the wedding group. Puffing my chest out, I stride through, a maharajah among his adoring subjects.

At the entrance to the Hall, I'm stopped short by the myriad of smells: rose-scented agarbathi; fried food; curry; hair oil; face powder; shoe polish; Lynx deodorant; body odour. Garlands of golden marigolds hang in criss-crossing arcs across the ceiling, releasing their own pungent scent into the already heady cocktail.

The noise is just as incredible – I had forgotten how Pakistanis love to shout when they talk. It worried me as a child when we went out visiting, thinking everyone was angry. It took years to realise this was just how they communicated: loudly and with gusto, like it was an Olympic sport. I kick myself for having forgotten the ear-plugs from the plane.

The whole neighbourhood must be in the vast room, sitting on white plastic chairs with purple bows tied at the back. I examine the women's section. There are too many people and it's impossible to spot Mother in the crowds. My stomach flutters. Part of me wants to turn around and retreat to the hotel. What am I going to say if I see her? How much small talk can I bring with me over these thousands of miles? It's going to be a minefield not to accidentally blurt something out. Saying "we" rather than "I" would instantly alert her.

Under a canopy on the stage, Shazia and Majid occupy matching thrones. They're decked out in their wedding finery – Shazia in a red-and-gold bridal outfit and an

Aladdin's cave of gold on her face, head, hands and arms; Majid in a cream-and-gold sherwani and matching pyjamas. I stop breathing for a few seconds as my mind tries to reconcile the young girl I've known all my life with the woman on stage.

Both have their faces hidden: Shazia's by the cowl of her dress and Majid's with an extravagant turban from which hang threads of white flowers. The imam kneels before them, the Qu'ran before him. Various family members sit on chairs on either side.

Shazia looks up. She spots me at the back of the Hall and waves excitedly at me. The canopy trembles perilously. I can't leave now. Mrs Chaudhry says something to Shazia, and she goes back to staring at her henna'd hands in her lap. Somewhere in the intricate pattern will be the initials "MH", woven into the design for her betrothed to find.

Something clicks inside me. Maaz Haqq. The same initials. A rush of sadness races through me, before I check myself and rein in my thoughts. This is Shazia's day.

*

The Posh and Becks of Blackburn rise from their thrones. The imam places Majid's hands over Shazia's. Majid's best man presents him with a ring, which he slips over Shazia's outstretched finger. Shazia explained in the car that the ring was a representation of the dowry from the husband to the wife before he's allowed to see her. With the "debt" now paid, Mrs Chaudhry reaches up and slides back the fabric covering Shazia's head.

I gasp. She looks just like Sridevi, the actress. Her hair is piled up in an elaborate construction. A sparkly gauze headdress trails down the back. Her make-up is immaculate – as heavy as stage make-up. She even has diamantés studded into her eyebrows. Majid could be Jackie Shroff, Sridevi's co-star. I wouldn't have been surprised if they'd broken out into a synchronised song-and-dance routine. The woman next to me hands me a square of kitchen paper, before dabbing at her eyes.

As the imam looks at each of them in turn, they give their acceptance: "Qabool hai", three times. The imam reads passages from the Qu'ran – all in Arabic. While the sounds are familiar, I don't know what the words mean, nor does the rest of the congregation, but it doesn't stop Mrs Chaudhry nodding as though she alone understands.

I search the room. Somehow, I've ended up sitting on the women's and children's side, the only man among the dupattas and chadars. There's no sign of Mother or Nabila.

On stage, another male family member presents a gloriously flashy gold pen to Shazia and Majid. As they sign the contract, the imam recites the Surah Fatiha, the opening chapter of the Qu'ran. He invites us to join in the seven short verses.

Bismilla iruhmaan nera heem – In the Name of Allah, the Most Compassionate, Most Merciful. Even I know the first verse. The more pious in the room know the remaining six and keep going, while I and the others bow our heads and cup our hands.

The imam passes the Qu'ran to Shazia and Majid. As they hold it between them, the two mothers-in-law stretch a dupatta over their children's heads, symbolically uniting the pair.

Shazia repeats her vows after the imam. "I, Shazia Asiya Chaudhry, offer you, Majid Sikandar Hashim, myself in marriage in accordance with the instructions of the Holy Qu'ran and the Holy Prophet, peace and blessing be upon him. I pledge, in honesty and with sincerity, to be for you a faithful wife." She told me she'd removed "obedient".

Majid's suit barely manages to stay fastened, his chest is so puffed up with pride and love. He matches the vows, in a voice shaking badly. And, just like that, two become one.

I can't sit still any longer. Shooting up, I put my thumb and forefinger into my mouth and fire off a series of ear-splitting whistles. A second later, the room joins in.

Forty

It's time to eat. But that's easier said than done. Getting all these people out of this room and into the next will take some doing. There's only one way in and out. The crowd bulges ineffectively at the door. I hang back, in no hurry now that the Nikah is over.

"Like a bad penny, here you are again."

I look round. An old woman glares at me, as old as Methuselah, bent forward in her wheelchair, with a face like a walnut and white hair covered by a black chadar. Her mouth works constantly, chewing something. She looks familiar, but I can't place her.

Then I spot the W-shaped cluster of moles on her cheek. "Mrs Kapoor!" I exclaim. I feel both joy and dismay at this thorn from my childhood. "I thought you were ... I mean, how lovely to see you."

She grimaces. "Where is your wife?" she said. "You have children? How old?"

For a moment, I'm drawn back to the dark interior of Khan's Korner Kabin. She asked the exact same questions to Mr H.

As I try to work out what to tell her, Mrs Kapoor chokes on whatever she's chewing. The equally elderly lady wheeling her thumps her on the back until the obstruction is dislodged. It is Mrs Mamood, Mrs Kapoor's faithful, if long-suffering, friend. She flashes a toothless smile at me.

"You are looking well," sighs Mrs Kapoor, as if it's painful to admit. "A few extra pounds, but haven't we all?" Bloody cheek, I think. "And how is she? That butterfly. Shameless, still dressing like a young girl. Is she here? Bhagwan, help her."

"Allah, Mrs Kapoor, Allah," interjects Mrs Mamood.

Mrs Kapoor spits out something onto the floor. "And where have you been hiding yourself? One minute you are here, there, everywhere: in my face, under my feet, behind my back. The next, you are gone and my life is safe from your bicyclette."

She takes something from the packet in her lap and tosses it in her mouth. "You have turned into a nice-looking boy." I allow myself a smile. "All things considering."

She's the same old Mrs Kapoor – the digs, the asides, the questions. The years haven't softened her. But I wouldn't want it any other way. She's a part of my past, which is exactly what I need right now: familiarity. A glow spreads inside me and I squeeze her gnarled hands. She looks surprised but not displeased.

"Mrs Kapoor, it's been lovely chatting to you," I say, "but I need to—"

"If you are not married," she interrupts, "I will find you a good rishtha. Do not worry, I will look after you. Just leave it all up to me. You are a good boy, thanks be to Bhagwan. You are like my own grandson."

"I have a partner, Mrs Kapoor – back in Australia, where I live now. But thank you for your kind offer."

At the word "partner", Mrs Kapoor's head rears back, like a cobra about to strike. Recognition triggers behind her eyes, her pupils skittering like bats around a lamppost. She spits out whatever she has in her mouth and I realise it's fried chickpeas. Unable to crunch them, she's been sucking the salt and chilli off them instead.

Scanning me up and down, she shoots out chickpeas from the side of her mouth before lifting a crooked finger at me. "*We behold what we are, and we are what we behold.*"

Raising her hand imperiously, she indicates to Mrs Mamood to move her on.

As Mrs Mamood passes, she whispers: "The Bhagavad Gita, beta. She did not just make that up. And forgive her manners – she has become addicted to chole. All that salt and chilli cannot be doing her any good. Yet, on she goes, praise be to Allah. And Bhagwan."

Mrs Kapoor turns in her chair, her mouth still moving, her gimlet eyes fixed on me.

*

After what seems like hours, I finally make it next door, a space even bigger than the first. This is the dining hall. It will offer several sittings until the entertainment begins. I'm sucked further into the room by the mass of people, pulled in by a kind of capillary action. We file down one side, while the group who've just eaten prepare to leave. Again, there is just the one entrance. God knows what would happen if there was a fire.

A sitting has just finished, with remnants of curries, samosas, pakoras and chapattis like roadkill on the tables. Happy diners roll out past us, the men belching loudly to show their appreciation. The women and children follow in their wake, chattering like starlings.

This room is devoid of colour and decoration – just white walls, strip lighting and easy-to-wipe vinyl floors.

I wince, thinking what a wasted opportunity. Benches and joined-up tables run the full length. Clearing the debris is a military operation: one group of turbaned teens dumps the scraps into bin bags; a second stacks the cutlery, crockery and glasses onto a trolley; and a third refreshes the tables by rolling huge bolts of paper from one end to the other before laying out for the next round of hungry guests.

My mouth salivates. I haven't had proper Pakistani food in a long time.

And that's when I see her. Mother. Dressed in red and gold, with a tiara on her head, blood-red roses threaded through her hair. In danger of upstaging the bride. A glow spreads through me. I call to her, but my voice is drowned out. She's with Nabila and a gaggle of children. It takes a few moments to realise they're my nieces and nephews: two boys and two girls. They're usually in the room when Nabila FaceTimes me, playing on their Game Boys or watching TV, but I've never met them for real. Is that Mohsin or Kamran? How old are they? When did I last speak to them? The eldest is Sofia. What's the youngest called? I can't remember. What kind of uncle does that make me? I push down the increasingly difficult to answer questions.

I'm too far down the queue to get to them: the line of diners is three wide and snakes down the length of the room. I'll need to wait until I've eaten before I can catch up with them. They are bound to be staying for the entertainment – Mother has never been one to forgo music.

Forty-one

"Wassup, shitface?"

Taleeb. He and Bilal, my nephew, join me at the table. I note with satisfaction Taleeb's shirt straining at the buttons. All the times he teased me about my puppy fat and now it's come back on him. I smile at Bilal, who wears a sweatshirt bearing the *Mamma Mia!* logo. He giggles.

Taleeb proffers a fist, which I instinctively go to clasp, before bumping it with my own fist. "Yes, sorry, it's been a bit mental," I say. "Work's busy and it costs a fortune to get back. Been saving up to do stuff around the house, too. Anyway, you're looking well."

"You calling me fat?"

I try not to blush. "No, I didn't mean—"

"Just kidding. I'm back at the gym, so should have these few pounds shifted soon."

A trio of turbaned helpers dole out chapattis, chicken curry, dhal, biryani, pakoras and samosas. Bilal grabs a pakora and nibbles at it, turning it like a squirrel with a nut.

"Do you know who this is, Bil?" says Taleeb to him. The boy leans into his father and smiles sheepishly. "It's your uncle Rafi. You were just one when you saw him last. He lives in Australia. Say hello."

"Are there kangaroos there?" asks Bilal, nibbling on his pakora.

"In the Outback, yes. Sometimes in the garden."

His eyes widen. "Can I come and see them?"

"Sure," I say. "Maybe your mummy and daddy can bring you soon?"

He seems pleased with that. "I saw you on TV. Daddy showed me." Taleeb kisses the top of his head before he wriggles down from the bench. "I can sing and dance, too. Look!" This kid's gonna go far, as Mr H would say. He moves in time to the beat of the music playing in the background, and he sings in perfect pitch, too.

When he finishes, I clap and do a little bow at the table. Bilal grins and curtsies.

Taleeb shakes his head, smiling. "No prizes for guessing who he gets it from."

Bilal trots back and shows me his pen, which boasts a fluffy pink feather at the end.

"Don't bother your uncle anymore, puthar. If you've finished eating, go and play with the others." Turning to me, he says: "So, how are you keeping?" He digs into his curry, demolishing the plate-sized chapatti in mere seconds. "Have you seen *Maam* yet?"

"I'm all right," I say. "A bit jet-lagged." I put down my metal drinking cup. "I saw her with Nabila earlier, but I might have to wait until tomorrow to see her properly. I can barely hear myself talk here."

"She never stops going on about you. You always were her favourite. And, boy, did we know it!" Taleeb knuckles my head and musses up my hair. I make a note to go to the bathroom before I go on stage. "What was it she used to call you? Her gulab jamun?"

"And burfi and rasmallai," I say, rolling my eyes.

We hoot at the dessert-based pet names.

"She loves seeing you on TV. She makes us tape every appearance. Bloody pain!"

TV? They must be showing repeats of *Sunset Strip*, the soap I starred in for a couple of years when I first got to Australia. "How is she?" I ask. "Without Dad, I mean."

Taleeb crunches down on a samosa, demolishing it in three big bites, a corner at a time. Some things don't change. "She's incredibly strong. She's doing okay. She always was tough, even behind all her silly clothes and make-up. I just don't think we realised."

He's wrong. I always knew. The mounds of washing in the sink. The thousands of chapattis she rolled out. The sacks of onions she chopped and cried over. Feeding and clothing three children on a budget. Bringing us up almost singlehandedly. Sharing her life with a man who remained a stranger to her. She was on her own then, as she is now.

"To be honest, it was tough for all of us," continues Taleeb. He sticks a hand up and the servers replenish his plate with more chapattis. "They didn't speak English well; I was the oldest, so I had to step in. Filling out forms, interpreting for them and translating official letters. Or enrolling myself at school and then doing the same for Nabila and you. Five years old, younger than Bilal, but already the man of the house. Can you imagine?"

The image takes me aback. "I can't," I say, shaking my head. I'd never thought about how life had been for Taleeb. As a child, I only knew him as my oppressor, someone I hated. I'd never considered the difficulties he might have faced or the things he did in the background that helped ease the journey for the rest of us. The rice lodges in my throat. I chase it down with a big gulp of spice-infused chai.

"You know she can't read or write?" says Taleeb. He digs into the gajrela – usually averse to vegetables, he has no issue with grated carrots cooked with sugar, milk and nuts.

I think about what Taleeb's just said. It makes more sense now: Mother's scribble of a signature on sick notes for school; asking Mrs Chaudhry to read the letters from Pakistan; the audio tapes we recorded once a month to send to relatives. While she may not always have understood me, I realise she had her own struggles.

The spoon clangs against Taleeb's teeth as he wolfs down the last of the sweet dessert. "So, you got a girlfriend? You getting married any day soon, or are you going to be a permanent bachelor?

My stomach contracts and I take another sip of chai. "No – no girlfriend."

I'm spared further questioning by the turbaned bearers passing out more desserts – buttery seviyan, made from vermicelli, and semolina-based halwa, studded with almonds, plump raisins and toasted coconut. Taleeb tucks in as though he's not eaten for a week.

I change the subject back to Mother. "Does she still make her own clothes?"

"A different outfit every day," says Taleeb, calling Bilal from where he's breakdancing with his friends so that he can try the puddings. "No change there."

I smile, reassured that the sun continues to rise in the east and set in the west.

"Do this one a favour?" says Taleeb, indicating Bilal, who's whispering something in his ear. "Sign his sweatshirt, yeah? He never takes it off."

"My pleasure." I take the feather-topped pen and, with a flourish, scrawl a message and my name across the title of the show. Bilal giggles as the pen loops across his chest.

*

Dessert bowls cleared, the whole table rises as one, to the relief of those waiting. I turn to Bilal. "Hey, buddy, I forgot to ask: what do you want to be when you grow up?"

Drawing in a big breath, he answers in excited gulps. "I want – I want – I want to be a . . . a . . . a policewoman!" He jumps up and down, performing star jumps.

Taleeb hugs the little boy and calls him his chandh ka tukra. Picking him up, he follows me out. There is another jam at the door. Like a game of Grandma's Footsteps, we shuffle forward in tiny movements. The music in the background has switched to '70s and '80s hits. Bilal sways in time to Donna Summer singing "I Feel Love".

"By the way, cool threads," says Taleeb. "I thought you were the groom." He guffaws.

"Your dad's a comedian – he should be on *New Faces*," I say to Bilal, who stares back at me blankly.

A crowd has gathered around us, excitedly calling out the name of the same Bollywood actor as earlier. Resigned to my fate, I reach for their pens to sign their napkins, but Taleeb isn't having it. "Buzz off!" It takes a few more choice words from him before they retreat.

"Come round as soon as you can," he says to me. "Khalida will want to see you. She'll never forgive me if you don't."

A brave soul thrusts an autograph book at me. I don't have the heart to say no, so I sign it with a flourish. *Much love, H. Roshan!* The man goes away happy.

"Are you staying for the entertainment?" I say to Taleeb. "I'm doing a few songs."

Taleeb shakes his head. "Would love to, mate, but Arsenal are playing Rovers. If I go now, I'll be home in time for kick-off. Anyway, I heard you plenty, back in the day."

"No worries. It's been great to see you," I say, meaning it. "And this little monkey here." I squeeze Bilal's cheek. He tickles me with the feather on his pen.

"Uncle Rafi, do you know this song?" Bilal sings along to the chorus of "Money, Money, Money" playing on the speakers as we exit.

Taleeb laughs. "Know the song? It was only your uncle's favourite band when he was your age!"

Bilal fist pumps the air.

"We saw the show when it came to Manchester," says Taleeb. "Not my bag, but the little one loved it. He's sung all the songs every day since. God help us!"

"He has impeccable taste," I say. "Just like his uncle."

Taleeb playfully punches my arm. "You've done well, mate. You were right to ignore me. We just didn't know how it would work out. No one from our background did what you did, so we had nothing to go on. We didn't want you wasting your time. Anyway, you proved us wrong. We're all dead proud of you. Even me." He gets me in a headlock and pretends to wrestle me. Bilal tells him off and he releases me. "This one's your biggest fan. Never stops mentioning you to his mates."

I take in the rare praise. The ten-year-old me would never have believed the day would come when Taleeb would give me his blessing.

I follow them out to the car park. A brisk wind has swept in, bringing with it a few flakes of snow. I shiver and cross my arms. Taleeb slips off his parka jacket and offers it to me. It reminds me of the coat the young boy wears in *East is East*.

Seeing my hesitation, Taleeb tuts and takes the coat and drapes it over my shoulders. Even though I must look like Liam Gallagher, it's blissfully warm. "I know it's not what you're normally used to," he says, "but needs must."

I give them both a final hug, then step back as Taleeb starts the engine.

"And if you need owt else," he says, through the window, "you know where we are."

Forty-two

I've barely put one foot in the Hall before Mrs Chaudhry zeroes in on me. She's changed into a sari seemingly made of sequins. The sparkly fabric gathers around her vertiginous stiletto heels, meaning she approaches with the quick, mincing walk of John Inman. "Come, puthar."

The room is transformed, with the chairs stacked and pushed to the edges and the central area cleared for dancing. The room is thick with heaving bodies. Disco lights pulse and throb. Glitterballs dangle and spin from the ceiling, making it look as though the room is being showered in coloured confetti.

I help Mrs Chaudhry up the stairs to the stage, one perilous step at a time. Behind us is an eight-piece group: "Bolly Good!" They're the main entertainment but will accompany me first, at Shazia's insistence. We all – including Mrs Chaudhry – take a bow to cheers, whistles and applause from the audience. Cameras click and whir and flashes ripple out around the room. Damn ... my hair ... I forgot to check it after Taleeb ruffled it. I quickly run a hand through it and hope for the best.

I manoeuvre behind the microphone stand, a few feet away from Shazia and Majid perched on their golden thrones. They have also changed, this time into Western clothes – Shazia in a flowing red dress and Majid in a navy-blue suit and orange shirt. Shazia giggles at something Majid says, before turning to me and kissing her palm and blowing the love my way; I catch it with my free hand, not caring if it looks corny.

Turning back to the crowd, I take in the scene. I'm home, centre-stage, about to entertain people who look like me but before whom I've never performed. As a child, I was forbidden to "make a show" of myself in front of the neighbours. Now, here I am, about to do just that, but with everyone's blessing. Looking out at the sea of expectant faces, my heart begins to flutter. Unlike in the theatre, there is no dimming of the lights. I can see all their hopes and expectations.

While the band does a final tune-up, I raise the microphone to my lips. I hear Mother's voice in my ear: "Tasting, tasting." When I repeat the words in an exaggerated Asian accent, waggling my head, the audience bursts into laughter and claps and hollers.

"Right," I say, "let's get this party started!"

*

I work my way through Bollywood numbers from the '70s and '80s – songs rich in melody by R. D. Burman, Bappi Lahiri and Kalyanji Anandji. The audience sings and claps along, thrilled to be taken down memory lane, while the youngsters dance enthusiastically even though they weren't born when the songs were hits. The room gets louder and louder, as the crowd joins in with the choruses. I've long abandoned my sherwani. I'm sweating under my kurta, but I don't care. I'm back on the stage, my natural home. The bodies in the room become a blur as everyone jumps up and down, flinging their arms into the air, returning to happier and simpler times. The very singing and dancing that Mother warned me would be my downfall is what brings this whole room and community together. Euphoria bubbles up through me. I breathe new life into the old songs and the audience wants more and more.

*

Half an hour later, after taking a bow to a round of camera flashes and boisterous applause, I turn to Shazia. She dances in front of her throne, alternately whistling with her thumb and forefinger and clapping loudly with her hands in the air, her gold bangles clacking and gathering at her elbow. Majid rushes over and lifts me up in a bear hug.

Mrs Chaudhry totters in their direction, motioning for them to sit down. Shazia gives one last whistle before reluctantly assuming the demure bride position. I blow her a kiss and take another bow. The audience cheers and stamps its feet, demanding an encore. They throw out names of popular songs.

I need no encouragement. I pick up the microphone and introduce the next number. "Aap jaisa koi meri—"

The crowd goes berserk, not letting me finish the title of the 1980 hit from the film *Qurbani*. I look to the band; they give me a thumbs up.

Halfway through the first verse, Shazia races to my side, ignoring her mother's cries to return to her husband. She grabs the microphone. She's enthusiastic and out of tune, but I don't care. Singing our hearts out, we're once more back in the floral-carpeted bedrooms of our childhoods, belting out numbers into our hairbrushes and imagining our names in lights.

*

After three more songs, I'm finally allowed to step away from the microphone stand. It's time for Bolly Good! to have their moment in the spotlight. I need to find Mother. I shake hands with the band, who head off for a quick break before their set begins.

I've barely stepped off the stage before I'm mobbed. The crowd swells around me like a wave breaking on a rock, wanting to gush about the performance, get my autograph and shake my hand, all the while talking about films and the Bollywood scene.

They take photos with me and thrust wedding invitations for me to sign. Despite my protestations, they insist I'm Hrithik Roshan. It's easier to give in. I answer questions about films I've never starred in and about co-stars I've never met.

For once, I'm happy to be who they want me to be.

Forty-three

This time, the cool air of the car park is a welcome break from the party. I pace the perimeter, winding down after the set. With the muted boom of the music pumping out from within the Hall, I don't hear Nabila until she grabs me from behind.

"You were amazing, bro!" she says, jumping up and down and shaking me like a bottle of champagne. "Fantastic show. And cool haircut. I'm not mad about the coat, though."

I'm back in Taleeb's parka, which I've zipped right up. I've no idea how Nabila's swanning around in just a salwaar kameez with a thin bubblegum pink cardie over the top.

"Hey, you!" I exclaim, turning and hugging her properly. She smells of curry, Vosene and Avon Moonwind – Mother's favourite talc. Which reminds me: "Where's *Maam*?"

"Don't worry, she's fine. She's still inside. She's been trying to find you all day but can't get past your army of adoring fans."

I grin. "Well, what can you do when you're catnip to the masses?"

She rolls her eyes. "Plus she likes the music."

I'm agog at the thought of Mother listening to "Push

It" by Salt-N-Pepa, as interpreted by Bolly Good!, which is currently leaking out of the door. Nabila goes to say something else, then stops.

"How are the little ones?" I ask, breaking the silence, linking arms and walking with her around the car park. She seems relieved at the conversation opener, visibly relaxing.

"Not so little now. Even Sajida's left nursery. Mohsin's seven, Kamran eight. Proper daddy's boys – he takes them every other Sunday to Ewood Park and I can turn off that blasted TV," she says. I shudder, remembering how *Grandstand* dominated our childhoods, the living room a no-go zone on Saturday afternoons. "And then there's Sofia: ten going on thirty. She's no doubt cornering some boy on the dance floor and refusing to let him go. A right little madam."

"Takes after her mum," I say, which gets me a slap.

She turns to me. "Anyway, never mind us," she says in a quieter voice, "how are *you*? How's life in Oz? Anything to tell me?" she asks, saying each word with the same care as she puts one jewelled, sandalled foot in front of the other. The wind whirls around us and we both shiver. I reluctantly offer her the parka, moving my hand at a glacial pace to the zip. I'm relieved when she says no.

"It's beginning to feel like home," I say. "Mind you, it's only taken ten years." I laugh.

"I hear the show's doing well. The kids are always singing the songs."

"It couldn't fail – tried and tested. I'd love to take the credit, but, you know me . . . modest to a fault."

Normally, she'd have giggled at this or rolled her eyes. She does neither. Instead, she unlinks her arm from mine. She's trembling. There's no way round it – I unzip the parka.

"Wait," she says. "There's something I have to tell you." She steps in front of me. "Something I have to ask you."

The wind pinches us with icy fingers, ruffling my hair and teasing her cardigan. She accepts the parka. I immediately regret my chivalry. There's no cold and damp like Northern cold and damp. My teeth chatter and I try to think of the beach back home.

Nabila opens her mouth, but then closes it, changing her mind.

"Go on," I say, nodding, "what did you want to ask me? And, no, I don't know any of the *Neighbours* cast, before you start."

Again, she doesn't laugh. Instead, her eyes search mine, her brow furrowed. Finally, she takes another big breath. A violent gust flares up. Her mouth moves, but the wind whisks away her words.

I move us to the side of the wedding venue, in the lea of the wind, away from the busy main door. I nod, encouraging her, even though something inside me tells me I don't want to hear what's to come.

"Is it true?" she says.

Just three words after that build-up? Part of me feels cheated. "Is what true?" I say in a light tone, belying the unease I feel inside.

She takes another breath. "What they say?"

Another three words.

I knit my eyebrows. "What who says?"

"A friend's brother who works on the airlines . . ." she begins. A party guest rolls past, speaking on her clamshell. We wait until she passes.

"What about your friend's brother?" I hiss, the words coming out harsher than intended.

Nabila looks at me, then up at the gibbous moon.

I sigh. Why's she being so cryptic? "Let's go inside. I'm freezing my tits off!"

She takes my hand. She's not normally demonstrative. I laugh nervously.

"Well," she says, "he said something happened on one of their planes recently."

I know where this is going. I don't want to hear it. "Come on, let's go and see *Maam*."

She drops my hand and looks me square in the eyes. "With a famous actor," she says.

I let out my breath. While I might have a successful theatre career in Australia, I'm hardly a famous actor. Not unless you mistake me for Hrithik Roshan.

Nabila continues. "Someone called Rafi Aziz and a member of the crew."

A wave of embarrassment and revulsion threatens to knock me off my feet. The blood drains from my face at the same time as adrenaline floods my body. I want to flee – far away, as though this conversation has never happened. But I'm finding it hard to breathe. I imagine I'm on stage, going through my vocal exercises. I force myself to stand tall, to take the cold night air down to my diaphragm. In. Out. In. Out. I can't stop shaking.

"I know," she says, taking my hand in hers again and squeezing it. "I've always known."

She's always known? Known what? What's to know? I sniff, then give a mirthless chuckle. I'm in denial. Should I laugh or cry? A day that should have been all about Shazia has quickly turned into the all-singing, all-dancing Rafi show. "Don't believe everything you hear," I say.

Stop it right now, says the angel on my left shoulder. *Lying isn't going to get you out of this. You know exactly what she means.*

I fall against the wall. "Whatever you've heard, it's—" I start, but she speaks over me.

"I know you're gay!" she snaps, as the wind dies down for a moment. The words echo around the early evening air. From around the corner, I hear the crunch of gravel, but whether by tyres or feet I don't know. Has someone heard us? I go to look, but Nabila stops me with a hand on my arm. "It's fine. Your secret's safe with me. Even if it is the talk of the airlines!"

I feel anything but safe. Despite the winter darkness, I'm totally exposed. She knows what happened on the plane. As does her friend. And her friend's brother. I cringe. And, more importantly, she knows something much bigger: that her young brother is gay. I've always been someone she's admired as my career's taken off. But how can she admire this part of me, which I've kept hidden from her and the rest of the family all these years?

"It's not true," I blurt out. I instantly hate myself for carrying on the pretence.

She looks at me, rolling her eyes. "I've always known. You don't need to lie to me."

I try to argue with her but realise I'm being ridiculous. She's not screaming and shouting. She's not throwing Bollywood-style histrionics. The only one with a problem here about my sexuality is me.

"I hope he was worth it," she says, tutting and shaking her head while rearranging the dupatta around her neck. "On a plane!"

"Don't!" I say, my hands over my ears. "It makes me sound like a teenage girl."

"Well . . ." she says, holding up her hands before breaking into a peal of laughter.

I'm momentarily affronted, then her contagious laughter grabs me and I join in. We only stop when our ribs hurt and our lungs cry out for air.

We slide down and sit on the cold tarmac with our legs outstretched, backs against the wall. The sherwani will be ruined, but I don't care. At the age of thirty, I've just come out to the first member of my family. Correction: I've been outed. The genie is well and truly out of the bottle. Light-headed and unburdened, I also can't shake the nagging ache behind my breastbone. I know from *The Arabian Nights*, which I loved as a child, that tales of genies rarely end happily ever after.

"Is that what made you leave?" she asks.

"Hm?" I say, coming out of my thoughts.

"The UK, I mean. Is that why you left? Because you were gay?"

I nod. It would have been impossible to figure out who I was with the scrutiny of not just Mother but the whole community on me. I'm reminded of something Mr H once said to me. "*You're a butterfly among the bricks.*" I had to leave to be able to spread my wings.

The squally wind deposits a sprinkling of raindrops on our heads. "And the crap weather!" I say, as we get up and stroll back to the Hall as fast as my upturned shoes and her jewelled sandals let us.

The wind is seriously up now, but I've stopped shivering. Confessing my Big Secret to Nabila has released all sorts of endorphins. I squeeze her hand.

"Does anyone else know?" she says, draping both our heads with her dupatta. Thankfully, the rain remains light, as the dupatta's about as effective as tissue paper.

"Just Shazia," I say.

Nabila nods. "You always were thick as thieves."

"She's known since college days. In fact, *she* told *me*. She said only an idiot wouldn't have guessed."

"She's right," says Nabila.

"Pardon me for being that obvious!" I say. I wipe the misty rain from my eyes. "Who else knows?" I'm really meaning does Taleeb know, but I can't bring myself to ask her directly. I never wanted his approval when I was a child, but I seem to want it now. It would mean he sees me as an equal, not someone he pities or holds in contempt. He's proud of the career I've forged, but I've never known what he thinks of me as a person.

She snorts. "It wasn't difficult. The signs were always there. Need I list them?" She doesn't mention Taleeb.

I tut. "What about *Maam*?"

We're almost at the main door, with the warmth and light from inside bleeding out into the night. Bolly Good! are just coming to the end of a medley of Asha Bhosle hits.

"What about her?"

Sometimes Nabila can be exceptionally thick. "Does she know I'm gay?!" I shout it out louder than I'd intended. It coincides with a break in the music. There are a few cars with their engines running and people milling around the entrance, but the wind would have whipped my words away.

"No, she doesn't," says Nabila. "You're her golden boy. You can do no wrong."

A golden boy with feet of clay. "Should I tell her?"

Nabila shrugs. "That's up to you. It's not an easy one. She still worries about what other people will think," she says. "About everything."

I picture Mother from when I'd glimpsed her earlier in the Hall, still beautiful in her mid-fifties, wearing a shimmering salwaar kameez, with immaculate make-up, lips like cherries, hair teased into ringlets, eyes outlined with surma and a rose behind her ear. I remember how our mirror was always covered in wedding invitations, as everyone wanted the exotic butterfly in their midst, even if they didn't know her well.

A few moments later, we're at the door ourselves. Nabila removes the sodden dupatta from our heads and flings it over a hook in the vestibule. At the threshold, I step over a red rose on the floor, like the bleeding heart of the little nightingale from Oscar Wilde's fairytale. A few petals have come loose. I stop and stare. Nabila pulls me inside.

The band launch into an upbeat Bollywood number. Shazia rushes over, leaving Majid behind on his throne and ignoring Mrs Chaudhry's demands to get back. Her bridal jewellery glints under the laser lights. Whooping, she leads me with an ornately mehndi'd hand to the centre of the dance floor. The crowds part. Shazia and I assume our starting positions, ready to cut some shapes as we've been practising in our FaceTime sessions – a medley of Bollywood numbers, mirroring the synchronised dancing of Jeetendra and Sridevi in films like *Himmatwala* and *Tohfa*. Three, two, one, go!

I lose myself in the music and moves. For now, nothing else matters.

Forty-four

The next day, after a much-needed lie-in, I return to the old neighbourhood. I should go and see Mother, but I can't face her. Not yet. With my conversation with Nabila last night still in the forefront of my mind, my emotions are all over the place and I don't trust myself not to blurt it out in front of Mother. Nabila has taken it well, but there's no reason to assume Mother will. She has form. I turn off my phone, just to be safe, in case she rings.

I step outside swaddled in my quilted jacket and Taleeb's parka on top, with a jauntily striped scarf and rainbow-fingered woollen gloves. I don't care how I look; it's whatever it takes to keep warm.

I want to visit a couple of former haunts. First stop, KKK. It takes a good hour to walk there from the hotel. When I get there, I look around to make sure I'm in the right place. For the shop is no longer there. Gone is the old hand-painted "Khan's Korner Kabin" with its Ks highlighted in different colours. A shiny new imposter sits in its place.

One Stop Shop
Convenience Store

Nabila said that after multiple requests from a minimart chain, Mr Khan had finally succumbed and sold up – but only if they took him on with the sale. He looks most officious in his uniform, his salwaar kameez replaced by a uniform, a headset with a microphone and a green tabard that reminds me of *Prisoner Cell Block H*.

The interior is also unrecognisable – bright, spacious and sanitary. The meat section has gone; in its place, a floor-to-ceiling chiller cabinet full of ready meals, frozen veg and plastic packs of samosas, bhajis and kebabs ready to heat up at home. Unlike most things remembered from my childhood, the store seems bigger.

As I take it in, including a section for newspapers and magazines, the front page of the *Lancashire Evening Telegraph* catches my eye:

"SLUM HOUSING CLEARANCE!" blares out the headline.

Underneath: "Audley Range compulsory purchase – houses not fit for habitation."

Ignoring the stencilled sign over the shelves ("You read, you pay"), I grab a paper. As I read, the paper trembles in my hands. The entire neighbourhood is up for demolition. The Edwardian stock has failed to keep pace with the modern age and the council can't justify spending more money on it. They're holding talks, but the plan is to offer the largely Asian community a fixed sum of money to move on. Every house will be torn down, replaced by a neighbourhood that, in the artist's impression, looks like *Brookside*.

I slump against the magazine rack, sending a *TV Times* flying. I'm trembling, aghast at the thought of the streets of my childhood being bulldozed out of existence.

Mr Khan trots over. "Thirty pence," he barks, snatching the magazine off the floor and pointing at the paper in my hand, before warning me breakages must be paid for.

*

"Oh my god! Rafi?"

I stare at the young Asian woman behind the till as she scans the newspaper. She has a choppy bob, dyed electric blue; piercings all the way down her ears; upper lip painted the same shade as a red pepper, the lower, green; and chunky signet rings on her fingers.

"Rafi," she repeats. "It's me!" I must still look blank as she rolls her heavily mascaraed eyes. "Ashiqah!"

My heart leaps. A part of my childhood has caught up with me. "Ashiqah! No way! What are you doing here?"

"I could ask you the same thing." She shoots out from behind the counter and throws her arms around me, clasping me tight, her rings digging into my back. I breathe in a heady mix of Poison by Dior, Irn-Bru and Silk Cuts.

I haven't seen Ashiqah in years. After turning eighteen, she fled to Manchester, determined to live her own life rather than the one her parents had mapped out for her. I left for Australia a few years after, and I haven't seen her since. I struggle to reconcile this feisty woman with the punk hair with the smug ten-year-old with the pretzel hairdo.

She appraises me from head to toe. "Looking good, Raf – I don't know what you've been doing, but it suits you."

I point at her piercings. "Look at you! I just – I just can't... you look fab!"

She laughs. "What are you doing back? They say you live in Australia now?"

"I do. I was back for a friend's wedding. Shazia. Do you remember her?"

She gives another laugh. "Of course. You gave her that terrible haircut."

I snort. "How come everyone still goes on about that? How's your mum?"

It's Ashiqah's turn to snort. "Insufferable. Living like a queen. They have a chain of electrical shops now, called AC/DC. Like a budget version of Curry's – korma to their madras. You'll see them everywhere."

I'd spotted a branch at the airport, the logo a plug with an electrical flash behind it.

"They're rolling in it," she says. "Big house in Pleasington. Electric gates. Three cars. Cleaner. The shop's everywhere. I can't bloody escape her!"

I marvel at Mrs Ibrahim's entrepreneurial spirit – from selling plastic Taj Mahals and clocks shaped like giant watches to running a multi-million-pound enterprise.

"One minute, Raf," says Ashiqah. "Just having a fag, Mr Khan! Back in five."

Grabbing her cigarettes and lighter, she motions for me to follow her out the back.

*

Ashiqah lights up, puffing hard and not talking for a few seconds while she gets the full nicotine hit. "So, are you seeing anyone?" she says, getting straight to it, waving at me with the cigarette. "Nice-looking fella like you's not gonna be single."

I hesitate. I can be truthful without going into details and I can use they/them pronouns to avoid gendering them. "Actually, there *is* someone."

She grins like an SMS smiley. "I knew it. What's he like?"

I break into a coughing fit. Am I that transparent? Does the whole world know I'm gay? "What makes you think it's a he?"

She rolls her eyes. "Puh-lease. How long's it been?"

"Five years and counting." The feeling of pride is tinged by guilt, as Pedro's name badge suddenly flashes into my mind, as it did in my face during our seedy toilet encounter. I force myself to think of home and the man waiting for me.

She takes another drag. "I'm made up for you."

"Ah, thank you," I say. She seems content to leave the conversation there, which is fine with me. I'm still getting used to sailing these new waters. "Anyway, how about you – anyone special?" I ask her.

"Still working my way through the frogs." She tips ash into a plant pot. "You think they're the one, then you find out they're married, or they've been in for GBH, or they're proper mummy's boys. What is it with men and their mothers?"

She's asking the wrong person.

She blows a smoke ring at me. "Talking of which, how's your mum?"

"I'll catch her tomorrow. I'm sure she's fine, but I can't

face her just yet. She's bound to ask me if I'm seeing someone. It's the question du jour."

"God, yes. What will you tell her?" she asks, drawing one of her arms around her waist, the other one vertical against her body, the cigarette at her lips.

"I don't know. While she's thrilled for me in so many ways, it always comes back to the same thing: what the neighbours will say."

"God, those fucking neighbours," spits Ashiqah. "It's all they care about. Not whether their children are happy or not. It's only about what other people think."

She lights another cigarette, her nails clacking on the lighter. Her sleek bob bristles. Seeing me staring, she laughs. "I just had enough of being told what to do." That doesn't surprise me. Ashiqah had always been a rebel, even back at school. "Bad girls have way more fun. That's why I was best friends with Iz. We were two peas in a pod."

I haven't thought about Izmat in many a year. "You still in touch?"

She nods. "She's properly pissed off her folks. Only gone and married a Jamaican!"

I laugh in disbelief. Not at Izmat having a Black partner, but the fact that the Asian community, having experienced so much racism, still has issues with its own racism.

Ashiqah continues: "Iz got out, and so did I. I couldn't stay and let them marry me off to some one-eyed freak from Jhelum."

I snort. "Was that in the mix?"

"They had a whole list of inbreds lined up for me."

"Ashiqah!" I tell her off, scandalised.

She blows another smoke ring at me. "We had so many rows. In the end, I told them to marry the buggers themselves if it meant that much to them."

I chuckle. I remember the precocious, ten-year-old Ashiqah arguing the point with Mrs Entwistle about the ABBA competition. I'm thrilled she's grown into an equally bolshy woman.

"The hypocrisy of it," she continues. "They say a woman's gone haraab just because she wants to date like a normal person, or wear jeans or cut her hair short. But a man can get away with all sorts of shit, as long as he goes to the mosque. Fuck that!"

She stomps her cigarette under her stacked, multi-buckled Goth boot. Smoke puffs out of her nostrils like an angry dragon.

"What made you come back to Blackburn?" I ask Ashiqah.

"I know it sounds daft, but I just really missed the old place. And with Mum and Dad safely out the way behind the gates of their moti mahal, it was the right time to return."

I nod. In Melbourne, I'll see a warehouse that reminds me of the mills, or I'll long for sarsaparilla sweets from the market or to feel the uneven cobbles under my feet.

Ashiqah points to the paper. "They're going to knock it all down. Can you believe it? I'll be out of a job and back on the dole. And everyone here sent packing, too."

A shiver runs through me. All those lives suddenly uprooted. To go where? I can't believe it's being allowed to happen. "Can no one stop them?" I ask.

"They tried. But the council's determined. Says the area's beyond saving."

This surprises me. Solidly built, the houses have plenty of life left in them. Most just need a lick of paint and a bit of upkeep. "They were happy enough for all this time."

"Yeah, well, no doubt someone's getting a backhander.

Probably some Blairite," she spits. I stare at her. "Don't even get me started. He's no different to the Tory scum." She tips out another cigarette from her packet with such force that the entire contents empty out.

Scooping them up for her, I ask if she needs to head back inside. She gives me a withering look. "You did the right thing by getting out of here," she says, lighting up again and leaning back against the wall. "They'd never have let you be yourself. None of them."

She's right. The community is too entrenched in its views to allow outliers to flourish. I'd have been expected to marry a girl from Pakistan, have loads of kids and repeat the same patterns for my own children when they were old enough.

"The oldies cling onto views they brought over with them on the boats," she continues. "But I'm pretty sure Pakistan's moved on, not locked in bloody amber."

From inside the shop, Mr Khan calls for Ashiqah. She flips a finger in his direction and leisurely drags on her cigarette. "Anyway, that's enough of me being a mardy cow," she says. "What's going on with you? What pays the bills?"

I tell her I trained to be a musical director but missed performing too much. How various lucky breaks helped me rise to the top relatively quickly. When I mention my current show, her prickly exterior crumbles and she sways on the spot, arms raised, belting out "Dancing Queen".

"Bravo!" I say, clapping. She can still whack out a tune.

"No, you were always the better singer," she concedes. Seeing the shocked expression on my face, she laughs, exhaling smoke. "But I couldn't let you always get your own way, could I? Right, no rest for the wicked. Mr No-Khan-Do's a bugger for clock-watching."

She flicks the rest of her cigarette into the flowerpot. We go inside. Mr Khan glares at us. Ignoring him, Ashiqah climbs behind the counter, needing a few goes, no doubt weighted down by her multi-buckled, heavy-soled Goth/biker boots. Oblivious to the queue, she pulls out a hand mirror and reapplies her lipstick – both shades – before looking at me for approval. I give her a thumbs up.

*

It's a short walk from the shop to the gates of St Matthew's. I pass several walls with graffiti on them. "Muzzies out!", "Taliban go home!" The NF logos may have gone, but the hate remains.

The school is smaller than I remember: just two wings and a central hall. Time has wrought its effect even here. The original mullioned windows have been replaced with featureless uPVC replacements. A safety mesh now covers the gargoyles on walls and roof. Thankfully, the shuttle weathervane remains. I salute it on Father's behalf.

A sign displays the school's name in Comic Sans font. Mr Brindle's name has been replaced by a "Ms Okebuye BSc, MA, NPQH". I run my hands over the stone wall surrounding the school, feeling the bumps and ridges through my gloved fingers. Sliding down the wall, I crouch on my haunches. I close my eyes. I hear the shrieks and shouts of excited children running around, the thwack of skipping ropes, the call of chanting games.

This need to connect to my past has become stronger over the years. The longer I stay away from Blackburn, the more I feel it pulling me back: an urgency to hold onto my early memories in case the past becomes a distant land.

A truck rolls by, its hissing air brakes returning me to the present.

Forty-five

The next day, the phone in the room wakes me up, its shrill ring cutting through my jet-lagged dreams.

"Hello?" I croak, expecting it to be Reception. I pull the cotton sheets closer around me, not wanting to wake up just yet.

"Time you were up, Smelly." It's Taleeb. How old is he? Then I remember my conversation with Nabila. Oh God, there are worse names he could be calling me right now. Has she told him? Is that why he's calling? I sit up in a hurry. I try to speak, but nothing comes out.

"Wakey-wakey. You there?" says Taleeb. "*Maam*'s been on the phone. Wants to see her favourite son. No change there! I'll pick you up. See you in half an hour."

"Wait? What? Where?" I'm still groggy.

Taleeb brushes off my questions. "It's your own fault for staying in a fancy hotel a million miles away from civilisation. Travelodge not good enough for you?"

I don't rise to it. Comfort is king when you've been flying long distance. I glance at the bedside clock. It's barely nine. Mother's keen! Mind you, she always was an early riser.

Before I can say anything smart back, Taleeb's put the phone down.

*

I feel like a child in Taleeb's car, a tank-like BMW. "How was the footie the other night?" I say, in between bites of the croissant I've nabbed from the dining room.

"Tight," he says, pulling out of the hotel car park without indicating. "Three subs, lots of fouls from Arsenal, but Rovers got them on penalties and corners."

I have no idea what any of that means, but nod anyway. "Hey, where's the fire?" I say, as we get so close to the Clio in front that I can read the Arabic prayer on its rear window.

He chuckles and eases back a fraction. "So, how was the show? Bilal wouldn't stop singing ABBA songs all evening. In the end, Khalida had to bribe him with fish fingers and chips to make him stop."

Relieved that we're on safer ground, I fill him in on the evening. Taleeb simply nods and keeps his eyes fixed on the road ahead, making it impossible for me to read his thoughts. He doesn't seem to know. If he did, he'd have said something by now. That's fine with me. I'm happy to be temporarily back in my closet.

We turn off the dual carriageway, into a smaller residential road. A few spindly cherry trees have now been planted on the pavements, I notice. It'll be a few months before they come out with their pink blossom. The flowers make me think of Mother. I'm excited and a bit nervous. It's been five years, with increasingly fewer phone calls as my career took off. Plus, we were never the same with each other after Mr H's death. I could never forgive her for how she'd spoken about him. Yes, I'd gone to the Conservatoire with her blessing and I'd made a living singing and dancing, which she'd also accepted once she realised it came with fame and fortune and something to lord it over with the neighbours, but the axis of our relationship had shifted permanently.

Taleeb turns into Lower Audley Street, his hands most definitely not in the ten to two position on the wheel. He hasn't used the indicator once during the whole journey. I stop myself from pointing it out. No one likes a backseat driver.

"Nabila called me," he says, turning to me. My heart is squeezed in a vice. Here it comes. The judgement from on high. The sneering comments. The teasing and bullying and name-calling. I'm ten years old again.

"Could you . . . could you keep your eyes on the road?" I say, genuinely worried about our safety and also trying to change the subject. I can't have this conversation. Not here, trapped like this. He makes me feel guilty, even though I have nothing to feel guilty about.

He chuckles and turns back round. "She said you'd chatted. About stuff."

My cheeks burn. I feel my heart thudding through my shirt and jumper. I'm surprised I don't see the fabric pulsing in and out, like in a cartoon. I need to get out, but the seatbelt traps me in the massive leather seat. I'm a grown man of thirty, yet I'm sweating and feeling like I've done something wrong.

"Oh yes?" I manage to spit out. "I mean, yes, we did."

"We've always known," he says, deceptively casual.

I clutch the seatbelt tighter. Wait for it. Here they come: the nasty little digs, the homophobic slurs, the holier-than-thou proclamations, the—

"And it's fine."

What the . . .

It takes a moment for me to register what he's just said.

I allow myself to exhale. Of all the things I'd expected Taleeb to say to me when I'd imagined coming out to him, "It's fine" was not one of them. This man who'd taunted me mercilessly when I was a child was now accepting me for being myself. I tilt my head, first one way, then the other, trying to shake sense into what he's just said.

"Well, that's something," I say. For once, I'm lost for words. The mini football boots hanging off the rearview mirror swing back and forth. Then I ask the question that's been niggling away at me. "Does *Maam* know?"

"We've not said owt to her, if that's what you mean. Although, you're hardly subtle."

"What's that supposed to mean?" I snap, instantly on the defensive. *You sound like a girl. You even* walk *like a girl.*

A tinny ringtone of Eminem's "Will the Real Slim Shady" fills the car. "That's probably her now." He flips open his phone. "Yeah, he's with me. Two minutes. Bye."

I can hardly blame Mother for wanting to see me. It's been two days since I landed. She'll have made a hundred and one dishes. No wonder Taleeb and Nabila get sick of the prodigal son. But arranging such an early morning visit is still a bit over-the-top. I say this to Taleeb. He shrugs. "Don't ask me. You know what she's like. Once she gets something in her mind . . ."

We're a couple of streets away. I notice a house with boarded-up windows. Then another. And another. I go to ask Taleeb about them, but he screeches off Windham Street into Baines Street with one final spin of the steering wheel. As he judders to a halt, he turns to me. "I don't mind what you are," he says, as though I might be a walrus. "Just be safe. You're still my little bro. Just take care, yeah? No silly risks – know what I mean?"

I force down the eyebrow that's dying to shoot up. I've never known Taleeb be so considerate. I nod.

"If she asks, though," he continues, "I probably wouldn't say. What she doesn't know can't harm her, right? It'll kill her if she finds out."

Just what I don't need to hear. Bollywood-style violins screech in my ears as the camera pans in and out of my face. But he's got a point. It's one thing telling Nabila – and, even then, my hand was forced – but quite another telling Mother. If she thought me dressing up as Agnetha when I was a child was bad, she'll have a heart attack at me living not just "in sin" but with a man, and not an Asian man but a white one. What would the neighbours say?

*

The house smells exactly as I remember: a mix of spices, overlaid with the floral scents of Glade and Daz. Mother is in the front room, sitting at one end of the sofa. It's covered in a busy fabric that reminds me of a Persian rug. Mother has barely aged. Her hair's greyer, and she has a few more lines around her eyes, but she makes up for it with a vibrant salwaar kameez of peacock green and beetle blue.

She looks up briefly, before averting her gaze. I'm taken aback. Her eyes are red, like she's been crying. She pats the sofa, indicating for me to take a seat. Normally, she'd have flown over and clung to me like iron filings to a magnet, sobbing with joy. Not today. She remains seated.

"What's happened, *Maam*?" I ask, wanting to go over and hug her, but not getting a good vibe. I sit down. "Is everything okay?"

As I perch on the end of the plastic-covered sofa awaiting a reply, my eyes scan the room: wall hangings of calligraphic Islamic text, an illuminated clock with a waterfall effect, gold-speckled curtains with fancy frills and pelmets and, over the mantelpiece, a mock-Rococo mirror festooned with peacock feathers, dried flowers and beaded necklaces.

Taleeb clears his throat. "Right, I'm off. *Maam*, let me know if you need anything from Tesco's later."

The door slams shut behind him. Inside the room, the glowing clock counts down the seconds. Mother stares at her hands in her lap. She still hasn't said a word. I clasp and unclasp my fingers, unconsciously matching her movements.

"So ..." I offer, finally breaking the silence. "How are you?"

She sniffs but doesn't answer. She turns her head away even further, almost peering over her shoulder, owl-like, at the wall behind.

I try again. "Is the clock new? I don't recognise it."

"I don't recognise my own son!" she shrieks from nowhere, whipping her head round. I jump. Her face is tomato-red, her eyes bulging, her mouth set in a hard line. Her dupatta slips down from around her neck. She tugs it off and flings it across the room.

She knows, she knows, she bloody well knows! The taunt cycles through my head. But how? Nabila wouldn't have said anything to her. Nor Taleeb, from our conversation in the car. And yet, something was wrong here. I put my hands out, as if calming a snarling dog. "The new haircut?" I joke. "It's not to everyone's taste, but it'll grow back."

She doesn't laugh. "Hai Allah, if that was my only problem. You have killed me. Your own mother. My own flesh and blood. How will I ever show my face in public again? I am ruined!" She beats her chest. I get up, to stop her, but she screams at me to sit back down.

Even though I know where this is going, I stall for time. "Would you like me to get you—"

"Why did you come back?" she says. I look at her aghast. I'm reminded of something Taleeb once said, when he asked Mother if they could send me back. "You have torn out my heart. Your own mother, who has brought you up, looked after you, fed you . . ."

As she reels off a list of things she's done for me over the years, I take a moment to gather my thoughts. She clearly knows. I don't know who's told her, but that doesn't matter now. Her shoulders heave up and down as sobs rack through her body. The only other time I've seen her this upset is when she caught me up in full make-up at KKK's. But this is much worse. I feel myself shrivel. I try to talk, but she waves my stammering away.

"Is it true?" she asks. She glares at me, wiping the tears angrily from her eyes.

"Is what true?" I say, getting up and offering her tissues from the jewelled box on the table. She knocks it from my hand. Tissues fly up into the air.

"I heard you," she says. "With Nabila. Shouting it to the world!"

My heart sinks. Me and my stupid big mouth. Why did I have to yell it out?

"Is it true?!" she repeats. She falls back on the sofa, propelled by the force of her words. She sobs miserably into her elbow, not having her dupatta at hand.

I want to deny it. But she's so upset, we've gone past the point of no return. It's pointless putting her through this and then pretending it isn't so.

"Yes," I say. I can barely hear myself, so I say it again, louder. "Yes." I sit up straight.

Her whole body goes into a rictus. For a moment, she

doesn't move or speak or cry. Then she shrieks, a sound that goes through my very marrow. She thumps her chest again, the vibrations travelling through the sofa and up my body.

"*Maam*, stop, you'll hurt yourself!" I get up, but she dismisses me.

"Not as much as you have hurt me."

I'm reminded of a Shakespeare line: *How sharper than a serpent's tooth it is to have a thankless child.* I protest. But she isn't having any of it. She shoos me away, grabbing her dupatta from the floor and pressing it to her mouth, venting several times into it.

I fetch a tumbler of water from the kitchen. She is bright red and hyperventilating. She rears away from the glass. "I cannot accept anything from you. You are pleeth!"

I drop the glass and its contents on the carpet. *Tainted.* A word full of meanings, none of them good. Not for the first time, tears of heat prick my eyes. I blink rapidly.

"It was all his fault," she wails. "He taught you bad things. And look what happened to him. He caught a terrible disease and died. No family, no friends at his bedside. An outcast, going straight to Jahannam, with all the other sinners."

"You take that back!" I shout, appalled at her words, each worse than the previous.

She shakes a finger at me. "If I had been stricter with you when you were little, this would never have happened. Allah is testing me. When everyone said you were going haraab, I would not listen. But now this is how you repay me! Bathameez child!"

Each accusation is like a slap to my face. I recoil, tears running down my cheeks. I hate myself for feeling like this and for her seeing me like this. Her face is contorted in rage. It's hard to imagine how she could have ever loved me.

"Stop! Why are you saying these awful things?" I say. "You haven't seen me in five years and you can't even hug me? How did we get to this?"

She tosses her head back violently. "My kaleja went cold when I heard you with your sister. How do you think I felt? My own son. I felt like I had died."

I can't believe she can harbour so much venom and not see how she's upsetting me. And yet I can. She was just as horrific when Mr H was dying and she called it out as an act of God. "You call yourself a good Muslim, but you're—"

"Ya Allah!" she shrieks, grabbing her ears. "So much gunaah. Someone like you using that word. Thoba, thoba!"

I am aghast. "Someone like me?!"

"Keep your voice down! What will the neighbours say?"

Her perennial worry. The neighbours. "I couldn't give a FUCK what they think," I say. We both gasp. The "f word" hangs in the air between us like an exploded bomb.

She shuffles to the end of the settee, putting as much distance between us as she can. "I should never have come to this godforsaken country," she says bitterly. "Your father is to blame. They do not have your kind in Pakistan."

My kind? The only thing she is right about is there's no expression in Punjabi for "gay". How can she understand who I am when there isn't even a word for it? While I rack my brain for an appropriate phrase, she continues her tirade. Each awful word lands like artillery fire, tearing holes in me one by one until I can breathe no more.

"There are no gays in Pakistan," she states at the end, as though this is a fact.

"They're hardly likely to shout about it," I manage to say weakly. "Not in a country where they would be stoned to death, or worse."

"Your brother is not a gay. Why should you be? I have brought you up the same."

She's forgetting the truth. She happily indulged me in all my dressing-up whims as a child while Taleeb was encouraged to explore his love of sports, with her full blessing. Not that it made me gay or Taleeb straight, but her memory is selective. Taleeb and I were not brought up the same.

She snatches an Indian film magazine off the table. "Look at all these beautiful girls," she says, suddenly charming. "There will be even more beautiful girls in Mirpur. Why not you and me go and take a holiday there, and do your rishtha? It is not too late."

She wants to get me married off? I look at her askance, as though she's speaking another language. "I have a partner already," I say. "I don't want a wife."

She talks over me and my words land on deaf ears. "If we had only got you married before you went to university, this would never have happened."

"I don't think it would have made a difference."

"I do not mind if you want to marry a gori," she says, as if making a huge sacrifice. "As long as she converts, then all is good. Yes, yes, this is possible." She says the last sentence to herself, weighing up her Sophie's choice of me marrying a white woman versus me being gay.

"I have a partner," I repeat, suddenly overcome with tiredness. A mixture of jetlag, the emotions of the wedding and now this back and forth with Mother.

Her eyes light up with hope. She trots over, her bangles jangling and the ghungroos around her ankles chinkling with each baby step. She sits next to me, a beaming smile on her face. She grabs my hands. "Why ever did you not say?" She hugs me. "What is her name?"

"His name," I mutter into her shoulder, before I can stop myself.

We both go rigid.

She backs away again, her face distorted into a look of pure disgust.

"We've been together five years now," I say, hoping this will count for something. She pulls a fresh face of horror, as though I've just stabbed her through the heart afresh.

Before I can say anything else, she grabs the telephone and holds it aloft, like a sword. "I will call the moulwi saab. He will drive it out."

It? I pull my own face of disgust. "There's nothing to drive out."

"If your father was still alive," she says, spitting out each word, "this would kill him."

My blood rises into my head, making me dizzy. "There are organisations we can talk to," I say. "Other parents who have gay children, who—"

"You will burn in fire, harami child! Is that what you want?"

I'm taken aback at the forcefulness of her voice. Growing up, the threat of a fiery Hell was often thrown at us when we misbehaved. Mother is still ruled by the same fears.

She starts to cry again. "My little one. An eternity of Hellfire. How can I leave this Earth knowing you are damned? Please, puthar, do it for me. Save yourself while you can. Repent. Ask Allah for forgiveness. What kind of mother would I be if I didn't try?"

I feel a sudden wave of compassion for her, knowing she means well by all of this. But I can't share her fears. I have only one life to live, and it's right now. Mr H taught me that. Surely, she understands I don't have the same fears and worries that she does? I may be her son, brought up by her, but I've moved on, and not just geographically.

As I shift position in my seat, my rainbow-coloured woollen gloves drop to the floor. Mother sits back as though they're radioactive, an accusatory look on her face. She stares at the Paisley-patterned cravat around my throat, as if seeing it anew. "So, you dress up as a woman? Still, after all these years. Like the khusras back home. Those bagherat – exposing themselves for money. Thoba, thoba. What a burden to carry. Ya Allah, what will become of me?"

In desperation, she's reached for the only thing she can relate to – the eunuchs who live in communal houses all over Pakistan and India, dancing and singing at weddings and birthdays, baring their bodies if payment isn't received.

"For goodness' sake, I'm not a khusra!" I yell, frustrated.

She flinches, as though I'm the one who's put this idea into her head.

I break it down as simply as I can. "I like men. Like Taleeb likes women." This goes down badly, but I plough on. "I lie with other men ... as though with a woman." Which is possibly the worst thing I can say, judging by her reaction.

She screams, throwing herself back against the sofa as if I've physically assaulted her. "Get out!" she says, her cheeks on fire. "Harami boy. Get out!"

My ears flush red. I stand up, swiping my gloves from the floor. I make for the door, but then turn around. As much as she's crushed me – more than she has ever done before – I can't leave things like this. "Please, *Maam*, I'm still me. Your jalebi. Your gulab jamun."

She looks at me as though I'm talking a different language. "I do not know *who* you are!" She holds her dupatta up to her face again, shielding herself from me.

My legs are like lead. Waves of grief course through me like a fever.

I try one more time. "You've done nothing wrong. I've done nothing wrong. This is just the way I am. I can't be any other way."

She shakes her head. "You have killed me. Your father, too, if he was alive. He sacrificed everything for this? For you to run around in women's clothes and kissy-kissy with other men? You have killed us both."

I can't breathe. I can't move. I can't see. Who is this woman? A voice in my head answers me: she was always thus. For all her colour, all her flowers, all her flamboyance, this is who she's always been.

"I'm your son!" I insist, one last time. "Doesn't that mean anything to you?"

She hides behind her dupatta. "You are dead to me. I have only one son now."

At that, she turns her back on me, her shoulders going up and down as she sobs into her dupatta. I call out, but she just cries even louder.

I know it is finished. The rage and fire leave me as quickly as they had flared up.

I stagger outside with the unsteady gait of an injured animal.

Forty-six

Even in my weakened state, I manage the steep incline of Windham Street, my wobbly feet crossing in front of one another until I can't go any further. I find myself at the canal, staring into the murky water. I had to get away from her and that house, the scene of so much happiness and also so much sadness. I can't even bring myself to think of her as Mother. Just she. Her.

I lean against the stone wall of the bridge, trying to get air into my lungs. Her words go round and round my head. I wince at their cruelty. I try to shake them out, but they keep coming back, louder, more strident, like in an overwrought Bollywood film. I squeeze my head between my hands, willing her voice to be quiet. It makes no difference. She attacks me over and over with her barbs. I groan and sink to the floor. A runner on the towpath stops to ask if I'm okay. I wave him way.

Why, oh why, did I admit everything? I could have lied and just said no to her question. She'd have been none the wiser. Yes, she'd have heard rumours, but they'd have died. Life would have gone on as normal. She was unlikely to fly to Australia and our two lives could have remained separate. I'd come back every few years, she'd kill the fatted calf in celebration, and I'd just deflect any questions about meeting the right girl or settling down. Why did I even tell Nabila? Why the fuck did I tell any of them the truth?

A deep, guttural cry wells up from within me and ricochets around the deserted canal side. A goose takes off nearby, honking in alarm, its feet treading water, wings flapping. I stare after it, hating it, envious of its ability to escape trouble so easily.

I could throw myself into the sludge-coloured water of the canal. End it all, like a Bollywood heroine jumping down a well to escape her pursuer. But I remember the water is only four feet deep. I'd have to walk to a lock to have a real chance. I tell myself off for even having such thoughts. I've done nothing wrong. I have nothing to atone for.

The strip of vegetation just before the canal is winter-brown and devoid of life. I get up and walk over to it. I squat down, my knees cracking, then lie on my back on a damp bed of dried stalks. They creak and splinter beneath me. The earth is rock hard and bumpy, and the cold permeates my layers in seconds. I don't care. I imagine myself sinking deep into the iron-cold earth. I deserve to die. I've brought this upon myself. Whoever said honesty was the best policy was a fucking liar. Taleeb was right. I should have kept my fucking mouth shut.

Two swear words in quick succession. I chastise myself. I close my eyes and curl into a tight ball on the ground, trying to blot out the image of her face distorted by hate like the ageing portrait of Dorian Gray. I have to think calming thoughts. After a few moments, David's handsome face slides into view. It morphs into his younger self. Here we are, ten years old and on the canal side. Looking up at the moon. Holding hands. Breath rising as we lay on the ground among insects chirping and bats flying overhead. David leaning over me. His lips on mine. His breath inside me.

*

I get up and begin walking. Then I break into a jog. And then a run. Heading west along the towpath, not stopping until, an hour later, I'm at Pleasington Cemetery.

I locate Father's grave, high up in the grounds, under a large oak tree in the Muslim section of the cemetery. From below, the cries of footballers on the playing fields. I brush away the autumn leaves that have settled on the grave. Cupping my hands together, I bow my head, sending up kalimahs and prayers remembered from childhood. When I'm done, I blow into my hands and wipe my palms over my face and head, sending the prayers on their way to wherever he is now.

I tell him what I've been up to these last few years. Why I'm back in Blackburn. How I remember funny stories he told us as kids. How I have a lifelong love of auctions. How I know he loved us even in his absence from the house for most of our lives. How, with each passing year, I see more of him in the mirror looking back at me.

Before I leave, I take a tissue from my pocket and wipe his headstone clean. I stand back, reading the epitaph one last time. Removing a glove, I kiss my fingertips and touch them to the cold, unyielding granite. "I know you'd understand, Dad." Then: "I love you. Even if I didn't always tell you." The branches of the oak tree creak and groan overhead.

*

In the northernmost part of the Muslim section, I stand before a different stone.

In Loving Memory Of
MAAZ HAQQ
Born 1 January 1952
Died 10 March 1982
Aged 30 years
May Allah bless his soul

I'd learned the location of the grave by accident thanks to a snippet in a page of the *Lancashire Evening Telegraph* she had used to line the changher. His name had leaped out through the butter-blotted paper and I'd taken it out for my box of memories. The piece had attributed Mr H's death to "complications following a car accident on the motorway". There had been no mention of any illness.

It was only years later that I learned the truth. Googling his name, an article had popped up in the *Bay Area Reporter*. Mr H's partner, Andrew, had set up an AIDS foundation in his name. A disease virtually unknown at the time, followed by years of misinformation and distrust, but now with combination therapy it's no longer a death sentence. Not for the first time, I sigh at the unfairness of it all. Had Mr H been born just two decades later, he would still be here. Even today, seeing a checked shirt, catching an old Jeetendra film on cable, or hearing a full-throated laugh and he's back in the room with me. I blink away the tears. Mr H wouldn't want me to mourn him.

Someone has recently laid white roses on his headstone. My heart soars. He is remembered! He is still loved. But, who? I look over my shoulder, but no one else is here. The glowering grey skies and brisk wind have stopped most people from venturing outdoors.

I read the inscription again and shake my head: thirty years old. Way too young. When I was ten, Mr H had seemed like a proper grown-up. Now here I am, the same age as him and only half the man he was.

I crouch down. "Hello, Mr H. Just me. Long time. It seems like another world since we . . . well . . . Things are going great in the show. I wish you could see it. You'd love it."

I take out the same pink handkerchief I've carried all these years. "I still have it. It brings me luck." I pause. "But I don't think it's working anymore." I return it to my pocket and, with a sigh, I fill him in on what's happened. I fancy I hear his surprised and concerned exclamations in return, his voice rising in outrage on my behalf.

When I finish, I wait in silence. The wind plays with my hair. I shiver. Overhead, a pair of crows rise up, cawing and chasing a lone heron that glides past like a ghost. Despite its determined attackers, the heron doesn't change its trajectory, remaining true to its course. The crows eventually give up, tiring of the chase.

"Did I do the right thing?" I ask Mr H. "What do I do now? Have I spoiled things forever? How can I make things right with her? Should I not have told her the truth?"

A memory flashes into my mind. We were rehearsing for my audition and I was panicking, sure the panel wouldn't take me seriously. I suggested pretending I was from a posh school, with middle-class parents. Mr H had let me finish before sitting me down. "They're gonna love you for being you, buddy. I promise. You don't need to be anyone else. If they don't, then they need their heads examined. Just remember: to thine own self be true."

To thine own self be true.

I turn the words over in my mind, taking them apart

and then putting them back together again. *To thine own self be true.*

Well, that's what I've done, and we are where we are. I might not have got the outcome I wanted, but at least I can hold my head up high and say I've been honest about who I am.

When my knees can't take it anymore, I get up. "Thank you, Mr H. For everything."

I walk away, a new lightness washing over me. I will live in the truth. My truth. In the words of *The News of the World*, I'm in my own "kiss and tell" story. It's the least I owe David. Again, as with today, it might not go down well, but at least I'll have said my truth.

There are no more answers to be found here. Not in this graveyard among the sleeping ghosts, not at St Matthew's school gates and empty playgrounds, not among the streets and houses of my childhood whose fate is already on borrowed time. Just one more day and I'll be home again.

Forty-seven

I reluctantly hand the parka back to Taleeb. As hideously unfashionable as it is, I've grown attached to its comforting warmth. He takes my case and steers me inside Departures.

"Are you sure you won't stay a bit longer?" he asks, scanning the display boards. "Try and patch things up with her?"

I shake my head. "There's no point. She's made her mind up. Nothing I can say or do to make her change it. She called me pleeth."

Taleeb winces. He squeezes my arm. "Don't give up on her. She's an older generation, that's all. It'll just take her time to get her head around it."

"We both know that's not going to happen," I say. "At least, not anytime soon."

We swerve out of the way of a runaway trolley containing a stack of cases.

"Don't take this the wrong way," begins Taleeb, which instantly gets my hackles up, "but when it gets tough, you tend to run and hide. Like you did to that Conservatory."

"Conservatoire," I correct him. "And I didn't run away. I had to get out or go under. It wasn't like I had a choice."

My voice has got sharper. I tell myself to calm down.

This is neither the time nor the place to fall out with Taleeb. Having already lost Mother, I can't afford to lose him too.

We walk to Check-in and drop off my case. As it trundles off onto the moving belt and disappears out of sight, I feel myself lightening inside. In just a few days, I'll be back home – where I belong.

We make our way to the Security gates. This is as far as Taleeb can take me. Beyond the scanners and counters, I spot a branch of AC/DC in the shops on the other side. I make a note to pop in once I'm through.

A young boy carrying a helium balloon runs past us, hollering. I turn to Taleeb. "Promise me something?" I say, stopping and looking at him directly.

He looks at me, wary. "Sure, what you got?"

"Bilal. Will you promise me you'll always support him? No matter what?"

Taleeb's eyes grow shiny. After a few seconds, he nods. "Of course, bro."

I feel my shoulders relax. Even in this new century, Bilal is likely to face similar challenges to what I did. But, with the right support he can overcome them – without needing to, in his father's words, run away.

Just before I go through Security, Taleeb grabs me in a hug. He smells of parathas, hair wax and damp wool.

*

I sleep for most of the way back. Having upgraded to business class, I have no immediate neighbours. I stretch out on the bed, slipping down my eye mask, pop on the noise-cancelling headphones I bought from AC/DC for a very reasonable price, and bury myself under Taleeb's parka. Noticing my reluctance to part with it, he'd handed it back to me just before he left. I embrace its familiar warmth, the cover of darkness and the security of silence. There's no Eulalia and Chuck to keep me company on this flight but I smile, wondering where their journey will take them. Where will mine?

*

When I land on the other side, I check my Nokia. There are several messages, but only one that makes my heart leap.

"Cant w8 2 CU soon. Milo & I hv missed U! Hugz n :-*"

A huge smile breaks across my face. After the soul-sapping relay of connecting flights from Manchester to Melbourne, including a delay for some reason, it's just what I need to see. I stride down the corridor with renewed energy.

Not even Passport Control on this side can dampen my spirits. I have nothing to hide. I walk through with my head held high.

As the doors slide open, I scan the crowds. Signs abound, including one that makes me laugh: "Welcome home, John, you old drongo!"

Walking down the gauntlet of eager family members and taxi drivers, I wheel my case behind me, my head darting around, looking for the one face that means the most to me. I begin to walk faster, the suitcase's wheels squeaking in protest behind me.

And then I see him. Taller than his immediate neighbours, his conker-coloured hair making me go weak at the knees, just as it did the first time I saw it. My thumping heart goes into overdrive and my feet pick up pace.

He has a banner up: "Back at you, Raffy!" He knows any misspelling of my name winds me up. I laugh out loud. An overwhelming rush of love floods my body.

I call his name. He's engaged in conversation with the

woman next to him and doesn't hear me. I put a finger and thumb in my mouth and whistle.

He looks in my direction and, like the morning sun, a huge grin breaks across his handsome face. I see his green eyes sparkling even from this distance. He dives into the throng of holidaymakers and home-comers, running up and lifting me up in his arms.

A symphony of flutes and violins strikes up in my head. The crowd disappears, blurred out by the cinecamera as it focuses on just the two of us. He whirls me round and round, and the camera slowly pans away, twisting and swirling, soaring heavenwards.

When he finally sets me back down to earth, the camera zooms in to frame our faces in profile. The sun sets behind us. A heron flies past, a dart across the fiery surface.

I say his name: "David. My very own David."

He cups my face in his strong hands. He smells of sunshine, surf and leather. Everything unfolds in slow motion. The director moves in for a tighter crop. As our faces approach, the camera circles around us. Brown eyes blend into green and back again. Heads tilt gently down. Noses slide past each other sideways until our lips meet. The sweeping strings and fluttering woodwind are joined by the driving rhythm of tabla drums.

When we finally break apart, I take a deep breath. I take his face in my hands. He looks at me with such love in his eyes. But I need to do this. He'll understand.

"I've something to tell you."

PART THREE
WHEN ALL IS SAID AND DONE

Forty-eight

The call comes in the middle of the night. My phone ringtone blares out the Europop earworm of Clean Bandit's "Solo". I wait for David to answer it. He hates this song. He also knows I like my sleep. But Demi Lovato keeps singing. Then I remember: he's not here.

Sighing, I roll over and grab my phone. I slide the green icon to the right and mutter something unintelligible.

"Rafi? Can you hear me?" It's Nabila. Her voice is woolly and it takes me a while to pick out the words. "Where are you?" she asks.

"Home. In bed. What's up? Everything okay?" I reach over without thinking, but of course the bed's empty. I try to remain calm, even while my heart beats so fast I'm convinced it'll burst out of my chest.

Nabila doesn't answer. I hear Ajaz's voice in the background, saying something.

"Hello? You still there?" I say into the phone.

Another pause. "Sorry. I'm so sorry." She begins to cry.

I'm wide awake now. "What's up? Are you all right?"

More tears and the sounds of Ajaz comforting her. "She's gone, Rafi. She's gone."

"Who?"

"Mother," she sobs.

When I was younger, I used to imagine what it'd be like if anything happened to Mother. Imagining myself having Bollywood-style histrionics as my world suddenly shrank and I was left rudderless without her. But, after all this time, and with all the bad water that's passed between us, I don't feel a thing. Nabila might as well have told me a neighbour had died. I feel nothing. There is no trembling in my hands as I hold the phone against my ear. No ragged breath. No tears.

Nabila continues in fits and starts. "It was sudden. She was in hospital." Hospital? I sit up straighter. Why didn't anyone tell me? "Said she had a pain in her stomach. The doctor thinks it was an ulcer, but isn't sure. One minute, she was fine, then . . ." She breaks down in more tears.

This is not how it was supposed to end. Although it's been eighteen years since she cut me loose, perhaps we could have made amends one day. Go back to how we used to be. But now she's carried out the ultimate scene-stealer – she's run offstage before the end of the performance. Instead of sadness, I feel rage. She's cheated me. My body begins to tremble. Once again, I long for a hug from David.

"They won't let us take her home either," says Nabila, before more sobs spill out of the receiver like the chirps of an insect. Ajaz takes over and fills me in. His words wash over me. After a few minutes, I notice he's no longer talking. A response is needed, so I say yes. I don't know what his question was.

After he hangs up, I look at my phone, as though expecting it to say something else. So, Mother has gone. She didn't want to know me when she was alive. I don't need her now. I need to get back to sleep. We've a big dress rehearsal for the new show and I need to be all cylinders firing. I shut my eyes.

It takes me longer to drop back to sleep than I'd thought.

I wake a few hours later, the tears erupting out of me like a volcano, my body contorted in grief. I reach over, but the bed remains empty.

*

In the cold light of a new morning, my mood has hardened. "I'm not going," I state unequivocally. David is back, having done another long shift at the hospital. We're at the breakfast bar. I'm playing with my Cornflakes, while David is by the toaster, buttering a bagel. "It would be hypocritical. I haven't spoken to the woman for almost two decades."

David stops his scraping. "*The woman?* Really, Rafi? I had a whole family in the ward last night, begging me to save their mum. And I couldn't. Just hear yourself."

I growl. "You know what I mean."

He comes over and places a hand on mine. "Listen, you've every right to be angry. You guys didn't end things well the last time you were there. I get it. She said some truly awful things, and no wonder you were upset with her. But this'll be your last chance to say goodbye. And the show here can run itself," he says, pre-empting my objections on that front. "They can get Jonathan to be stand-in director, no?"

Conflicting thoughts race through my head. If only I hadn't left it so long. If only I had called just to hear her voice. But then she could have called me. And she never apologised for the things she said when she last saw me. But if only . . .

I chide myself. This isn't a Bollywood film; this is real life. There are no "if only"s.

I squash the flakes in the bowl with the back of the

spoon. "It's no good. Even if I wanted to go, it'd be too late. Her body'll be buried within twenty-four hours."

"Normally, yes," says David. "But, since your mum died in hospital, cause of death unknown, Nabila said they're doing a post-mortem and it could take a couple of weeks. So, we have time to get back for the funeral. I really think you need to be there. It's your final chance to make peace."

His words reach me faintly, like he's in a different room. But I understand his point. If I can't forgive Mother, even in death, what does that say about me? I've held onto the hurt for so long it's difficult to think in any other way. She and I haven't spoken since I left. Several times, I picked up the phone, determined to reach out, but then I'd remember her last words. *You are dead to me. I have only one son now.* The distance between us wasn't just geographical. It was an infinite chasm that nothing could bridge.

I pick up on David's choice of words. "*We?*" I say. "Will you come with me? Really?"

Forty-nine

David wants to join us at the mosque, but I tell him he'll feel out of place, being the only white person there. After some persuasion, he agrees to wait for me at the hotel. A part of me wonders if it's me who's worried. What other people will think if they see me with a white man. Stoning me silently with their stares. Am I all that different from her, after all? I shake it off. David would just feel a bit weird, I tell myself.

Nabila, Taleeb and I walk to the Green Street Masjid, which is purpose-built, with a shiny green dome topped off with a golden crescent. It's so different to when we were kids and we used to pray in converted houses. As I enter, we are greeted by the smell of incense and the sound of splashing water from mourners performing ablutions before a bank of taps. We join them, kicking off our shoes and rolling up our sleeves. Nabila detours off to the women's washing area around the back.

The rooms are perfunctory: white, lino-floored, cool under my now bare feet, with minimal decoration. Everything is saved for the prayer hall, which boasts chandeliers, rich fabrics and calligraphic tapestries. The intricate design of the green-and-blue carpet incorporates serried rows of kneeling spaces. Nabila points out the metal folding chair on which Mother sat when no longer able to prostrate herself. To my surprise, tears prick my eyes. I tell myself off for crying over an inanimate object.

We enter into a smaller prayer room, which smells of paint. Taleeb and I join the men sitting cross-legged along one side, their heads bowed, with piles of date pits before them, each pit denoting a prayer. Nabila sits with the women on the other side.

Mourners pass and shake our hands, giving condolences. "It is in God's will," they intone, before embracing us. They share stories about Mother, breathing new life into her, filling in the image I have of her, which has grown fainter over the years of estrangement.

There are people I haven't seen for years: extended family members from Blackburn, Birmingham and London; shopkeepers, taxi drivers, mosque elders, neighbours; and school friends, whose names unlock happy memories even while I struggle to recognise their grown-up faces.

*

Mother's body is brought into the main prayer room in an open coffin so we can pay our final respects. She has been ritually cleansed and dressed in simple white linen. Her hair is braided and covered with a white dupatta. Someone – Nabila? – has threaded bramble roses through her hair and dabbed a beauty spot above her lip. I gulp deeply, feeling a fist rising in my throat. My eyes are stinging and I blink rapidly. Even in death she has flowers in her hair.

The last time I saw Mother, her face was scrunched up in rage and disgust at me. Now it's serene. I see her as she once was. Her mouth is slightly open. It is at once her, and at the same time not – someone with a likeness playing the part. Like her beloved Noor Jehan. I feel a mix of love, anger and disappointment. Mostly love. I can no longer hold onto the hurt. I have to let it go. I forgive her.

As the imam finishes his prayers, we all press forward and circle the coffin – men on the inside and Nabila with the women on the outside. Shazia props up Nabila on one side, while two tall girls support her on the other side: Sajida and Sofia, the spitting images of Nabila. I've seen them grow up on the screen, when they've joined Skype calls with their mum. I haven't been in the same room as them since Shazia's wedding. In front of me, I spot Ajaz and the boys, Mohsin and Kamran – both towering a good two inches over their father. Seeing this visible proof of the passage of time, a twinge of guilt shoots through me. But I tell myself to get it together. This isn't the place to make amends.

We all move as one, a mass of humanity slowly orbiting around the coffin, hands upraised, sending prayers to guide Mother's soul to heaven. I reach out to touch the coffin, expecting a connection, to feel something deeper, but under my touch there's just smooth wood. She is gone. The flower that once bloomed so brightly among us will bloom here no more.

*

A flotilla of cars take the mourners to the cemetery in Pleasington, where Dad is also buried. Taleeb and I walk together among the cortege of male mourners. The sun is out and our white, cotton salwaar kameez are effective foils to the summer heat. Nabila has stayed behind at the mosque – women aren't allowed for this final part of the funeral rites. She had made her displeasure known.

We gather around the burial plot, which is one of about

twenty newly dug graves. They will all soon be filled, and marked with black headstones and gold-engraved Islamic calligraphy. We pull prayer caps on our heads, faces bowed, hands cupped, eyes closed. The loamy scent of the newly turned soil fills my nostrils. A falling leaf brushes against my cheek, and for a moment, she is back, the pansies in her hair tickling my skin.

While Mother is lowered into the ground, the priest starts speaking in Arabic. The last rites. I remember the sounds even after all these years since we laid Father to rest. They give me comfort, even though I don't understand the words. The mourners join in, their white salwaar kameez rippling and gusting like the sails of a mighty armada. All paying tribute to her. So many of them. She must have been well beloved and at the heart of this community, I whisper to Taleeb. He nods silently.

I say my own prayers for her, in English. I want the words to mean something. "I'm sorry I wasn't the son you wanted me to be. But I was always *your* son. You made me. I never stopped loving you. I'm sorry I didn't come back. I know I hurt you. But you also hurt me." I stop myself. Now is not the time. "Farewell, *Maam*. May you rest in peace. Allah be with you."

Taleeb and I drop three handfuls of earth on top of the coffin before the other mourners take up shovels and begin to fill in the hole. I throw a lone red rose in there. Then we walk away, without looking back. Footballers play on the pitches that spread out below, Pakistani teams taking on white teams from out of town, their voices floating up in the wind.

Fifty

David asks me why we haven't seen much of Taleeb and Nabila since the funeral.

I explain to him the mourning will last for forty days and forty nights. Funeral-goers will visit Nabila and Taleeb in their respective houses, bringing food, condolences and prayers. But that we should keep a low profile. Despite the passage of time, the community remains conservative and will struggle seeing a white face in the house, let alone a gay couple. Nabila and Taleeb have enough to contend with, without fielding awkward questions.

David accepts this and after a lazy morning at the hotel, we head out for an explore. There are two days left before we fly back to Melbourne. Despite the general air of sadness, I want to show David around some of the streets he might remember from when he was here. But, with so much time having passed, I don't quite know what to expect anymore.

The main thing I notice is that a lot of the young people have swapped jeans and T-shirts for Islamic dress. When growing up, I'd see this only when I went to mosque. Now hijabs are commonplace on the girls, beards and salwaar kameez on the boys. Shazia said that alongside the airport effect last time I was here, it was one of the enduring legacies of 9/11 – a need for the youth to reconnect and publicly own their faith.

I feel vulnerable, not only because of my Andy Warhol T-shirt and bright red shorts, but also because I'm walking with a white man, not a common sight in the neighbourhood. I put a little distance between David and me. He notices and asks if I'm all right. I nod. He bridges the gap. I take his hand and squeeze it.

We've had to work at closing the gap that appeared between us when I'd returned the last time and told him all about Pedro. I'd expected him to laugh it off. He hadn't. He'd walked out. He asked what was left if the trust had gone? It had taken many months of work and couples counselling to get us back on an even keel. I haven't strayed since, nor have I had the desire. I get all my extracurricular attention from my adoring audiences.

When we pass a group of young guys, I expect verbal abuse or a disapproving look from the heavily made-up young women in their hijabs. I imagine everyone's staring at us, judging, but they don't give us a second glance. The prejudice, this time, I realise, is mine.

As our meander through memory lane continues, we pass an abandoned mill. An image of Father springs up in my mind, leaving the house with his metal tiffin tins stacked one on top of the other, and I smile. Waterfall Mills – an idyllic name for a building that would have been anything but. We pass another. Also empty, the looms long silent. These brick titans taunt the town, too large and expensive to convert into anything else, reminding everyone of what they'd lost. I'm saddened by the smashed-in windows, the roofs pitted with huge holes, weeds sprouting from the brick walls. It's impossible to imagine the noise and industry that once thronged inside them. David says they would make great luxury flats.

Reaching Lower Audley, where we all once lived, we look around, unsure if it's the right place. Unlike the mills, Lower Audley has entirely vanished. The only sign it was ever there is in the name of the road: Lower Audley Street. The neighbourhood itself has been wiped off the map. We stand at the edge, where we'd have pedalled furiously along the flat bit of Windham Street before it climbed up to the canal, but now there's no such entrance. Everything is different. Despite the yellow, *Brookside*-style residences that have replaced the red two-up-two-downs, the estate has no name, as though it's ashamed of how it came into being.

I take in the new streets with disbelief and anger, shaking my head. So many lives uprooted. A community torn apart and sent who knows where. Nabila, Taleeb and Mother moved to Higher Audley, but others migrated further away. And all because the houses were allowed to fall apart through a lack of care and foresight, not unlike my relationship with Mother.

It's impossible now to even visualise what used to be here – where there were houses, there are now paths; where roads, there are now green spaces. Baines Street, Coronation Street, Pilkington Street, Pitt Street, Helen Street, Meadow Street – I chant their names in my head, bringing them back to life, at least in my imagination. Streets remembered by one generation, forgotten or never known by the next. The only constant is the canal, somewhere out there. First Father, now Mother, both gone.

"Each time I think I'm on steady ground, it turns into quicksand," I say to David.

Of course, I knew the compulsory purchase order had

gone ahead, all those years ago. Nabila had kept me informed by email. But it's still a shock to see its effects with my own eyes. I'm a stranger in my own past.

David puts an arm around me. This time, I welcome its reassuring weight.

"Come on," he says, winking at me. "The canal will still be there."

And we venture into the maze of yellow bricks.

*

We smell the canal before we come to it. The brackish scent of the water, stirred up by the warmth of the early afternoon sun, draws us to it like a tractor beam.

"It hasn't changed one bit," says David, pointing at the henna-brown water. "I didn't think I'd recognise it after all this time, but it's just the same."

"Thank God something is," I say.

"Remember the last time we were here?"

"I've never forgotten. For those few hours, I was the happiest person alive." I take his hand, a warm glow spreading through me.

David meshes his fingers with mine. He leads me into the familiar patch of vegetation, which is still here, somehow having escaped the jaws of the bulldozers, greedy developers and weedkillers. It's overgrown with nettles and brambles, with rosebay willowherb and thistles as tall as we are. Not most people's idea of verdant beauty, but, to me, it's as splendid as Fitzroy Gardens back home.

He stops in the middle, shielded by overhanging branches. He turns me round and drops on one knee. For a second, I think he's collapsed, but then a grin appears on his face. The big galah – what's he up to?

"Stop messing around," I say. "What are you playing at?"

In one swift motion, he retrieves something from the pocket of his shorts and takes hold of my hand. His grip is clammy, despite his assured manner. I can guess what's coming and I'm rooted to the spot. This was the last thing I expected this morning. From the canal on the other side, a splash followed by the croaking of a coot.

"Rafi Aziz," he says, looking up at me, his green eyes unblinking and holding my gaze, "it's high time I made an honest man of you." I don't quite believe what I'm hearing. I'm so used to people leaving me. Is this a joke? My eyes start feeling hot and prickly again. I might cry. "You can be a right diva. You always think you're right. You never take the garbage out. But you're *my* diva. Will you marry me?"

A firework explodes inside my head, my heart, my whole being. My mouth drops open. Every part of me is on fire. A Bollywood orchestra strikes up in my head. It takes a few seconds for me to react. I can't speak, so I simply nod.

David slips a silver band on my finger, the metal cool against my skin. I bring it up to my face. It's unadorned and honest, like him. Outside of our green sanctuary, the coot chases something on the water. Nearby, a car starts up. Kids race by on the other side on their bikes. Nothing stays the same. The world is in flux. But the ring remains on my finger. And David is still before me.

As he stands up, he cups my face and kisses me. An electric charge shoots up my spine. It's like we're kissing for the first time, that same dizzying feeling from all those years ago. He tastes of mint, ketchup and apples. I run my fingers through his hair. How many times did I think of him back then? How many nights did I cry myself to sleep and wonder about his life down under? Well, I have Friends Reunited to thank for bringing us back together. I kiss David deeply. My husband-to-be. Holding each other, we sway to unheard music in our Eden of green, unwilling to let the present become the past just yet.

Fifty-one

Next day, braving the blustery rain, we call on Ashiqah. With the One Stop Shop bulldozed along with everything else, and Mr Khan finally forced to hang up his tabard, she bit the bullet and bought her own shop: The Global Supermarket, with a globe symbol replacing the "o". It's the size of a mini-mart, with aisles, tubs and shelves fit to bursting with Pakistani, English and Eastern European produce. She's also got a proper working meat counter too, just like in KKK, but with better lighting and concessions to health and safety. When she claps eyes on David, her mouth forms a perfect O. A part of her past has walked into the store, the boy of ten now fifty. He admires her pink bob and kaftan, both of which I say make her look like Zandra Rhodes. She thumps me, then jokes we're the new Mrs Kapoors and Mrs Mamoods. To my delight, she says Mrs Kapoor is still going – ever-caustic and still with a taste for fried chickpeas.

We then lunch with Shazia. We're greeted by her excited screams, engulfed in her delight and the spicy aroma of biryani. Although she's seen and spoken to David online, this is the first time they've met. She flings herself on him, refusing to let go, Majid eventually having to prise her off. They're parents to six children, who are proudly paraded before us. She regales us with their academic achievements while Majid looks on proudly.

Shazia is resplendent in an ornately embroidered sapphire salwaar kameez. She designs them herself, selling them to boutiques all across the Northwest. Her well-stocked detached house is a testament to her success, from the swan tables and diamanté-studded dining chairs to the chandeliers and floor-to-ceiling painted portrait of her and Majid gazing lovingly at each other.

I give her a big squeeze. She squeals, her face lighting up. "What's that for?"

"Just for being you," I say. "Don't ever change."

*

I leave David with Shazia and Majid. They're driving him to Blackpool. He's obsessed with it after seeing it on *Strictly*, which we watch on iPlayer using a VPN. That leaves me free to do the task I've been putting off. Going through Mother's belongings to see if there's anything I want to take back with me.

I can't face going there directly, so I walk into town, to kill some time and help clear my head. I pass a shop window displaying vividly coloured bolts of fabric in the window. For a few seconds, I glimpse her inside, a scarlet dupatta over her head, a beringed finger pointing at various clothes, a nod or shake indicating approval or rejection. Despite being fixed by her gimlet eye, the assistant measures out lengths with a flourish against the metre rule glued to his worktop.

I trip on a piece of pavement. When I look back, the shop is empty once more, the only sign of life a neon sign in the door: "Closed". I shiver, despite the sunshine.

*

The house is yellow, like chickpea flour. Red bricks have fallen out of fashion, along with the mills and terraces they once made up. Weeds run rampant in the garden. Mother used to pay passing tinkers a few pounds to keep on top of them. The house is a squat two-storey, ex-council, in a small terrace on the main road. It has none of the character of our former houses. There is no ornamentation, just boxy, uninterrupted lines.

I'd got the key from Nabila earlier in the week. After a few moments of hesitation, I let myself in. For some reason, I leave the door ajar, unable to close it behind me. What am I scared of? Being stuck in here with Mother's ghost?

Nabila said Mother moved houses two or three more times after the Lower Audley demolition. This is the first time I'm setting foot inside this one. Despite that, it instantly feels familiar. The same mulligatawny soup of ornaments and nick-nacks everywhere; the heavily decorated dressing table mirror on the wall; the floral carpets and wallpapers; sofas kitted out in hand-sewn covers with frilly edges; even the smell of curry and hot oil that still hangs in the air.

As I walk around, images blur in my mind. So strong is her presence, with the modest acquisitions of her life all around, I'm transported back to Baines Street. The filmmaker in my head plays tricks on me, projecting the old house's irregular Edwardian spaces and soaring ceilings onto these simple square rooms.

I hear her in every room. The kitchen plays the percussion of her metal spoon as she scrapes and stirs the sizzling contents of her pans. The lounge strikes up with the rattle of her sewing machine in the corner, stitching its way through enough fabric to clothe the neighbourhood. The hallway takes up the melody, echoing the sound of her laughter.

I touch the wallpaper, tracing the faded pink and orange trellises. From the market, she used to find matching garlands to dress the panelled kitchen door, and they do the same in this house, hanging like a shroud, the plastic blossoms having randomly dropped off over the years. I pick one up and put it in my pocket. More fake flowers trail dustily around the mirror. As I stare at my reflection, I half expect to see her appear over my shoulder, perfecting her intricate eye make-up or dabbing a beauty spot onto her cheek.

I close my eyes. The bedlam that inevitably followed in her wake has segued into an unnatural calm. I can hear my heartbeat and, over its soothing thud, a faint, high-pitched whine, as though of the inner workings of the house.

A breeze steals in through the open door. I catch her girl-woman voice on the wind. A song from one of her favourite films whose title now eludes me. A woman singing about the magic her beloved has wrought over her.

The song fades. A smile crosses my face at the same time as a hand squeezes my heart. With stumbling steps, I follow her ghost through the door, into the kitchen.

The cupboard doors hang at angles, like crooked teeth. The one-handled rolling pin lies abandoned on the worktop, having shaped thousands of chapattis in its life. A pan of oil squats on the hob, its sides encrusted from years of churning out pakoras and samosas. The front hob is switched off – the Eternal Flame finally extinguished. A lump forms in my throat. I close my eyes again. I'm pirouetting across the floor, my Jesus sandals covering the pockmarked lino. Mother joins in, waltzing with me while the curry pans spit and sizzle.

Sighing, I open my eyes. I look to the stairs at the back. Once more, my imagination overlays them with the dark, covered stairs of the old house. How many times did she climb them, removing herself from reality, singing in her thin, girl-woman voice, finding release and comfort in the lyrics of her beloved Bollywood numbers? The slow ascent, the sad melody trailing behind her, the final few words silenced as the bedroom door shut.

We would not see her again for the remainder of the evening.

Understanding came only in later years: she was singing not for pleasure but in sorrow, driven to her bed to wrestle with whatever demons had taken residence in her mind. Her deep-rooted homesickness was never assuaged, no matter how many times she moved house. A part of herself was forever adrift in the sun and dust of her homeland.

The bedrooms are empty. Nabila must have had them cleared in readiness to sell the house. The floral carpets boast bright patches where the beds protected them from the light. The only piece of furniture is a rickety wardrobe in the main bedroom. It's empty. As I close the door, I spot something on top of the wardrobe, pushed to the back: Mother's Qu'ran, wrapped in an envelope of cloth – kept in the highest place in the house. I reach up and retrieve the holy book, placing it carefully in the tote bag Nabila has lent me.

When I return through the lounge, I stop and crouch by the sofa, reaching into the space underneath. We always used this area as extra storage when we were kids. I'm sure Mother would have continued doing the same. But nothing. More emptiness and dust.

I'm about to give up when my fingertips brush against

something. I pull it out. It's my old toy piano. I can't believe it. I was sure it would have been binned a long time ago. Blowing off the dust, I rest my adult fingers on the child-sized keys.

Minutes pass. I daren't depress the wooden keys. What if they don't work?

Eventually, I pick out an ABBA song. I play the verse of "SOS", which I remember could be played entirely on the white keys. The back of my neck prickles as the familiar bell-like tones ring out. I can't finish the song, as my fingers stumble too much. My heart is beating fast. She kept it. All these years. For a woman who'd shown little sentimentality, not having kept any of our school drawings or books or milk teeth or baby shoes, the fact she'd held on to this one thing . . . she had still cared. Cared enough to not have thrown it away.

It takes a while for that to sink in. Outside, the traffic rumbles past; inside, my heart keeps time like a metronome to the dying echoes of the piano melody.

On a hunch, I switch on my phone torch and shine it under the sofa. There: a tattered shoe box against the wall. Getting down on my front, I stretch my arm into the void and grab it. I meet resistance; the box is full. I drag it out, throwing up dust devils before it.

Sitting with my back to the sofa, legs stretched before me, I place the box across my knees. I count to three, then take the lid off. Inside are about a dozen cassette tapes with Mother's spidery marks on the labels. It's not Urdu – Taleeb had said she couldn't read or write – but a script of Mother's own making. As kids, we would make recordings to send to relatives in Pakistan. But I don't know what's on these tapes, or who they're for. Maybe they were for Mother herself, an oral diary, a way of recording her experiences or offloading her anxieties? Or for Ammi, but in that case, why hadn't she posted them?

There's an old Philips tape recorder in the box. I take it out. Which cassette should I play? I haven't time to go through all of them. I'll take them back with me to Australia, where I can listen to them properly. For now, I go for the tape with the writing on the label that looks the most recent – where the ink is the darkest. I figure this will be the one she's recorded last.

I plug the cable into a nearby socket, then press the Eject button to open the lid. I slip the cassette in, push down the lid, which gives a reassuring click, and press Play.

Fifty-two

"*My darling boy. I hope you are well. How I long to see your face again. It has been many years since your laughter and songs gladdened my heart. Where have you gone?*"

Her voice fills the room, sounding frailer than I remember. She speaks in Punjabi, which I translate in my head. While I don't catch every word, I understand enough. I press Pause. It's been almost two decades since I've heard her speak. Tears well up in my eyes. Images flash through my mind, but at double the normal speed, like a chase in a black-and-white silent movie.

I focus on the words rather than her voice. What does she mean where have I gone? She knows full well where I am. And she's been missing me? That should make me feel better, but it doesn't. I press Play again.

"*I am old now. Nabila tells me I still have many years ahead of me. That is fine for her to say, when she has just turned... oh, how old is she now? I can never remember. For myself, I prefer to count in weeks, or even days. I can then fool myself into thinking I have more time. I am older than Ammi was when she...*"

She drifts off, and the tape spools on. A breeze races through the house and I wish I'd shut the door. I shift in my seated position on the floor, crossing and uncrossing my legs at the ankles.

"*Her youngest has just left for university,*" she continues, the timeline confirming that she's recorded this recently. "*I remember when you went away. I thought my heart was being torn from my chest. Why did you have to leave me, my little bulbul? My youngest. My precious jewel. Oh, how I have missed you. Days without end, nights without comfort.*"

I chuckle. I know David would tell me off for being so heartless, but this is the Mother I remember. Ever the Bollywood drama queen.

"*Where was I? My memory is not what it was. Dr Khartoum looks at me with his big glasses and worried eyes. But I am just old. Though not as old as her!*"

I chuckle again – she must mean her nemesis, Mrs Kapoor.

"*I hope you are both happy, my bulbul.*" Both? I sit up and my finger accidentally hits the Pause button. That's a massive development, considering the words she said to me the last time we were in the same room. I press Play, hoping to hear more. Vexingly, she changes topic. "*That woman! She reminds me of Baboon-Faced Sanam from the next village. She was also very . . . is this still recording? Tasting, tasting. One, two, three . . .*"

I have no idea who or what Mother is talking about. She always was maddening.

"*It is okay, I know – Mrs Kapoor told me,*" she continues. Told her what? And how come Mrs Kapoor is always at the centre of things, even after all these years? "*I would not give her the pleasure. I said I was proud of you and looking forward to meeting your . . . your friend.*" I hold my breath, but she doesn't elaborate.

I rewind the tape a little and listen to it again. *Your friend*. She must mean David.

The hairs on the back of my neck stand up and my scalp prickles. She'd made her peace. She'd offered an olive branch, but I just hadn't been around to receive it. She had accepted David. I let out a sob, and it takes a few moments before I can compose myself.

I said I was proud of you and looking forward to meeting your friend.

Oh, Mother, why couldn't you have told me that in life? Just fourteen little words. Why let so much bad blood come between us?

I stop myself. It's pointless trying to reverse the clock. I don't know what journey she went on to change her mind about me and David, but I'm ecstatic to hear her reach out like this over the years.

I press Play.

"*Oh, the look on her face when I offered her snuff! You'd think I was trying to poison her.*" Mrs Ibrahim? "*She walked away, her mouth chewing paan like the cows back home chewing the grass.*" No, Mrs Kapoor!

As she talks, I notice her voice lifts whenever she mentions her band of old enemies, Mrs Ibrahim, Mrs Kapoor and Mrs Mamood, keeping each other young with their gossip and insults. A bit like me with Ashiqah when we were kids, hating each other but needing each other so that we could validate ourselves.

The tape winds on in silence for a minute or so. Just as I'm about to hit the Fast Forward button, Mother's voice comes on again.

"*Now, where was I? Oh yes, that's right. Puthar, I always knew. I may not have had words for it, but a mother knows. You were so different from the others. A gentle boy. You loved music even when you were inside me. You would settle as soon as I began to sing. I could not hide who you were from yourself or from others. I thought if you could change, I could stop you from being hurt."*

Her voice has lost its bounce. Silence for another minute or so.

Then: *"But I see now I was wrong."*

I stab Pause and blink in disbelief. I actually shake my head, unable to take in what I've just heard. Mother never admitted she was wrong, but here she is, stating just that.

"If you are the gay-shay, then so be it. Nobody is perfect. My Taleeb has a temper. Nabila has her—"

I jab Rewind, without hitting Stop, then Play. I repeat this four times. My jaw drops lower with each listen. I never thought I'd hear Mother say the "g" word, let alone get her acceptance of the situation – albeit a slightly reluctant one. I lean back against the sofa, marvelling at this unexpected turn of events.

"Nabila has her pride, the silly girl. Son, I am too old to understand this new world. I am a simple village girl. In Mirpur, we . . . we . . . where was I? I had something to tell you. What was it? My mind has . . . oh yes, your friend, I cannot think of her name – dark girl – she has met a nice young man! He is a Pathan, but you cannot have everything. She seems happy and that is what matters. You and her playing together in the back garden. And now look at her – a big house, fancy clothes and her own car. Wah-wah! No wonder her mother goes around with a smile on her face."

I wince. I don't think Shazia, award-winning businesswoman, wife and mother of six, would appreciate being reduced to the colour of her skin.

Mother talks like she lived her life, veering from topic

to topic, her voice dying as she forgets a thread, coming back with relish when she picks up another totally different thread. I don't know whether to be impressed or concerned.

"My darling boy, I wear a smile just as wide when I talk about you. I am so proud of you. For who you have become. How you bring so much joy to so many people. Nabila shows me your videos and songs on the Yoo-hoo. My heart swells until I fear it will burst."

My own heart threatens to do the same and I bite my lip. Why couldn't she have told me this before? I fight down the anger building inside me. I shake my head at the wasted years, the lost opportunities to make amends. Why couldn't she have joined Nabila for even one of our Face-Times? Maybe she feared my reaction. That I might not want to speak to her. Or she was afraid to see me with David, having her suspicions confirmed, which would once again challenge her deeply held beliefs. I'll never know.

"Okay, so you did not become a doctor or lawyer – and you always did wear your hair too long!" I feel my goodwill slipping further. *"Your father, Allah be with him, told me to let you be. He said he would not step in the way of anyone else's dreams again."* I pause the tape. Again? It sounds like Father also did some soul-searching over the years.

"He often hummed your songs when working – or whistled, and then I would have to tell him no more as he was eating my head." I snort at the curious Pakistani expression. *"He was a good man. I know that now."* I can hear the smile in her voice and I smile in return, bemused, wondering what they've done with the old Mother. She normally didn't have a positive word to say about Father. *"I realise he was as much a stranger to this new world as*

I was. No one to show us anything. Just the cold. The grey streets. Words without meaning. I was lost. But so was he. I could have . . . I wish I had been a better . . ."

The tape winds on for a few seconds in silence. Then she returns.

"Your father and I could not give you and your sister and brother much. But there was always love. Of that, we had plenty. For all of you." Another pause. *"The child is no more. You are a man. But how I long to take you in my lap and stroke your hair and kiss your cheeks. Forgive me, son. I was no more than a child myself."*

We are both now crying. I'd vowed not to blub again, but she gets me every time, even from the grave. I'm mourning what's passed. What might have been. But both of us were too stubborn to try and mend what had broken. Where has it got us? Deadlock. Decades of silence robbing us of new memories. Years eaten up, gone in the blink of an eye.

It takes a few minutes to compose myself.

"It is eight o'clock already? Where is my cardigan? I need to drop off my garam masala to your sister. She says no one else makes it the same. And Khalida wanted to get my advice on her sewing machine. Ai-hai-hai, always so much to do."

There are the sounds of rustling and moving about. It must be the end, but then she returns to the microphone and continues speaking.

"She is a good mother – Nabila – but she uses too much salt. And she has a heavy hand with the chilli. She will give them all heart attacks!"

The rest of the tape continues in this disjointed way.

—*"Hello, tasting, tasting. Is it working?"*
—*"The doctor says I am ill, but what does he know?*

His pills take away my words, I am sure of that. But he will not have my memories. I lay them down. What else can I do?"

—*"Be happy, my darling. Khush raho, beta. I only ever wanted you to be happy. Does not every mother want that?"*

Tears run down my face. Why is she saying this now? Why couldn't she have told me when we still had time? I roar at the futility of it. I bang the heel of my fist into my forehead. "Stupid, stupid, stupid!" I mouth noiselessly, my jaw cracking. It's too painful to continue listening. I reach for Stop.

"Think of me fondly, my son. Even when I could not understand, oh beat of my heart – when harsh words and dark clouds drove us apart, and when the ocean put even more distance between us – know this: your mother loved you."

I hurl the recorder across the room. It bounces on the carpet, rolling over and over like a Formula One car coming off the track. I hug my knees, head tucked between them. The tape keeps spooling, its tick counting down the seconds. Her girl-woman voice floats through the room as she starts to sing. The ghostly melody of a song by her beloved Mohammed Rafi. And then the recorder clicks shut.

Out of tape. Out of words. Out of time.

*

It takes a while before I can compose myself. I wipe my face and get up on slightly shaky legs like a newborn calf. I collect the recorder from where I've thrown it, unplug it and return it to the shoe box. As I do, I notice something nestled behind the cassettes – a rose, desiccated, the colour of dried kidney beans. I stare at it, mesmerised. My imagination saturates the rose with a rich crimson, bringing it back to life. I pick it up, but the stem is brittle and the flower head drops off. I manage to catch it in my other hand. To my dismay, it crumbles into loose petals in my palm.

Lifting my arm, I arc my hand over my head, unfurling my fingers, letting the papery petals fall like blood-red rain.

I send up a prayer, in Punjabi: "May flowers bloom forever in your hair. May the songs never leave your heart. Sending you all my love, my dear, wonderful and always perplexing *Maam*. Allah bless you."

Tucking the shoe box under my arm, I leave the house, shutting and locking the door behind me. Just as at the cemetery, I don't look back.

Fifty-three

Nabila barely has time to lead me into the front room before I pummel her with my questions. "Why didn't you tell me? Why did you keep quiet about it? Why have I had to find out by listening to a tape?" I rattle the box of cassettes at her.

Nabila squints at me. "Tell you what? Listen, sit, let me get you some—"

"Tell me what? Are you fucking kidding me?" I shout. Nabila flinches, but I don't care. "That she'd accepted me!" I yell. The blood thumps in my head and I sway on my feet.

She takes a step back. From the lounge, I hear the fanfare of *Who Wants to be a Millionaire?* I'm guessing Ajaz and some of the kids are home. I correct myself. The "kids" are in their late teens to late twenties. The two eldest have their own houses.

In a slightly less loud voice, I add: "I can't believe you didn't tell me."

She shrugs. "Oh, that. Look, first thing first – I can rustle you up a paratha, if you're hungry. It won't be as good as hers, but—"

"How long did she . . . did you . . . why didn't you . . ." I struggle to speak, frustration cluttering my words.

Despite it being summer, the room is cold and the fire is on. Nabila sits on the sofa and motions for me to do the same. I remain standing. "She was old," she says, as though the three words explain everything. She picks up a cushion and pats it into shape.

"I know she was old, but what's that got to do with anything?" I say, trying not to let my voice rise in volume.

"Well, I don't know what's on those tapes," she says, pointing to the shoe box, "but if it's her talking on them, you can't believe everything you hear. She was old. You know what old people are like. They ramble."

Yes, and that explains some of the lapses in her memory on the tape, I think. But she sounded perfectly lucid for much of it.

"For how long?" I ask.

"How long has she been old?"

I snatch the cushion from Nabila and hurl it with force. It narrowly misses toppling a plastic gardenia on a plant stand in the corner. "How long had she forgiven me?"

Nabila reaches for the mosaic table between us and offers me a plate of biscuits. It's all I can do not to knock them from her, too. I snatch a chocolate bourbon, if only to give my hands something to hold.

Nabila retrieves the cushion. "She softened over the years," she agrees, her hands back in her lap, clasped, while she gazes into the far distance. "That's true."

I stare at her, open-mouthed. "Years? Years?!" I get up, then force myself to sit. "How long?"

Her eyes look up, as if doing a calculation. After a few seconds, she answers. "It was when they did that special on musical legends. She caught it on the box and that sparked something off in her. It was just before Sajida went away. So a year?" She ignores my gasp. "Mrs Kapoor then mentioned something to her. And she asked me if it was true – that you were living with someone – and what could I say?"

"A year ago?" I say, my eyes narrowed in disbelief. "She said this a whole year ago? What the hell!" I realise I'm shouting again. "How could you have kept that from me?"

"Keep it down. Saj and Mo are in the lounge – they don't need to hear this," she says, getting up to shut the door. "What good would it have done? You weren't here. You could hardly just fly back. Me and T just had to get on with things. Simple as."

I'm astonished at her glibness. "That's no excuse! And don't try to make me feel guilty!" I'm still shouting, unable to hide my anger and irritation. I've crushed the bourbon into earth-like crumbs. I drop them onto the plate. "She makes her peace with who I am, and you don't think to tell me – not once, not even when I—"

"And what would you have done?" Nabila sits back down, glaring at me. "Flown back and run around the tree with her while singing a song?"

I grind my teeth. "Don't be ridiculous. We could have repaired things. Let bygones be bygones. I'd have had a few more years with her. I could have bought her a nice house, made her life comfortable, flown her over to see us in Australia. She never even saw me perform."

"She saw you at school and then—"

"She didn't see me on stage!" I snap. I feel the veins in my neck throb. I must calm down. "And now she's dead. Lying there, like a statue, never to open her eyes again."

Nabila waves dismissively at me. "I see you've not lost your sense of drama. Don't you think me and T looked into all that, Mr Hot Shot? None of those things are cheap. And she wouldn't accept it, in any case. You know how proud she was. I tried talking to you about her, every time I called, but you always came back with stuff about the house or work or the bloody dog."

A fresh surge of fury rises in me. Before I can retort, she cuts in over me. "You'd shut me down whenever I mentioned her. Or you'd end the call. You know how many times I rang back and it went straight to voicemail?" She looks me up and down. "I spoke to David more times than I did you. It was him that told me he'd moved out for a month after your last visit. The man's a saint – I wouldn't have taken you back!"

I protest, but she silences me with a stare every bit as scary as the ones she used to give me when we were children. "Then your calls became less and less. Just twice a year, lately – *if* we were lucky."

She stresses the "if".

The vein in my forehead throbs and twitches, joining those in my neck. I don't recognise any of what she's saying. But my inner voice pleads otherwise. Why else is a flush creeping up my neck? I protest. "Don't make out I'm some heartless, self-obsessed—"

"Well, if the shoe fits."

My mouth flops open. I shake my head and blink as if to dispel the negative images she's painting of me.

Nabila flicks on the TV in the corner. An Indian soap opera on Zee TV fills the screen. Before I can tell her to switch it off, she turns up the volume. "I'm happy for you," she shouts, "I really am – and you've done great. But you—"

I leap up. "Don't patronise me! She and I might have ended badly, but she was still my mum. I would have come over and made things right."

Nabila points the remote control at me, no doubt

wishing she could use it to mute me. "Really? You didn't even fly over for the births of any of your nieces and nephews. And you've only met them once, at Shazia's wedding, and briefly at that. You were too worried about your beloved audience wanting an encore! When she was young, Sajida thought you only existed inside the TV, as we only ever saw you on a DVD recording of this show or that. And you only came back for Dad's funeral because it coincided with a business trip."

I want to deny the charges, but I can't. The hot flush now advances to my face. A litmus test of truth, which I'm failing badly. I press back into the armchair, squirming. "You know I can't just drop everything. I don't have that kind of job. But this was important. I would have made the effort." As soon as I say it, I know it sounds wrong. As though I didn't think the births of my nieces and nephews were important.

She shakes her head, her nostrils flaring. "Don't come here saying it would all have been fine if only you'd known – that's not how this works."

"You should have told me," I repeat for the umpteenth time. "I deserved that much!"

Her mobile goes off. She snatches it up. "Yes? No, I'm fine. It's only your uncle. The other one. I'll be in soon." She jabs the phone to end the call and glares at me. "Saj," she says, as though this explains everything. I'm too annoyed to laugh at the ludicrous situation of her daughter ringing her from the next room to check on her.

Nabila grabs the remote and mutes the TV. "I told you, I tried. Many, many, many times." She bends down a finger with each "many", ticking them off. "And keep your voice down – Ajaz is still asleep."

"So, let me get this straight," I continue, trying to keep

340

my voice calm, "you're mindful of what Ajaz hears and doesn't hear, but not your own brother?"

She scoffs. "Now you're just being ridiculous."

I refuse to back down. "I was her son!"

The phone rings again. She ends the call without taking it.

"I told you, keep your voice down!" she warns me.

It's a red rag to a bull. "I blame you! You always hated that I was her favourite. I had a right to know! I would have—"

"You had a right? You had a RIGHT?! You were on the other side of the fucking world!" she shrieks.

It's as though she's slapped me. I've never heard her swear before. Over the years, I'd been aware of resentment about me pursuing my dreams while she followed the path set out for her. Little comments here and there, but nothing like this. My jaw drops. Her words rebound in my ear.

Seeing the shock on my face, Nabila touches me on the elbow. "I get it, I really do. I know it didn't end well between you and her. You needed to work. Make a name for yourself. It can't have been easy doing that on your own, all the way out there. I'm not blaming you. Nor does T. You had to do what you had to do to survive."

I grind my teeth, arms folded, unable to even look at her. I'm angry, but, as with the guilt, I don't know who it's directed at – her or myself? I can't argue with what she's saying, and yet I feel like she's being unfair. That she's choosing to highlight the things that fit her narrative while ignoring others that challenge it.

She continues: "But while you were away, life back here moved on. T and me had families to raise. Mother got old and we had to keep an eye on her. You're right, she was largely fine, but you know what old people are like.

They have their moments." She sniffs and yanks a tissue from the gold box on the table. "We asked her many times to join us on a Skype with you. But you know what she was like – never good with technology. She'd get coy and say she'd wait for you to come back and see you in person. Then she'd talk about her usual stuff: clothes, songs, flowers. And she put all her love into the little ones."

My stomach contracts. The wasted years. And all for what? Just so I could maintain my foolish pride? Where had that got me? An orphan with a mother preserved in aspic, her face contorted in rage, her cruel words cutting me like Shia flails, the years not lessening their effect.

I slump back into the chair. Nabila is right. I walked out on Mother. On all of them. Fed up with the judgements, being told I was haram. Just as in childhood, I'd stormed off in a sulk, but I'd held onto this grudge for years. I stayed away, unable to face further conflict. The grown-up me should have been squaring up to it, seeing it as a necessary evil to mend bridges. And all the while, time ticked on and stole Mother from me.

The fire hisses and gutters, but I'm cold inside. How is this house so bloody freezing, even in the middle of summer? Nabila's eyes are fixed on the TV, and she pulls at her lower lip. From the lounge, Chis Tarrant is about to ask the contestant the sixty-four thousand pound question.

Noticing me shivering, Nabila turns the fire all the way up. The flames leap over the ceramic tiles. She offers to get me one of Ajaz's sweatshirts, but I shake my head. She asks if I'd like some Vimto or masala chai, but again I refuse. I don't trust my trembling hands.

She sits back down. "You know she lived here with us for the last few months?"

This is the first I know about it. Nabila and I last spoke

a couple of months ago. Presumably, Mother had moved in by then? Had Nabila tried to tell me about it and I'd batted it away, as I'd done whenever Mother's name came up? Anyway, there's no point beating myself up about it now. I can't turn back time. "Since when?" I ask.

"Since she left the chip pan on and went for a walk round the block."

My mouth drops open. "Oh my God! Was she okay? And the house?"

She nods. "Alhamdalillah. A neighbour spotted smoke. The door was open, so he was able to get the pan out. But, after that, me and T decided it was safer for her to move in with us."

Me and T. I flinch. Those three words, again, tripping off her tongue so easily. She and Taleeb are a unit. I don't belong. I try not to take the omission personally.

"I don't know how you did it," I say to Nabila, as she returns from the kitchen with a glass of water for me and a mug of chai for herself. The cardamom and cinnamon in the tea smells comforting, and I regret having turned it down.

Reaching for the biscuits on the table, she takes a Malted Milk, easing back on the sofa. "You just do," she says. "One day at a time." She dips the biscuit in her tea. Her eyes are puffy and her hair scraped back and held in place with an elastic band. She has dark circles under her eyes and her face is clear of make-up. Worry lines crease her forehead. Guilt once more courses through me. She's had enough to deal with these last few days, months, years, without me berating her for keeping things from me.

"Are you all right, sis? Can I help with anything? Just say." I immediately regret it, as once more I realise I mean to offer pecuniary assistance. What had she called me earlier? Mr Hot Shot? Well, she's right. I understand the value of money but nothing else.

Nabila waves a hand. "It's fine. We're good. It's just nice to see you after all these years. What will be, will be, Insha'Allah." She takes a slurp of tea. "At least she's happy now – the doctor said she wouldn't have felt a thing."

I send up a kalimah. I remember how the centuries-old Arabic words had given me comfort at her funeral. "She'll be giving Dad a hard time up there," I say, pointing at the ceiling. "You know what she was like, once she got an idea into her head."

Nabila nods. "Nagging him to fix a socket or to stop whistling or to get out from under her foots!" She did an uncanny impression of her shooing Father out of the kitchen.

We burst out laughing. Nabila sets her mug down on the table and tea sloshes over the rim. For some reason, we find this hysterical and cackle like a couple of kookaburras. Ajaz pops his head in and asks if we're okay. His concerned expression sets us off even more. He tuts, mutters something about "those mad Azizes" and leaves us to it.

When we finally stop, exhausted, our ribs hurting, the air feels warmer in the room. I'm no longer shivering. I can breathe again without it hurting.

"You know, I *will* have that tea," I say. "If the offer's still going?"

She smiles. As she passes, she squeezes my shoulder. I lay my hand on hers.

Fifty-four

I sit cross-legged amid a mound of clothes, phone chargers and documentation. It's a good job we're in a suite, as I can keep all this clutter away from the bedroom. We're going to need a good sleep if we're to get up early enough to catch the flight back.

My phone pings. It's a WhatsApp from David. They're on their way home. More pings come through in quick succession: photos, including a selfie of him, Shazia and Majid at the top of Blackpool Tower, a close-up of a smiling donkey and a polystyrene tray of fish and chips. My stomach growls and I realise how hungry I am. I call Reception for a Caesar salad.

My phone pings again. "What now?" I chuckle, sure it's going to be another photo from their packed day.

I check my screen. It's Taleeb.

"Sup bro? Hope packing ok. Come ours when David back. Khalida cooking dinner. Wont take no. Nabila & Ajaz joining. T"

I hadn't planned on an evening out on our last day before we fly back to Oz tomorrow. But now I'm looking forward to seeing everyone again. The family all together. And Khalida's amazing food, which is even better than Mother's. "Sorry, *Maam*, but it is," I say.

I pick up the phone and cancel the salad. I resume the packing with renewed vigour.

*

We're gathered around Taleeb's dining table, which, like everything else in his life, is supersized. It fills the room, leaving little space for the chairs to come out before they hit the wall. David and I sit next to each other, then Nabila and Ajaz, and Taleeb and Khalida opposite. Khalida fusses around us, making sure we have chapattis, piling up the biryani and going back and forth into the kitchen to return with a never-ending supply of dishes.

The table heaves with food, so I ask her to sit, but she won't hear of it. "You are our mehmaan," she says, filling my water glass. "What would people think if I let you go back without making sure you've eaten properly? Look how skinny you are!"

Taleeb looks about to say something, but a glare from Khalida and he continues chewing. I smile wryly. Always, even now, they fear what other people will say.

Nabila nods, sucking on an orange segment to cut through the richness of the curry. "We had to mark it," she says. "We couldn't let you leave tomorrow without a get-together and celebrating Mother's life too. She loved biryani."

"She made a great biryani," agrees Ajaz, shovelling a huge spoonful into his mouth. "Darling, did she not show you how to make it properly?"

"Bloody cheek!" says Nabila, slapping him on the shoulder. He laughs and gnaws away on a chicken drumstick. "Sorry, folks, can't take him anywhere."

Taleeb motions around the table. "*Maam* would have wanted this. All of us back together, in the same room, in the same country." He raises his metal glass. "To *Maam*!" We all chink our glasses.

"So, Rafi," says Nabila, reaching over to nab a kebab from the platter, "what plans for you guys next? Anything you want to tell us?" She looks from me to David and back again.

I've no idea what she's on about. I help myself to more chicken dhansak, which is sweet and sour, in a thick lentil sauce, just how I like it.

She points a kebab-speared fork at my hand. "Little bro, I has eyes."

"You has bad grammar," I say.

"More eyes than a spider," says Ajaz. "Doesn't miss a trick, believe me."

"Some people need to be kept an eye on, *believe me*," she says.

Taleeb looks at my hand. "So, he still bites his nails? Big deal. Bilal does the same."

"How is—" I begin, before Nabila slams the table.

"The ring!" she yells, making us all jump. "Look!" She reaches over, grabbing my hand and raising it into the air, like I've won gold at the Olympics.

Taleeb finally notices the silver band. He whistles under his breath. "Nice one, bro. Put it there! Khalida! Come see what your favourite brother-in-law's gone and done."

"Her *only* brother-in-law," I correct him.

Khalida rushes in, blowing her cheeks. "Oof, what is it? I've got to keep an eye on the samosas else they'll . . ." She breaks off as Taleeb waves my hand at her, the overhead light catching the ring and making it glint.

As Khalida screams and inspects the ring, Taleeb gets to his feet. "A toast, to my little bro. Not so little now, mind.

And to David, who's taken him off our hands. Good luck, mate, and thank you!"

Laughing, we clink our steel cups of water, Fanta and Diet Coke together.

Taleeb sits back down. "Meri jaan," he says to Khalida, "could you ease off the chilli when you make this again? It's just a bit—"

Khalida grabs a chapatti and smacks him over the head with it, which makes the rest of us roar. As she heads back to the kitchen, she congratulates us again on our engagement. The others join in.

"Well, I can't take any credit," I say, nodding at David. "The decision was taken out of my hands."

"Someone had to do the right thing," says David. "Leave it to Rafi and I'd still be waiting when they're measuring me for my coffin."

There's an awkward silence, the reference to death reminding us of the week that's been. Khalida breaks it by returning with a towering mound of samosas. We all exclaim at the Pendle Hill of pastries.

"Eat, eat," she says, waggling her head. "Before they get cold."

Ajaz grabs one, opening his mouth as wide as possible to see if he can fit a whole one in there. Nabila smacks him on the shoulder and he laughs.

I turn to David. "Hey, mister!" I mock-protest, not thrilled at how I'm being portrayed. "Not fair. I was coming round to it. But I've been busy."

"You're always busy!" David, Nabila and Taleeb exclaim in unison.

I roll my eyes. They're in it together. Out to get me. But it's true. I haven't got to where I am by kicking my heels.

Khalida tells them off, as they're now sharing stories of

what I was like as a child and how I'm no different as a grown man of nearly fifty. She finally sits down and helps herself to a child's portion of rice and a spoonful of curry. She manages a mouthful before going round and topping everyone up.

"When's the big day?" asks Nabila, lifting my hand again and scrutinising the ring.

David and I both splutter, her question taking us unawares.

I change the subject. "Hey, does this remind you of something?" I say. They look at me blankly. "Another time we had a dinner, all of us? When David came around. Remember?"

David guffaws. "Oh god, I was so nervous. I'd never eaten Pakistani food before. But your mum was so good to me."

"She came in and gave you a small wooden fork," says Nabila. "I remember that."

"And your hand was on my leg the whole time, and no one saw," I add, grabbing his thigh under the table.

Taleeb remains quiet. I look at him, encouraging him to add his own memory. He clears his throat. "Yeah, well, it wasn't my finest hour. Sorry about that, David."

David waves away his apology. "No worries, mate. I just remember you bringing up Mum's divorce. I wanted to deck you!"

Taleeb grimaces and apologises again. He turns to me. "So, when's the wedding? Don't keep us in suspense."

"Oh, we haven't decided anything yet," I say. "Could you pass me the okra?" I feel a hot flush creeping up my neck. I'm not used to my siblings being so open with me. I don't even think I've fully processed what the ring means. The week has been a blur of emotions and I need time to work through them.

"To be fair," says David, coming to my rescue, "I only gave Raf the ring a few days ago. But a big fat Ozzie wedding is definitely on the cards." I raise an eyebrow. He nods. "You don't get married after twenty-odd years of being together without a proper celebration. I want the works. Big band. Big hair. But maybe not the big dress."

Taleeb guffaws and gives David another high five. I shake my head at them both.

"Do we?" I say to David, dabbing at my mouth with my napkin. "Shouldn't we talk about it? Can we afford it? What with everything else we—"

"You bet your bottom dollar we can afford it. You're directing more and more shows. I've just been promoted. Nothing but the best for me and my man."

Tears spring to my eyes. I sniff and pretend it's the spiciness of the food. I'm engaged to be married! How did that happen? David's right; if it had been left to me, I'd have dithered and come up with a thousand-and-one excuses. I take his hand and squeeze it hard. He squeezes back.

The doorbell rings and Khalida gets up to answer it.

"Well, I'd best get saving the airfares now, I suppose," says Nabila, biting into a samosa. "Might have to remortgage!"

"You'll fly over as our guests," says David. "Wouldn't dream of hearing otherwise. Would we?" I nod in agreement. He turns to Taleeb. "And you too, bud."

"Deal." They hug across the table.

"We can firm up plans when ..." I begin, but before I can continue, the door opens and a handsome young man in his late twenties rolls in. He has a nose stud in his left nostril, an asymmetric haircut wrapped in a colourful bandanna and what looks like a tartan skirt over a pair of impossibly tight jeans.

"Hello, son! This is a nice surprise," says Taleeb, getting up to hug Bilal. "I thought you'd forgotten us."

"Hey, Pops. I heard Uncle Raf and David were over, so I had to swing by. Good to see you both! Looking sharp, Uncle Raf. You too, David."

Before we can get up from our chairs, he hugs us from behind. He smells of Tic Tacs, expensive moisturiser and a top note of weed. I note his fingernails, painted glossy black. Various bands of paper and plastic encircle his wrists, markers of good times had at festivals and clubs.

"Let's get a proper look at my favourite nephew," I say. I rise and take him in, holding him by the shoulders. A big grin breaks across my face. Even though we chat regularly online, it's still good to see Bilal in the flesh. He's grown into a striking young man, and he towers a good couple of inches over me.

"You here for a few more days?" he says. "Mom, could I get some of your masala chai? Starbucks makes it like shit. Sorry, my bad! Anyway, Uncle Raf, I really want to show you my studio. I'm working on a new piece, which I know you'll find sick."

I've seen the studio online, on Bilal's Instagram account. He's getting a name for himself as a sculptor, specialising in using "found" objects and recycled materials. A recent set of pictures he posted to Insta showed a life-sized family unit, two parents and two children, made entirely of household rubbish.

"That sounds great, Bil, but—"

"Great! Dad can drive you there. Can't you, Pops?"

"Oh, *can* Pops?" says Taleeb, raising an eyebrow. "Salford via the corner shop for some milk? No problem." Turning to Khalida, he adds: "This is what happens when you treat them like little princes. Spare the rod and all that."

Khalida flicks her dupatta at him and hands Bilal a plate teetering with samosas and pakoras. I feel a pang of sadness and recognition, reminded of how much Mother used to spoil me like this.

Bilal whips his head away with a staccato tango-like movement. "Fried food only at weekends, Mom. You know that."

"But today is Friday," she says. Then, more slowly, "Fry-day."

Ajaz laughs like it's the funniest thing, while the rest of us groan. She clucks, before returning to the kitchen to prepare more food.

"I'd have loved to, Bil," I say, "but we fly back tomorrow. Early start. Next time, though – I promise."

Bilal nods and squeezes my shoulder. He asks if I'll at least give him a song. I feign embarrassment, but Bilal won't hear of it. "I can't take two nos in the same night, Uncle Raf. A song for your favourite nephew, please."

So, I rise from my seat and clear my throat. "Okay, you've twisted my arm." They all laugh. "This one's for Bil – and also for *Maam*, who gave her love of music to me."

Quietly at first, then louder, I sing an old R. D. Burman number, "Kiski Sadayen Mujhko Bulaye", from the film *Red Rose* – a romantic number between Poonam Dhillon and Rajesh Khanna, about a lover calling out to his beloved. It was one of Mother's favourites.

It's been many years since I've sung it, but I still know all the words. Taleeb grumbles the food will get cold, but Khalida tells him off and encourages me to continue. Ajaz begins stamping out the beat. Before long, everyone's joining in with the words. I open my eyes. Even Taleeb claps to the rhythm, albeit badly, and with a slightly embarrassed air.

When the song finishes, I take a bow, and they applaud.

"And now, time for a toast," says David, rattling a spoon against his glass.

Pushing their chairs back, the others stand up, drinks in hand. Bilal switches the main light off and takes a Zippo to the candles on the table.

"Mom!" shouts Bilal. "You're going to miss it."

Khalida comes running from the kitchen, bearing a tureen of jewelled sath range chawal, my favourite rice dish. She lays it before me. "What's happening?"

Bilal pours her a lassi. "A toast."

"Toast? Really?" she says, taken aback. "Okay, I can go and make—"

"Mooooooooooom, you're so cute." Bilal grabs her in a hug, kissing the top of her head and lifting her off her feet. She squeals and tells him off, blushing like a little girl.

"To us!" says David. All six glasses clink together.

"To family!" say Taleeb and Khalida, catching each other's eye. Clink!

"To *Maam*!" says Nabila. Clink!

"To better food!" says Ajaz, getting a nudge in the ribs from Nabila. He laughs and kisses her. Clink!

"To John Lewis's make-up counter!" says Bilal. Clink!

I pause for a moment. "To the future!" Clink!

As we sit back down, the camera in my mind whirs into action once more. Our excited chatter ebbs away as strings fade in and take over. The camera pans around the table in a slow circle, focusing on each of us in turn. David reaches for another chapatti. I chuckle as Nabila tells a funny story about Mother. Ajaz fills in the details, including doing the voices, which makes everyone guffaw. Taleeb adds his own memories. Khalida comes back from the kitchen with another steaming plate. She whispers something in Bilal's ear. He smiles, hugs her, grabs a samosa and chomps it in three bites, just like his father.

As the credits roll, they ask me for an encore. I take David's hand and launch into Nusrat Fateh Ali Khan's "Mere Rashke Qamar", a romantic hit from the 2017 film *Baadshaho*. The song tells of the moon's envy as the lovers first clap eyes on each other. Nabila tells me Mother adored the song. I sing louder. Ajaz thumps out the beat of the driving drums on the table. Then, as one, we rise to our feet. Singing. Dancing. Laughing.

The orchestra swells. The camera pulls away. The room recedes, before slowly fading to black.

Acknowledgements

Like most debut novels, *Northern Boy* has been years in the making. Rafi and Mother's intertwined stories have been in my head for a long time, and I owe a huge thank you to the team at Unbound for sharing my vision, trusting my words and giving them the best home they could have.

I'm so glad I entered the Unbound Firsts competition and that Aliya Gulamani, editorial lead, saw potential in the story. She totally got my vision for the book, as did my fabulous editor, Marissa Constantinou, who from the beginning saw Rafi's world as I did and whose expert advice and guidance let the story really breathe. Both are the best champions one could hope for.

And I want to give a shout out to Zahra Barri, my fellow winner of the Unbound Firsts competition, whose book *Daughters of the Nile* is out now too, so do check it out – it's fabulous!

A huge thanks to my agent, Robert Caskie, who believed in Rafi, Shazia and co. from the outset. He has seen many iterations of this book, and his unwavering support has meant the world, and kept me going even when I thought I had no more to give. An equally big thank you to Gillian Stern, who, along with Robert, gave crucial developmental edits to get the book into the shape it needed to be.

Many others in the industry have proven to be champions along the way, giving encouragement and advice. Notable mentions go to Ella Kahn, who saw Rafi's story right at the beginning and who helped shape the narrative, and Gillian Green, who gave valuable feedback through various drafts. And to Amy Fitzgerald, who fell in love with Rafi at the start and gave me the impetus to keep going.

Rafi's journey began with Spread the Word, when I won a place on their inaugural London Writers' Awards in 2018. Thank you to the amazing team of Ruth Harrison, Bobby Nayyar, Eva Lewin and Laura Kenwright. And to my LWA buddies: Arun Das, Esther Poyer and my writer-in-crime Chris Simpson, for edits, laughs and mortifying exclamations ("Oh – we thought you were dead!").

Also thank you to the team at Creative Future Writers' Awards, especially Matt Freidson, where Rafi and Mother first came to public light in 2019 in a prizewinning short story, "A Home from Home". And to Aki Schilz and Joe Sedgwick from The Literary Consultancy, for always having my back.

And then there are my writer friends, in real life and online. A huge shout-out to my fellow Megaphoners: Nazima Pathan, Munira Jannath, Alka Handa, Abimbola Fashola, Ten The Goi and Zareena Subhani, and Leila Rasheed and Stephanie King for running this amazing writers' group.

A massive thank you to writing buddies Matt Cowan and Christina Tolan, both of whom read and re-read drafts of *Northern Boy* and always came back with great ideas – rather than sending me off with a flea in my ear! And a shout-out to our pals on the Curtis Brown Creative "Edit and Pitch Your Novel" course, who saw the genesis of the story and whose feedback gave the book va-va-voom.

Hugs to dear friends Franca Tranza, Alexander Mark Rogers, Gareth Williams and Richard Bocock, there from the start of this writing journey. And to fellow Northerner Anne Connolly, who was in St Winifred's School Choir and who really did get to meet ABBA – several times!

Eternal thanks to my brothers and sisters, for rubbing off my corners, and to my unique, colourful, eccentric, wonderful mother. This book is for her and women like her, who often don't have a voice.

To Mrs Müller, Mr Brindle, Mrs Battersby and Miss Newton, who took we Punjabi-speaking, working-class sons and daughters of weavers, seamstresses, taxi drivers and mill and factory workers, and released us into the world, five years later, able to speak English, read widely, write in copperplate and with the confidence to face the challenges that would hit us harder than children from more privileged backgrounds: no thanks can ever be enough.

And to Blackburn, which made me what I am. To the lost streets of my childhood, to halcyon days and to happy memories growing up among the cobbles and terraces. This Northern boy salutes you.

And, finally, to Gary, for having helped in immeasurable ways to get this book out there, not least for wielding a brutal pen and telling me to get rid of almost a third of an earlier draft! You are everything and more. Without you, this wouldn't have been possible. Thank you for allowing me to be.

Scan here for the official *Northern Boy* playlist.